M. V. PRII

Copyright © 2022 Mattew V. Prindle

All rights reserved. No part of this book may be reproduced or used in any manner without the prior written permission of the copyright owner, except for the use of brief quotations in a book review.

Bob the Wizard

Acknowledgements

Bob the Wizard was a labor of love, and not just mine. I could not have done it without help. My wife Caulette provided inspiration and encouragement. My mother Angalene and my good friend Patrick McCleery provided invaluable editing and feedback. My father David and my friend Noreen Garrison generously provided pro bono proofreading. Finally, this final product wouldn't be in your hands (or on your screen) without the brilliant work from my cover artist, Sean Mauss, who provided the cover, internal maps, and formatting. May you all stay vigilant.

-M. V. Prindle

M. V. PRINDLE

BOB THE WIZARD

BOB the WIZARD

TABLE OF CONTENTS

CHAPTER TWENTY-TWO:
    CONTINGENCY 255

CHAPTER TWENTY-THREE:
    OATH 269

CHAPTER TWENTY-FOUR:
    FALLEN HEROES 284

PART THREE: 300

CHAPTER TWENTY-FIVE:
    SICK AND TIRED 301

CHAPTER TWENTY-SIX:
    FIRESIDE 313

CHAPTER TWENTY-SEVEN:
    WHO WE ARE WHEN WE WAKE 325

CHAPTER TWENTY-EIGHT:
    TORFUL 340

CHAPTER TWENTY-NINE:
    NINTH CASTLE 354

CHAPTER THIRTY:
    BRIDGES 371

CHAPTER THIRTY-ONE:
    THE SILENT STALKER 385

CHAPTER THIRTY-TWO:
    ASH AND ALLIANCE 396

M. V. PRINDLE

Table of Contents

CHAPTER THIRTY-THREE:
    KEYSTONE 410

CHAPTER THIRTY-FOUR:
    WEAPONS 419

CHAPTER THIRTY-FIVE:
    FACING THE DEMON 434

CHAPTER THIRTY-SIX:
    GATES 445

BOB THE WIZARD

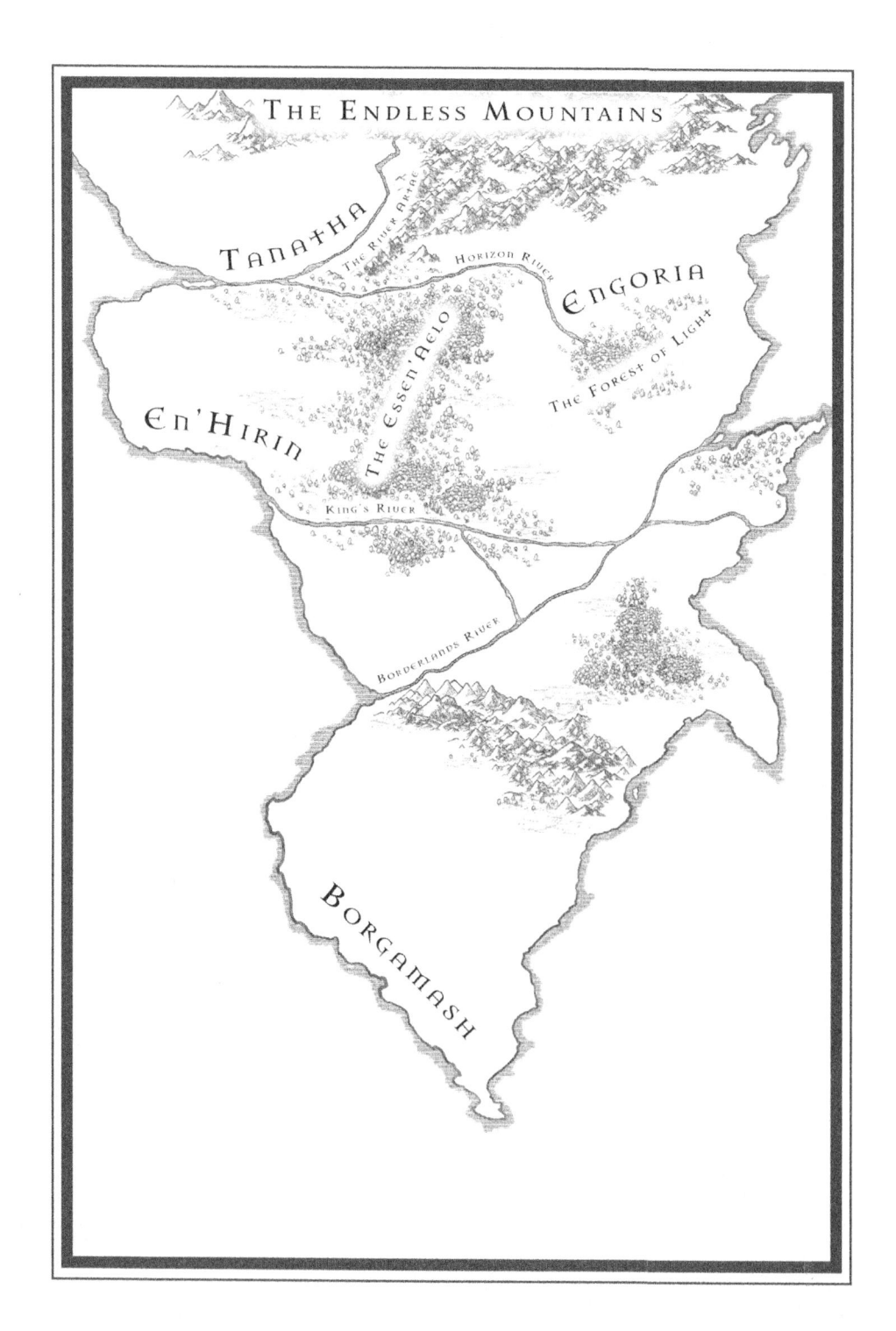

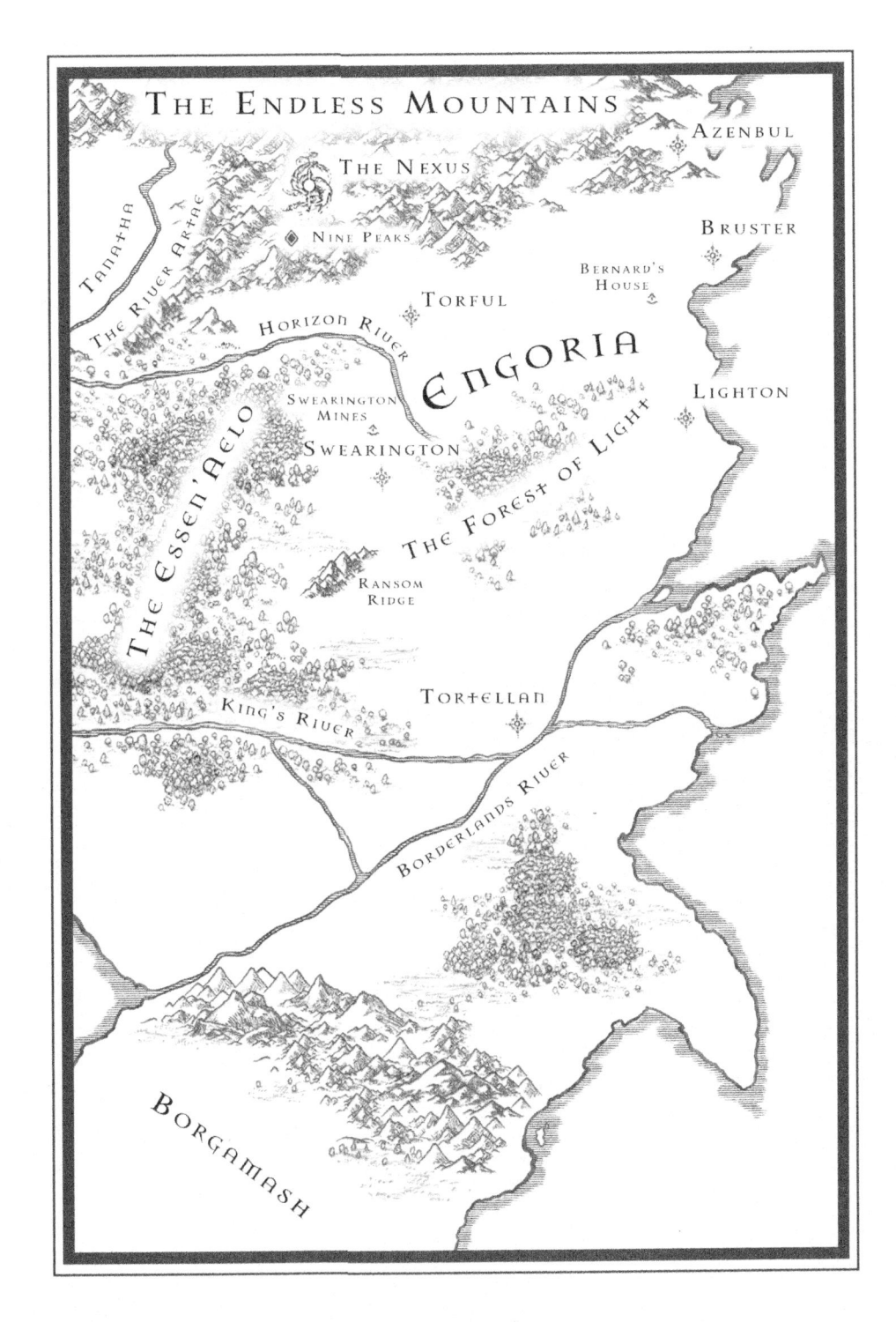

M. V. PRINDLE

BOB THE WIZARD

M. V. PRINDLE

PROLOGUE:
HOW THINGS CAME TO BE THIS WAY

Anna had lost her father to cancer and her mother to the slow decline of Alzheimer's, so she knew a thing or two about loss. She'd once told Bob, as they lay entwined and staring at the bedroom ceiling, that no one actually understood loss. No one, not even her, not even someone who'd lost everything. No one understood it, she said, and that's why people said they're sorry for your loss. Not that they weren't sorry, usually they were. But the thing they were most sorry for was something they couldn't put their finger on, maybe weren't even aware of. It was that they couldn't explain how someone could be there one moment and gone the next. The finality of it was just too much for them. They liked to pretend that death wasn't real, that people who were dead weren't really gone. Some people, like Anna's sister, actually talked aloud to their dead relatives as if they were there in the room. Most people didn't go that far, but they still played games with themselves. Told themselves things, so they wouldn't think about death, at least not the ultimate finality of it.

Losing Anna had destroyed Bob from the inside out. After she and Daniel were dead, Bob found himself talking to her, which of course made him think of her speech about people not understanding loss. Sometimes he'd chuckle about it. Sometimes he'd struggle not to weep. Such were the vicissitudes of grief.

If he'd given himself time to process the murders of his wife and son and what they meant for him, he might have decided Anna had been wrong. But as it was, he'd been consumed by utter rage. He'd plunged headfirst after the murderer with nothing more than a backpack, a pistol, and a strange object called a Gatekey, gifted to him by a creature that named itself Rashindon before it died in his living room.

Then came his first Gate. Then another, then another. They all blurred together. Bob was still in shock. He didn't sleep for four days during that first stretch, with nothing but nicotine in his body most of the way. At some point he came out of a Gate into a dim silver room full of dozens of other Gates. He had a long conversation with a holographic computer image that for some reason kept referring to him by his first initial, **R.** The computer said that he was in an Astraversal Waystation. Bob started by asking what the fuck that meant. If not for that conversation, he wouldn't have been able to continue the pursuit, as the computer—which said many things Bob didn't fully understand—informed him which Gate Galvidon had walked through only one day previous.

Since then, mostly Bob's thoughts were occupied with what was right in front of him. He had to eat, get enough water, and he couldn't run out of tobacco. A man could only take so much punishment. And of course, there was the hunt. Most of the places the Gates brought him to were occupied by people. He asked after Galvidon. *Have you seen a Gray Man? Big black eyes, little horns?* In some places, where it seemed appropriate, he'd add, *Looks like a demon.* The trail was easy enough, mainly because the Gatekey glowed something fierce whenever a Gate was nearby.

When he did think about his wife and son, he tried to focus on Anna. The simple truth was, thinking about Daniel was too painful. He could sense the grief for his son, like the itch of someone watching him, but he tried his best to keep it at bay. It was too vast. If he even looked in its direction, it might crush him. In the moments when he found himself thinking of Daniel, he knew that Anna was right. Loss is too incomprehensible. What kind of world would let that happen to a nine-year-old child?

Anger was easier than grief.

No world he'd seen since leaving Earth had presented a paradise. Bob grew calloused to the suffering that he saw. His focus was singular. Galvidon would die. Bob wasn't sure he believed in justice anymore, but anyway it wasn't about justice. It was about making Galvidon suffer. Some egghead once said that for every action, there is an equal and opposite reaction. Galvidon killed Bob's family. Bob was the reaction. Simple as

M. V. PRINDLE

that.

There was no turning back now. He was lost in a forest of worlds connected by, as far as Bob could tell, a magical highway called the Astraverse. He'd find and kill the Gray Man, or he'd die trying.

On the plus side, he didn't miss being a garbage man.

BOB the WIZARD

Part One:
Traveler

"Life is like riding a bicycle. To keep your balance, you must keep moving."

-Albert Einstein

M. V. PRINDLE

CHAPTER ONE:
CHASING THE DEMON

In all his travels across the Astraverse, Bob had been in many tight spots, but none quite so precarious as this. Hanging off the side of a skyscraper had a way of putting things in perspective. The wind tugged at his mane of black hair and bushy beard, whipped at his black leather trench coat as if angry he'd dared to climb so high. The brown backpack he carried also protested his position, pulling on his shoulders toward the hard asphalt far below. As his coat swayed, the sawed-off shotgun tied within it clunked heavily against the concrete building. Bob wanted a cigarette, and seriously considered trying to light one. He might have actually given in to the urge, but angry yells from inside a nearby window impressed upon him a need to hurry. Below, the vast city sprawled beneath him. Sun glinted off the other skyscrapers and winked off passing cars as they zipped through the air in invisible traffic lanes. Cars didn't fly where he came from—his world, his Earth. Then again, Bob hadn't seen his Earth in a long time.

The yelling from inside the building, muted by wind and traffic noises, was growing closer, and Bob heard a door slam open somewhere. He was on a shallow concrete ledge, gripping a banister, and was hesitant to remove his hands to grab the Gatekey from inside his coat. But there was nothing for it; the voices were just inside, right behind him, and the window blew out. Glass pelted against the leather on his back, probably getting into his thick hair. A white-hot beam hissed over his shoulder, warming his neck. They were shooting at him. Of course they were. Bob jumped.

Or rather, he fell on purpose. The air was thick and tried to tumble

BOB THE WIZARD

him. Plummeting, he fumbled for the Gatekey in the inside breast pocket of his coat. He gripped it and took it out, the wind doing its best to tear the object from his grasp. The Gatekey was glowing, but not quite enough. He was almost there. Whose idea was it to put an Astral Gate in the middle of the sky? It was a first for Bob, who would like to strangle the person who'd decided on the Gate's location. Had anyone really decided? Bob didn't know who built them, and now was not a good time for contemplation. The Gatekey—a large bronze key with odd, intricate details—flared and became like a little sun, shining so brightly that Bob would have been forced to squint had he not already been doing so because of the violent wind. It was time. Hand buffeted, body rotating, clothes and hair twisting and whipping about, Bob reached out with the glowing Gatekey, as if for a lock, and turned his hand.

Then, everything shifted. He fell a few feet, landing hard on soft grass. He bounced—the sawed-off clanging against his hip, the backpack roughly thumping his back—and rolled to a stop. Still clutching the now-dimmed Gatekey, he stared up at a blue, unpolluted sky. Grasshoppers, or something like them, buzzed and chirped in the tall grass around him.

"Fuckin' A," groaned Bob. He'd rolled onto his back, which was far from comfortable since the backpack was rather full. He sat up, puffing out breath, blood rushing to his head. A rough sigh escaped his throat, scratchy and raw. He staggered to his feet, swaying, bits of grass and dirt clinging to his hair and clothes. Looking around, he tucked away the Gatekey and rummaged in an outside coat pocket. He pulled out a rectangular pack of cigarettes—some strange brand from the world he'd just escaped. The cigarettes were miraculously undamaged.

"Would you look at that," he muttered, and put one between his lips, drawing a metal lighter from another pocket with practiced swiftness. He snapped his fingers over the little wheel on the lighter and pressed the resulting flame to the end of the cigarette, sucking in the tobacco with relish. The lighter closed with a snap.

He hadn't known for sure he'd find a safe landing on the other side of the Gate. If he hadn't seen Galvidon make the jump a few hours prior, he would never have even found it. Bob had tracked the Gray Man down but failed to catch him. Again. He buried his frustration.

M. V. PRINDLE

"Now then," he said, "where the fuck am I?"

A grassy meadow sprawled around him, maple and birch trees here and there, gently rolling hills stretching into the distance. Much of the grass was bright green and came up to his ankles, and there were swathes of pale grass the color of his khakis. This variety seemed to grow in thick, shoulder-height stalks that susurrated in the wind. Happily singing birds flitted about the trees and dove for insects. The sun was high and seemed a little bigger than the one from his Earth, but it was hard to tell. He puffed his cigarette and took it all in, trying to relax and let his body settle from the fall. Then, the butt of the cigarette smoldering in his mouth, winking at the smoke, he took off his pack and rooted around. He came out with a shoestring, which he held, and a pair of black, plastic sunglasses, which he slid onto his face. He spit out the butt and twisted his black steel-toed boot over it. After zipping his pack and readjusting it onto his shoulders, he took the Gatekey out of the trench coat's left breast pocket.

He held up the key, inspecting it. It had ceased to glow, which meant the Gate had only been one-way. Some of them were two-way. You never could tell until you went through one. The Gates were sometimes invisible, and on those occasions, the Gatekey's glow was the only way to know if one was near. The key itself was bronze, about seven inches long. There was a little green meter on its shaft—like some batteries had on Bob's Earth—and it was depleted. There were other things about the Gatekey, tiny buttons and symbols, but he didn't worry about those now. Bob's concern was the depleted meter. He slipped the shoestring through the round hole on the back end of the key and tied it around his neck. Exposing the Gatekey to sunlight was the only way he knew of to recharge it, and now was a good time; there was plenty of sun and no one was around. He chose the tallest hill he could see as a destination and crunched his way through the grass.

A brown rabbit zigzagged past him. He considered taking out the sawed-off and trying to shoot the little bugger, but he wasn't hungry yet, and besides, it would probably just get away. He trudged to the hill's apex, lit another smoke. It was warm under the sun, but a pleasant breeze wafted at the hill's crest. He surveyed the area. There was a forest to the east. At least, he thought it was east. It was hard to judge direction in a new world. Everywhere was different.

BOB THE WIZARD

When Bob had first begun traveling, he'd assumed he was moving from planet to planet, but that wasn't the whole story. Some of the places he went weren't planets, exactly. They were just... realms. One place had literal edges that dropped off into space. Another, as far as he could tell, was an endless stone labyrinth. Yet another had been divided by some arcane force into concentric circles, each with different geologies and inhabitants. Some realms he visited had their own ideas about time and distance, about up and down, about life and death. Most of them, however, had been more or less like his own Earth, and populated by humans. Some instead boasted humanlike creatures. Oddly, he'd never had problems with language, though he doubted all the people in these places spoke English. He thought it was something about the Gatekey—somehow, it let him communicate with intelligent beings anywhere he went. In any case, he'd never stayed in any of those places long enough to learn much about them. He wasn't a tourist.

So, there was that forest to the maybe-east. To the distant maybe-north, the rolling hills seemed to give way to foothills and mountains. To the maybe-west the grassy hills stretched as far as he could see. A half-mile from the foot of the hill upon which Bob now stood, to the maybe-north, was an unpaved road—a well-worn path of tan pebbles running from the western hill-country eastward into the forest. Bob stamped out his cigarette and made for it.

He saw another rabbit, and a buck the size of a small horse. Both fled at his approach. At least there was plenty of food if he was willing to work for it. Finally, he approached the road, glancing both ways along its length. Neither direction was particularly inviting. The forest to the east was a dark green line that petered off as it spread northward. The road seemed to pass through a peninsula of trees that grew from the forest's main body to the south. In the inner gloom of the woods, tiny points of light seemed to twinkle like fireflies. To Bob's left, the hills grew gradually upward, obfuscating what lay beyond.

He stood in the heat, indecisive, and inspected the pack of cigarettes. Only five left. He put the pack away. Just as he was deciding to walk into the forest—it being at least some kind of thing he could get to—a wagon trundled out of the thick of the trees along the path, headed toward him. The rattling vehicle was built from sanded wooden planks, its bed protected by a canvas covering, and altogether was about the size of the

M. V. PRINDLE

pickup truck Bob had owned once upon a time. It was pulled by two harnessed horses, one chestnut-brown and the other black. As the wagon approached, Bob saw it was driven by a fellow of late middle age. His short brown hair poked out from under a wide-brimmed straw hat and the sun reflected off his dirty white woolen pants and tunic. His face was lined and weathered. The man and his wagon came upon Bob standing in the road and pulled to a stop, the horses snorting and clopping. The man stroked a graying beard and eyed him warily.

"Ahoy there," said Bob, putting on a smile. "Fine day and all."

"You a bandit?" asked the man, squinting. "Don't have nothing. Just some veggies and such."

"Oh, no sir," said Bob. "I hate bandits." It was the truth.

The man's eyes moved up and down over Bob, taking in his trench coat, unkempt hair, his sunglasses. "You look funny," said the man.

"Well, you aren't winning any beauty contests yourself." Bob spat off to the side of the road.

That brought a smirk to the older man's face. "Funny clothes," he said. "That a cloak? Looks like a cloak. You a wizard?"

Bob searched the other man's face. He didn't seem to be joking, so Bob considered the question. Unconsciously, his hand reached up to the Gatekey on his neck as he thought of all the things he could not explain. "Well, I suppose so," he said. "I do know a thing or two about magic."

"That so?" said the man, seemingly impressed. "What's that on your eyes? Can you even see?"

Bob remembered the sunglasses and took them off. He turned them around so the man could see the backs of the lenses. "See just fine. Makes the sun less blinding."

"Huh. Where you off to, Wizard?"

"Not really sure. I'm a bit new around here. Came from… distant lands. Across the ocean." This was Bob's go-to excuse. If he was in a world that had oceans, that's what he told people who asked. *I'm from across the ocean.* He hadn't seen any oceans yet, but this place seemed near enough to his Earth, so he went for it. "I'm looking for a man. Well, not a man exactly. He's worse. He'd be even more funny looking than me. Would've come through here just a few hours ago. You seen such a man?"

The guy shook his head. "Can't say I have. What do you mean, 'not a man, exactly'? He an elf?"

Again, Bob studied the man for a trace of irony and found none. Wizards and elves? Bob already couldn't wait to get out of here. He replaced the sunglasses on his face, sighing. "No, not an elf. More like a, I don't know, like a demon."

The man's eyes widened. "Can't say I seen no demons! What you want with this one?"

"Well," said Bob, "I'd like to kill his ass."

This seemed to relax the guy. "Oh, well that's good. Say, I can't sit here all-day flapping jaws. Got to get on up to Swearington. This path's not so safe lately. I figure a man who kills demons could kill bandits just as well. You want to ride along?"

"Fuckin' A," replied Bob, grinning. The wagoner looked confused. "I mean, yes sir, I'd appreciate a lift very much."

"Right then, hop on. Name's Willis Bailey, by the by."

Bob hefted himself up to sit next to Willis. "Oh, uh, I'm Bob." They shook hands.

Willis scoffed. "Ha. Bob the Wizard. Alright then. Hyah!" He whipped the reins, and the wagon resumed its journey into the hills.

The ride was bumpy, like sitting on the drier in the laundry room. Bob noticed, propped on Willis's left, a small crossbow, fully cranked and loaded and ready to fire. The front panel of the wagon and the angle had obscured it during their introduction. Bob was glad he hadn't offended the guy—he was unsure he could've pulled the sawed-off in time if things had gotten ugly. But Willis seemed okay, so never mind.

"So, Willis," said Bob, raising his voice over the clopping of the horses and the rattle of the wagon, "veggies, huh?"

"Yeah, and some odds and ends. Bringing them to Market Circle, you know. Last trip from the harvest. First load for the King, second for the Liege Lord, and the last load I can sell for my own sake. Could sell it in Lighton, but Swearington's got higher prices, being Engoria's center of commerce and all. Say, can I try them fancy eye things?"

Bob smiled, taking off the sunglasses and passing them over. Willis put them on carefully as the wagon's movement bounced his hand. At first, the farmer threw his head back in shock. Then, looking around at the hills and the occasional tree, he laughed. "A man could get used to this," he said.

"Keep them," said Bob.

"No, I couldn't—"

"Yeah, sure, keep them. As payment for the ride."

Willis pushed out his lower lip. "Alright then. What else they do? They let me see those demons?"

Bob chuckled. "No, no. Just keep the sun out of your eyes."

"Well, that's magic enough, I suppose. Thanks, Bob the Wizard."

Bob waved his hand. "Don't mention it. Though, I wouldn't mind if you'd answer a few questions. For a weary traveler. What do you say?"

Willis shrugged. "I'll answer best I can. Just you keep an eye out for trouble."

"Deal," said Bob, and cleared his throat. "Always best to start with the basics. What do you call this world?"

The farmer's sidelong glance was apparent even through the sunglasses. "The world? World's called Hub. Where'd you say you're from, again?"

"Across the—"

"Across the ocean, yeah. Alright, Bob the Wizard from across the ocean, what else?"

"Hub, huh? Why's it called that?" The wagon crested a hill and the road flattened out some as they approached the next rise. The tall stalks of grass whispered around them.

"Why's it called…? I don't know. Just what we call it. Why's anything called anything? Why you called Bob?"

"Short for Robert," said Bob.

Willis snorted. "Bit of a smartass, aren't you?"

"I'll ask the questions here," replied Bob, smirking. He saw Willis shake his head, amusement and frustration warring on his face. "For example," he pressed, "what country are we in?"

Willis scratched his neck. "Country? Well, I think you mean to ask what kingdom. If you do mean that, well then, you're in Engoria."

The wagon rattled over a pothole. "Engoria," repeated Bob, trying out the word. Willis said nothing, and the conversation lapsed. Bob gazed across the rolling hills of grass, spotting more wildlife. He saw a few more deer, and a long green snake slithered from the road into the grass. He thought he saw one of those firefly-like lights darting around a large maple. Bob stared at the tree, but the little flying light, if it had been there at all, was gone.

The horses were working to pull the wagon up a particularly steep hill, at the crest of which the road would pass between two large mounds of craggy rock that jutted from the grass like a giant's knuckles. A large birch stood at the summit of the mound on the left. The hill's height barred any attempt to see beyond it.

"So, who's this demon fellow?" asked Willis.

"He's a murderous bastard," said Bob. "Killed my wife and son. Been chasing him ever since."

Willis looked uncomfortable. "Right sorry to hear. Sorry for your loss."

"Thanks. It was a while ago now. Don't know, years maybe. Time is sometimes hard to track."

"Not when you're farming. Crops tell time better than any calendar when you see them every day."

"I'll take your word for it. Never was a farmer," said Bob. "Say Willis, you ever heard of something called Astral Gates?"

Willis grunted. "That some kind of church thing?"

"Uh, no, never mind." It had been worth a shot.

Willis adjusted the sunglasses. "You been doing it all alone?"

Bob's mind had begun to wander. "What's that?"

"Chasing this demon fellow. Said what he did to your family was years ago, but here you are, still chasing. I may be a simple old farmer, but I can add two and two. You been chasing this demon the whole time. So my question is: you been doing it all alone?"

Bob stared across the sea of grass as it rippled in the wind. "That I have, Willis. That I have."

"That's a shame. People need other people. I reckon even Bob the Wizard needs a hand now and then."

"Two hands is usually enough," said Bob dismissively. He'd already decided to like Willis, but he found advice exasperating—especially concerning the matter of finding Galvidon.

"What'll you do after?"

"After?" repeated Bob absently.

"After you get him," said the farmer. "What'll you do then?"

"Haven't thought that far ahead," said Bob. "Finding him is my whole life now." It had been a long while since he'd talked about himself, and his words rang unpleasantly true to his own ears.

"If it were me," mused Farmer Willis, "I'd start a new family. Or find one. Everybody needs a family."

Bob had no reply. For so long, finding Galvidon was the only thing that'd mattered. As a result, Bob now felt at a distance from other people. He couldn't see himself ever having another family. Besides, Anna and Daniel were his family. Now they were gone.

The wagon creaked up to the crest of the hill. The two craggy mounds rose up on either side, throwing shadows. The horses spat and snorted. As they reached the crest, a flit of movement by the tall birch caught Bob's eye.

Willis said something, but Bob didn't hear. There was the sharp whistle of disturbed air, then an arrow shaft was protruding from Willis's chest. Just before flinging himself off the wagon and into the grass, Bob glimpsed the farmer fumble for the crossbow. Bob struck the ground, rolled, threw his weight to minimize the pressure on the backpack. The leather of his coat protecting his arms from friction, he skidded and flopped among a patch of khaki-colored stalks.

The horses must have been exhausted from the climb because the wagon rolled to a stop. The animals' nervous snorts mixed in Bob's ears with the shouts of men and the ring of unsheathed metal weapons. Bob, heart hammering, had already taken off his pack and untied the sawed-off from inside the trench coat. It was an old weapon with two triggers—one for each barrel. The shotgun was currently loaded for diversity, with one barrel holding a slug and the other a shell of buckshot. Bob grabbed the ammo belt from his pack and draped it over his shoulder, leaving the pack where it lay. Breathing as evenly as he could, he moved in a crouch, inching through the stalks of grass to get a view of the attackers.

The halted wagon partially obscured his view. He could see four men, and one of them looked…blue. They all wore rough leather armor over woolen clothing and bore shortswords, axes, or daggers. Bob could see no bows, so the arrow must have come from an assailant that was out of his line of sight. One of the men had blue skin and pointed ears. Bob remembered what Willis had asked him when he'd described Galvidon as not really being a man. *He an elf?* Apparently, this world had blue elves, and they weren't above being bandits. The armed men approached the wagon, and all but the blue elf had a crazed, desperate look about them. The elf simply looked determined.

Bob heard the gurgling voice of Willis mutter curses and there was a loud *thwap*. Bob saw a large dirty man bearing an axe get struck in the head with a crossbow bolt. Blood shot from the wound in a quick spout and the bandit crumpled to the dirt road.

"Shit!" yelled one of the bandits. "He isn't dead!"

There was another sharp whistle and a thump, and Bob knew Willis had taken another arrow. He was surely dead now. The black horse reared up, whinnying, and kicked out at a man with a shortsword, causing him to stumble backwards. Bob sprang onto the road, cocking back both hammers on the sawed-off. The arrows had come from the southwest, so once Bob reached the wagon's rear, he moved around its eastern side, keeping the vehicle between him and the shooter. The bandits on the road were rounding the wagon, careful of the horses, which were both twitching and stomping. Two men came around the wagon's front side toward Bob, spotting him. The man with the shortsword who had stumbled away from the horse scowled and raised his weapon. The other, bearing a notched dagger, grinned and ran at Bob, screaming.

Bob pulled the shotgun's right trigger and a slug blasted through the man's skull, leather skullcap and all, clean through to the other side. He spun, blood and brains spiraling out both sides of his head. A stream of red, goopy matter splattered the canvas on the wagon and streaked across the sword-wielder's shirt. The gun's report was enormously loud, echoing across the hills. Bob heard curses and yells of alarm from the other side of the wagon. The sword-wielder was horror-struck. His hands trembled as his head jerked from the dead Bandit to the blood on the wagon to Bob. Bob wasted no time and pulled the other trigger. The buckshot took the guy's head off, splattering it to fleshy bits that rained in a radial mist of gore.

Sensing the imminent approach of the remaining assailants, Bob rounded to the front of the wagon. He was careful not to break cover. The archer was somewhere in the grass on the vehicle's other side. Bob cracked the breech on his weapon and deftly removed the spent shells in a plume of gun smoke. The brass on the shells seared his fingertips as he tossed them. He grabbed two more at random from the ammo belt around his chest and inserted them into the barrels. The breech clicked shut. Bob cocked the hammers just as two men came around from the wagon's rear.

One of them was the blue guy. They both looked shocked and confused. Bob figured the loud sounds had mystified them—and seeing their friends' heads turned to hamburger had probably done nothing for their confidence.

BOB THE WIZARD

Bob leveled both barrels at them. "Ahoy there, fuckers," he said. "Seeing as how you killed my good friend Willis, I ought to end your days outright. But I'll give you a chance. Run the fuck away, and I won't do to you what I did to them."

The bandit that wasn't blue dropped his axe and bolted, sprinting east down the road without so much as a goodbye. The elf eyed the dead bandits and then met Bob's stare. He dashed. The sawed-off roared—but Bob missed. He must have loaded a slug, and this guy was fast. The blue elf was on him, bringing down his sword in a deft killing stroke. But Bob was fast too, and he pulled the other trigger. An explosion of buckshot launched his attacker backward through the air.

The horses had had enough and began to drag the wagon down the road. The blue guy lay prone several yards away, dying. Doing his best to ignore the gurgles, Bob turned to jog after the wagon.

"Woah, now," he called to the horses. "Woah there, easy, easy."

They slowed but didn't stop, and Bob hauled himself onto the wagon as it moved. He plopped down next to the dead form of Willis the Farmer. Bob set his gun down on the wooden panels and pulled on the reins, speaking more calming nonsense. The horses halted, and he craned to peer south. At the height of a hill, maybe a quarter mile away, he could see another blue elf, standing tall in the grass. He had regal features—a long nose and a square, hairless jawline. His piercing eyes shone with cold, deeply seated rage. In his hands was a longbow, well-made from hewn branches. They stared at each other, Bob and the archer, for a long moment, sizing each other up. Then, the blue elf turned and vanished into the khaki-grass.

Bob turned to the corpse of the farmer. "Well Willis, this has turned out to be a pretty fucked up day."

CHAPTER TWO:
REST FOR A FOOL

The blue archer gone, Bob nudged the horses westward down the path. Willis's corpse bounced and slid into a heap at the floor of the wagon's cab. After only a few yards, Bob reigned the animals in again and sat for a moment under the sun, thinking. He sighed and hopped off the wagon, rounding to its rear gate, which creaked open when he unlatched it.

There he found bags of barley, corn, turnips, and radishes. There was a shovel made from a curved iron plate crudely bolted to a hefty wooden dowel, a few other gardening implements, a bale of hay, a few small tins of sugar and salt, and three large sewn bladders that were corked at the top. At first Bob feared the bladders might contain wine or beer—if it was alcohol, he might actually drink it. He popped open a cork and sniffed. To his relief, it was water. He drank greedily.

After pocketing a tin of sugar, he unenthusiastically ate half a radish and then brought the bale of hay around to the horses, patting them each reassuringly on their flanks before going back for his backpack. The elf he'd shot—the one that'd almost sliced him with a sword—lay a dozen yards behind him on the road. A ragged crimson hole sat in his midsection like a mouth, the surrounding area peppered with little round wounds. The two men, their identities now unidentifiable due to their pulverized heads, lay partly in the grass nearby. They were already gathering flies. God rest their souls, or whatever.

Bob discarded the spent shell casings from the sawed-off and reloaded as before—slug in the right barrel, buckshot in the left. Not counting those two shells, he had four slugs and eight shells of buckshot remaining. He stuffed the ammo belt back in the backpack, pulled out some jerky and munched on it, then returned to the wagon, picking up the shortsword, axe and daggers from the dead bandits on the way. He deposited the weapons in the vehicle's bed.

As he came around to the cab, Bob scanned the horizon to make sure he was still alone. Satisfied, he returned his attention to the wagon. He stared at it. Something told him he should just leave it, proceed on foot to the city Willis said he was heading toward. What was it called again? Swearington, that was it. Anyway, he was used to walking. No big deal. Besides, the wagon wasn't his. Taking it would be stealing. Did that matter? And who would know? Bob couldn't fool himself into thinking he didn't need the wagon's contents—surely, he'd be able to sell off what he didn't eat, and money was always helpful. He might need it to bribe someone for information on Galvidon's whereabouts. If he didn't take the wagon, he'd shortly run out of food and probably end up stealing something else. And what would happen to the horses if he just left them here?

He almost forgot to check the Gatekey around his neck, which, after about an hour and a half in the sun, was almost fully charged. At least, Bob thought it had been that long. Jumping between worlds was hell on his internal clock: a kind of cosmic jetlag. He opened the sugar tin, and it was full of cubes. He popped a couple in his mouth and then fed the rest to the horses. Bob thought about the bandit's ambush, and wondered why, if they wanted the contents of the wagon, they hadn't just shot the horses to prevent its escape. Then he reconsidered. Horses were valuable. The bastards were probably hoping to steal them, too. He decided that he'd better get a move on, since the men—and elves—that'd killed Willis probably had a camp nearby, and the blue archer was probably heading back there now. If it was close, more of those sorry excuses for human beings—and elves—might be coming to this very spot to finish what they started. Briefly, he considered trying to bury Willis with the shovel, but decided he didn't have time. He dumped the farmer's body unceremoniously in the grass on the side of the road.

"Sorry pal," he muttered. The corpse had two arrows protruding from its chest. Bob snatched back his sunglasses, wiped some blood off in the grass, and replaced them on his own face. He returned to the wagon and propped Willis's crossbow by his leg as the farmer had done. He scanned around for men—and elves.

Bob shook his head. "Fucking elves, man. Fucking blue elves. That's a first." He whipped the reins and the wagon rolled on toward Swearington.

It took about an hour of driving through hills until he saw signs of civilization. The land began to even out, though he could still see hills in the distance to the north. The bushy patches of tall, khaki-colored grass were left behind and the short, green variety lay across the landscape like a blanket. He soon realized that it had been cropped by livestock, namely sheep, which moved in flocks behind low wooden fences along the road. Bob saw men and women out in the fields or around their wooden hovels, tending the sheep or scything barley or beating laundry dangling on lines. Like Willis had, they all wore dirty, rough-spun wool.

Beneath a distant pall of smoke, an enormous medieval city began to take shape on the horizon. To the southeast, he could see the birches and maples growing more heavily with other trees and underbrush—the beginnings of a forest. A group of men carved at large trunks with axes, hefted fallen trees onto wagons pulled by donkeys. Skin colors ranged from sunburned white to almond brown, and all the workers seemed to have dark hair, ranging from brown to black. He saw no elves.

Bob drew stares. *You look funny*, he remembered Willis saying. Bob did his best to seem as if he were perfectly comfortable, grinning back at his onlookers and waving. Hard, accusatory looks were set on the workers' faces. "Oh, don't mind me," muttered Bob. "Just Bob the Wizard, passing through."

A shadow passed overhead. Bob glanced up, expecting a storm cloud or flock of birds. But high above him, gliding through the air on giant, leathery wings, was a monstrous silhouette—just a dark shape, the sun glaring above it. It appeared to be an enormous flying animal, long and snake-like, with a triangular head and a finned tail. It flapped its great wings, miles above the rolling green, and then passed away toward the mountains in the north.

When Bob looked down again, he saw that many of the workers, farmers, and animal-tenders were peering to the sky as well. The horses pulling the wagon snorted and twitched, and for a moment there was a nervous stillness all around. Then the long shadow passed away and everyone went back to their tasks.

"Was that what I think it was?" Bob asked the horses.

He didn't even want to think it, but wouldn't it fit with the elves and talk of wizards? He sighed and lit a cigarette, hoping again that Galvidon would soon flee this world called Hub, like he had all the others so far. That way, Bob could find the nearest Astral Gate and leave this world behind.

Swearington was impressive from the outside. Long, crenellated walls, thrice the height of a man, wrapped its perimeter. Snapping and dancing in the air, hung on pikes from rooftops and wall-mounts, were great banners. There seemed to be two varieties, always arranged with one above the other. The top banner featured a black turtle from above, on a deep green field, enclosed in a golden rectangle. The bottom displayed a white fist on a black field, surrounded by a white circle. Bob guessed, based on their relative positions, that the turtle was the symbol of the nation or kingdom, and the fist was the symbol of the city or province. He was sure that he would find out, whether he liked it or not. If he was going to catch Galvidon, he'd have to start asking around—and in a place like this, with relatively low technology, the only people who would have any kind of knowledge outside of their trade would be the leadership.

The road hardened to cobble as the horses pressed onward. The city loomed up on Bob's right. Beyond it, to the northeast, he could just make out the glitter of a huge lake. He passed a small gate at a section of wall where the sheep farmers seemed to mill through in both directions, carrying burdens of wool, or wood, or vegetables. The road seemed to be leading him to a much larger gate as it continued westward. Ahead, Bob saw another wagon trundling through the guarded sally port that led through the wall into Swearington proper.

As he drew closer to the large, iron sally port, he saw that beneath the crenelated wall of gray stone, there was a shallow moat tracing the wall's underside. It passed under the bridge and sally port that extended from Swearington's interior, yet was dry and empty, forgotten. The gate stood open, flanked by a pair of guards. They wore black and white, steel armor—shining breastplates, half-gauntlets, and greaves over chain and boiled leather. On their heads were skullcaps, and in their hands were halberds two feet taller than they. Green capes adorned their backs, and small versions of the black and white banners—displaying a fist—hung from the heads of their weapons. They bore dour expressions, which Bob decided was partly because it was their job to look intimidating, and partly because it must have been uncomfortably hot under all that armor.

The horses slowed as Bob approached the gate. The guards were eying him. He lifted the Gatekey from his chest and glanced at it. The little green meter was fully charged. He tucked it back into his shirt as the wagon pulled to a stop. The guard on the left was much taller than the other, his nose crooked, his face clean-shaven. The shorter one on the right had a close-cropped beard. Both men had dark brown hair.

Bob scratched his beard. "Ahoy there," he called, smiling.

"Where you coming from?" asked the tall guard on the left, sounding bored.

"Just got some crops for Market Circle."

"Never seen you before," said the short guard on the right.

"Well, truth is, I'm new around here. Doing a favor for a friend. Willis is his name. He put me up for the night, so in exchange I'm driving his crops to the market."

"He's letting you sell his crops?" said Tall, his brow rising.

"I've got a gift for commerce," said Bob.

"You look funny," declared Short, scowling.

"I'm a wizard," said Bob. He hoped this explanation would fly with the guards like it had with Willis.

Short looked doubtful. "That so?"

"What's that on your eyes?" demanded Tall. "Can you even see?"

"Wizard glasses," said Bob. "Keeps the sun off."

"Wizard glasses?" said Short. "I never heard of no wizard glasses."

"You know a lot of wizards?" asked Bob.

Tall snickered.

"Well, no," Short admitted. "How do they work?"

"Wizards?" asked Bob innocently.

Tall scowled. "The *glasses*. How do the *glasses* work, he wants to know!"

Bob shrugged. "Magic. How else?"

"You sure you can see?" asked Tall.

"Don't look magic to me," said Short.

Bob was unsure whether to be amused or frustrated. The Astraverse seemed bent on taking his sunglasses today. He slipped them off his face and leaned over the cab's front panel, holding them out toward Tall. The guard hesitated.

"Go ahead," said Bob, "perfectly safe."

Tall approached the wagon, halberd held high like a flag, and reached his gauntleted hand to take the sunglasses. His armor jingled like a piggy bank.

Tall got the glasses onto his face with some difficulty. He wore thin chainmail under his skullcap, so the earpieces flapped out, but the glasses clung to his head like a frightened bat. Tall seemed to blink and staggered back a bit. "By the Sun!" he exclaimed.

Short took alarm to this and jangled forward, lowering his halberd menacingly. The horses snorted indignantly and shifted around.

"Oh, calm down, Lem," said Tall. "Just surprised, is all. It's quite nice, really." He moved his head around, taking in the world anew. He waved his free hand in front of his face. "Amazing! Everything's all dim, but I can see fine!"

Short—or rather, Lem—lifted his weapon back to standing and clanked over to Tall. "I want to try."

"You boys have fun with those," said Bob. "Can I go in?"

"Yeah, sure, Wizard," said Tall, handing the sunglasses to Lem. "But don't be casting no spells or nothing. Illegal, you know. King Flaire's orders."

"Not that we ever seen no magic," grumbled Lem.

"I hear you," said Bob, but he was already an afterthought to the two guards, who were fully enamored by the sunglasses. He got the horses moving under the gate and through the sally port. At a sudden thought, he swiveled. "Hey," he called, "who's in charge of this place anyway?"

"That's Lord Mannix," Bob heard Tall yell after him.

As the wagon passed through the far side of the port and into the courtyard, the guards' laughter rang out behind him.

The road continued through the courtyard. Bob passed a barracks and saw more guards milling around. They paid him no mind. Bob could hear the ringing of metal on metal, rhythmic and sharp. Soon he approached an outdoor smithy where a large muscular man, arms exposed outside his leather apron, pounded a rod of glowing metal into shape with a hammer. Two young men cinched pieces of hardened leather together. One of them looked up from his work at Bob, seemed about to call a greeting, but then scowled instead. The wagon trundled past a large canvas tent with its flaps wide open. Inside it, behind a grizzled merchant, dead birds—pheasants, maybe—hung from hooks. The merchant called to him, claiming the best prices north of Royal River.

The path wound through the courtyard in a wide semicircle around Swearington's outskirts. It took him west before doubling back eastward. There were smaller roads crossing the main thoroughfare, but Bob feared getting lost, so he took no detours. Along the way, he passed guard towers, women who seemed to be making wool, more smithies, and a noisy tavern called the Swear House. Occasionally, the looming tip of an enormous keep peeked at him from the center of the city.

Finally, sweating so profusely he thought he might take off his coat—something he rarely did in strange places—he reached an inn. A wooden sign painted with the words *The Fool's Rest* creaked in the breeze. Bob gratefully pulled the horses to a stop and swung himself down from the high driver's seat. He retrieved a couple of radishes from the bed of the wagon and offered them to the horses, who seemed about as eager to eat them as he'd been. They dejectedly began munching anyway.

"Soon you'll be nice and comfy in a stall," he told them. "Just have some business to attend first. Don't go anywhere." The animals flipped their tails in reply. Bob walked up to the Fool's Rest, its great oaken door standing slightly ajar.

Hesitant, Bob pushed open the heavy door, revealing an interior of carved wooden chairs, plush red pillows, and leafy plants on the rafters that wove down support beams like ivy. An embroidered mat sat atop the clean, woodgrain floor. Across from the entrance lay a long welcome desk of polished mahogany. Upon it sat an unlit lantern, a little bronze bell, a leather-bound book with its pages open, and a curled-up orange cat. Behind the desk stood a beautiful young lady, straight brown hair held back with a painted wooden headband. She wore a blue dress and a white apron. The floor creaked as Bob entered and she looked up from absently petting the cat. Bob stood in the doorway, momentarily speechless. He was suddenly, keenly aware of being dirty, sweaty, and smelly. He unconsciously squeezed his armpits closer to his midsection.

"Hello, traveler," said the woman. "Welcome to the Fool's Rest. Do you wish to rent a room?"

"I…" Bob cleared his throat. She looked so much like Anna.

"Cat got your tongue?" she asked breezily. She scratched the cat under the chin, and the feline raised its head, purring. "Do you have his tongue, kitty?" She chuckled.

"I, uh… Yes, a room would be nice. Do you have somewhere I could get a bath? I'm a bit…uh, travel-worn." He cleared his throat again.

"Yes, we have a bath room. An extra silver. Would you like it prepared?"

"I have no silver, I'm afraid. Just crops to sell at Market Circle. Would you take barter?"

"Why, certainly. Have you any barley? We simply can't get enough. Sweet barley is our most popular breakfast."

"Oh, yes, got plenty. How much for a room and a bath?"

"One moment, I'll have to confer with my father."

She ducked away into a back room. The orange cat eyed him suspiciously and then hopped away. Bob was left to awkwardly look around the room like a museum patron. At least it was pleasantly cool.

After a few minutes, the young woman that looked like Anna returned with an old man. He squinted, holding his daughter's arm as a guide. Only a few wispy white hairs remained upon his head, and his lips seemed perpetually puckered.

"Hello there," said the man in a tremulous voice. He doddered behind the desk and extended a wrinkled hand. "Name's Gerald Sun. I'm the owner of Fool's Rest. The Head Fool, you might say." He grinned, revealing only a few teeth.

Bob stepped forward and shook the old man's hand, chuckling. "Robert Caplan, friends call me Bob." He had long discarded the notion that he should give a false name. He was from across the Astraverse—it wasn't as if Gerald could look up his social security number.

"Jenna tells me you're looking to trade. Says you got barley."

"Yeah, if you'd take some off my hands for a room and bath, I'd appreciate it." Bob was making a conscious effort not to curse. It seemed like a poor time for profanity, but it was no small strain. "Also got some corn, turnips, radishes, a bit of sugar and some salt. Planning to unload at Market Circle tomorrow—which I'll, uh, need directions to."

The old man narrowed his eyes and suddenly Jenna seemed clouded in concern. Bob shifted on his feet, uncomfortable. "Mr. Caplan," said Gerald, "your list of crops sounds an awful lot like it came from Bailey Farm out near Lighton."

The lie came easily. "Met the Baileys. Nice folk. Put me up for a couple days. Willis sent me up with his last load, so he could relax." He smiled, but he was suddenly very worried. He hadn't counted on Farmer Willis being such a well-known figure. Who knew a farmer could have so many friends?

Gerald and Jenna's suspicion appeared to deflate. It was probably that detail about the final load that saved Bob, at least for now. He needed to get to this Mannix fellow and figure out where to go to find Galvidon, and he needed to do it soon. The longer he stayed in Swearington, the more likely he was to fall under suspicion. He hadn't killed poor Willis, but he *was* guilty of stealing the man's wagon. Best to be gone before anyone found out. He suddenly wished he'd taken the time to better hide those bodies. He'd been so concerned about getting away before more bandits arrived, he hadn't considered the need to cover up evidence. Just habit, he supposed. He followed Galvidon and damn the consequences. Doubt trickled down Bob's spine and he shook it off. He told himself what he always did: that he'd be gone before the consequences of his actions could catch up to him.

Before he could bathe, there was business. Gerald ended up with all the barley in the wagon, trading Bob money in the form of gold, silver, and copper coins. Trusting Gerald and Jenna to give him a fair deal, he paid no attention to the precise value of the currency. After a promised bath and a room for the night, he came away with three gold, six silver, and a handful of coppers. He expected to have to pay for at least one more night at the Fool's Rest, so that was two silvers reserved, three if he wanted a second bath.

The horses were irate by the time Bob had them pull the wagon around to the back of the inn. They twitched their ears and glared at him wearily. He had to coax them with more sugar cubes to accompany him to the nearby stable. The ostler was a grumpy asshole named Samuel that bitched at Bob about the state of the horses. Bob had to retell the lie about Willis taking him in, because Samuel clearly knew the horses well. The chestnut-brown horse was Abigail, apparently, and the black horse was called Shade.

Bob gave up Abigail and Shade to Samuel's stable, where he was sure their remaining tack was removed, and they were watered and rubbed down. That cost him a full five more silvers, and by the time it was all said and done, the sun was going down. Bob doubted that Lord Mannix would take visitors in the dark, and besides, he was sleepy and sore. The Fool's Rest was waiting. After a quick and tepid bath, Bob was exhausted. He ascended the staircase to his room, catching a glimpse of Jenna, still beautiful. He fell asleep thinking of Anna and had nightmares full of death.

CHAPTER THREE:
OATH KEEP

The morning light filtered through the shuttered windows of the Fool's Rest. Bob woke up earlier than he'd like—not because of the light, but because the day was already warm and sultry. His room, though cooler than outside, was not exactly air conditioned. The morning's chores involved eating the famous sweetened barley for breakfast, dressing in the off-white, rough-spun outfit he'd purchased from Gerald the night before, cleaning the sawed-off with some gun oil from his pack, and donning his filthy trench coat. Warm as the day was, several important items were concealed within the coat, including his weapons. The Gatekey still hung around his neck on a shoestring, and had through the night, its green meter still fully charged and ready. Using any of its abilities might draw unwanted attention, but he'd do it, if he had to. Maybe then, the city of Swearington would take his status as a wizard more seriously. Not that he really believed in magic. The power of the Gatekey simply came from technology beyond his understanding. Nevertheless, when it came to the hunt for Galvidon, Bob was not above employing theatrics.

That a cloak? Looks like a cloak. Willis's words came back to him. *You a wizard?*

And then, the guards had mentioned something about the king outlawing magic. Yet when Bob had claimed to be a wizard to both Willis and the guards, neither party had seemed to fear him. What exactly was this illegal magic people seemed to believe in? Bob didn't really want to find out, but he had to blend in long enough to get to Galvidon. If blending in meant pretending to be a wizard, then fuck it, Bob was in.

Not interested in dealing with Samuel the Ostler, Bob left the horses and entered the roadways of Swearington on foot. He drew stares from citizens as he passed them. There was something else both Farmer Willis and the guards had said. *You look funny.* Bob avoided eye contact if at all possible. As he walked, he checked a roughly drawn map of the city he'd bought from Jenna for three coppers. He planned on setting up a stall at Market Circle if he didn't find compelling news of Galvidon. He'd need supplies for his travels, and turnips and radishes were not what he'd call essentials. As he wound his way toward the city's heart, the last cigarette from the previous world smoldered on his lips. He'd smoked the other three the night before in his room before bed, and finding tobacco—or a satisfactory analogue—was a priority. Shit, Hub seemed close enough to his Earth in plenty of ways. Bob had *better* be able to get his hands on some tobacco, or he'd be one seriously grouchy wizard.

He checked the map again. The entire northeast section of the city, labeled *the Sun's Quarter*, seemed to be separated from the rest by one wall stretching from the keep northward, and another wall eastward. This was probably where the nobles lived, or whatever they called themselves. The rich people. Anyway, Bob had no need to go there. The path from the Fool's Rest to Oath Keep—so it was labeled—seemed to zigzag northwesterly through a no-man's land between the huge swathe of Shadow Quarter in Swearington's northwest and the commercial district surrounding South Gate. The gray-and-white, cobbled streets, often lined with horse shit, weaved around shanties and stonework stores.

Bob passed more than one fenced lot that seemed to house piles of yellow and black stone rubble. Draped over them from poles were canopies of patchwork hides or canvas—some measure of protection against the elements. Beyond the looming keep, ominous buildings billowed plumes of black smoke from chimneys, adding a faint tinge of burning metal to Swearington's aroma of shit and sweat. The closer to the city's center he got, the more clouded with black smoke the sky became, dimming the streets, turning the heat into a stifling blanket.

There were churches, each displaying a shining sun as their icon. Bob, disinterested, barely noticed them. He passed carriages and wagons, stalls and alleys, beggars and whores, taverns and inns—all of it filthy and uninviting. Bob realized he'd been staying in Swearington's version of a fancy hotel.

M. V. PRINDLE

As he approached Oath Keep's main entrance, an odd little shop caught his eye. Its sign proclaimed it to be *Abernathy's Apothecary*, and it sat across the cobbled road from one of the covered rubble-piles. An odd assortment of sun-bleached knickknacks was displayed behind its cloudy windows. Bob marked it, both mentally and on the map, as a place to search for tobacco.

Finally, he rounded a street corner, and the keep came into view. It's structure and splendor were a stark contrast to the messy squalor that made up what Bob had seen of Swearington. It sat six or seven stories high, and upon its walls were multicolored, stained-glass windows depicting strange happenings that Bob didn't care to understand. The keep's upper sections held several high, crenelated platforms for defense, and a few stone balconies enclosed by ornate balustrades and shaded by thatched roofs. It appeared to have two main wings, and atop the main tower flew snapping, black and white banners. The keep's fine stonework glistened in the sunlight, daring Bob to approach it.

There was an outer wall, but the barred-iron gate lay invitingly open. Through it, Bob could see the inner courtyard, paved in immaculate cobbles and ringed at the edges with bright green grass. A carved sign of polished wood labeled *Oath Keep* was set in a frame atop the arch of the gate. Bob passed under the arch into the courtyard, and for a moment stood alone, letting the ambient sounds of Swearington play in his ears.

Stone steps, shallow but wide, led up to the keep's main entrance—a large pair of oaken doors flanked by support columns. No guards to stop him, Bob tentatively pushed open the ornate double doors. They creaked. He glimpsed a darkened atrium lit by filtered sunlight shining in through both stained-glass and smaller, open-air windows. A moment passed, and when no one stopped him, he strolled on in.

Between a pair of armored guards, a large marble dais dominated the atrium from the room's center. A high ceiling extended all the way to the top story and was surrounded by white bannisters on every floor. Bob saw a blue-skinned elf woman with red and purple hair. She carried a pile of scrolls toward the dais, clad in a simple brown dress that was little more than a sack. Upon the dais was a high seat, and upon it sat a lofty middle-aged man busily writing away with a quill. The scratches of the quill echoed in the great chamber like secrets. The guards, who were dressed identically to the two at South Gate, made no move to intercept Bob. Though, they did favor him with a familiar look of disapproval.

The double doors swung shut naturally with a clamor. Bob's footfalls produced an echo. The writing man did not look up as Bob approached his seat. There was something about the guy that seemed different to Bob, though he couldn't quite place it. Then it came. This man, sitting atop the dais on a high-backed marble chair lined with black cushions, wearing billowing black and white robes and scratching away with a quill, was blond. It dawned on Bob just then that every human he'd seen since arriving on Hub had brown or black hair—but not this man. His primly cut and combed hair was quite blond. The dim light softly reflected off the man's round, clean shaven face. Bob cleared his throat loudly.

"Yes?" said the blond man without looking up. "What?" He was still scratching. The elf woman deposited her scrolls at the bottom of the dais and slinked away. The two guards remained motionless, staring at Bob as if he were a bug.

"Are you Lord Mannix?" asked Bob in the most diplomatic tone he could muster.

"What? Don't be ridiculous," said the blond man. He glanced up at Bob and stopped writing. The room fell silent. Bob was keenly aware of his own breathing. "Who... what... are you?" he demanded. He was clearly irritated. Just as clearly, Bob saw that he was a man who held authority, whether or not he was Mannix. He glared at Bob with the air of a man who didn't need to make threats, simply because everyone knew not to fuck with him.

"I apologize, uh... my lord." Bob waited to see if his chosen honorific would be corrected. The man just kept staring at him, so Bob blundered forward. "I am Robert Caplan, known around here as Bob the Wizard. I'm a traveler from faraway lands, and I seek the council of Lord Mannix, who I understand to be the supreme authority in Swearington. May I ask, my lord...who I am addressing?"

The blond man sat up straight, hands to the hems of his robe. "You have the pleasure of addressing Archlector Stephen Carosel. I am Logistics Counselor to Lord Mannix. Furthermore, for the city of Swearington, I am executive of treasures and municipal infrastructure." He narrowed his eyes. "I must say it is easy to tell that you are not from here, Darkhair. Your hair is long like a woman's, you appear to lack hygiene in regard to facial hair, and your cloak is of a queer fashion I have never seen. You say you are a wizard. I have my doubts. I have met wizards and witnessed their magic, Mr. Caplan, and you, apart from simply being odd, have nothing in common with them." He seemed to consider a hidden thought. "Unless you are as criminal as you appear, in which case you might as well be a wizard. Now. *Are* you a criminal?"

Bob was certain that he was. No use admitting it. "Of course not, sir," he grated. "And... I mean no offense." Man, those words were hard to get out. "I'm a simple traveler who's come a long way. I seek any information that you, or the esteemed Lord Mannix, could provide."

The Archlector displayed a cagey look. "I see. And you can pay?"

"Pay... pay what?"

Carosel chuckled. "Lord Mannix and I are busy men. You have already wasted minutes of my time. Regardless of how far you've traveled, I shall provide no information, nor shall I call Lord Mannix down from his chambers at the behest of a Darkhair, without substantial incentive. One hundred gold pieces."

Bob laughed. "My lord, I don't have even close to—"

"Yes, quite right. Off with you." Lord Carosel waved his hand dismissively and returned to scratching with his quill. Bob quietly seethed. Anna had a word for irredeemable men. *Douchebags*, she called them. Bob was confidant she'd agree, he was currently dealing with a Grade-A douchebag.

The guards took a step forward. The looks in their eyes had changed. They were hesitant, nervous. Perhaps they were less convinced than Stephen Carosel that Bob was not a wizard. It didn't matter—Carosel had inadvertently given away that Mannix was here, somewhere in the keep, and Bob had a fully charged Gatekey. Bob was not going to allow this pompous blond douchebag to get in his way. He turned his back on the guards and flung open the double doors, allowing them to slam noisily against the walls. He trotted out into the sunlight, smiling the ill grin of a man with a secret weapon.

BOB THE WIZARD

Bob kept the sawed-off tied inside the trench coat on his right side. On his left, there was a pair of slim, steel, seven-inch combat knives in plastic sheathes. He didn't use them often in combat because, for one, the gun was a much better close-range weapon, and for another, he was far from an expert in blade-combat. Mostly, he used the knives for practical purposes—skinning animals, cutting cords, that sort of thing. Although he had killed some people in self-defense since he started his hunt for Galvidon, and he planned on murdering that alien-looking son of a bitch at the first opportunity, he wasn't an assassin. He sometimes thought that if he ever needed to kill someone quietly—really needed to—the knives would do the trick. But there was another thing Bob figured the knives could do that the shotgun couldn't: scare the shit out of an asshole medieval lord. Waving the gun around wouldn't have the desired effect—this Mannix fucker probably had no idea what a gun was and would therefore likely just scoff. Bob would have to blow his head off, and then he'd be in even deeper shit than he was now. Anyway, it was probably best to leave intimidation as a last resort. Outside Oath Keep, Bob patted his left side to reassure himself the blades were still there.

Carosel had said he wouldn't call Mannix *down from his chambers*. Bob had an idea that meant Mannix was somewhere near the top of the structure. He'd moved around to a side street outside the keep's wall. From there, he could still see the upper half of the tower section. He surveyed the building. A horse-drawn carriage passed behind him. The horses and the driver ignored him, but there was a fresh lump of manure adding its aroma to the air after the carriage passed. It seemed appropriate after talking to Archlector Carosel.

Bob fingered the Gatekey. "Not a wizard, huh?" he muttered. He'd never thought of himself in those terms before he'd met Farmer Willis. He remembered a bizarre conversation with a dying creature named Rashindon, next to the corpses of his wife and son. Rashindon had said that he, Bob, was special in some way. Bob had no idea what that was supposed to mean. But now, about to use one of the Gatekey's powers, he wondered. Someone from his Earth had once said that any technology, sufficiently advanced, was indistinguishable from magic. And if the people of Hub saw what the Gatekey could do, they'd damn sure think it *was* magic. So maybe he really was a wizard after all. At least, he'd like to think so.

Eyes fixed on the highest visible balcony, Bob pressed one of the tiny buttons on the Gatekey. For less than a second, the world blurred around him. Then, everything sharpened, and he was standing safely behind the railing of the balcony atop the keep.

"Eat shit, Carosel," he muttered, and reached for the door that led into Oath Keep.

There was a circle of frosted glass set into the door. Just beyond was a stone veranda and a pair of wicker chairs. Beyond that was a hallway lined with doorways and empty sconces. To Bob's left, the hallway curved onto a shadowed indoor balcony. He softly pulled the door shut behind him and stepped into the hallway. He could hear a man humming in a deep timbre.

Suddenly, a set of doors cattycorner to the veranda opened to Bob's right. A young elf woman stepped out of it—different than the one that'd been carrying scrolls to the Archlector downstairs. She wore the same simple brown dress, and she seemed to be adjusting it here and there, as if making sure it was on right. Her hair was a bright shock of red the color of wine, and on her neck was a mark that was unmistakable—a hickey. She glanced up and saw Bob standing in the hallway and froze, eyes wide, hand still on the strap of her sack-like dress. Bob just smiled at her and winked, bringing his finger up to his lips in a friendly shushing gesture. She stared for a moment, then came to some silent conclusion. She finished straightening her clothes and walked easily past him down the hall toward the indoor balcony. Bob could hear the humming man behind the very door that she had exited. He strode to the door and opened it with confidence, stepping into the room.

It was a lavish bedchamber, full of silks and oil paintings and rich woods. A fellow about Bob's age, back turned, sat on a king-sized bed. He appeared to be dressing and was presently putting on boots. His hair was a short, golden blond, slightly curly. The humming trailed off.

"Forget something, sweet one?" His tone was dismissive but not cruel.

"You've stolen my heart," said Bob.

BOB THE WIZARD

The man whirled. He had a long, proud face, his nose slightly hooked, and a square jaw covered in a close-cropped beard that produced a healthy sheen. For his part, once he saw Bob, he relaxed a little and resumed tying his boot, seemingly unworried.

"Are you an assassin?" asked the man nonchalantly.

"Probably not," said Bob. "But I do want to speak with Mannix. You him?"

"Lord Fulton Mannix, at your service." He finished tying the boot and moved on to buttoning his shirt. Unlike Carosel, it appeared that he was not the robe-wearing type. He wore fine leather pants and a shirt of white silk. "And how did you manage to get all the way up here?"

"Magic," intoned Bob theatrically. When Mannix did not reply, he continued. "Lord Mannix, I need information, and if someone in this stinking city has it, it's you. I'm after a man named Galvidon. He's exceptionally dangerous and would appear very strange to you—gray skin, large black eyes, head too big. Little horns." Bob tapped a spot just above his eyebrow. "You seen him?"

Mannix gave Bob a look of appraisal. Having buttoned his shirt, he proceeded to tuck it in. "Who are you again?"

"They call me Bob the Wizard. I'm a traveler. This man I seek is very dangerous, I can't stress that enough. If you know anything, it's in your best interest to tell me. He'll kill your people as he pleases and then leave."

"There were some murders just yesterday." Having finished with his shirt, the Lord of Swearington grabbed a pair of black suspenders from the bed and attached them to his pants. "And we found the body of a farmer on the East Road just this morning." Bob noticed he didn't mention the dead bandits. Mannix pulled up his suspenders with practiced efficiency. "But this is Engoria," he said, sighing. "There is always death. It's the way of things." He snatched up a long green coat from a nearby plush chair and slid it on, checking his reflection in a nearby ornate mirror, straightening the folds of his coat. "I certainly have not seen a horned man. Though, you are a stranger here, it seems. Perhaps you are the danger you claim to seek." He gave Bob a pointed look, eyebrow raised. "Now, if you will excuse me, I really must be going. You'll magic your way out, I'm sure. Quite impressive, really, getting in here." He gave Bob an affectionate pat on the shoulder, and then he was out the door.

Bob stood speechless. He hadn't even taken out the knives. But what was he to do? If he threatened the man, he'd only end up a pariah, unable to investigate further. The rebellious anger he'd felt just a few minutes ago had already evaporated. Fulton Mannix was so… well, nice. Still, perhaps he'd been lying. Maybe Mannix *had* seen Galvidon, and he was covering it up for some reason. But why? These Engorians seemed to consider people with dark hair to be lower class. It appeared that elves were little more than servants. Why wouldn't they extend their prejudice to Galvidon? Bob supposed he'd stay in the city a few days, ask around on the streets. Maybe he'd poke into those murders Mannix had spoken of. Frustrated, Bob sighed and left the room.

The city stretched below him from his vantage on the balcony. The air smelled much better from up there, but Bob could still detect the faint odor of burning metal. He saw the plumes of black smoke curling from those strange buildings in Swearington's northern half, the haphazardly placed piles of black and yellow rock. In the sky, storm clouds approached from the northwest.

Bob was irritable and shaky and was having trouble thinking straight. He needed a cigarette. The apothecary shop he'd seen on the way to Oath Keep was not visible, hidden by the dirty sprawl of the city's heart. His inner addict urged him to try to teleport to the apothecary, but he'd never attempted such a thing—only places that he could immediately see were safe to jump to with the Gatekey. What if he ended up in a wall or something? What if he disappeared and never appeared? No, not a risk worth taking for nicotine. He picked a spot as far away as he could see, down on the street. Seeing no people walking by his target, he pushed the appropriate button on the Gatekey.

The world blurred and then coalesced. His sudden appearance on the street startled a nearby beggar. There was someone here, after all.

The man was sitting in shadow under a blanket and jumped when he saw Bob. "Sun above! Where did you come from?"

Bob shrugged. "Teleported from the keep."

BOB THE WIZARD

The beggar narrowed his eyes, then shrugged. "Spare a coin?"

"You seen a gray man with big black eyes and horns around here?"

"What?" The beggar shook his head.

Sighing, Bob walked on without proffering a coin. No disrespect to the guy, but Bob needed his coins.

"Funny-looking bastard," murmured the beggar.

Bob turned the street-corner, desperately hoping Abernathy's Apothecary had some tobacco.

M. V. PRINDLE

CHAPTER FOUR:
MARKET CIRCLE

Abernathy turned out to be Justin Abernathy, an aging and semi-pleasant blond fellow that bragged—not unjustifiably—over his collection of smoking implements, when Bob inquired. Apparently a resident of the Sun's Quarter, Mr. Abernathy bemoaned his struggle as a small-business owner.

"Harder than it used to be," he grumbled to Bob. "Kissed by the Sun or not, I'm barely getting through. It's Martimus and his damn war, you ask me. Finnigus Flaire was a good king, but this son of his…" Abernathy trailed off, glancing at the ceiling as if someone up there might be watching. "Well, never mind. Shouldn't speak ill of the King, even if he is a fat, lazy, warmongering sack of…" he cleared his throat. "Tobacco, you said? Right this way, sir."

Hand-carved pipes sat in rows on the shelf, each a work of art. Abernathy claimed it was the finest collection in all of Engoria. Bob, lack of nicotine unpleasantly derailing his thoughts, was unable to bask in their beauty. He chose the first one that stood out to him. It was, in Bob's estimation, a very wizardly pipe: a six-inch stem and bowl carved into the shape of a dragon. He still had his lighter, but it would run out of fuel eventually, so he bought two boxes of long, slender matches to go with the dragon pipe and a two-ounce pouch of tobacco. Abernathy invited him to try it out right there in the store, and Bob did so gratefully. The shop owner had to show him the trick to lighting the odd matches, which involved gripping the head in a small square of sandpaper that came with the box. Once the pipe was lit, Bob assured the man he was a satisfied customer, bid him thanks and farewell, and left Abernathy's Apothecary puffing away, an entire gold coin lighter than when he'd entered.

Through Swearington's winding streets, he found his way back to the Fool's Rest. The pipe would take some getting used to. The tobacco was unfiltered and hardly processed. After only a few minutes of smoking, Bob's head was swimming and he was coughing like an amateur. Still, he felt his irritation ebb away, his shakiness vanish, his scattered thoughts line up in neat little rows. Once in his room, he sat happily cursing to himself between hacking coughs.

Gerald Sun and his daughter Jenna were conspicuously absent, so Bob went out to find another kitchen. He returned to the Rest through sheets of rain, his belly full of stew, his purse depressingly light. He told himself he'd make more than enough coin at Market Circle the following day and tamped more raw tobacco into his stately dragon pipe. He chuckled, feeling very wizardly. There were a series of outhouses behind the Rest, and he thanked the God he could no longer believe in that he'd brought his own toilet paper. He fell asleep thinking about pompous blond men and managed to avoid nightmares.

In the morning, Gerald and Jenna were still nowhere to be found. Frowning, Bob ate some trail mix and jerky from his pack and headed out to the stable where he'd left Abigail and Shade. Despite obvious reluctance on the part of Samuel the Ostler, Bob returned to the Fool's Rest with the horses, and hitched them to the wagon. He sat in the cab and studied the map. His destination lay due east, just inside of Darkhair's Gate, where he'd seen farmers moving to-and-fro while approaching South Gate on the East Road.

Half an hour later he arrived at Market Circle—a bustling cul-de-sac full of tents and wagons, shouts and ringing bells. Bob paid a fee of six coppers to a haughty blonde woman for rights to a space. Abigail and Shade trotted the wagon through an ever-growing crowd. By the time Bob set up the wagon so that it resembled a stall, the day was already approaching noon. He was sweating and the horses were irritated. He leaned up against the side of the makeshift stall, lit his pipe, and waited for customers.

The Gatekey, having been used to teleport twice since Bob's arrival, was completely drained. Then the rain clouds had rolled in, obscuring the sun. The little green meter on the large bronze key was entirely depleted. The sun was out now, and aside from a few evaporating puddles, Swearington's cobbles were already bone dry. Bob wore the Gatekey around his neck, silently willing the meter to fill, but it made slow progress.

For a couple of hours, Bob smiled at potential customers as they approached his stall. Most of them were dark-haired. Many told him that he looked funny. Three inquired as to why his hair was so long. One attempted to sell him a shaving kit—which he briefly considered—and five asked him where he'd gotten his cloak, and if they could get one. He puffed on the dragon pipe in what he hoped was a mysterious and wizardly manner, doing his best to placate them with vague responses. He sold most of the corn and a few of the radishes. The turnips remained untouched in the wagon, but he unloaded the rest of his salt. After a few hours, Bob's coin purse was full of silver and copper coins. After a purchase, or when it became clear that a patron was not going to buy anything, Bob asked casually if they had seen a strange-looking man with big black eyes, gray skin, and little horns. They all gave him sidelong looks and scurried away.

All, except the woman who bought the last of his corn. It was well into the afternoon by then, and the green meter on the Gatekey had almost—but not quite—reached the halfway mark. This woman was old, and her hair—which Bob did not doubt used to be dark—had gone a bold gray. She walked hunched over, a crude cane helping her along. Her dress was woolen and died a faded pink color, with matching bonnet. She was a shrewd haggler, and Bob eventually let the corn go for less than he had to other buyers, partially because he admired her persistence, and partially just because he was tired of haggling.

"Alright," he said, "twist my arm, why don't you." He grinned, stuffing her payment into his bulging purse.

The old woman released a shrill, two-fingered whistle, and a boy of about twelve came running over like a trained animal. "Haul this bag up to your father," she told him. "And don't spill a kernel or my cane will find your backside!"

"Yes'm," said the boy, not looking at her, and dragged away the canvas bag, stumbling comically.

"Seems like a good kid," said Bob absently, packing tobacco into the pipe.

"He's got shit for brains, just like his father. Least he can follow orders."

Bob chuckled. "I like your style. Whereabouts you from around here?"

"Over in the pastures. Awful place. Smells like a sheep's ass."

"City smells like a horse's ass. Only pleasant place is right here in the outer city. Away from all the assess."

"Oh, I wouldn't say that. Some assess right over there." She gestured with her cane and Bob turned to see in the milling crowd, of all people, Lord Fulton Mannix. Surrounding him were a handful of armored guards and two other men with the same golden blond hair that Bob had come to associate with the word *douchebags*. The guards all carried halberds, and the douchebags were decked out in silks and snappy black coats, shortswords at their hips in gleaming scabbards.

"Met him yesterday," said Bob to the old woman. "Didn't seem that bad. Not like that Carosel fucker. Now *he* was an ass."

The woman shook her head. "Carosel's a pig, that's so, but that Mannix is a snake. Don't trust those smiles and winks, he'll bite your ass soon as you turn around."

Bob considered. Perhaps he'd let the man get away too easily. "Good to know. Say, got a quick question for you, ma'am."

"Don't you ma'am me, young man. Reminds me I'm old. Name's Hilda Fields. Call me Hilda, or my cane will find *your* backside."

Bob extended his hand and shook her bony palm. "Robert Caplan. Friends call me Bob, so call me Bob, Hilda."

"Very well, Bob, what's the question? Got to be off to watch that boy and his father before they do something stupid." She eyed her family where their wagon was parked across the circle.

Bob cleared his throat. "You seen a strange looking fellow around? Big, black eyes, gray skin, little horns?" He tapped his forehead above an eyebrow.

Hilda glanced toward Mannix and his entourage and lowered her voice. "Sure enough. Few days ago. A man and his wife was killed out in the pastures, maybe you've heard. Happened to be my neighbors. Stabbed to death. Nasty business. I don't get much sleep, you see, on account of my hip. Was out on the porch the night they was killed. Now, my house and theirs aren't so close, and I didn't know they was dead until the next day when they was found. But that night, I saw that fellow you describe. Terrible looking man. Saw him on my property, sneaking away from the neighbors. Thought he was a rustler, maybe. Had a mind to wake my idiot son in law. Then the odd looking fellow, he done flew off into the sky. Didn't think much of it until the next day."

"You didn't think anything of a flying man with horns?" Bob withdrew a match and held it with the sandpaper square.

She scowled. "Listen here, sonny. Bob, I mean. I been living out in them pastures my whole life, and I seen much stranger things than that. Sometimes the faeries come. Sometimes bandits. Now and then a fucking dragon will swoop out of the sky for my sheep. So no, some asshole with horns don't really rattle my cage."

Bob was nodding thoughtfully.

"Anyhow, hope the knowledge does you good. Got to get off." She hobbled away on her cane, faster than Bob would have thought, and started shouting at the boy that he'd put the bag of corn in upside down. Bob smirked, the match popping to light in his hands. As he was poised to light the pipe, he heard the heavy clank of armored footfalls approaching.

"Bob the Wizard," said Fulton Mannix. The guards were glaring, and the two blond cronies rested their hands on pommels.

Bob's heart started pounding. He didn't want to be afraid of this smooth-talking bastard, but he was. He did his best to hide it, bringing the flame on the match to the dragon pipe and drawing in breath. He held for a moment, then blew a billow of smoke into Mannix's bearded face. For his part, the Lord of Swearington didn't blink. His easy smirk remained undaunted.

"The Great Blond Mannix," said Bob. "To what do I owe the pleasure of your attention?"

"I'm afraid I must arrest you for murder," Mannix stated impassively. The two other douchebags tightened their grips on their pommels. Passersby began to gather at a safe distance to watch.

With his free hand, Bob idly gripped the Gatekey still hanging from his neck. If he was lucky, it might have reached a half-charge, which would be enough to get him a good jump.

"Murder? Me? I think you've got it wrong. Trespassing, sure. Being disrespectful to blonds, absolutely. Being far, far too good looking for this shithole, I mean, if you say so. But I couldn't hurt a fly if I tried. Isn't in my nature." He puffed casually on the pipe and glanced away. Hilda Fields stared curiously from the onlookers.

The lord's smirk didn't waver. He was in control and he knew it. "I could arrest you for any reason. That is my prerogative, Darkhair. However, it so happens that I have witnesses claiming you rode into town, not only with Willis Bailey's horses, but with his crops as well. Strange. Willis Bailey was found dead on the East Road just after your arrival. Then there is the small matter of the stabbings in the pasture. Tell me, Master Bob, when we search you, will we find knives?"

Bob's pulse was pounding. He was full of adrenaline; small details stood out—little blond hairs in Mannix's nose, beads of sweat on the guards' foreheads. Hilda Fields looking on, hand to her chest, real concern in her eyes.

"Might be that you would. But I'd sooner stab myself than a man and wife in their own home." As soon as he said it, he knew it was a mistake.

Mannix raised his eyebrows. "Interesting that you know the details of the murders."

"Now, wait a minute, I—"

"Take him."

Bob frantically pressed the button on the Gatekey. Nothing happened. God damn mother fucking rain blocked the fucking sun. The douchebags drew their swords and the guards rushed to grab him. There was a split second in which he almost reached inside his coat for the sawed-off, but he knew he'd never get it out in time. Gauntleted hands gripped him roughly by the arms and held him fast. He fumbled and dropped the dragon pipe. The guards pushed him to his knees.

"Everybody's got knives," protested Bob. He saw one on the lord's belt. "You've got a knife. Maybe you killed those people."

Mannix's infuriating smirk didn't waver. He gave a curt nod and an armored fist crashed into Bob's stomach. It sucked the air right out of his lungs, and his bowels gave an alarming lurch, threatening to release. Pain shot through his abdomen.

"That's quite enough, master Bob," said Mannix. "I do believe I've indulged your mouth well beyond the limits of propriety."

Bob's shoulders were bent at unnatural angles. All he could see was boots and gravel, but he heard men rummaging through Willis's wagon behind him.

"Take his purse," said Mannix.

"What's all this?" It was the voice of Hilda Fields. "This man hasn't done nothing. Been standing here for hours. Sold me corn."

Bob coughed roughly and spat up phlegm. He could see Mannix turn.

"Not that it's your concern, Ms. Fields," said the lord, "but this man is responsible for three murders. That we know of." Rough hands snatched the coin purse from Bob's waist. Bob felt the unmistakable sensation of a gauntleted fist clank against the sawed-off inside his trench coat. The guard hesitated, then tried to yank it free.

"It's tied in, dumbass," mumbled Bob, still out of breath.

"Seems unlikely," said Hilda to Mannix. "I seen the murderer myself. You know he got my neighbors. Seen him right after the fact, flying away. Wasn't this man."

"Take him away," said Mannix, ignoring Hilda.

"My lord," said the guard who was searching Bob. He had managed to untie the shotgun and was proffering it to Mannix. "What, in the name of the Sun, is *this*?"

BOB THE WIZARD

The hands holding him slackened a bit, and Bob was able to lift his head.

Mannix's eyes narrowed, the smirk finally wavering. He gingerly accepted the firearm, holding it by the barrel at its center of gravity. "I've no idea," Mannix murmured. The safety was on, but it was loaded.

"Careful with that," said Bob. "It's a wizard's weapon. Likely to blow you up, if you're not careful."

The guards looked nervous. One of the douchebags had returned from the wagon, Willis's crossbow planted on his hip, business end pointed to the sky. He eyed the shotgun with a kind of eagerness. Mannix handed the gun to the crony, and the man took it in his free hand, barrel pointed toward him. Bob willed the shotgun to go off in his hands. Sadly, the weapon's safety remained engaged.

The other douchebag returned. "Spots of blood in the wagon bed," he said. "Dried blood sprayed all over one side of the canvas."

"Give it to *her*," said Bob. "Give the wagon and the rest of the crops to Ms. Fields. You got no use for them." Hilda was still standing at the fore of the onlookers, her lined face set in a deep scowl.

Mannix chuckled. "Bit late for altruism, murderer. This is all now property of the King. And this spectacle has gone on long enough. Back to your shopping, citizens! Daylight won't last forever!" In fact, the sun was on its way to setting. Lord Mannix turned to his entourage. "We'll finish searching him at the keep. Don't lose your grip on him. He's slippery." He started to turn away, but then his eyes alighted on Bob's chest.

Bob's pulse started up again. It was just a key. Nothing to worry about. Just a key.

But Mannix reached his hand down and cradled the Gatekey for a moment. He yanked it forcefully off Bob's neck and the string snapped, stinging the sides of Bob's neck. Bob was pulled roughly to his feet and could only watch, with sharpening horror, as Mannix pocketed the Gatekey.

CHAPTER FIVE:
THE NEW NORMAL

Water dripped somewhere. A sliver of natural light the size of a Bible spine struggled down from a slit in the dank stone wall above Bob's head. He sat in near-darkness, staring through heavy iron bars over the narrow corridor into an empty cell across from his own. Really, it was the only thing to look at, but Bob didn't really see it; he was lost in his own head. They had stripped him naked and taken everything—the trench coat, the knives, the gun, the tobacco, the money, and most importantly, the Gatekey.

Worse—the moment Bob was thrown into a cold, hard chamber in the underbelly of Oath Keep, Mannix had presented him with his backpack, which he'd left at the Fool's Rest. Mannix had mentioned witnesses saying that Bob had the Bailey's property, and Gerald and Jenna had known that he had it. He should have seen it sooner. In his arrogance, Bob had thought his lie about taking Willis Bailey's final load to market had been convincing. He knew now, it hadn't worked for a second. They'd bought the barley, saving them a trip to market, and had turned around to rat him out to the authorities. This, Bob saw now, explained their absence from the Rest. To add insult to injury, next to his backpack on a crude wooden table, Mannix had placed Bob's sunglasses. No doubt the guards who had let Bob in the front gate had been seen wearing them and had been forced to explain where they'd gotten them. Bob found himself dully hoping they hadn't been punished too severely.

Mannix was not stupid, and since Bob had claimed the sawed-off a powerful wizard's weapon, the Lord of Swearington had ordered it taken away somewhere far away from Bob. So, when faced with scowls and halberds, Bob had no choice but to undress as ordered. He was no slouch in a brawl, but he stood no chance, unarmed, against several armored men with bladed weapons, and he knew it.

Bob had been a fool, he now realized. He'd spent too much time getting away with things—using the Gatekey to go where he wanted, when he wanted. Lying whenever it suited him. Chasing after Galvidon with tunnel-vision like a weak-nosed bloodhound. The guards had given him a single-piece tunic to wear. Like many things around here, it seemed to be made of wool, and that made sense. There were more sheep around than people. And here was Bob, herded and shorn. One of the sheep.

The water dripped again, somewhere Bob couldn't see. God, he was thirsty. But that wasn't his body's most insistent desire. It had only been a couple of hours since his capture, but already, he had trouble focusing his thoughts. He needed tobacco, and he needed it badly. He sat with his legs pulled up under his arms, clenching and unclenching his fists, picturing what it would feel like to get a nice long pull on the pipe. Or, better yet, a cigarette. Hub—he hated this place. He never should have taken the Gatekey from Rashindon.

The Gatekey. He'd been in shock, his grief wavering on the horizon, waiting to crash down upon him and sweep him away. He remembered taking the Gatekey from Rashindon's strange gray hand, the bodies of Anna and Daniel still cooling a few yards away. Why? The strange creature Rashindon, the same kind of thing as Galvidon, whatever it was, had said confusing things, amazing things. Bob had latched on to his story like a man in a storm clinging to a tree. He needed an explanation, for things to make sense, a purpose. In the cell under Oath Keep, Bob began to rock back and forth. He saw Daniel as a toddler, smiling. Anna on their wedding night. Then the memory of their empty, dead faces invaded and washed away the good memories, replaced them with fear, with confusion, with hatred. He should have stayed. He should have called the police, planned their funerals, tried to move on. Now, he couldn't. The events of that evening had propelled him on his strange journey, led him to this moment, here, in a dark cell, a single sliver of light, no family, no friends, no hope, and no fucking cigarettes. The water dripped. Somewhere.

M. V. PRINDLE

The sky was a black sheath, and Bob was being roughly tossed into the back of a wagon. The bed was not covered with canvas the way Willis's had been—it was more of a hard-floored wooden box covered in crumpled linens and bits of straw. It had no windows, but Bob was beyond caring. He had passively allowed himself to be drug from his cell, up a winding staircase, through the central atrium in which he'd had a pleasant conversation with a pompous asshole named Carosel, and out the big double doors that he himself had slammed open in a show of defiance. None of that defiance was left now. He assumed, even dimly hoped, that he was being marched to his execution. The faces of Anna and Daniel swam once again into his mind's eye. He had long stopped believing in heaven, but now he dared to wish that it was real. Maybe he'd been wrong. Maybe he could see them again. If nothing else, death was preferable to his current state of misery.

But it seemed death was not yet allowed to him. Instead, he was shoved into a mobile wooden box that stunk of sweat and piss. The wagon began to move, and Bob was jostled and bounced, his teeth clattering, his muscles aching. He once again began to feel desperate for nicotine. He covered his face in his hands, frustration and despair boiling his guts, blotting out all ability to reason. He had forgotten that *wanting* could be so strong a state. It came in waves, covering everything, making him unable to feel anything else. He found himself chewing on one of his knuckles, hard enough to draw a trickle of blood.

He had kicked booze years ago, long before he started hopping worlds, even years before the deaths of Anna and Daniel. The seductive liquid had damn near ruined his life. He had almost gotten through the Austin Police Department's Training Academy before totaling his car on the way to the final exam. Perhaps he put too much vodka in his coffee that morning, or maybe it was the half bottle of whiskey the night before, not quite out of his system. Probably, it was both. If there was one thing more embarrassing and disgusting than a drunk wannabe cop, it was a drunk father, and Anna had almost left him. She had almost taken a two-year-old Daniel and split, filed for divorce and child support. Only his vow to never take another drink had made her hesitate, and then, only barely. But he'd proven it, never touched the stuff again, not even after they'd died. But this—being beaten and stripped and falsely accused of murder, put in a rattling, stinking cage and driven God knew where—this was different. Quitting the booze had been like dragging himself out of Hell. This was like getting thrown down into it.

The wagon continued to rattle, and eventually, the grip of need began to lessen for a time. The steady jostle, the rhythmic clopping of hooves, and Bob's mental and emotional exhaustion all conspired to lull him into a stuporous doze. In half-dreams, he kept seeing Mannix's smirk, seeing himself packing a pipe full of tobacco. When the rattling of the wagon slowed and stopped, when the rear gate squeaked roughly open and moonlight poured in, Bob was unsure if he was afraid or relieved. His nerves felt frayed; everything was sharp and painful, but also dull and far away. He was pulled out of the wooden prison, none too gently.

His senses dully registered disturbed earth, moonlight glinting off long tools propped against a shack, a pungent metallic odor. The hands under his arms felt like vices. Someone opened a bolt in a door. It shrieked with rust. He was tossed inside a room.

"Bed four," said a voice behind him, and the bolt shrieked again.

Bob surveyed the dark room. There were tiny slits near the roof, letting in moonlight. Someone within the room said something brusquely in a language Bob didn't recognize.

"What?" mumbled Bob stupidly, afraid to move.

"Over here, newcomer," said the voice, hushed and strangely accented.

He walked toward it. After a few steps, he saw an empty pallet on the floor, little more than a few strips of cloth. The moonlight outlined the shapes of sleeping men on either side of it. Bob sat on the pallet, then lay, staring at the deep blackness that shrouded the ceiling.

"Now sleep," said the voice, from right next to him. It was neither friendly, nor hostile. It was resigned, hollow. "Work at first light."

Bob stared into the empty darkness. Mannix's smirk seemed to be there. So was Daniel's dead face, and Anna's. He saw Willis on the road. *Everybody needs a family.* The hard looks of bandits, greedy, hungry. Their bodies being sundered into bloody rags by shotgun blasts. Staring into the shadows, staring at the past, Bob drifted into unconsciousness.

M. V. PRINDLE

"Wake up! Wake up, you Blueskin bastards! Thirty minutes for breakfast! Get up! Worthless cunts!"

It was a harsh voice, uncaring. It cut through the fog of Bob's nightmares like a hot knife. Sunlight streamed through the slits near the ceiling. Bob's head throbbed. He needed to piss. His bones ached. Sharp pains stabbed him in the places he'd been punched, kicked, bashed and jostled. The owner of the voice was clanging a bell. Each strike of the bell's clapper against its hollow carapace sent a needle into Bob's temples.

"Last warning! Thirty minutes, you useless piles of shit! Up!"

Bob groaned and sat up. The world seemed to tilt for a moment, and Bob wondered if he was hungover. No, not hungover, much worse than that. His head moved automatically around the room. He was in some kind of shed, about the size of the living room in the house he and Anna had shared for three years before she died. The walls were plates of rusted metal, naked support beams riveted down to hold it together. He remembered being in the box, remembered the strange voice from inside the darkened shed. No chance all of that was part of the nightmares. It was all too real, impressing itself upon him with harsh immediacy. The only door to the single-room construct was hanging open, morning light flooding in. He vaguely supposed that it was soft light, but it still seemed to stab his eyeballs. His stomach rumbled. Despite everything, he was hungry. Had that awful voice said something about breakfast? He wasn't sure if that was part of his dreams. The voices owner seemed to have departed. None of the sorry-looking men around him could have had the balls to yell like that, he could tell by their bearing, by their clothes, by the expressions on their downcast faces. Blue faces. It struck Bob like a sunrise. They were elves.

Blue skin of various hues, all around him, some a light cornflower, some a brilliant azure, others still a dark royal, like the color his uniform would have been at the Department. Pointed ears sat beneath hair of strange colors: lime green, deep crimson, startling purple. Each of the elves wore thin woolen rags like those Bob had been given in the cell under Oath Keep. Presently. they filed out the door, scowling or distant, not even looking at Bob, paying him no mind. Shaking and bruised, he lifted himself off the ragged pallet and took his place at the rear of the line. God, he had to piss.

BOB THE WIZARD

He ambled out into the growing daylight behind a string of dirty elves. He saw a man, short and stalky, hair dark brown, deep scars across his face, wearing a thick padded coat— gambeson, Bob thought it was called—a kind of linen armor. The man's scarred face was set in a rigid scowl. In one hand he held a bell, in the other a short whip. The owner of the angry voice, then.

To his left, Bob saw a line of elves at a ditch that was carved in the earth, their backs to him. It was clear what they were up to, and he cantered quickly to join them. At the ditch, he pulled his trousers down a few inches and commenced his business. The whole area reeked, but that was to be expected. As yesterday's liquid left his body, he turned to the man—elf, he was an elf—to his right, and said softly, "Hey friend, can I get some tobacco around here?" The elf, his skin a darker, royal tone, gave him a sidelong look but said nothing, finishing his task and walking away.

"Twenty-five minutes you ugly blue assholes!" came the voice that had woken him.

The bell clanged a few times, and Bob winced as the sound lanced into his head. Relieved of one of his myriad problems, he found his way to a line forming at an erected stall. It was the same rusted, riveted metal as the shack he'd slept in, but long and open-faced. It reminded Bob of the cafeteria line at school when he was a child. Behind it were a group of dour looking elf women, haggard and tired, worrying over pots and pans, serving up bowls of something with a ladle. One of them seemed to be in charge of distribution. She didn't look up—she simply filled a bowl and stuck her arm out, waiting for the next in line to relieve her of it. The line progressed quickly. Each elf that got a bowl moved away slurping as soon as the food was in hand.

Eventually it was Bob's turn. He took a steaming bowl gratefully and said thank you. He stepped away from the stall and brought it to his lips, sniffing. It smelled alright. He took a sip. It was a kind of thick gray broth, rather tasteless. Needed salt, but it was hot, and that was something. Bob gulped it down quickly and after his final swallow, began a coughing fit. The few elves that were nearby moved even farther away. Bob hacked and wheezed, coughing up a ball of sticky phlegm. He noticed that the earth seemed disturbed, as if tilled, but there were no crops. He remembered flashes from the night before—tools, gleaming in the moonlight. What was this place?

"Twenty minutes!" yelled the scarred man. He seemed bored.

Bob coughed a few more times and glanced around. The elves were standing idly and staring at the horizon or stretching. Some stood in a cluster, whispering. None of them looked at him once. Bob approached the man with the bell. He was still hungry, his body still ached, but he felt generally improved from his state upon waking.

"Ahoy," said Bob, and coughed. "What's all this, then? Why am I here?"

The man regarded him for a moment, and then suddenly there was a sharp crack across Bob's shoulder and pain flared through him, bringing him to his knees. "Quiet slave! Speak when spoken to! This asshole. This fucking asshole." He spat.

Bob clutched his shoulder and took a few paces back, out of the man's reach. "Well, you're a lousy fucking conversationalist," he muttered. The scarred man glared at him and Bob saw nothing but malice in his eyes. Bob slunk away.

Out of habit, his hand reached for his chest where the Gatekey would be but gripped nothing. Then, his brain working more or less okay for the first time in a while, something dawned on him. He could understand what the man was saying. Either the Gatekey was somehow transmitting to him from far away, which seemed unlikely, or they actually spoke English on Hub. At least, the humans in Engoria did. Curious. Still, a riddle to be solved another day.

Bob spent his remaining minutes of relative freedom in line at a well for water. It was warm and tasted metallic, but it seemed clean enough. Afterward, the scarred man began shouting and clanging his bell, and Bob followed the blue-skinned elves as they filed away.

The procession made its way over a hill. They were walking east. Bob saw little sign of vegetation, and even less of animal life. The day began to heat, though a pleasant breeze ruffled his hair and soothed his skin. After about half a mile, they crested another hill, this one tall and rocky. At first, Bob thought they'd come upon a cliff, that perhaps they'd be thrown, one by one, over the side to their deaths. He remembered his despair the previous night, and now, in the light of day, such sentiments seemed weak and ridiculous. He found that he very much wanted to live. To his relief, death was not yet in the cards: upon closer inspection, Bob found he was not on a cliff at all, but a deep gorge dug into the earth at a steep incline—a quarry, maybe. He had a sudden craving for a cigarette but did his best to push it down, clenching his fists and setting his jaw.

At the insistence of the bell, they made their way down the incline. Dust and pebbles scattered with each step. The ground began to even out as they reached the base of the slant. Finally, they came to a large, cavernous mouth set into a gravelly mound of earth. Framed by wooden planks, it seemed to lead into utter blackness. Someone handed Bob a heavy pickaxe. At some point the group had been joined by a number of dark-haired men. They were armed with daggers or hand axes, and each had a short whip tied to their belt. They wore deep frowns and light, sleeveless shirts. Two of the elves were given lanterns and they began to descend into the darkness. Even Scarface was quiet now, and the only sounds were muted puffs of breath and the crunch of footfalls on rough earth. As he descended, Bob glanced over his shoulder, past the group of dark-haired men, and saw, with growing unease, the daylight shrink and die away behind him.

M. V. PRINDLE

CHAPTER SIX:
DIGGERS

Iron. That's what they were doing inside the earth—mining iron. And, Bob soon discovered, iron ore was black and yellow. Bob remembered seeing vast, covered piles of it throughout Swearington. At least, the ore was black and yellow in good light, but down in the cramped, stuffy dark, it was almost indistinguishable from the rest of the rock. The elf slaves and their Darkhair masters must have been at it a long time before Bob's arrival—they seemed to see the ore where Bob couldn't.

The iron appeared in the sediment in long streaks. The miners' job was to follow these streaks wherever they led, necessitating tunnels that twisted and turned through Engoria's underbelly. Digging out the ore was a laborious chore of its own, hauling it out to the thick carts another, but by far the scariest part of the job was clearing a new section of earth.

This involved heating a section of cavern with controlled fires, and then sending in a group of slaves, carrying buckets of water, to splash out the fire and wet the walls as fast as possible. The temperature change caused the rock and packed earth to weaken, allowing the slaves to beat and dig it away. All the while, more slaves pulled out the excess earth, what the slavers called overburden—or *mullock*—and hauled it out to the surface to scatter as evenly as possible around the area. Sometimes, when Bob and the elves were in a particularly tight place, the slavers wheeled a huge bellows to the mine's mouth and attached it to sections of pipe. The pipe was then strung all the way into a tight chamber. A couple of slaves usually got the unfortunate job of pumping the bellows, sending air through the pipe and down to the enclosed workers, preventing their suffocation.

BOB THE WIZARD

Bob was unsure how long he'd been at it. Weeks, he thought, but it already felt like eternity. The first few days had been the worst. He'd had to constantly pause for coughing fits, which were even less pleasant in the cramped, dusty corridors.

He was perpetually hungry. He and the elves were only served two meager meals a day—almost always the gray broth—once as they woke, and once after the day's work was done. Occasionally, there were vegetables to be had. They were old, and Bob had to pick off the dead, black parts of them. He'd never been one for vegetables, but by the time the first round had come, he was so tired of that tasteless gray liquid that it felt like a privilege to eat something new.

He still had cravings for a cigarette, but they became distant things, like the lasting impression of a nightmare. His mind began to conflate freedom with tobacco, and while hauling rocks or swinging a pickaxe, he'd envision himself free and bathed, sitting in a comfortable chair—often the one with black cushions that Archlector Carosel had been sitting in—lighting the dragon pipe with a long match, and puff, puff, puffing away. It was a dream that seemed more unattainable every day, but he didn't allow himself to let go of it. One day, he would escape and continue his search for Galvidon. One day, he would retrieve the Gatekey from Mannix. When it happened, he swore to himself, he'd be more careful from then on. He would never allow himself to get so overconfident again. Now he knew—with bitter, exhausted certainty—the consequences of thinking himself beyond the reach of the Astraverse and its machinations.

He grew thinner. His muscles became hard and dense. His beard, already bushy and scraggly, grew almost to his chest. One of the elves had cut his hair for him. It was a kind of half-measure, a haircut with a knife, but Bob was surprised at how expertly the blue man shortened his hair with such a small blade. It was under supervision, of course—the Darkhairs nearby with ready whips. Bob supposed that one does not simply give a slave a knife and walk away. But there seemed to be very little danger in the elves. They did their work with diligence and without complaint. Not that they were happy. On the contrary, Bob had never been around a group so despondent and morose. Still, he was curious about them. For their part, they mostly ignored him.

Bob awoke each day with no one to talk to. To the Darkhairs, he was just another slave. To the elves, he was an intruder. They offered no camaraderie, no encouragement. They barely even looked at him. Bob was apart from everyone, an island. For Bob, it was a familiar arrangement.

Then one day, in a narrow tunnel with an armful of ore, Bob had collapsed to his knees with wheezing coughs, large gobs of yellow phlegm escaping his esophagus. One of the elves, a sinewy man with bright-azure skin and winding, purple locks, had placed a hand on Bob's shoulder. He felt a tapping on his back, like the comfort a mother might give an infant.

"You alright?" said the elf in a stilted accent. His voice was firm but quiet.

Bob responded by nodding and coughing some more, pounding on his own chest.

"You sick?" The elf crouched on his haunches.

Bob spat. "You might say that. Don't worry, nothing contagious."

The elf raised an eyebrow. "I do not know this word."

"Contagious. It means… you can catch it. I'm saying, you can't get sick from me."

The elf nodded thoughtfully. "That is good. I am sick enough from this work."

Bob turned to look at him, but he was already walking back to the earthen wall.

The encounter got him thinking about the Gatekey again, and the humans on Hub speaking English. Once he'd talked to the elf with purple hair, he began to pay closer attention to what the elves said to each other in quiet murmurs. When they spoke to the whip-wielding slavers, they spoke English. Some of them seemed to speak it very well. Others, not at all. But when the elves spoke to one another, they did so in their own language. He tried speaking to other elves occasionally. If he asked something about the work, they'd give a terse response and look away. If he asked them something personal, they'd just ignore him. He supposed that they hated him for being a human, a member of the race that had enslaved them, and for that, he couldn't blame them. He wondered about the circumstances of their enslavement. How long had it been like this? Did the common people of Engoria know there were slaves providing them with iron ore? Where had the elves come from, and how did they end up here? He thought back to his first few days in Engoria: the two blue-skinned bandits that had seemed to have a different attitude than their human counterparts, the total lack of elves in the pastures or inside the city of Swearington, the female elves he'd seen at Oath Keep, one carrying scrolls for Carosel, another leaving Mannix's personal chambers. In Engoria, they were clearly not held in the same regard as humans, and Bob sensed a long history between them and the humans of Hub. But what was it? And did it matter? The days and questions blurred together.

Some days after the purple-haired elf had spoken to him, Bob found himself working alongside the guy. The nearby slavers moved to another area and on impulse, Bob approached the elf. The clinks and clanks of metal tools echoed in the dark chamber. The blue slave was tapping away at a streak of iron with a small hammer and chisel. He glanced up as Bob approached but kept working.

"My name is Bob." He extended a hand. "What's your name?"

The elf kept hammering and for a moment Bob thought he'd ignore him the way the other elves did. But then the elf looked around for slavers and put down the hammer.

"I am called Torael," he said quietly, and took Bob's hand.

They shook, and Torael watched the process as if it were new to him. Maybe it was new, or maybe he just couldn't believe he was shaking hands with a human. Bob couldn't think of anything else to say just then, and besides, one of the Darkhairs was making his way over, so Bob just gave Torael a nod and a weak smile and went back to hauling ore.

Bob's days were spent digging, swinging unwieldy metal tools into rocks, hauling heavy burdens of ore, and avoiding slavers. Aside from the first time he'd tried to approach Scarface, he'd gotten a few other lashings from the Darkhairs—for moving too slowly, for being in the way, for putting a clutch of ore down on the wrong cart, and of course, for talking back. After only the first whip across his back for saying something glib, he began to keep his witticisms to himself. Mostly. No sense of humor, slavers. More often than not, he simply went from place to place, doing what was expected, and thinking.

He thought about escape. He thought about Anna and Daniel. Sometimes he passed the hours of the day by replaying memories in his mind—the first time he and Anna had taken Daniel to a movie theater, the time he and Anna had made love in the bed of his truck, the time before Danny was born when Anna's sister had stayed with them after leaving her husband and the three of them were up all night, drinking, playing board games, and talking. The memories sometimes seemed more vivid and real than the dark, musty monotony of being forced to mine for metal with a group of blue men that hardly even looked at him. But escape—that was what he thought about most. He thought about running, but that was no good. The men here had horses, no doubt crossbows or some other ranged weapons stashed away somewhere. And Bob didn't know the land, didn't know where to go. He could fight, but he would lose, and he knew it. The only possibility, he decided, was to get help. If he could, he would have to somehow win over these elves, or at least some of them, and stage a mutiny. It seemed farfetched, and he knew that for it to work, it would take a long time to implement. But time, it seemed, was one thing he had plenty of—time to think, to wish, to regret, to remember, to feel pain and exhaustion.

By night, he mostly dreamt of his family. The good memories he relived by day never seemed to show up in the hours of darkness while his eyes were closed and his breathing even. Only the bad ones replayed, again and again—waking up in the hospital after the crash that ended all hope of becoming a police officer, fighting with Anna drunk, fighting with her sober, sleepless nights worrying about his infant son, and then, horribly, all of those worries coming true and worse. In his dreams, he saw Galvidon standing over their ruined bodies, Galvidon and Rashindon fiercely fighting, making a ruin of his living room. Galvidon triumphing and fleeing into the night. It replayed over and over in his dreams, and he woke often, heart hammering, in the blackness of a metal shed, moonlight filtering in through little slits, surrounded by the sleeping blue forms of his fellow slaves. But he didn't cry out. Absurdly, he felt like that's what Galvidon wanted—for him to cry out in fear. He was past despair now. Now, when he woke, he would clench his fists and grit his teeth, allow himself to fall back into dreams knowing—somehow, some time—he would get his revenge on that ugly gray bastard.

―◉―

Uncountable days after Torael had first spoken to Bob, the troupe set up for a blast. Most of the iron throughout the revealed chambers had been pulled out, so they were preparing to create a new chamber. The trouble was, the band of iron in the sediment trailed at a downward angle, deeper into the packed earth and heavy rock. The latest chamber they'd been working was low and cramped. The previous day, Bob had worked the bellows, sending air to the group of elves inside. On this day, Bob and Torael were on the back half of the blasting crew—a group of five sent with large buckets to extinguish the fires set by the crew's front half. A small blaze had been set on carefully placed oil, and one of the Darkhairs gingerly worked the bellows, allowing enough oxygen into the tight chamber for the fire to burn.

The chamber baked Bob's skin. Layers of sweat seemed to boil on his forehead. He and the elves advanced toward the flame like hunters upon dangerous prey—cautious, but with the confidence of a pack. They tossed their buckets as evenly as possible, and a great billow of steam erupted, filling the tight chamber and forcing Bob into an all-too-familiar coughing fit. Even now, in the depths of the earth, long removed from the habit, he longed for a pull on the dragon pipe.

Two meager lanterns hung on metal hooks that had been beaten into the rocks, casting barely enough light to see by. Bob turned to venture back through the tunnels, to let the water do its work. The sudden temperature change should soften the earth enough to dig up a new chamber, to allow the slaves to laboriously pull the mullock out with shovels and pickaxes over the next day or so. But something was wrong. As he approached the narrow escape route, the tight cavern began to tremble.

Bob told himself it was just a little jostle—the earth settling, maybe. But as he stepped further, he saw flecks of the earthen ceiling begin to crumble and shower downward. Everything seemed to vibrate. Torael was just ahead of him, gripping the wall for balance. Another of the elves brushed past Bob, bolting for the mouth of the entrance. Bob glanced back at the rest of the dousing crew. Panic scrabbled for purchase in his chest.

"Go!" he yelled, but they were already going.

They tried to move, ducking their heads against falling debris. The ground rebelled against their efforts, shaking and rumbling with displeasure.

There was a great, booming crack from the walls, the ceiling. Huge chunks of dark rock begin to topple above the entrance to the chamber. Time seemed to slow, and Bob saw, as if watching a film frame by frame, a cluster of massive earthen boulders descend.

"Look out!" he screamed, tugging on Torael's arm just as the elf began to enter the chamber's mouth.

In a brief instant, Torael stumbling backward on top of him, Bob caught a horrible glimpse of an elf being crushed from above as if by a great, dark fist. Dirt and dust suffused the air. Bob was pinned under Torael and was pretty sure he lay on top of another elf. The two lanterns flickered, and one was put out by a tumult of swirling particles. The rumbling and crashing finally stopped, but Bob, Torael, and three other elves lay in the tight corridor in a tangle. The air was thick with matter. Their final source of light flickered precariously.

Torael muttered something Bob didn't understand and hauled himself to standing. Bob did the same, hearing grumbles in the elf language from behind him. He saw that the mouth of the entrance was completely blocked, filled with a jagged stack of rock and earth, as if no one had ever cleared the area, had not taken pains to construct a tunnel at all. They were trapped.

"Fuckin' A," said Bob.

Torael gave him a quizzical look, then apparently decided to ignore the comment. His blue face was caked with patches of dirt and streaked with sweat. Bob figured he didn't look much better. "This is most-bad situation," said the purple-haired elf. He bent down to where the pipe that connected to the bellows poked out feebly from the collapsed entrance. "No air coming," he said, shaking his head. "Most-bad situation."

One of the other elves said something to Torael. He seemed angry, almost shouting. Bob couldn't blame him for his ire. This was a definite damper on his own plans of escape. Then again… if they did end up getting out of this alive, Bob had an opportunity to build some trust here. But the getting out alive part, that had to be first priority. He wouldn't die in a hole with Galvidon still out there somewhere.

There was more room back down the corridor, where they'd set the fires. The chamber was still warm and the section that had been burned was soft and damp. They still had some equipment, so they could dig out some of it, but there were two problems with that. The first was that they had very little room to put any mullock they moved. If they piled it in the corridor, it would only hinder attempts at rescue. The second problem was that the softened section was on the floor and low on the wall of the chamber, so they'd only be digging further downward, rather than upward to freedom. Bob surveyed the chamber and one of the elves caught his eye. He had stringy, bright yellow hair, and was short for an elf, about six inches shorter than Bob, but he was well-muscled. He seemed to be cradling his right arm. In the dim lantern-light, Bob could see an angry welt covering the entire forearm. Then he noticed several chunks of rock along the floor. Some were little more than pebbles, others the size of a softball. He craned his neck upward.

To his relief, there was a small break in the chamber's upper section, and there seemed to be a soft light filtering through it—daylight. He couldn't see straight into the sky, but he assumed that there was some kind of haphazard series of breaks in the rocky earth that eventually led to the surface.

"Torael," he said. The elf turned from a hushed conversation with the rest of the blue-skinned dousing crew. "Not as most-bad as all that. Look." He pointed up to the flickering crack. "Air."

Torael stepped over to where Bob was standing and saw what he was pointing at. He nodded slightly and said something in his native language. "Here," he called to the other elves, and when they saw it, they seemed to breathe a collective sigh of relief. Torael looked to Bob. "Now we must worry of water."

Bob pointed to the buckets on the floor that they had hauled in to douse the fire. One was upside down, and two were filled with dirt, rock and ash. The other three had a small amount of water at the bottom. It was dirty and spare, but it was better than nothing. "Do you think they will rescue us?" asked Bob, indicating the corridor for clarity.

"Help us?" Torael arched an eyebrow. "No. But they will help the mine. It is their money." He pointed to the streak of iron, nearly depleted and running into the ground at an angle. Bob supposed he was right. The Engorians had expended resources and time to build the mine this far in, chasing the iron. They wouldn't want to lose it now. Still, they might not hurry. The lives of four slaves might not be worth the trouble. So, Bob figured, it was their job to stay alive long enough for the mining crews to dig them out.

"Look at the bright side," Bob said to the elves, raising his hands expansively. "No more work today!"

Torael cracked a smile.

BOB THE WIZARD

CHAPTER SEVEN:
BOB TELLS A STORY

The water in the buckets was gone after only a few hours. Not surprising, really. There were five of them, and very little of the life-sustaining liquid. Still, they had a day or two before they were in serious trouble, so the first night they spent in the collapsed chamber—what Bob now thought of as *the Cave*—was relatively comfortable. They had no blankets, but it was warm. They had no bedrolls, but they were used to sleeping on a hard surface. They had no food, but they were used to being hungry. To Bob, it almost felt like a vacation.

He finally learned the names of the other three surviving elves. The stalky yellow-haired elf with the bruise on his arm was named Hirrell. His skin was cornflower blue, and he was, as far as Bob could tell, the most jovial elf in the Cave. He smiled the most often, chuckled at things, and seemed undisturbed by his wound.

"Will heal," he said, shrugging. "I am tough."

Then there were Fan and Gorrelai. Both had dark navy skin and deep green hair, though Fan's was cropped short, hugging his skull, and Gorrelai had dreadlocks sprouting from his head like a fern. Fan was about as tall as Bob, a few inches shy of six feet, and was lithe and graceful, like a dancer. Gorrelai, by contrast, was six and half feet tall and rippled with taut, heavy muscle. It seemed to Bob that they were brothers or cousins. They stayed close to one another, and Fan seemed to be a translator for Gorrelai, who spoke little to no English. Gorrelai was always scowling, and it turned out he'd been the one that had been shouting angrily when the cave collapsed. It was a sensible reaction to being a slave, to being trapped in a mine, but Bob soon saw that it was his reaction to everything. Bob wandered if the elf would have a different attitude if he were not a slave. Nonetheless, he derived some amusement from the big elf's cursing and angry grumbles. He didn't understand a word of it, of course, but he very much sympathized with the sentiment.

After a few hours of being trapped, the flickering light from the crack in the Cave's ceiling began to fade. Bob looked down to find the elves sitting in a circle, legs crossed, facing one another. Torael caught his eye.

"Come," said the elf. "Sit."

He gestured to a small space on the floor between Fan and Hirrell. Bob shrugged and complied, glancing around at the seated slaves. They had closed their eyes, resting their hands on their knees. Bob furrowed his brow.

Gorrelai began to speak in a low chant. Torael softly translated for Bob's benefit.

"We pray to the spirits for our friend, Paulsin. His body is now for the earth. Spirits of earth, thank you for your gift of soil, so that the plants may grow. We pray to your strength. Spirits of the air, thank you for your gift of wind, so that we may breathe the breath of life. We pray to your…" Torael seemed to be searching for the right word. "…always changing," he finished. "Spirits of the sun, thank you for your gift of warmth, so that all may know life. We pray to your brightness. Spirits of mind, thank you for our thoughts, so that we may know when our wishes are granted. We pray to your…" Again, Torael struggled, searching for an English word he knew that would align with the proper meaning. "…deep thinking. We ask for your aid, we ask for Paulsin. Earth, embrace him, air, carry him, sun, warm him, mind, think him. We pray the same for ourselves. May the spirits guide him home."

Fan and Hirrell intoned this last line in unison. "*Et tessat sheeram sheral.*"

His English translation complete, Torael also repeated the line in his native language. Then four sets of eyes looked at Bob expectantly.

"*Et tessat sheeram sheral,*" said Bob, with as much respect as he could muster. The elves seemed satisfied and appeared to relax.

"We have no fires to light for him," said Torael to Bob. "Or we would do so."

An awkward silence followed. To fill it, Bob said, "I didn't know—um, Paulsin, was it? I didn't know him. I just hope, after I'm dead, there's someone around to care as much for me as you all do for him."

Gorrelai muttered something angrily that nobody bothered to translate. Torael's sharp brown eyes were studying Bob. "Bob," said the elf after a moment, "you saved my life." The other elves all nodded in agreement, though Gorrelai muttered again.

Bob glanced at the angry elf. "What?"

Fan rolled his eyes, as if tired of Gorrelai's attitude. "He says, you do not have to save Torael if your people do not dig in mine. He says your good deed does not make their bad deeds better."

Bob looked Gorrelai in the eye. "I understand. And I agree. But these are not my people. I come from far away. I admit, there are plenty of shitty people where I come from too, but I care for them as much as I care for the Engorians."

Fan translated. Gorrelai responded, sounding curious.

"He asks, where do you come from," said Fan. Hirrell laughed, showing slightly crooked teeth.

Bob looked at him. "What?" he asked the stalky elf.

Hirrell hesitated. "He… He calls you 'Sora Kelai'. This means, 'face hair.'"

Bob stroked his beard, tilting his head in appreciation. "Well, if the shoe fits…"

"This is what we call you before I know your name," said Torael. "En'harae do not have hair on face. You have… much."

Hirrell chuckled again, cupping his hands below his face as if holding a burden there. "Yes," he said. "Much."

"Wait," said Bob. "What is… 'In Hair-eye?'"

"En'harae," said Torael. "This is the name for our people." He held a

64

hand to his own chest. "I am one. En'hari." He indicated the other three. "We are many. En'harae."

"Not..." said Bob, "not elves?"

Hirrell chuckled, Fan shook his head in exasperation, and Gorrelai went on a tirade, stiffly gesturing.

"No, no, no," said Torael, smiling slightly. "This is a name humans call us. They think we are like people from their stories. We do not like this name. We find it.... not nice."

"Offensive," said Bob. "Got it. En'harae it is." He made a mental note never to refer to them as elves aloud, though he knew he'd have a hard time not *thinking* of them as elves. "Anyway, this charming En'hari asked where I come from. That's a bit hard to answer." Bob thought for a moment, and considered what lie he could tell, or some half-truth that they would believe. He glanced around the dark Cave, at the guttering lantern, at the rocky debris and earthen walls, at the faces of his fellow slaves. He decided to try the truth. "I come from... another world." He concentrated, trying to find were to start. He'd never had to explain all this to anyone. "The world," he gestured expansively, "Hub, is only one world of many. Where I come from, there are no dragons, no En'harae in the whole world. My people look up at a different sky than we do here. In my world, your sky doesn't exist." He waited for them to scoff, to call him crazy, to call him a liar, but they just looked at him, intent, awaiting more. He cleared his throat. "In my world, I had a job. One night, I came home—"

"What's your job?" Hirrell interrupted. Fan was softly translating for Gorrelai. He stopped at Hirrell's question, curious.

Bob considered. Well, he was telling the truth, so why stop now? "Before—a long time ago—I wanted to be a police officer. That's a person who enforces the law. But... I had an accident. I made a mistake, a big one. So, after, I was... I was a garbage man." He waited for their derision.

It was Fan who spoke. "What is this, this garbage man? You make garbage?"

Bob chuckled and shook his head. "On my world—Earth, we call it—I come from a country that has many resources. So many, we have too much of everything. There are big buildings full of food to buy, vehicles that drive on hard roads, big houses, powerful weapons, and many kinds of toys. People have so much food that they spend a lot of money on toys. These kinds of things, our food, our toys, they come wrapped in packages. We throw the packages away. Garbage. We make a lot of trash. So much that it piles up in our cans and we put it out in front of our houses. Garbage men come to take the trash and move it away from everyone, so it doesn't get in the way."

There was a pause. Fan was translating for Gorrelai. Torael looked thoughtful, his azure skin reflecting the dim flickering light in red and orange flashes. "So, in this country, everyone is rich?"

"No, not everyone. In fact, there are many, many poor. But the rich ones have so much, they don't know what to do with it all, and a lot of people have a lot, but aren't thought of as rich. We call them the middle class."

"Are you one who is rich?" asked Hirrell.

"No, I'm one of those middle-class people."

"This garbage man," said Torael, "this is a noble profession?"

Bob laughed. "No. Not really. It probably should be. But no one really even thinks about us. They're too busy working and playing with toys. I became one because, I suppose, in some ways it suited me, and because I couldn't become a policeman anymore."

"Because you made mistake," said Fan.

Bob nodded.

"Apologies," said Torael. "Before you speak of garbage men, you were telling of coming home from work."

Bob ran his hands down the length of his beard. A familiar deep frustration was seething in his guts. He pushed back an urge to cry. He'd come this far in his story, and he wanted to gain the trust of the En'harae, partially because it was his plan for escape, but also because he was alone. He'd been alone for so long, he'd forgotten what it was like to have friends, to have people to commiserate with, to laugh with. He didn't know if the elves would be his friends, but they were a damn sight more pleasant than most of the humans he'd met on Hub. He pushed away his fear, cleared his throat and began his story again.

"I came home while the sun was setting. I was dirty, sweaty, and stinking like garbage. That was all normal. I was in my pickup truck—that's like a wagon that doesn't need horses—and I pulled up into the driveway of my little house, just like I always did. Turned back to get the mail out of the mailbox, and when I was walking to the door, I saw that it was open.

"Now, I don't know how it is where you folks come from, but in my neighborhood, you kept your front door locked all the time. You never knew what kind of asshole might try to break in and steal your expensive toys, or worse, try to hurt you. So, I guess I don't need to say that the door hanging open like that was a bad sign, right off. I got scared, nervous, and dropped the mail. I owned weapons, but they were all in the house, see, so I was unarmed, and the first thing I got to thinking was that there was someone in the house who shouldn't be there. I told myself to calm down, that it was probably just an accident. Anna—that's my wife—she'd probably left it open after coming out to water the lawn, or see a neighbor, or something. It's happened before. But when I got closer, I knew my hopes were all wrong. The doorknob was broken clean off like somebody kicked it in. Now, I had a phone. That's like, a little device you use to talk to people far away. I had it, but I was scared, and worried about Anna and my son, Daniel, who at this time of evening would be home and about to eat dinner.

"I wanted to call out their names. See if they were okay, you know? But I held back. I was afraid of who might still be there. I didn't want to let on that I was there. So I crept in, careful not to nudge the door and give myself away. Now, my house was small by the standards of my country, but it was still a good size. No second story, but a few rooms separated by good walls. Just inside the door was a kind of entrance area, to hang up your coat, set things by the door, that kind of thing. You had to walk a ways before you could see into the living room. Soon as I walked far enough, I saw him there. Looked like a demon. In my world, no such thing as demons, never were. But there he was, back to me, skin all gray, head a little too big, wearing strange clothing, like armor. I froze, looking at him, he was so strange. Took me a moment to see the real trouble—to see what he was doing.

BOB THE WIZARD

"Seemed to be cleaning a blade—wiping it off with a rag. That's when I saw... when I saw..." Bob's breath hitched. The eyes of the elves were set upon him, unwavering. Fan's low voice, which had been gently overlapping Bob's, ended a sentence as he finished his translation. The lantern on the wall guttered and faded, almost out. Bob took a deep breath. "Anna and Daniel," a tear pushed its way down his cheek, "they were dead, the both of them, slumped on the couch, stabbed so many times…" He started weeping in earnest, eyes stinging. The lantern guttered a final flare of light and went out, leaving them in darkness. "There was blood all over the floor, all over the furniture. I cried out. Fuck the sneaking, it was too late. I yelled, I fell down, I cried. The demon turned to face me. He had eyes that were full black and too big, and little horns, like a goat, on his forehead. He just sort of cocked his head at me like I was a bug. I got mad, furious. Who the fuck was *he*? Just come into my house and kill the people I love? I was going to attack him, to fight him, and if I died too, well, what the fuck? Better than being alive without my wife and son.

"But when I got to my feet, suddenly there was another one, another gray man. His clothes were different. Before I knew it, the second one, he threw himself at the first. They fought, slashed at each other with blades, shot at each other with strange weapons I'd never seen. It was all I could do to get out of the way. I tried to help, I wanted to help, but I couldn't. They moved too fast and looked too much alike to me. Which one should I attack? Even so, I managed to run into my bedroom to get a gun. I heard them crashing around the living room and talking in a strange language. I got the trigger guard off my little .38 and came down the hall. The first one, I could tell it was him now, I saw him stab the other one in the chest. This first one, he looked at me, and I raised my gun. He cocked his head again, trying to decide what to make of me, looked like. I was about to pull the trigger but then he was gone—vanished. I don't mean he ran, I mean one second he was there and the next he wasn't."

The steady sound of Fan's translation ebbed away. All five of them sat in the dark. Hirrell murmured something in the En'hari language that sounded like a question. After a moment, he cleared his throat and spoke hoarsely in English. "What did you do next?"

Bob was too deep in it to turn back now. He plunged ahead. "I walked into the room to get a closer look at Anna and Daniel. But the second gray man was still alive. He spoke to me in my language, in a strange accent—not from my world, but not like yours, either. 'Robert James Caplan,' he said. That's my full name. I approached him, feeling numb, still in shock. I can't remember what I did with that .38, must have put it down. Took it with me later and lost it somewhere in another world, but that's getting ahead. This gray man said his name was Rashindon, said he was from something called a Protectorate. It had some second name I don't recall. He said he came to find Galvidon—that was the other one's name, the one that killed my family. Said Galvidon was from some Order, had a fancy name of its own. 'Your family is special,' he said. 'They carry the Blood of the Electum.' Now, before you ask, I have no fucking idea what that means. Said *I* was special too, but that Galvidon couldn't see it. Didn't explain why. I figure he didn't have time for details. He was in a bad way. Pressed something into my hand, a big key with little buttons, called it a Gatekey. Told me to go west until it glowed like the sun, then press this certain button and turn it like I was unlocking a door. Said that's where Galvidon was going. Said if I wanted answers, I had to follow him. 'Go prepared,' he told me, 'Galvidon is formidable.' Well, I figured he was right, considering Galvidon had just killed three people in my house and then disappeared like a ghost. Then Rashindon died, right there, holding my hand. Those were his last words: 'Galvidon is formidable.' Well, like I said, I was well into being fully in shock, but I was also still angry. I was going to kill that horned motherfucker. I packed weapons and food and some other supplies. Money, too, for all the good it did me. I went west, and that key started to glow something fierce. I pushed that button like Rashindon said, and poof, I found myself in another place, far, far away from my world, and not much like it.

"For the next long while—could be years, it's hard to tell—I followed Galvidon in and out of different worlds. Only confronted him once, and the bastard brushed me off like I wasn't important. Not even sure he recognized me. But I kept after him, asking questions, learning to track, learning to survive on my own. Went through supplies, picked up more where I could, usually keeping a low profile. That went on for a long time, and well, you might say I got cocky. I learned some of the Gatekey's tricks—turns out it can do all kinds of things, like make you go from one place to another really fast. I figure that's how Galvidon was able to disappear from my living room. Anyway, after all that, I ended up here, on Hub, in Engoria. Galvidon has already killed two people—that I know of—in this world. And they've pinned it on me. Lord Mannix arrested me and took the Gatekey, sent me here. I don't know if he really believes I did it, or if I was just a convenient way to lay the blame. Anyway, now my only hope is to catch up with Galvidon before he leaves this place for good and I lose him forever." Bob let out a sigh. "And that's my story, more or less."

Fan's translation trailed away. They all sat in silence, unable to see each other. Finally, Torael said. "Bob, this is amazing story."

"Do you believe me?"

"Yes. How to make up such things? Besides, I have seen magic. It is from the *Tessat*. The spirits. Our *Tessaeshi* use it often. Very rare, but sometimes there are outsiders who can hear the spirits. The En'harae, we call them *Teserae*, but the humans, with their silly stories, they call them wizards. This Galvidon, he sounds like a wizard. A very evil wizard."

"But you are good wizard," said Hirrell. "Try to kill evil wizard."

I'm not really a wizard, Bob almost said. Instead, he just nodded noncommittally.

For a dozen heartbeats, no one spoke. Then Gorrelai said something without his usual ire. Fan spoke for him. "We understand your loss, Face Hair. We too have lost our families. The humans have taken everything from us." Gorrelai continued. "I see now that I was wrong about you. I see you, I think, this is a criminal. They put him with us because he is low, like they see us to be low. But now I see, you are like us. You have been cheated, your family killed. You are En'hari."

Bob didn't know what to say to that. Another long moment passed, this time broken by Torael. "We must sleep. Is too dark anyway. Maybe tomorrow they dig us out."

The other En'harae murmured their assent, and there were soft scuffles as everyone blindly stretched out in their own space on the rocky ground. It was warm enough, and Bob was exhausted. Once his eyes were shut, the things he'd told the En'harae began to replay in his mind. He realized that in his telling, wrapped up in the emotion of the memories, he'd neglected to explain several things, like what a what a .38 was. But it didn't seem to matter, they were smart, he could see that much, and they had understood the most important parts.

And he wanted them to understand. Did he seek their approval only because he needed their help to escape? Or was it because, after being alone for so long, he was desperate to connect with another person? Questions he couldn't answer. He began to drift into unconsciousness. He was pulled from the edge of sleep by Torael's voice, speaking softly.

"Bob?"

"Yeah?"

"Thank you for saving my life."

"Anytime, brother," said Bob, and then there was silence.

Galvidon's face swam in Bob's vision like the afterimage of a camera flash. Rashindon's last words rolled across his mind. *Galvidon is formidable.* He awoke in utter darkness and for a brief moment, had the sensation that he was falling. His hands instinctively flew to the earth on either side of him and the feeling passed as the steady rock returned his bearings. The nightmare faded, and Bob heard the rhythms of breathing around him in the Cave.

A heavy sigh escaped him, and he rolled over to try to regain the comfort of sleep. Just before his eyes closed, a tiny sparkle of light drew his bleary attention toward the ceiling. A pinpoint of white light, like a star escaped from the heavens, circled and danced above him in the Cave. It was the only source of light on an otherwise empty black canvas, and Bob was once again struck by a sense of imbalance. He watched the little light hover this way and that, wondering if its movements were intelligent or simply random. He began to suspect he might still be dreaming. Then, as quickly as it came, the point of light swooped up and disappeared into the crack in the Cave's ceiling. Curious but also tired, Bob once again allowed his eyes to close to the threat of horrible dreams.

CHAPTER EIGHT:
BOB HEARS A STORY

Bob woke to the sound of shifting rock. Suddenly hopeful, his eyes snapped open. First, he was disappointed to find the four En'harae at work moving bits of rock from the collapsed tunnel. Then, he was relieved. It was silly, he knew, to feel relief that the sounds of pebbles shifting and rocks clunking weren't the sounds of rescue. If they weren't rescued soon, they'd die. Nevertheless, he still relished the time spent here, not working, communicating freely with the elves. He saw Fan, his navy skin looking wan in the morning light stuttering through the crack in the ceiling. The lithe, green-haired elf had climbed halfway up the jagged wall of fallen debris and was handing a chunk of stone down to Hirrell. They hadn't made much progress, but Bob decided that—despite wanting to elongate his vacation—doing something was better than doing nothing. Even if they weren't able to move enough of the blockage to escape, any progress made on their end might make their rescuers' job easier.

His stomach grumbled as he sat up. He was sore from sleeping on the rocky earth, so he stood and stretched. The last thing he wanted to do, first thing after waking, was manual labor, but he figured the En'harae felt the same way.

"Need a hand?" he said, shuffling over to the Cave's plugged mouth.

Torael handed him a heavy chunk of stone and his muscles immediately protested, but he gamely accepted the burden and dumped it in a growing pile in one of the chamber's corners. So far, the work of his companions only seemed to be making the earthen room more cramped. The four elves were muttering to each other in their language, and Bob waited for what seemed like a lull in the conversation before he spoke again.

"So, I'm thinking, I told you my story, and we're all stuck here together, and I don't know much about you." Bob took another rock and walked it to the pile. "Or your people. I'd like that to change. What do you say?"

"What you have in mind?" asked Torael, wiping sweat from his brow with the back of his wrist.

"Well," said Bob, thoughtful, "let's start with where you come from."

"Ah," said Fan from a perch on the mound of rubble. "He wishes to hear of En'hirin."

"Very well, Bob, if you wish," said Torael. "En'hirin is our country. It is west of this horrible place. It is full of beautiful forest, calm rivers, a large coast full of tasty fish."

"Don't forget plains," said Hirrell. "My tribe, Lae'N'glee, lives on plains. Torael is Ellaren, so he forgets."

Torael smirked and nodded his assent.

"But everywhere, there is great song and poetry, many spirits," said Fan.

"And women," said Hirrell wistfully. "En'hirin has most beautiful women, you believe."

Bob thought of the blue women in Oath Keep and nodded. "I believe."

"We do not live in stone houses like humans," said Torael. "The Tessaeshi have made great temples of wood, but most En'harae do not live there. Most tribes live in canvas houses around the rivers. We can move them when the animals move."

"What kind of animals?" asked Bob, setting down a burden.

Torael shrugged. "Many kinds."

"Like *chess'no baka*," said Fan, and Gorrelai nodded silently. "They live on the grass in great numbers, and we hunt them and eat their meat and use their bones and skin and fur. They have great spirits to protect them, and we must honor them, or the spirits are mad and attack us."

Torael handed another stone to Bob, looking thoughtful. "I do not know your word for *chess'no baka*. They are large, hairy beasts, big heads, long tusks. They travel in herds."

"Bison, maybe," said Bob, though that didn't seem exactly right. Bison didn't have tusks. Maybe Torael had misspoken. Anyway, their story seemed familiar. He marveled that, no matter how far from Earth he traveled in the Astraverse, he still found so many similarities to his home. People, it seemed, followed similar patterns across time and space. He idly wondered if there were some underlying reason for these similarities—a cause—or if it was just that the Astraverse followed patterns. "There are... were... people on my world who seem like you. They were in my country."

Hirrell perked up. "What happened to them?"

Bob scowled. "Well, there are some left, but not really. My ancestors came to their country with powerful weapons and unknown diseases and killed them, took their land, and built a nation on it. It's a great shame in our history."

Gorrelai asked a question and Fan responded with many words. Bob patiently moved rocks into the pile, waiting. It seemed they had moved all the smaller stones from the mouth of the entrance, and those remaining were huge and seemed immovable. At least there were now significant gaps in the rubble. Finally, Fan finished answering Gorrelai, and Gorrelai responded in his characteristic spiteful tone.

Torael seemed to be nodding in agreement. "Yes," said the purple-haired elf. "He says, this story you tell, of people from your world, it is what happens to us. Humans come, kill us, take our land. The spirits cannot stop their armor and weapons."

"But this is not all," said Fan. "There is much war for us."

Bob thought of the American natives. "Do your tribes fight one another?"

Hirrell looked surprised. "Fight one another? No! We fight the Gez

Kar."

Bob must have looked confused, because Torael began explaining. As he did so, all five of them moved to the center of the Cave, having no rocks left to move, and sat down for a rest. "En'hirin is west of here, past many miles, through the Essen'aelo."

"Essen'aelo is a great forest," interjected Fan. "Humans call it Shepherd's Forest because the southern part stretches east, where it borders many farmlands." Bob recalled the beginnings of a great forest to the west as he approached Swearington on the East Road.

Torael continued. "This is so. And the Essen'aelo was much bigger when we were children. But anyway, we were speaking of En'hirin. Far to the south of our country is Borgamash. There, in Borgamash, there are more humans. They are different from those here in Engoria. Skin is darker, more respect for spirits. We have no trouble with them, but they have trouble with Engoria."

"Engoria very much trouble for many," said Hirrell.

Torael nodded. "To the west of our country, long, beautiful coast."

"Many fish," said Fan, grinning at the thought.

"For many years," said Torael, "when we were children, we have these fish, and the chess'no baka, and we trade. Mostly we have trade with other tribes, but also with Borgamash. They know spirits. They are humans, but we have not much trouble with them. We trade some with Engoria, but they do not like us. They worship a god of the sun, their Solanus." At this name, Gorrelai spat angrily. "They treat us like we are low, like we do not know things. But for a long time, there is peace with them. But to the north of our country, east of Endless Mountains, there is a place of jungles and fiery mountains called Tanatha. Gez Kar live there. They know spirits, but they are not friendly. They fight us, they fight everyone that get close. They defend their territory with much death and anger."

The other elves were nodding, save for Gorrelai, who simply scowled. Despite not speaking English, he seemed to understand much of it when others spoke it. The big elf said something.

"Yes," said Fan. "Now there is New Tanatha. This land was once ours as well. The Gez Kar live there now."

Bob was trying to keep up. "These Gez Kar," he asked, "they're humans?"

Torael shook his head. "No, they are much worse to look upon. No metal weapons or armor, but they don't need. They are very strong, and have claws and teeth, and some, natural armor on bodies. I do not know words for what they are. They are like… lizard? Scales on skin, long faces with many teeth. Some have shells, some not. But all are nasty and hate us, and hate humans—or so we think for long time. We fight the Gez Kar, they come from north to raid and we fight, they go back, and we watch. They come again, we fight again. This is the way for us, for our parents, for their parents too."

Bob was a little shaken. He knew this world was a strange place—he'd seen a dragon, after all—but lizard-people? He could scarcely imagine trying to fight a giant, intelligent lizard without even a gun. He shook his head. "These Gez Kar sound awful. Big fucking lizards? I don't want to meet them. But what did you mean, you *thought* they hated humans?"

"Many years ago," said Torael, "when our fathers were young and strong, the Gez Kar come. We fight like usual, but bad fighting, many dead. Our fathers, they learn new thing. Gez Kar have king."

"*Very* big fucking lizard," said Hirrell.

Torael nodded. "This is new, no king before, just many tribes like us. Like you ask about us, the Gez Kar tribes always fighting each other, so they don't fight us as much, yes? But this king, they call him Forr Ghaway, he is smart for Gez Kar. He organize, he scare other tribes, with much killing, to do what he say. The Gez Kar come to En'hirin's north, we fight them, but there are so many, is very bad war." Here, Gorrelai spoke a short burst of speech. Torael bowed his head for a moment. "Yes, I get to that part. Forr Ghaway, I say he is smart king. Well, he talk to Engoria's king."

Bob thought back to his conversation with Justin Abernathy. "Martimus? That's him, right? Martimus Something."

"Martimus Flaire, son of Finnigus Flaire," agreed Fan. "King of Engoria."

"Engoria King is stupid," said Hirrell, and made a face.

"Yes," said Torael, "but greedy, and for some reason, he likes turtles."

Bob remembered the banners flying above Swearington. One had displayed a white fist. But the other had featured a black turtle. He stroked his beard thoughtfully. Perhaps the turtle was the symbol of Engoria's King. "Yeah," he said, "it's on the flag."

"Anyway," continued Torael, "stupid, greedy King Flaire likes turtles. Forr Ghaway, he have shell, he look like turtle, little bit."

"Nasty turtle," said Hirrell. "Not cute turtle."

"So, King Flaire make a deal with Forr Ghaway. Our fathers, they do not know this. They fight Gez Kar, they don't lose, but there is much death—our numbers go down. Many years of fighting. Our fathers, they die in war. We grow strong, we fight Gez Kar. King Flaire tell us Engoria will help us fight. There is a great battle at foot of Still Mountains. En'hari tribes united, fighting the armies of Forr Ghaway. We wait for help from Engoria, but they no come. Much death. Then, while we recover, Engoria comes. We think, they have finally come to help. But, while we are still weak, they attack us." Gorrelai spewed a string of curses. Bob knew curses when he heard them. "They attack us, we are surprised. We fight. Gez Kar come, we cannot fight both. We lose. Engoria and Tanatha, they split En'hirin for spoils. Most of our people now live as vassals. Some En'harae become slaves to Gez Kar, and some…" he spread his hands.

Bob's beard felt rough and knotty. His stomach rumbled again. "You were betrayed. That's shitty. I'm sorry."

"We will take En'hirin back," said Fan quietly. Gorrelai said something and pounded a hand to his chest. "There are En'harae gathered even now—"

Fan was interrupted by a heavy cracking noise at the mouth of the Cave. All five heads turned. Pebbles dribbled and clattered from the large stones at the chamber's entrance. They could hear muffled voices and the scraping of metal on rock. They were being rescued.

Now was Bob's chance to build a foundation for escape. He spoke quickly in a low voice. "Listen," he looked them each in the eye in turn, even Gorrelai, "the Gatekey that was taken from me, it's very powerful, but not anyone can use it. I don't understand all the rules, but I know it responds to me while ignoring others. Without it, I'm just Bob, a slave, like you. But with it in my possession, I'm more. I'm Bob the Wizard. If you can help me get it back, I can use its power to help your people. We can escape this mine together, bring as many elves… um, En'harae as we can, and figure out a way to get the Gatekey back. If you help me, I promise to help you win back your country from the Engorians and the Gez Kar."

Bits of rock crumbled away from the rubble at the entrance. The sounds of hammering and scraping grew loud in the small chamber. The shouting voices of slavers filtered through the earth and stone. One of the large boulders cracked. Fan, Gorrelai and Hirrell looked to Torael, who was staring at Bob with discerning eyes. The air grew thick with dust. Slowly, Torael extended a hand in a recognizable gesture of goodwill. Bob took his hand and shook. Hirrell made a whooping noise, Fan chuckled, and Gorrelai nodded.

"Very well, Bob the Wizard," said Torael, barely audible above the clamor of their rescue. "We help each other. But we will need a good plan."

<hr>

The days that followed were mostly uneventful—certainly no occurrences as exciting as the collapse in the Cave. However, while not engaged in grueling slave-work, Bob was not idle. There wasn't much discussion among the En'harae about a plan of escape, but he'd successfully ingratiated himself into their good graces. Torael seemed to have some measure of leadership, that much was clear. Whether it was natural ability, or some station he'd held before enslavement, Bob was unsure, but the other elves seemed to follow his example. After the Cave, the En'harae mostly treated Bob well.

It wasn't just Torael's influence that raised Bob's standing among the slaves. Once, the day after the rescue, a brawny elf had approached at evening meal, scowling and sneering at Bob as he sat slurping his meager dinner. The elf was a burly fellow, one of the biggest Bob had seen, and he spoke in broken English, heavily accented.

"I hungry, Sora Kelai," he rumbled. "You human so small, give dinner for me."

Before Bob knew what was happening, the elf had reached down and grabbed him by the front of his shirt and pulled him to standing. It was all Bob could do to prevent the rest of his gruel from spilling. He just looked the elf in his beady brown eyes, considering the best course of action. He was about to say something when a dry branch cracked Bob's assailant on the head from behind. Bob, finding himself released, watched with fascination and satisfaction as Gorrelai descended on the bully like a cat after a particularly muscular mouse. He shouted and kicked at his ribs and arms. The bully scampered away as Gorrelai spat after him. Gorrelai turned to Bob and nodded—a gesture Bob returned—before walking away and muttering to himself. Yes, Bob saw, it certainly paid to have friends.

And he'd begun to take lessons from Torael, learning Hari, the language of the En'harae. Each night, after the slaves were herded into their sheds, Bob and Torael would quietly have discussions, practicing language, trading tidbits about their lives and the lives of their people. After only about a week, Bob found himself able to understand much of what the elves were saying around him. The Hari language was interesting. Bob learned that the En'harae referred to the planet Hub—if indeed it was a planet—as *Devoh Sheral*, which translated to, *the Great Home*. He learned that the word to indicate oneself—*I*, in English—was *en*. The word for a single elf—*En'hari*—directly translated to, *"I, being with you."* Or, more simply, *"I am with you."* The word for the entire people—*En'harae*—was, *"I am with us."* And the word for their country—*En'hirin*—meant, *"I am with the land."* Bob marveled at how language could shape people's view of the world.

In addition, he learned that the En'harae had a caste system. However, unlike that of the Engorians, it had nothing to do with physical appearance, and was mostly about division of labor. Upon reaching the age of adulthood, which Bob gathered to be about fourteen years old—though, it was hard to tell how long a year was here compared to a year on his Earth—a young En'hari would choose a vocation—a *Kafeh*—that would determine their path in life from then on. One could become a hunter, or a cook, or a shaman, or an artist. There were many vocations. He learned that Gorrelai belonged to the *Gasheera*, the warrior caste.

"Wait, wait," said Bob, confused. "I thought you were all warriors."

"We have to be," replied Torael. "Big war, everyone must fight. But this is not our normal way. For a long time, only Gasheera fight Gez Kar. Once Forr Ghaway come, everyone fights. No choice."

When Bob asked Torael what his Kafeh was, he deftly moved the conversation to another topic. Bob noticed the evasion but didn't press.

At night, he'd sometimes wake with the face of Galvidon swimming in his mind's eye. On more than one occasion, in the dim moonlight filtering through the slits near the shed's roof, he noticed the dancing point of light had returned, perhaps to watch him. He remembered the old peasant woman from the market, Hilda Fields. *Sometimes the faeries come.* Bob wondered if the little dancing light was a faerie, and if so, why it kept showing up while he was sleeping. What did it want? The third time he saw it, he thought to call out to it, but didn't. No use waking the other slaves—who needed their rest—or worse, drawing the attention of the slavers. So, Bob did what he always did after waking from a nightmare. He swore to himself that he'd find and kill Galvidon, that he'd make him pay for what he'd done, and he drifted back to sleep, desperately clinging to plans of revenge.

Once, while in the midst of a ten-hour stretch of swinging a pickaxe, he was overcome by the feeling that the rocks were trying to tell him something. He stared dumbly at the rock face for several minutes. Could he really hear that? He could swear the rocks were singing. A slaver walked by and Bob snapped out of it. He convinced himself that it was just dehydration. Just his mind getting away from him. After all, it had stopped. He got back to work.

Then one day, Bob woke to the usual sounds of a bell rudely clanging and Scarface yelling insults. As alarm clocks went, it was an effective one, but it had reached the point of mundanity for Bob. As he woke, stiff and sore but with his lessons in Hari still fresh in mind, he marveled at how a person could get used to anything. The slaver's scurrilous voice had become something of a bore, and it took Bob longer each morning to pull himself off his pallet. If only Scarface came with a snooze button.

The day soon proved itself to be irregular. During breakfast, Bob thought he heard strange sounds in the air—the hiss and rumble of a crowd, like a sports stadium just over the hills. Bob began to wonder if he were imagining things. But no, the En'harae heard it too. He saw their pointed ears perk, their heads cock, their eyes narrow.

At the tail end of mealtime, Scarface began to shout about something he never had before. "Alright, you louse-ridden sheep fuckers! Get off your lazy shitters and up to the hill! You're going to see what real fucking men look like! You'll know real glory, if you ain't too fucking stupid to understand!"

In the far distance, Bob saw other groups of slaves already being marched up the scraggly slopes to the northeast. From where he stood, they looked like ants. Bob allowed himself to be herded. Scarface wouldn't quit with the bell, but Bob had already learned to tune it out, as if it were a cranky air conditioner.

The morning sun was out in earnest, but the air was cool, and light picked off the sparse trees across the open ground, reflecting sharp greens that stood out starkly from the dull colors of the mining grounds. The sounds of a large crowd swelled, revealing rhythmic shouts, the tromping of booted feet, and the rippling of canvas in the wind. Bob, and the other slaves in his troupe of about forty, huddled together as they reached the crest of a large slope. Bob found himself standing beside Fan and Hirrell. He would have looked around for Torael and Gorrelai, but the sight on the plain below unfolded and demanded attention.

To the north of the mining grounds was an expanse of grassy plain—a kind of long, shallow valley running east to west that cut through the hills. Marching across it was an army. The deep greens of Engoria were prominent on armor and clothing. Banners snapped and shifted, many of which bearing the turtle crest of the Engorian King. Bob saw a few in black-and-white that bore the fist of Swearington, and several others he didn't recognize. It was a throng of soldiers—a couple thousand, by Bob's estimation—accompanied by horses and flocks of sheep, by hundreds of carts and a dozen war machines. Catapults and siege towers were pulled by donkeys or horses or blue-skinned slaves. Regiments of archers were preceded by pikemen and infantrymen. Riders in impressive plate armor flanked the clanking, stomping crowds on proud destriers or sinewy coursers. Some men led their mounts on foot. Dogs darted under legs and around the flocks of sheep, tongues lolling and fur bristling.

BOB THE WIZARD

Shouts and cries and babbling filled the air, and stomping feet vibrated the earth. They marched westward toward what Bob understood to be miles of hills, then Shepherd's Forest—the Essen'aelo—and finally En'hirin, the homeland of the En'harae.

"Fucking beautiful sight, you worms," said Scarface. "More men to bring true civilization to your stinking shithole. You should be grateful. They're going to build you real cities! Show you how to farm and build roads! You blue fuckers should be on your knees thanking them! Worthless savages!"

Bob didn't need to look at the faces of Fan and Hirrell to sense their resentment and exasperation. The troupe stood for long minutes, watching the sprawling procession of "civilization," pass them by on the rolling plain below. The army left churned earth in its wake—the grass and flowers torn and tossed, the trees bent or broken, large clods of brown earth and animal feces scattered across the ground that had, only moments before, been luscious and untouched nature. Bob was disgusted by the whole affair but was not above being thankful for a reprieve under the sun. The time it took to witness the passing of the Engorian army was time not spent digging and hauling, under whips and insults. When the last of the throng passed, Scarface bid them turn around and get to work.

As they crunched down the hill back to the mining grounds, pebbles and loose earth skidding and hopping around their feet, the troupe was approached from the southeast by a pair of armored men. Bob could see the wagon they'd arrived in, parked in the middle-distance, alongside Horizon Road. The two men wore the black and white of the Swearington Guard, and one of the slavers sauntered over to meet them. Bob listened to Fan and Hirrell mutter to each other in Hari but watched the slaver as he nodded curtly to the guards and jogged back to the group, where he spoke to Scarface. The head slaver pushed his way through the slaves like a bull and stopped in front of Bob, who stared at him impassively.

"You, Darkhair," growled Scarface. "You will go with those men. Now."

Bob gave the guards a sidelong glance. "Why?"

Like a striking snake, Scarface lashed his short whip across Bob's shoulder. A raking sting spread across his back and he cried out despite himself.

"You don't fucking ask questions!" bellowed Scarface. "You fucking Darkhair bastard! A man that gets himself thrown in with *this* stinking lot! Even worse than a Blueskin! You're a fucking disgrace. Get out of my sight!"

Even as the sting on his back thrummed, Bob was tempted to point out that Scarface had dark hair too. Instead, he tromped off, a little unsteady, toward the waiting guards. When he reached them, rubbing at his shoulder and back, he gave them a quizzical look.

"What is it, then?"

"You're to come with us, *slave*," said one, sneering. "A guest will arrive shortly at Oath Keep who wants to talk to you."

BOB THE WIZARD

CHAPTER NINE:
WANT

A guest, they'd said. *Wants to talk to you*, they'd said. Jostled as he was in another windowless box on the back of a wagon, Bob had a hard time putting his speculations in order. Thin lines of sunlight wavered and shifted across his vision, streaming in through tiny cracks and chinks in his mobile cage. It reminded him absurdly of a dance floor at a bar. Not that he'd spent much time dancing. Bars, sure. Dancing, no. He could almost picture a spinning Disco ball fixed on the ceiling and caught himself chuckling in the stuffy half-darkness. Who could possibly want to talk to him? Apart from the En'harae slaves, he had no friends in Engoria. Surely not Gerald and Jenna at the Fool's Rest, they'd turned him in for murder. Hilda Fields was nice enough—well, not nice, exactly, but they'd gotten along—but she was just a sheep farmer and held no sway over Mannix. He dared hope that there had been more murders, that his name had been cleared. A sorry thing to hope for, but there it was.

It occurred to Bob that Mannix might want to ply him for information. Mannix had the Gatekey, after all, and the sawed-off. Maybe the Lord of Swearington intended to torture him until he divulged their secrets. Bob pictured himself lecturing Mannix on the use of the shotgun.

Well, you just put that round, open end up to your head—yes, like that. Now, you pull the trigger…

Bob chuckled again. He was having far too much fun for a slave in a box. As far as the Gatekey went, Mannix could torture him until the end of time, and it wouldn't matter. Whatever was *special* about Bob—as Rashindon had said—the Gatekey somehow knew. It wouldn't work for other people. Bob didn't like to think about it, but he'd had the Gatekey taken from him before. The strange object was keyed into him somehow, like one of those fancy doors in science fiction movies that only opened once they scanned the right person's eyeball.

Special, Rashindon had said. Anna had called him that often. When he did something thoughtful, she'd say, *you're a special kind of man*. When he bungled a small task, like folding the laundry wrong, she'd also say, *you're a special kind of man*, but in an entirely different tone. After he'd wrecked the car—breaking his nose and two ribs, destroying the future he'd thought he'd have—she'd said, *you're a special kind of stupid*. Maybe that's what Rashindon had meant: that Bob was a special kind of stupid. It was a hard assessment to argue with, as a slave in a bouncing box lit by an imaginary disco ball. He pictured the dying alien in his living room, pressing the Gatekey into his hand, and saying, *you're a special kind of stupid, Bob*.

Bob barked a laugh. There wasn't much else he could do. The alternative was to sink into despair, the way he'd done the night they'd first taken him out to the mine. He could either choose to see the funny side or lose his sense of humor entirely. And wouldn't Galvidon like that—Bob, losing hope?

The jostling of the wagon shifted its pattern, and the muted sounds of Swearington began to reach him. There was a long series of starts and stops as the wagon made its way through city-traffic. Finally, the wagon wheels struck smooth stone and pulled to a stop. Bob was still smirking to himself as the wagon's rear panels opened and sunlight streamed in, framing the outlines of the two guards. They motioned for him to exit, and he did so willingly enough, grateful to stretch his legs after over an hour of sitting in a cramped box. Sure enough, Oath Keep reached up to the sky before him. The courtyard's polished cobbles were hard beneath the soles of his tattered shoes. From just over the inner wall to the west and north, the ramshackle slums of Shadow Quarter peeked at the courtyard. The guards shoved and prodded him along, up the stone steps and through the double doors of the main entrance. In the huge inner atrium, Archlector Stephen Carosel sat scratching atop his dais.

"Hey there, friend," called Bob as he was shoved leftward from the entrance toward a descending spiral staircase. "I know you missed me!"

BOB THE WIZARD

The golden-haired Archlector glanced up and scowled just as Bob passed out of the room.

<hr />

He was in a cell again. That fucking water was dripping somewhere. The grimy gray walls were jagged and neglected. There was a rotting wooden bench to sit on, a rotting pallet of cloth upon which to sleep. It was chilly, and Bob's worn slave's rags did little to guard against the cold. He sat for a few minutes, briskly rubbing at his arms, before he heard the creak of the door that led into the dungeon. He heard the jangle of mail, the click of heavy boots, and Lord Fulton Mannix came striding into view.

The Lord of Swearington wore a forest green tunic under a vest of chain and a dagger at his belt. His lush blond hair was well combed, his short beard well clipped. There was something off about him though, something different. As Bob looked him in the eye, he realized what it was—he was not smiling. His face was stern and set, and his eyes seemed almost to worry. No trace of mirth touched his expression. If Bob didn't know better, he might think the man was afraid. What had made the light-haired lord so nervous? Bob supposed he should just shut his mouth and wait to find out.

Suddenly the Lord's expression changed, like a dark cloud passing away from the sun. He was smiling again—that self-important smirk—and he began to stroll back and forth before the bars of the cell. He clucked his tongue.

"Bob the Wizard," he mused. "We meet again."

Bob watched him, waiting. The buoyant mood he'd worked himself into had faded.

Mannix stopped directly in front of him, his body cocked to the side, eying Bob like a window shopper. "No reply? No retort? Nothing amusing to say?" He raised an eyebrow and tapped his chin thoughtfully. "Perhaps your time as a slave has indeed taught you something."

Bob stared, and Fulton Mannix stared right back. After a few seconds, Bob gave in. "What do you want?" he said shortly.

Mannix tapped his chin again. "Yes, yes. What do I want. Do you know a man... well, a person, called Galvidon? Strange fellow, a bit frightening. Had the displeasure of meeting him shortly after your arrest. Ah, I see from your face that you do know him. Well, he knows you too. At least, he's heard of you. Seems the Darkhairs have been whispering about you. Someone claims to have seen you disappear from the street and reappear on my balcony. A neat trick, I'd wondered how you did it. Seems I underestimated you." Mannix paused, and Bob wondered if the blond Lord was waiting for a thank you.

Gee whiz, Mr. Mannix, I sure do appreciate the compliment.

Bob just continued to stare. Internally, he was quite alarmed at the mention of Galvidon. He was excited by the news that the Gray Man was still on Hub. That meant Bob hadn't lost his trail. But he was also afraid. He was unarmed, alone in a cell, and the creature that had murdered Anna and Daniel might be the guest the guards had mentioned.

Mannix seemed to understand that Bob was still not going to speak. "At any rate, it seems this Galvidon has made his way to Tortellan, had audience with King Flaire, and convinced him of some scheme. I have not been provided with the details." Mannix scowled, and Bob was satisfied to see the blond man's discomfiture at being excluded. "Not that Martimus and I see eye-to-eye on much. At any rate, it seems that, in a short time, the King has become quite enamored with your gray friend. Made him a Counselor. An unheard-of thing, to elevate a foreigner to such a position after only a few weeks, but here we are." Bob was sitting on the wooden bench, knees drawn up to his chest. Mannix got down on his haunches and put his hands on the rusted iron bars of the cell, looking Bob in the eye. "Do you know where your key is?"

Bob blinked. "You have it."

"It's special, isn't it? I can tell when I hold it, when I look at it. It has power." Mannix's blue eyes shone in the dim light of the dungeon, hungry and wide. Bob remained silent. "You don't seem to be magically disappearing from that cell on your own. I wonder, could the key have something to do with it?" Mannix lifted his eyebrows, almost triumphant, before narrowing his eyes as he continued. "This Galvidon, he will ask you for it. He has already sent a message ahead, telling me to relinquish it to him." Mannix lifted his hands and spread his palms. "But I don't have it." His smirk was hard and conspiratorial. "I don't know what he's talking about. Do you? What key? This man had no key." He indicated Bob through the bars with one hand. "Tell me Bob, what happened to the key?"

Bob rolled his eyes. "You have it," he repeated. "Lord Mannix," he added.

Mannix stood and threw up his hands. "I see being a slave has dulled your mind after all! Not much for subtlety, are you? You will tell Galvidon that you have no key. You never had a key, do you understand?"

"Why would I do that?" Bob's throat was dry, and a suspicion was beginning to dawn on him. He tested his theory. "I'm thirsty," said Bob, with as much authority as he could muster.

Mannix raised an eyebrow, his smirk unwavering. He trotted a few paces to the dungeon entrance and rapped his knuckles sharply upon the door. A moment later it opened, and a guard's head appeared, peeking into the dank chamber. "Bring us some water, Darkhair," said Mannix good-naturedly.

"Sir!" spouted the guard and swiftly disappeared behind the doorframe. He appeared a few moments later with a bucket and a ladle, which he handed to the Lord of Swearington before swiftly making his exit. Mannix casually carried the bucket over to the front of Bob's cell and placed it on the floor with the ladle inside. He smiled and gestured to it like a waiter. Bob got to his feet slowly, taking his time, and made his way over to the bucket. It appeared to be full of clean water, so he reached through the bars, glancing at Mannix all the while, and brought the ladle to his lips. The water was cool and refreshing. He sipped at first but was soon gulping it down by the ladleful. When his thirst was quenched, he returned to the bench and sat. Mannix was eying him like an eager child.

"So, Bob the Wizard, what happened to the key?"

"It's getting fuzzy," said Bob. "But I think I remember that you took it from me."

Mannix's smirk dipped slightly, threatened to become a frown, but he resisted, and it resurfaced. "I see. And what might allow you to remember that you never had it?"

"Why don't you just kill me?" asked Bob. He could hardly believe the words escaping his mouth, but still they continued. "Why go through the trouble to bribe me? Surely killing me would be easier."

Mannix brought a hand to his eyes, as if disappointed that a dog had peed on the carpet. "What was I just saying about subtlety? As much as I might like to, I can't kill you. As I said, King Flaire likes this Galvidon fellow, and Galvidon wants the key. If I kill you, I'll clearly be implicated. It's common knowledge I sent you to the mines. Any fool will see that your death meant that I was covering something up. Galvidon will know I have it." He looked at Bob. "I want you to show me how to use it. I want to know how it works. For that to happen…" he lowered his voice. "Galvidon must not know I have it."

Part of Bob was amused by this turn of events. He despised Mannix—his obvious hunger for power, his superior attitude, the fact that he'd thrown Bob into slavery. But no amount of dislike could measure up to how he felt about Galvidon. Galvidon was his reason for existence. Without Galvidon, he wouldn't be here, would never have arrived on Hub. Bob would never tell him what he wanted to know, never tell him where the Gatekey was. That would be suicide—if not literally, it would mean the death of his quest. Without the Gatekey, Bob would never be able to follow the Gray Man to the next world, never avenge the deaths of his wife and son. So, the fact that Mannix was attempting to bargain with Bob for something that Bob would already have done, well, that was a little funny. Still, he had to be careful. He needed that Gatekey. He had to let Mannix keep it from Galvidon, because getting it back from the Lord of Swearington, difficult as that may be, would be a damn sight easier than getting it from the Gray Man. Yet, he couldn't give in to Mannix too easily. If he played it right, he could get some advantage that could help him later.

"Oh, I don't know," said Bob, scratching his beard. "Galvidon is a hard man to fool. And scary. One look at him, I might lose hope, you know? Might just tell him everything. A man needs hope. Tell me, *Fulton*, what do I have to hope for?"

Mannix winced at the use of his first name but recovered quickly. "Surely the life of a slave is not an easy one," he said, examining his fingernails.

"Then let me go. I'll tell Galvidon what you want, and then you let me go."

Mannix snorted. "No, no, that wouldn't do at all. If I lost you, that would be as bad as killing you. Lord Mannix, what has happened to the prisoner? I'm sorry, my King, I seem to have misplaced him." He chuckled. "Besides, I need you here, for your knowledge."

Bob's mind was racing, but thinking was difficult. He was hungry and working in the mines had taken a toll on his body. No matter what he told Galvidon, if he even lived through that encounter, sooner or later Mannix would find out that Bob couldn't help him use the Gatekey. He shuddered to think what means the blond lord might implement to try and ply out the information. Perpetual incarceration, certainly, and perhaps torture. He had to find a way out of this, and soon.

"I could use some food, and a good blanket, and a change of clothes." He paused. "And some tobacco, with a pipe."

Mannix's eyes sparkled. "Why, of course. The food and the blanket I will provide shortly. We will wait on the clothes and tobacco until after you speak with Galvidon tomorrow. We should keep up appearances, after all. No need for Galvidon to know we've become friends." At this last, Bob glared at the Lord of Swearington like one might look at dogshit on one's shoe. Mannix didn't seem to notice. "But I do feel the necessity of warning you, *friend*, that should you renege on our arrangement and tell Galvidon what happened to the key, I'm afraid I shall become enraged, and your life would be forfeit."

"Goes without saying."

"Good. Before I go, is there anything else?"

Bob stroked his beard. There *was* something else—the one thing that might actually help him get out of here—but he needed to frame it the right way, in a manner that wouldn't arouse suspicion. When he told Mannix what he wanted, the lord smirked his smirk, winked, and agreed. Bob sighed and sat back in his cell, listening to the water drip as his captor exited the dungeon.

The food was the best he'd eaten in weeks. As he ate the roast mutton, fresh bread, and vegetable stew, he felt as though he'd never eaten anything better. There he was, in a dank cell underneath an aristocrat's keep in a world he wasn't born in, feeling like a king as he wolfed down his meal. They'd brought him spiced wine, but he'd asked for water instead, drawing an incredulous look from the attending guard.

"You drink it," said Bob, shrugging. "Just as long as you bring me some fucking water."

Once he was finished, the guard removed his leavings. Bob began to feel sleepy. He found the will to stay awake, standing and stretching, taking off his shoes to allow his bare feet to soak in the cold from the stone floor.

After a few minutes, the guard returned with what Bob had asked for from Mannix. It was the En'hari woman Bob had seen leaving Mannix's quarters when he'd snuck in through the balcony. She wore the same brown clothing that resembled a sack, and bore a tightlipped, disapproving stare.

"Stand away from the door," the guard commanded, although Bob was already sitting on the bench, well away from the cell's entrance. The guard ushered the woman into the cell by her arm and gave her a perfunctory shove before locking the bars in place. "You two have fun," he said, chuckling to himself, and made his exit.

Bob recognized her hair, so bright red it almost hurt his eyes. As she straitened her back and glared at him disdainfully, he noticed her eyes were a warm brown, her face sharp, accentuating her long, pointed ears and giving her a sleek appearance, like a fox.

Bob remained sitting and cleared his throat. "Do you recognize me?"

She hesitated, scowling down at him for a moment before nodding her head slightly.

"I'm Bob," he said. "What's your name?"

She remained silent.

"*En'do senna Sora Kelai*," he said in Hari. At this, her eyes widened, and her frown slackened.

"You speak my language poorly," she said, in perfect English. "You just said your name was Face Hair."

He responded in Hari. "*So it is. I was so named by my En'hari brothers.*"

"*They must not like you much.*" She switched to English. "What do you want with me? I hope you don't plan to touch me with those filthy hands."

Bob glanced down at his hands. They were, in fact, very dirty. He shook his head and responded in English. "I won't touch you, though you *are* very beautiful." As he spoke, he realized that, though he'd said it to soften her hostility, it was true. Being so close to her, alone, with implicit permission to do what he wanted to her, had awoken his body more than he cared to admit. He could almost see Anna standing behind her, coolly observing, waiting for him to do or say something that he'd regret. He averted his eyes from the elf woman. "You haven't told me your name."

She arched an eyebrow. "Ellaria. My name is Ellaria. Now what do you want?"

Bob was already speaking in a low voice, but he lowered it even further, and glanced around at the empty cells as if making sure no one was in them. "What I want is to get out of here."

Ellaria laughed, almost giggled. "Is that all? Good luck, Face Hair. What's that to do with me?"

Bob was beginning to have serious doubts about this course of action, but it was all he had, so he pressed on. "I made a deal with my fellow slaves, with the elves… I mean, the En'harae. We agreed, they'd help me get something back, an object I lost. In exchange, I'd help them liberate En'hirin." The blue-skinned woman studied him. Her brown eyes searched his face. "I was with a man, an En'hari, named Torael. He told me…" Bob dropped his voice to a whisper. "There is a resistance nearby, a group of fighters, who stand up to Engoria. Do you know of them?"

At the mention of Torael, her eyes widened, then darted about as if she were thinking rapidly. She returned the whisper. "What tribe?"

"What?"

"What tribe," she hissed. "Torael from what tribe?"

"Oh, I don't remember. El-something."

"Ellaren?"

"Yeah, that's the one."

She rubbed her eyes with thumb and forefinger. "What is your plan?"

"This resistance. Can you contact them?"

She sighed. "It will be difficult, but it can be done. I know someone."

"There is a man coming to talk with me tomorrow. Afterwards, Mannix will throw me back in the mines. But the object I need is here. If you can get the resistance to attack our troupe and free us, we can strike the keep quickly and retake the object. We can free you." Bob had no idea if he could pull that off, or if he did, how long it would take. But this was his only chance, so he stretched the truth.

She shuffled her feet, considering. "There are dozens of mines outside of Swearington. Which one?"

Bob shook his head. "About forty-five minutes by wagon down Horizon Road, due west of Swearington. I've made the trip twice. There are plenty of bumps in the road, but the wagon never turns. It's a straight shot."

"Very well," she whispered, and then, suddenly, she was yelling. "Guard! We are through here!" She turned to Bob. "Even if I thought you could get me out of here, which I don't, I wouldn't help you. But I will do it for Torael." Before Bob could respond, the dungeon door had creaked open, and the guard entered. Ellaria slapped Bob across the face. Tiny stars floated in his vision, and he covered his cheek in surprise. "Get your hands off me! Guard, get me away from this filthy animal before I vomit all over this dungeon!"

The guard, obviously confused, glanced from her to Bob. "You sure?" He was looking at Bob. Which slave ought he obey? It seemed the guard defaulted to favoring his own sex. When Bob nodded to him, he unlatched the cell, still wearing a stupefied look. Ellaria pushed her way out of the cell and stormed up the stairs. The guard relocked the cell and stared quizzically at Bob.

Bob shrugged. "Women."

Mannix had been kind—or fearful—enough to provide the blanket Bob had asked for, so despite the chilliness of the night, sleep was forthcoming. Unfortunately, so were nightmares. Again, he walked through his front door. Again, he was confronted by the corpses of Anna and Daniel. Again, Galvidon stood over them, his black eyes impassive, his knives glinting and dripping with red. And the dream shifted from precise memory as Galvidon approached him speaking in Mannix's voice. *What happened to the key?* The Gray Man plunged a dagger into Bob's chest and said, *not much for subtlety, are you?*

His eyes flickered open, and he reached for his chest, half expecting to find a mortal wound. Of course, it wasn't there—just his bony chest, all the fat worked away in the iron mines. But through the narrow, barred window of the cell, a familiar sight hovered. The little dancing point of light swirled into the cell like a wayward star.

"What do you want?" demanded Bob. "What are you?"

His voice was scratchy and barely audible to his own ears. The light paused in midflight and hovered, still and bright like a headlight in fog. Then, slowly it spiraled downward and approached him. As it settled in the air before his face, it resolved itself into a tiny flying woman. She was only three inches tall, bore two delicate, colorful wings like a butterfly, and of course seemed to glow from within, like a flashlight behind paper. Other than these curious attributes, she seemed completely human. Bob thought the word, *faerie*, but many of his preconceived notions about the creatures, gathered absentmindedly from stories he'd heard as a child, were challenged by her appearance. For instance, he didn't expect her to be wearing tiny, wire-rimmed glasses, or her shimmering golden hair to be tied back in a neat little ponytail, or for her to be wearing what seemed to be, as far as Bob was concerned, a long, white lab coat. Perhaps strangest of all, if only for its utter mundanity in the face of all her irregularities, she held a tiny notebook in one hand and a miniscule pen in the other.

Her flight was graceful and soundless, but when she spoke, her voice was clear and strident, as if from a full-sized person. "Finally saw me, huh, Bob? I suppose it was inevitable. A bit irritating, though. After all, when the thing you're observing notices you observing it, it invariably changes its behavior. Anyway, I suppose I've seen enough of you in your natural state to draw *some* conclusions, so I guess some interaction could yield more detailed data…"

The hand holding the pen reached up to adjust her glasses. "Tell me, why didn't you mate with the En'hari woman? That seemed to be your intent when you requested her presence. Are you not sexually active?" Her eyes ran across his body. "You seem physically mature. It was my understanding that human males cannot grow such an impressive amount of hair on their face until the age of maturity." She peered at him expectantly, her wings gently flapping, her pen poised above the notebook.

Bob was flabbergasted. He spoke slowly, one word at a time. "What… the… fuck?"

"Ah, profanity! I see I've made you uncomfortable. So sorry, I can be a bit zealous about my work, and sometimes I forget to engage in social customs. Allow me to introduce myself. Osivia Glenbrook, faerie scientist." Pressing the notebook to her chest, she held out one tiny hand to Bob. It was less than the size of one of his fingernails. Suddenly unsure that he'd ever actually awakened from his nightmare, he reached out his pinky finger. She grabbed it in her little outstretched hand and gave it a couple vigorous shakes.

"Faerie… scientist," he repeated dumbly. He rubbed his face vigorously. She was still there. "What the *fuck?*" he whispered.

Osivia cocked her head. "Oh my, I'm afraid my sudden appearance may have fried your brain." She began to speak slowly and loudly. "Me… Osivia… You… Bob."

Bob decided he had no choice but to accept that this was really happening. He sat up fully. "You've been watching me? Why?"

"Because you're interesting." She said this as if it were the most obvious thing in the world.

"I am?" He yawned.

"Well, I've been studying humans for a few years now." She spoke rapidly. "Not many faeries care to know things. And I mean, they *really* don't want to know things. But there's this school, right? It's just one. Just one school in our entire civilization, can you imagine?" She snorted laughter. "Anyway, it's called the Academy. I always wanted to go there. My parents didn't want me to, but they also didn't try very hard to stop me, so I went and enrolled, and I met some great faeries. Well, there were only ten professors, and I learned everything and graduated and now I'm off researching the world because, let's be honest, no other faeries are going to do it. So, mainly I've been studying humans because we live so close to them, and they're fascinating, you know? Well, you probably don't think so, being one of them. But I think so. And that brings me to you."

Bob was only halfway paying attention at this point. He'd decided Osivia was not a threat, and now he just wished she would be quiet so he could go back to sleep. "Me," he said dreamily.

"From what I've observed of humans, it seems most of their behavior is in pursuit of one of two things: sex, or violence. Plus, humans are hierarchical. They hate the other intelligent species and consider themselves superior. They even have internal hierarchies which elevate certain subgroups above others. Individuals with lighter hair seem to have a higher standing than those with darker hair. Males seem to dominate their social structure—*certainly* not a problem faeries have." She sniffed. "Anyway, I saw you save that En'hari's life. Compassion for another species! A behavior I have never before witnessed in a human! Fascinating! Why'd you do it?"

Bob had lain back down. Had he been fully awake, he might have thought more thoroughly about his response. He might have said that he'd saved Torael because he needed him to gain the elves' trust. He might've said that saving him was just instinct and had nothing to do with compassion. But at that moment, the self-reproving doubt he always carried—the cynical part of him that refused to acknowledge that Robert James Caplan, of all people, could be worth more than a squirt of shit—was asleep, and under it was the true Bob.

"World's better when we help each other," he mumbled.

M. V. PRINDLE

"Fascinating," he heard her say. There was a slight scribbling noise. "Now, tell me, why didn't you mate with the En'hari woman?"

Bob's response was a snore.

BOB THE WIZARD

CHAPTER TEN:
HOLD OUT

Bob awoke late in the morning, his stomach rumbling. He told himself in a vague, detached sort of way that the little glowing woman had been real. Sunlight filtered in through the pathetic windows, warming the cell. Birdsong mingled with the meaner sounds carried from just beyond the courtyard's wall—a bustling ambience of shouts, whinnies, and the clacks and creaks of wagons. Bob waited a few minutes, trying not to notice the renewed scent of horse shit that wafted through the windows. Shortly, the guard—a different fellow from the night previous—swung open the creaky dungeon door and brought Bob a meager breakfast. With a start, Bob realized that he recognized the armor-clad man. It was Tall, one of the guards he'd met at South Gate, to whom Bob had given his sunglasses. The man caught him looking and gave a perfunctory nod before tiredly saying, "away from the door, wizard."

"Took away the glasses, huh?"

"Almost got me in trouble, you did," mumbled Tall. "I warned you not to be using no magic."

"Wasn't the magic that got me in here," said Bob.

Tall set down a plate of boiled egg and old bread through the slot near the bottom of the cage door. "Not what folks are saying," he said quietly. "See, some people think the king done outlawed magic because them wizards were about to kick him off that throne. So, word gets around there's a real wizard in town, Darkhairs start to talking." Tall glanced at the entrance to this wing of the dungeon. The wooden door was firmly shut. "What was your name again?"

"Bob," answered Bob, eying the plate of food.

M. V. PRINDLE

"Bob the Wizard," mused Tall.

"I'm not here to overthrow the government."

Tall didn't seem to have heard. "Say, why you ain't magicked your way out of here?"

Bob tapped the side of his nose with one finger. "Biding my time."

Tall seemed to consider this as he exited through the creaky wooden door. Bob rolled his eyes and turned his attention to the food. He reflected that even this poor meal was an improvement to his daily slave broth.

After eating, he paced the cell and worried about the En'hari woman, Ellaria, and whether she'd taken steps to contact the resistance. He thought of how nice some tobacco would be and wondered if Mannix would really give him a pipe later. He wondered if Galvidon would kill him, if all his journeying up to this point would end with him bleeding to death in a cold cell while a faerie in a lab coat scribbled in a notebook.

At some point, Osivia the Faerie Scientist had returned. Bob glanced up at the tiny windows, and there she was. She was much harder to pick out in daylight. She came and went throughout the day, but was usually somewhere close, hovering, or lounging in the barred windows, reading over her notes, like a student waiting for class to begin.

Bob thought of Torael, wondering why Ellaria had said what she did. *I wouldn't help you. But I will do it for Torael.* He remembered wondering if the purple-haired elf had some kind of important position in En'hirin, and Ellaria's words seemed to reinforce that suspicion.

He thought of Anna and Daniel. A memory came to him, him and Daniel—little Danny five years old—running around the back yard, chasing each other with one of those inflatable balls from the grocery store.

You can't catch me Daddy! You can't catch me!

It wasn't long before Galvidon invaded his thoughts again, and then in his daydream it was the Gray Man, and not Daniel, running around his old back yard and screaming, *you can't catch me*. It would have been funny, if it wasn't so sad.

99

BOB THE WIZARD

The day passed so slowly Bob began to wonder if Galvidon would ever arrive. Had he changed his mind? Was Mannix mistaken? It was too much to hope for. This plodding anticipation was just another way for Galvidon to cause him misery. Bob wrung his hands. He scratched his beard, he sighed, he did push-ups, he tried to go back to sleep. He considered trying to talk to Osivia again but wasn't in the mood for her prying and prodding. There was a slanted divot in the floor in a corner at a rear wall, and he urinated down it, which did nothing to improve the smell of the air. Shafts of light came through the windows, shifting like luminous slugs across the cracked stone floor, ticking the time away in arduous slow motion, stone by stone. Finally, as the sun began to set, Bob was pulled from his trance by the telltale shifting of locks and creak of the wooden door.

Galvidon melted soundlessly out of the shadows in the corridor. He looked just as Bob remembered him—tall and sturdy, skin as gray as sheet rock, large eyes black like oil. Curved and lightly striated horns, roughly six inches long, protruded from his forehead. A pointed chin and angular eyebrows, an ill-defined nose, conspired with his skin color to give him the aspect of a shark. He wore black, chitinous armor that fit together in overlapping segments, like the skin of a centipede, and caught the light in dull reflections, like obsidian. Curious pouches hung from a belt on his hips, alongside some kind of pistol. His knives were holstered on his midsection inside crossed scabbards built into his armor. Thick boots, black and heavy, sheathed his feet. Despite all the gear on his person, his movements were silent and graceful, like a leopard.

Bob's breath quickened. His boredom was forgotten. Anger and hatred bubbled inside him, up from the base of his spine and into his stomach, into his esophagus, constricting his organs. His temples thrummed, his vision vibrated, his pulse hammered. Instinctively his hand reached inside a trench coat that was long taken for a gun that was not there. An involuntary growl escaped his throat.

Galvidon stood just outside the bars to the cell. Bob sat opposite him on the rotting bench. For a few moments, they regarded each other. Outside, the city sounds had died down to a low hum punctuated by the occasional distant whinny or clatter. Galvidon's black eyes rolled over him, though it was hard to tell exactly what he was looking at. The Gray Man cocked his head and broke the silence between them.

"You are the one called Bob the Wizard?"

His voice was rich and resonant, deeper than Bob expected. He had that strange accent Bob had described to the elves in the Cave—odd, otherworldly.

Scowling, Bob bit back a thousand scathing words. His mind churned with vitriolic accusations and insults, but logic held them back, barely. He had to choose his words carefully. He was at a disadvantage, and every word was precious, might decide whether or not he lived through this encounter, might determine if he could ply any useful information from Galvidon, his greatest enemy.

Bob swallowed. "You don't remember me, do you?" His voice had a hoarse, quavering quality he didn't like. He didn't want Galvidon to know how afraid he was, how eager, how elated.

"Should I?" asked the Gray Man. "You seem ordinary. Unremarkable. If not for the rumors surrounding you, I would not notice you, stepping on you in passing. Yet these rumors are troubling. They say you are a wizard. That you travel quickly through the air at will. Yet you are trapped in that cell, enslaved, alone, and you do not escape. I believe you had the aid of a device. An Astral Key." He paused, and Bob could feel those black eyes traveling over him, searching, analyzing. "Where is the Key, Bob the Wizard? Where did you acquire it?" He spoke without anger, but his tone demanded a response.

"I don't know what you're talking about."

Galvidon nodded, as if he had expected nothing else. "Tell me, why do you think I should recognize you? You speak with an accent foreign to Hub. Which realm are you from?"

Bob remained silent. His eyes stung, and he realized with resentment that he was struggling to hold back tears. He willed his jaw to remained clamped tightly shut, afraid of what might spill out if it opened. Behind the Gray Man, in one of the cell-windows, Osivia fluttered nervously. Galvidon's hand moved deliberately to one of the pouches on his belt and unfastened a strap. From it he slid a small cylindrical object, silver and black, bearing tiny dials and buttons. It reminded Bob of the Gatekey, though it was something else.

BOB THE WIZARD

Galvidon's black eyes narrowed. "Bob the Wizard," his tone was formal and commanding, "Where is the Key? Where did you acquire it?"

"I don't know what you're talking about," repeated Bob, his eyes fixed with fascination on the little cylinder in Galvidon's hand.

The Gray Man cocked his head and almost imperceptibly clicked something on the cylinder. Suddenly Bob's ears were full of a piercing buzz, his head felt as if it were being crushed, his muscles began to ache and twist inside him. His organs protested, he could feel each of his teeth, each of his fingernails and toenails, his nipples, his genitals. Everything had become a frayed nerve, a point of severe pain, and it only got worse every second. He tried to bring his hands to his head, but his muscles rebelled, and he flailed helplessly, falling to the cell floor, the agony in every part of him building to a crescendo.

Then it was over. The buzzing noise ceased abruptly, and the pain receded, though he was left sore and strained. Lying awkwardly on his back, Bob let out an involuntary, gurgling sigh. He was dimly aware of Galvidon repeating his questions.

Where is the Key? Where did you acquire it?

"Don't... know," managed Bob, still on the floor.

The buzz returned, and everything flared with pain once more, sharper now, each extremity trying to pry its way free from his body, his core thrumming in protest. Bob saw Anna's face, smiling at him, heard Daniel's voice echo in his ears.

You can't catch me, Daddy!

The second round of torture abated. Bob felt like he'd just traveled through a meat grinder. His arms and legs twitched of their own accord. This time, Galvidon turned away from the cell and gave Bob a full minute to recover. But the respite seemed over in a flash. Bob had struggled to his knees, and Galvidon turned calmly back to face him.

"Bob the Wizard," said the Gray Man. His formal tone had shifted—he seemed amused, entertained. A ghost of a smile twitched on his tight, lipless mouth. "Where is the Key? Where did you acquire it?"

Bob's hands found the bars of the cell and he arduously dragged himself up until he was face to face with Galvidon, looking into the dark depths of the Gray Man's emotionless eyes. His legs felt like jelly. This was the closest he'd ever been since that night on Earth, so long ago.

"Okay," he huffed. "Okay, I'll tell you. But you tell me something first."

Galvidon's smile was earnest now. "Impressive. Very well, Bob. Since you will spend the rest of your life a slave, working until you die while I continue to do great things, I will answer one question." He still held the torture device in one hand, and the other curled around an iron bar just above Bob's own hand. They were almost touching. So close.

Dizzy, Bob swallowed on a swollen throat and steadied himself. "Why…" he said, "why did you kill my family?" His voice broke, and he was angry at himself for that. He noticed Osivia was still there, in a window, watching intently, unmoving. The sun had departed at some point. Osivia's glow was muted, pulsing a dull orange.

"I see," said Galvidon, and nodded. "I see. I do not remember your family, Bob. I have killed so many, they all run together. But it doesn't matter if I killed them twenty cycles ago or yesterday, for I always kill for the same reason." His dark eyes flashed in the moonlight. "It is beyond your understanding, but I will try to explain. You see, Bob, there were not always so many realms. Before the Astraverse, there was only one realm. The First World—called the Anterior by humans, the Urdis Varin by my people—the original realm from which all other realms eventually sprung. A holy place indeed.

"The first sentient race there, we call the Precedentials—the First Ones. Truly, they were close to God. But, as all races do, they began primitive. They existed through millennia of wars and growth, but eventually, became a harmonious and prosperous society, with unified purpose—holy purpose. They built powerful machines, great and small. And over time, they began to evolve into disparate strains. The second races came to be—the adequate humans, of which you are one, and mighty Galon Var, of which I am one. Slowly, the Precedentials faded and were all but replaced by our two peoples, but their technology remained. Those First Ones that still lived—for there were still some—gathered their technological powers and their peerless knowledge and, with God's blessing, created the whole of the Astraverse. God warned a chosen few Precedentials of a great undoing coming to befall the Anterior—what would come to be called the Great Cataclysm. These chosen First Ones sought to bring forth Creation, so that life would continue if the Urdis Varin were obliterated."

Bob was surprised. Galvidon spoke with vehemence and authority. It was clear, no matter how much of it was true, that the Gray Man believed what he was saying. Bob didn't know what explanation for Anna and Daniel's murder he'd been expecting, but this wasn't it. He studied Galvidon as he continued.

"Fearing the Anterior would be destroyed utterly, the Precedentials seeded millions of worlds across the Astraverse with humans and Galon Var. Among this colonial multitude were a select few, chosen by the First Ones—and therefore by God, as well—for their bravery, intelligence, their ingenuity and strength. These blessed are called the Electum. Soon after the seeding, the Great Cataclysm came to pass, leaving the Urdis Varin in squalor and chaos. The remaining Precedentials were finally destroyed. Yet they had left a final test for us, their children. They protected their remaining technology with powerful gene-locks, so that only the Electum and their descendants could operate it. Those who remained on the Anterior were forsaken, left to fight amongst themselves and claw their way through the darkness. Eventually, thousands of cycles later, a society was rebuilt, humans and Galon Var working side by side, but still they could not use the legacy of the First Ones, for they themselves were not of the Electum." Here, Galvidon paused. He took a deep breath through his nose and straightened his posture. "Through the word of God, the Order of Tag-Nah was born. We dedicate ourselves to searching out the descendants of the Electum, all across the Astraverse, and determining their worthiness. The judgement of the Tag-Nah is the judgement of God. Most are unworthy. Others, the Tag Nah judge to be righteous. I am such a one. The Order found me at a young age in my realm, a distant place you would not know. They trained me, molded me, and dubbed me an Eliminator. I move across the realms, destroying the unworthy descendants of the Electum, lest any challenge God's decree that the Tag-Nah Order be supreme. You see, once I, and others like me, have finished our work, none will stand to oppose the glory of God. Only those whom the Order has chosen will wield the power of the First Ones.

With that power at our command, we shall unite the entire Astraverse in God's glory and bring unity to every corner of Creation."

Bob stood at the bars, jaw slackening and tightening in turns, trying to take this all in. One thing was clear to him. Galvidon was completely insane. He seemed to think he was on a holy quest. Seemed to think that murdering countless innocent people was *the right thing to do*. Revulsion and hatred churned in Bob's guts.

There was a sparkle in the Gray Man's otherwise empty eyes. He spoke again. "So you see Bob, though you weep for your family, you can take comfort in knowing they died for a holy purpose, for their sacrifice was crucial to the true salvation of every other sentient being across the Astraverse." The Gray Man paused and removed his hand from the bars. "Now, I don't know if you could fit all that into your brain, but I have more than answered your question. It is your turn. Tell me." The commanding tone returned. "Where is the Key? Where did you acquire it?"

"Yes, the 'Astral Key'. Well…" Bob cleared his throat. "Funny thing. It's in your mother's ass." He spat a mist of saliva in Galvidon's face. "You crazy, murdering fuck!"

The world erupted once again into a wash of buzzing and agony, and Bob lost track of everything—where he was, who he was. His vision was filled with blackness and sparkling lights that seared his brain with every flash. Distantly he heard screaming. In some deeply buried part of his consciousness, he thought the screaming was his own. Galvidon's questions repeated, but he couldn't tell if they had been asked again or if they were just replaying in his brain. Abruptly the pain and noise shut off to the sound of the dungeon door slamming open. His head swam, and he was fairly certain he was back on the floor. Mannix's voice floated into his ears as if through a deep wall of cotton.

"What's this?" demanded the Lord of Swearington. "What are you doing? I don't remember giving you permission to torture my prisoner! He is my property, you know. A valued slave! How can he haul rocks if you melt his brain, or whatever it is you're doing?"

"The King," said Galvidon in a level tone, "has given me the authority to—"

BOB THE WIZARD

"If the King wanted you to kill my slaves, surely he would have informed me. No, you may be a Councilor, for *some reason*, but I command this city, and that means I outrank you here. Look at him. If he hasn't told you whatever you want to know, he never will. No man could endure this and not give in! No. No, No! That's quite enough. You will kindly give up your interrogation and leave him to recover. I want him in the mines tomorrow, do you hear?"

Bob's eyelids felt glued together. Galvidon's voice was suddenly right next to his head. The Gray Man must've crouched down by the cell. He spoke in a low voice. "I don't think you are from here, Bob. I think you're from somewhere else, and I think you had an Astral Key. That should mean you carry the blood of the Electum. You have used the work of the First Ones, yet my instruments detect no trace of the Electum in your genetic makeup. Very curious. I must speak with the Order. They may want you alive. Rest well, Bob. We will meet again. This petty lord cannot protect you forever." When next he spoke, Galvidon's voice was strong and clear, and farther away. He must have been standing. "The King will hear of this." Not angry, just flat and stating facts.

"Be sure to tell him that you damaged my property," said Mannix. A few moments passed, and then Mannix muttered, "creepy bastard." Then, "Hey, Bob the Wizard, you alive?"

Bob struggled to open his eyes but couldn't. He wasn't sure how to answer; he was alive, but he felt like he was dying. Every part of his body screamed in protest. His breath came in shallow gasps. "Think...so," he managed.

"You didn't tell him, did you?" Mannix was anxious. "You held out?"

"Held out," agreed Bob in a croak.

Bob felt the lord's hand on his shoulder. He must have reached through the bars. Mannix gave him what was surely intended to be a fatherly pat, but it felt like bullets. "Good show, my boy! Good show. You've earned that tobacco."

Bob heard him pad out of the dungeon, heard the bolts latch into place. His muscles still screaming in agony, back still on the cold, hard stone floor, he pictured himself drawing breath on a pipe stem, and his mouth twisted into a twitching rictus. It was as close as he could get to a smile.

He lay on the heatless floor for a while, feeling like he'd been run over. His eyes finally opened after a bleary stretch of time, but afterward he just lay still and watched the moonlight drift across the ceiling in a glacial sweep. Eventually, Osivia fluttered down and hovered above his chest, her full radiance returned. She peered down at him through those miniscule spectacles, surrounded by a corona of yellow light, muttering to herself. She seemed to come to a decision. She opened her arms expansively, clapped her hands together, and rubbed them like a cook distributing spices to soup. Tiny dots of light dripped from her clasped hands like blobs of molten metal from a welder's torch, pattering onto Bob's face, neck, and chest. He immediately began to feel better. He sat up, still aching. His tongue still felt puffy in his mouth, like a dry sock, but he was noticeably improved. By the time a guard brought him dinner, he'd managed to pull himself onto the rags that passed for a bed.

It was another lavish meal of hot soup, fresh bread, and some kind of crisp, green vegetable slathered in butter. He was given a flagon of clear water, and clean clothes were laid on the floor before him. Best of all, there was a pipe, and not just any pipe, but his dragon pipe—the one he'd gotten from Abernathy's Apothecary. He stared at the little carving of the dragon while slurping down soup and munching on vegetables. He had a vague urge to thank Osivia for whatever she'd done to heal him, but she'd fluttered away somewhere.

After the meal, he pushed away the plate of food and lay back on the bed, intending to rest for a moment and then try his new clothes, smoke some tobacco. He fell asleep and dreamed of doing those things instead, dreamed he walked out of the cell into his old backyard, and Anna and Daniel were there, and so were Fan, Gorrelai, Hirrell, and Torael. The elves were barbecuing, and Osivia fluttered around with little Danny chasing her, laughing. Rashindon came out from the house and took a hot dog from Torael, and the Galon Var that had given Bob the Gatekey came up to him, munching on the frank and bun.

"You're special, Bob," he said between bites. "Different. He can't see

BOB THE WIZARD

it." Behind him, Osivia's tongue blew a raspberry at a giggling Daniel.

After a downgraded breakfast— it seemed Mannix's generosity only stretched so far— Bob changed into his new clothes and indulged in the gift of tobacco. The feeling of fresh garments was somewhat undercut by the fact that his body remained filthy, but the woolen trousers and rough-spun, linen shirt were still welcome. He even had a new pair of shoes—some kind of cheap leather, no doubt sheepskin. The first draw on the pipe set him into a fit of deep coughs. He considered that perhaps beginning the habit anew after being rid of it might be foolish. Such reservations didn't prevent him from proceeding.

He was only on his third draw when a pair of guards entered the dungeon to haul him away. He was mercifully allowed to keep the pipe and tobacco—thank God for small favors. A jittering wagon ride later, he found himself walking down a hill to the mining grounds.

In the strident light of morning, he saw the grounds with fresh eyes. There were the sheds where the slaves slept, and in the far distance to the north and east were other camps full of other troupes of slaves, meant for other entrances to the mines. Past the well at the grounds' center was the makeshift food stand where he and the En'harae were served meals. Halfway up the far hill to the west, where the milled earth gave way to grass, stood the slaver's cabin—made of sturdy wooden planks—where Scarface and his cronies spent their limited free time, resting their shitty, sadistic heads. Close to the cabin were three ramshackle sheds, the size of outhouses, that functioned as equipment stores. There was a horizontal railing for tying horses, complete with a trough. To the southwest of the grounds, brambles and rocky outcroppings folded into the rolling hills that were the trademark of the area. His was the final troupe in a long series, and Bob knew there were only a few acres of wilderness to the southwest before the vast forest of the Essen'aelo began.

The slaves were finishing breakfast. Many blue heads turned in Bob's direction as he trudged toward them flanked by guards.

"Sora Kelai!" someone shouted. *Face Hair.*

Many others took up the call. "Sora Kelai is back!"

Bob could sense the guards' discomfort as Bob was met with hails and smiling faces. He could see the slavers—a healthy distance from the filthy slaves—glowering at him, but he ignored them. He was inundated with greetings, and as he met the En'harae in earnest, hands clasped his shoulders, his elbows. The guards melted away and returned to their wagon.

Bob found himself facing Torael, his purple locks almost pink in the midmorning sun. The elf bore a smirk and cocked an eyebrow. "Sora Kelai," he said. "We thought you were dead."

"Not yet," said Bob, rubbing at his arms. He was still sore from Galvidon's interrogation.

"Welcome home."

"Home," mused Sora Kelai. He brought himself close and spoke softly into the En'hari's pointed ear. "Not for long, I hope. If all goes well, help is on the way."

BOB THE WIZARD

CHAPTER ELEVEN:
CHAINS

The slaves' good mood was short-lived. Soon, they were back in the shadowy depths, chasing after almost imperceptible strips of iron like moles after grubs. They dug and hauled, hauled and dug, and Bob, who was still recovering, felt his chest tighten and his limbs creak. He kept patting the pocket where his pipe and tobacco were kept, reassuring himself they were still there. He told the story of Oath Keep's dungeon to Torael in soft snatches. He was unsure whether to trust anyone else with plans of escape, spilling his secret only if no other En'harae— save Fan, Gorrelai, or Hirrell—were within earshot. Gorrelai seemed particularly interested, and stared at Bob at every opportunity, as if by looking at him, he could bring about his own freedom through sheer willpower.

Torael had a tale of his own. Apparently, the other slaves had been somewhat emboldened by Bob's habit of talking back to the slavers, despite the lashings he'd received. More often, since Bob had been taken to the keep, the En'harae laborers were likely to mumble or even shout in protest. It kept the slavers busy whipping backs and cuffing chins— much more frequently than before Bob had joined the troupe. This information tickled at Bob's pride, but nonetheless, he was wary. If one of the slaves went too far and was killed or permanently injured, he'd feel responsible. God knew the slaves had enough troubles, without Bob's infectious attitude adding to them. But the day closed without incident, and as the sun crawled down behind the reddening horizon, Bob and the other slaves returned to camp for evening meal. Bob finally had a chance to spend quality time with his pipe. He idly wondered if Osivia the Faerie was around somewhere. He didn't see her.

Another day passed. Then another. The sun cracked the sky on the morning of the next. Breakfast passed breezily, and the slaves were cheerful enough. Bob was sharing his pipe with Hirrell, who wanted to try. The yellow-haired elf sputtered and hacked, falling over sideways to peals of laughter from the other elves. Even Bob got a chuckle. He was distracted, telling himself he couldn't really hear a low hum emanating from the earth at his feet. The dirt was *not* singing to him. Ridiculous.

At breakfast's end, Scarface declared—in that vitriolic bark of his—that they'd need more firing and dousing crews to follow the iron. There was an outbreak of muttering. Assignments came down, and Bob and Gorrelai were to be on the dousing crew, along with three other En'harae Bob only knew in passing—Gurse, Morhaem, and Titchell.

As they gathered their equipment, Gorrelai muttered curses and swore oaths that even Bob, now with passing familiarity to Hari, gave sidelong glances at. The large, muscular elf became more agitated with each passing minute, and soon he was kicking over buckets, tossing pickaxes, and yelling. Bob tried to calm his irascible friend, but to no avail, and before long a gaggle of slavers arrived, led by a scowling Scarface.

"What's the fucking trouble here." Scarface didn't say it like a question. He followed Gorrelai's tantrum with eyes like little marbles. "This Blueskin crack a fucking axle?" He spoke to Bob, though Bob was sure that the other three elves in the crew spoke fair amounts of English. The other slaves, who'd begun preparations for the day around the equipment sheds, stopped what they were doing and peered over.

"It's all fine, sir," said Bob, as servile as he could muster. "He's just—"

A water bucket clanked noisily across the rough earth and its contents splashed chaotically through the air, splattering Scarface's legs. Gorrelai bellowed wordlessly.

The head slaver glanced down at himself, then turned back to stare at Bob. "Seems we've got a problem."

Bob could only watch as the slaver brought two fingers to his mouth and unleashed a piercing whistle. Several more Darkhair slavers made their way over from the other crews. The slaves grew jumpy, eying each other and their captors. One of the elves on the dousing crew—Gurse, Bob thought—tried saying something to Gorrelai, something about calming down. Gorrelai erupted into a tirade—more at the world at large than at Gurse. Bob was sure he caught the name Paulsin. That was the En'hari who'd been crushed to death by the collapsing tunnel.

"Hold him down, boys." Scarface looked like a man in his element.

Everyone had given Gorrelai a wide berth, and the slavers began to circle him. The big elf lashed out when one came near, and Bob didn't envy their task. Gorrelai's muscles rippled, his chest heaved. His nostrils snorted. He looked like a wild animal—rabid, maybe.

The first couple of men that got close enough to grab him got smashed in the face for their trouble. Whips snapped, and someone threw a shovel, and all the while Gorrelai bellowed curses and tussled and struggled, until finally there was a heap of dark-haired men with bloodied faces atop a twisting blue mountain.

Scarface sauntered over to the dogpile and began to bind Gorrelai's arms and legs with thick leather cord. Soon, they'd lifted a bound Gorrelai to his feet. Men held him up from behind. The elf had dark bruises all over, but his chest still heaved. He spoke in Hari, and Bob caught every word.

"We will free En'hirin from your dirty hands, and we will stand over your corpses. I had forgotten my strength. You'd tricked me into forgetting. But Sora Kelai has reminded me, we are strong and will not break. Before I am through, I will kill every last one of you." His eyes flashed defiantly as he was dragged away.

Many of the slaves who stood watching the spectacle turned to stare at Bob. He shrank his shoulders and tried to look unassuming. It was hard not to stand out in a crowd of blue people with brightly colored hair and pointed ears. It seemed like most of the Darkhairs didn't understand Gorrelai's words, and anyway were occupied with hauling him away. But Scarface turned his cold, cruel gaze upon Bob and seemed to measure him. Gorrelai's voice, still cursing the Engorians, faded away as he was dragged into the slavers' cabin. Scarface stood and stared at Bob—thoughtful, appraising, dangerous.

After that, spirits were decidedly low. Another slave was assigned to the dousing crew as a replacement for Gorrelai, but Bob was too distracted by his own thoughts to learn his name. He could hear the low murmur of soft discussions among the En'harae, but no one spoke to him, and he didn't mind. He was worried—about what would happen to Gorrelai, about whether the incident would change the elves' view of him, about what horrible things Scarface had been contemplating while those beady eyes were fixed on him. He only hoped that Ellaria had managed to contact the En'hari rebels in a timely fashion. He was more than eager to leave iron mining behind him.

The firing crew filed out of the mine entrance with sullen frowns, unable to look the dousing crew in the eyes. Bob wondered absently if Mannix had sent word down to the slavers, to give Bob the most dangerous jobs, in an effort to silence him, but thought better of it. Mannix was playing a deft game—attempting to hold onto the Gatekey and simultaneously stay in the good graces of the King. He'd already pissed off Galvidon, and having Bob killed after the Gray Man had declared that he and Bob would meet again might draw too much ire Mannix's way. The fact was, Mannix might even be upset if he learned that Bob was on another dousing crew. Not that Bob had a way to tattle on Scarface, even if he'd wanted to. Better to try to keep his head down and do as he was told. He'd already garnered more attention than he was comfortable with. Mannix seemed to want him here, in the mines, perhaps to break his spirit, to make his life so miserable that, eventually, Bob would be willing—eager—to become Mannix's personal lackey and teach him the secrets of the Gatekey. Well, Bob was cracking, slowly but surely, but not even Bob's broken spirit could teach Mannix the secrets of Galvidon's 'First Ones.'

Bob, Gurse, Morhaem, Titchell, and the nameless elf completed their task by heaving buckets of water onto the fires in the mine's inner chamber. No one spoke, and the work was carried out mechanically. As he made his way to the chamber's exit, Bob closed his eyes, waiting for the rumbles and quivering earth. But it never came. And, Bob realized, sometime around Gorrelai's outburst, he'd stopped hearing the strange songs of the earth and rocks. So, there was that.

Dinnertime was muted, and a haze of fear seemed to permeate the air. Fear, and tobacco smoke. His body no longer accustomed to the effects of nicotine, Bob received a pleasant, heady buzz as he puffed away at the dragon pipe. It was not enough to lift the shadowy pall that had eclipsed his mood. He absently turned over the carved smoking implement in his hands, staring at the ground. At some point Torael approached him, and they sat in silence for a while, not looking at each other.

"It is not your fault," said Torael at some point.

Bob grunted.

"Ever since… this," the En'hari gestured vaguely. "He has had a temper. I told him more than once it would be the death of him."

The silence seemed to weigh heavier after that. When Scarface rang his infernal bell to signal lights out, the slaves despondently made their way to the shacks. Bob and Torael shared no more words that night.

The ragged clanging of the bell tore through Bob's sleep. Scarface was shouting at them, as he did every morning, calling them worthless, calling them scum, shouting curses that Bob found strangely comforting. The head slaver would never know how much his profanity anchored Bob to sanity, reminded him who he was and what he was fighting for. Bad language was Bob's language, and each morning, hearing it galvanized him to wakefulness, motivated him to move forward. Probably not what Scarface intended.

Nevertheless, this morning was different. As the predawn light sifted in through the open door, through the little slits that passed for windows, Scarface's words settled on Bob's ears, and he remembered Gorrelai.

"Got a present for you blue bastards!" yelled the scarred slaver. "Special fun planned today! Pull your shit-stained asses out of your fucking stinking beds!"

Clang-clang, went the bell.

Present? Fun? Nothing good could come of those words, not when they came from the mouth of a slaver. Bob dreaded the day, but he made his way out of the shed anyway. The morning was crisp and cool, and the grounds looked much the same as they always did. One of the donkeys grazed lazily by the supply sheds. The breakfast stall stood open and ready to serve. The breeze tugged at Bob's hair and beard, and he walked with his hands under his arms for warmth.

"Morning, Ezela," he said to the blue-skinned woman behind the stall.

Her hollow eyes regarded him with tired resignation. He heard a line forming behind him. She slid his bowl across the rough wood of the stall's counter without a word.

Slurping his gruel, Bob laid eyes on Fan in the milling crowd. The thin En'hari looked even more downtrodden than everyone else, his eyes sunken into his navy-blue face, his short green hair wilted like underfed grass. Fan noticed Bob's attention and made his way over, clutching his bowl of breakfast but making no moves to consume it. Bob sat on one of the rickety benches that rung the gravelly yard, and Fan sat down next to him—careful and precise, like a perching avian. For a moment, they sat in silence.

Fan set his breakfast beside him on the bench. "He is my half-brother."

Bob didn't need to ask to know he was talking about Gorrelai.

"We share a father. Our father, Gaeren, was Gasheera, a warrior, and a good one. He died nine years ago, fighting the Gez Kar, in the Battle of the Still Mountains, right before Engoria marched on us for the first time. Gorrelai reminds me of him. Is like him, I mean. Tough, angry, but also noble, standing up for those smaller."

Bob nodded and sipped weakly at the remains of his breakfast. He wasn't sure what to say, or how to go about saying it. But it seemed Fan needed no encouragement.

"My mother was a dancer. Forijja, we say. A performer."

Bob remembered thinking Fan moved like a dancer, so this news didn't surprise him.

"Our father loved her. Gorrelai's mother, Mojinn, was Gasheera, like Gaeren. Gorrelai was born before me, and Mojinn died fighting Gez Kar, long before this war with the humans. Gorrelai grew up without her. Gaeren, he married my mother, and Gorrelai was angry." Fan smiled. "In those days, he was not so angry all the time, but his temper, it came out when Gaeren married my mother. They tell me, he avoided our hut and would not speak of us for many months. Then one day, the Gez Kar, they pushed very far into our lands, attacked our village. I was outside, gathering wood to bring back to my mother. The Gez Kar came upon me, and I was alone, young, afraid. I knew I would die. But then he came." Fan shifted in his seat and looked Bob in the eye. "Gorrelai, and a few other Gasheera, they arrived to meet the Gez Kar, and they saved me. He saved me. They defeated the Gez Kar that day. After, he began to arrive at our hut. He spoke to my mother, grudging at first, but over time, they became friends. He brought us gifts, he taught me lessons of war, though it is not my Kafeh. We became close, like true brothers, and our father was proud to see us side by side before he died." Fan stood up, leaving his food behind. "I will miss him, Sora Kelai."

Bob watched him go, wanting to say something, wishing he could find the words. But no words seemed enough. What could he do? He prepared his pipe, scowling.

He'd only managed a few desultory puffs before the slavers began to surround the yard. They were outnumbered by slaves three-to-one or more, but they were armored in padded vests and leather, armed with bladed weapons and whips. The bell began to clang from somewhere, and Bob and the other slaves craned their necks to look.

From the slavers' cabin, Scarface led Gorrelai by a chain. Flanking the muscular elf were two more slavers—Scarface's favorites, by all accounts—a pair of thick Darkhairs called Sonny and Jack. As a rule, Bob didn't bother to learn the slavers' names, but these two he knew. Apart from Scarface himself—whose real name escaped him—Sonny and Jack were the worst of the lot—cruel, strong, and surly. They had Gorrelai strung like an animal—hands bound in front of him with cord, chain clamped to an iron rung around his neck. He was naked save for a ragged loincloth. He'd been beaten badly, even more so than when he'd been carried off. The face of Fan's brother was swollen and yellowish, his lip misshapen, and one eye was forced closed by a welt. His body was streaked with ugly bruises. Although he stumbled when Scarface yanked his metal leash, he still managed to walk steadily and with his shoulders back, his tufts of green dreadlocks swaying in the gentle wind.

Bob tapped out the remainder of his pipe, replaced it in his pocket, and stood. Scarface led Gorrelai into the yard like an unruly horse. Sonny and Jack took places in the circle of slavers surrounding the quiet crowd of En'harae. Scarface bore a gentle smile as he walked, like a man who kept a joke to himself. Calmly, the head slaver lashed the end of the chain around an iron rung that was built into the side of the breakfast stall. He turned and addressed the gathering.

"Surprise!" he declared, his smile broadening. "It's occurred to me recently that you lot maybe forgot who's in charge round these here mines. Occurred to me maybe you thought the good work you do for Engoria is optional. Maybe forgot the God in the Sun looks down upon you with disgust for how backward you are. Fucking tragic, it is, to forget your place. Well, sure as a beast shits in the forest, I aim to remind you."

He flipped a three-tailed whip off his belt. It was shorter than the whips the slavers usually carried, and each of its tails bore a metal bead the size of a marble. "Thing is, haven't had much trouble with Blueskins doing what they're told, for most of the time I had the pleasure to be here leading them. Not much trouble, for a long while."

He looked at Bob and his smile vanished. His eyes met Bob's and held them. Worry and fear bubbled in Bob's guts, but also anger. He hated this man and had no intention of cowing to his stare. When Scarface spoke again, his voice was hard with repressed fury.

"Only one thing worse than a Blueskin that don't know his place. One thing, and that's a Darkhair who thinks he's more than he is. A man who consorts with Blueskins and treats them like they ain't just scum." The slaver's eyes shone. "And what's more, word from the keep comes down that he *fucked* one." A murmur went up among the elves. "That's right, had a girl brought to him in the dungeons, didn't he?"

"Now, wait a minute—" began Bob, but Scarface was in his face already.

"Shut your stinking hole!" the slaver screamed at him. He was so close Bob could feel his hot breath on his cheeks. "You haven't done nothing but fuck up our peace since you got here! You're an instigator, a fraternizer, a Sun-cursed traitor to your own people! To good folks, who know which way is up. Well now, I figure there's one way to remind you who you are…" he held up the whip and Bob braced himself for a blow. "And who *they* are."

The whip was in Bob's hand. Scarface had put it there. Bob stared

BOB THE WIZARD

dumbly down at it, his mouth working, trying to say something, anything, that could rescue him from what was about to happen. Cold dread flushed through his bones. His heart jackhammered in his chest, his breath caught, and sweat prickled his armpits. Scarface stood there, taut and erect, eyes blazing with satisfaction.

"What…" Bob managed. "I can't…"

The slaver pointed to the chained form of Gorrelai without turning. The En'hari's wide, naked, navy-blue back was exposed and facing them. "The penalty for insubordinate behavior from a slave is ten lashes," said Scarface, quietly now. No one else spoke. The scarred man's voice was clear in the morning air. "And we'll add five for the equipment he fucked up. You'll whip him, Bob the Wizard."

"I… I won't."

Scarface strode purposefully across the lawn. All the En'harae were staring at Bob. Among them, Fan's eyes were hard and unbelieving. The head slaver made a curt gesture, and to Bob's rising horror, Sonny kicked at the back of Torael's legs, and the purple-haired elf dropped to his knees. Several slavers drew their weapons. Scarface produced a dagger and held it to Torael's throat, knife against skin. He glared at Bob.

"You'll whip him," repeated the slaver, commanding, "or this one dies. Loss of one slave's a small price to pay for the obedience of the others."

Torael's eyes found Bob's, and to his amazement, displayed no trace of fear. He was calm, accepting. Bob's hand trembled around the whip. Fearful whispers broke out among the En'harae. Ever so slightly, Torael gave a nod.

Gorrelai spoke. His voice was thick, but the Hari phrase he uttered was clearly audible. "*Do it, Sora Kelai.*"

Bob felt his legs move. They strode as if on their own toward Gorrelai. He was a few feet away then, in striking distance, and his hand raised the whip. Fan was staring, they all were, staring at Bob. The whip came down with a sharp crack. Three stripes of blood, thin and angry, erupted on Gorrelai's back. The big elf cried out, a short deep grunt.

"*Do it,*" said Gorrelai again, and Bob felt himself comply. Red lines lashed across blue flesh.

"*Do it.*"

Bob found himself screaming—a long, guttural cry, like the roar of a trapped animal. The whip came down again. Again. Tears poured from his eyes. He hated this, he hated himself, he hated the slavers, and Mannix, and Galvidon. They would all pay. The whip cracked again. Gorrelai's cries mixed with Bob's. The elf's wide back had become tattered and frayed, like ripped cloth, bloody and ragged. The whip stilled. Bob had lost count. His breath heaved.

"Not done yet," said Scarface. "More."

Another tear pushed its way down Bob's cheek and settled in his beard. Knife still at his neck, Torael was now crying also, though his face remained impassive, regal. Tears were its only feature. The whip came up.

There was a sharp whistle. Bob's head snapped around at the noise. The fletched shaft of an arrow was protruding from Scarface's neck. Surprise covered the slavers face as he reached up to grab it. He opened his mouth as if to speak, and a gush of blood sprayed out instead. Scarface collapsed, and the yard became chaos.

BOB THE WIZARD

CHAPTER TWELVE:
ESSEN'AELO

Bob had been in fights. He'd killed, seen others killed. He'd even fought on one side of a conflict against another—but nothing more serious than what he'd call a skirmish. He had never been in a *battle*—a churning mess of two large groups, each intent on wiping out the other. What was more, his experience was limited to two kinds of conflicts: brawls and gunfights. He had no experience with sword fighting or guessing the trajectory of arrows. But, Bob knew better than most: there's a first time for everything.

His first instinct was to drop to the ground to avoid gunfire, and that's what he did. The three-tailed whip, it's tiny round heads now livid with Gorrelai's blood, fell forgotten to the broken earth. Bob found himself chest-down in the gravel and dirt, his hands covering his head as the sounds of the battle erupted. There were several *thwips* as more arrows broke the air, shouts and screams of rage or surprise, swords rasping from scabbards, thuds and grunts. Realizing his mistake, he peeked around from his prone position. The hidden archers—which had come, of course, from the southwest—seemed to have focused on the slavers near Torael. As Bob looked on, he saw the purple-haired elf snatch a shortsword from a fallen slaver and deftly cut down another with a swing of biting steel.

Bob clambered to his feet, stumbling on his way to Gorrelai and the breakfast stall. "Hold on," he muttered, but his voice was lost among the shouts and scuffles.

The big, navy elf was leaning against the chain that held fast in the wood of the stall. Bob glanced around frantically, adrenaline sharpening his senses. A slaver thumped to the ground next to him, shoved over by a group of En'hari slaves. The man fumbled his sword, dropping it to the side. The slaves dogpiled him, pounding at his face to avoid the thick linen and leather covering his torso.

Bob grabbed the sword. "I've got the bastard," he said loudly.

One of the slaves noticed him and jumped away, patting his comrades' shoulders. When they were clear, Bob raised the sword, point downward, like a black-bearded King Arthur, ready to plunge Excalibur back into the Stone.

The slaver, face bloody and blue, began to stir. His eyes widened. "No, stop," he croaked, but Bob didn't stop.

He dropped his full weight behind the blade, and it punched through the layers of light armor and into the man's chest, through his back into the rough earth. The man jerked, blood splattering from his mouth and welling up to soak the fabric around the wound. Bob did his best to ignore it. Compassion for the enemy had no place at a time like this, Bob knew that much. He planted his foot on the slaver's body and, with no small effort, tugged the sword free.

"Sora Kelai!" cheered one of the slaves, and they ran off.

Bob turned back to Gorrelai, who held out his bound hands. Bob sheared away the leather cord, careful to avoid cutting his friend. "Stand back," he said, and gestured to make himself clear. The big elf knew what he was up to well enough, and stepped back to the length of the chain, pulling it taught. His blue legs were shaking, and drying tears streaked his dirty face. Bob hacked at the base of the hook in the stall. After three good whacks, the hook pulled free, the wood too battered to hold. The sword came away with an ugly notch near its tip.

Suddenly Bob had to dodge away from a strike. It was Sonny, his short brown hair in muddy disarray, splatters of blood across his broad, grizzled face. He was coming at Bob with a sword of his own. Sonny wielded it with confidence, and it was only luck and adrenaline that kept Bob from being chopped in half. He struck back with the notched blade but felt it fly from his hands. He'd probably have died then if it weren't for Gorrelai, who bull-rushed the slaver from the side, shoulder connecting under the arm, lifting him clear off the ground and slamming him onto his back. Gorrelai had wrapped the chain around his fists and set to work beating Sonny to death with heavy, crushing blows of bunched, metal rungs.

Bob swiveled around, searching for the next threat. He saw several unfamiliar En'harae, clad in armor similar to what the slavers were wearing. Oddly, he also saw a human—a man he didn't recognize—fighting alongside the elves. Bob started to relax. The situation seemed well in hand. Most of the slavers were down, and those remaining were vastly outnumbered. A pair of armed and armored En'harae worked alongside the new man, the three of them overwhelming a wounded slaver with quick jabs and slashes. The man, burly and muscular, looked a little like a big, powerful version of Bob. He had a thick black beard, though his was trimmed short. The man hefted a huge, kite-shaped shield—almost the size of a basketball backboard—and he threw his weight behind it, smashing into a slaver as Bob watched, staggering him and sending him reeling to the ground. Where Torael had been held at knifepoint, three dead slavers lay, Scarface among them, their bodies peppered with arrows, giving them the appearance of bloody, morbid porcupines. Nearby, a group of unarmed slaves looked on, cheering and tossing rocks, as Torael, shirtless and shoeless, danced around a slaver's blade, severed his hand, and stabbed him through the neck with an effortless thrust.

Bob found Gorrelai standing next to him, apparently having finished the brutal attack on Sonny. The big elf put an arm around his shoulder, leaning on him, the bloody chain still fastened to the collar on his neck and wrapped on his hands. Bob shifted under the weight, but it was reassuring, in a way, a good kind of pressure, to feel Gorrelai alive, there with him. Still, his surly friend was in a bad way. His back was still bleeding, his green and yellow bruises cracked and turgid.

The two of them stood for a moment and watched the bloodshed. Gorrelai spoke in a strained voice, the Hari syllables slurred in his swollen mouth. *"A beautiful sight, Sora Kelai, to see these men cut down. Most beautiful thing I've seen in years. But damn the spirits, my back hurts."*

Bob glanced at him, and despite the En'hari's face being a swollen mess, Bob was sure there was a twinkle in his eye. Bob smirked, and Gorrelai's face split into a grin. Then, they were both laughing. It began as a chuckle, then grew to the deep, hearty laugh of those that had gone through hell and come out together. After the final slaver was put down and Torael strode across the yard to them, they were still laughing.

As Torael walked up, two others were close behind. The big, bearded man with the kite-shield sauntered at Torael's back, and a somber looking En'hari carrying a bow approached from a hill to the southwest. Torael turned and embraced the bow-carrier, and they exchanged soft words in Hari that Bob didn't catch. This elf—there was something familiar about him, but Bob couldn't quite place it. He was flush with the elation of victory, and tasted freedom on his tongue, though they still stood on the grounds that had been his prison.

Torael turned from the other En'hari and began to speak. "I am guessing," said the purple-haired elf, "that we may thank you for this rescue, Sora Kelai." He was spattered with dirt and blood, his exposed skin glistening with sweat, but he still managed to look noble. He held his head high, his shoulders back, and gripped the pilfered sword at his side with an agile familiarity that bespoke a deadly potential.

Bob was staring at the elf that had come off the hill, trying to decide why he looked so familiar. "I suppose," Bob said to Torael. "Like I said before, I spoke to a slave at Oath Keep, while Mannix had me in the dungeon. Asked her to get a message to these folks." He nodded to the two behind Torael. The rest of the rescuers seemed to be herding the slaves southward. "Ellaria, that was her name. I guess she came through." He looked sheepishly at his friend. "That must be where the rumor came from Scarface was talking about, but I didn't—I mean, we just talked. Me asking her down there, it was just a pretense, and…"

Torael placed a hand on Bob's arm. "It's alright, my friend. I would never trust his words."

Bob barely held back a sigh of relief. The burly man with the kite shield had moved to support Gorrelai.

Torael indicated the somber elf behind him. "Sora Kelai, this is my brother, Kelael."

Kelael glared at Bob in a way that made him uncomfortable. So familiar…

"But," said Torael curiously, "I do not know *this* man." He gestured at the large, bearded shield-bearer.

Looking at him holding up Gorrelai, Bob realized how huge the guy really was. Approaching seven feet if he was an inch, his muscles looked like ropes of flesh-colored metal. He was even bigger than Gorrelai.

"He is Harold," said Kelael, still giving Bob a hard look.

Harold nodded to Bob as he and Gorrelai began to climb the grassy scree, following the other slaves. When Bob returned his eyes to Kelael, his mind belched up what had been stuck in its throat. He remembered where he'd seen the elf before. It was off in the distance, atop a grassy hill, bow in hand. Bob had been standing next to Farmer Willis's wagon, next to the man's corpse. The blue archer.

Bob's eyes narrowed, and Kelael stared right back, unflinching. He was shorter than Torael, his skin a shade darker, his frame a fraction wider, but they shared the same proud, regal features, the same sure bearing. Had Bob spared this elf a thought since his first day on Hub, he might have made the connection sooner. The way Kelael was looking at him, Bob had the idea that the En'hari had no trouble remembering their first encounter. Bob recalled the wagon ride, talking to Willis, giving him the sunglasses. He remembered a deadly arrow swiftly parting air to strike the farmer. After Bob had shot three of the attackers, there was the blue archer, cold eyes boring into him from a distance. Yes, this was him alright. Bob held his gaze.

"You're a good shot," he said to Kelael. "Thanks for showing up."

"This was not for you," said Kelael, unmoved.

"Should we gather our Gasheera and advance to the keep?" said Torael. "You have helped us, and we have an agreement to regain your magic key."

Bob turned his attention back to Torael. "I don't know. Are you up for that?"

"Perhaps it is best, for surprise. Once we leave, Mannix will know of our escape. He will then be ready."

"I don't think he'll expect us to attack him at all. He's too fucking arrogant for that. But he will look for us, he'll hunt us down. He'll be angry with you for escaping, but even more angry at me. He wants me to teach him... my magic."

Kelael sneered. "He already looks. He cannot find us. He does not know how to see us."

Bob had no idea what that was supposed to mean. *He does not know how to see us.* He let it slide. "Alright, if you think we can take him right away, then—"

There was a flash of movement from above. Bob craned his neck and saw a swift glowing object, like a little star, darting down from the sky toward them. He reached for his gun, which of course he didn't have, but then he realized it was a faerie. Not any faerie, but his biggest fan—Osivia Glenbrook. She pulled up short between the three faces of Bob, Kelael, and Torael. Bob could almost hear the screeching noise, like a race car pulling its handbrake.

"Bob!" She was panting. "Bob the Wizard! They're coming!"

Torael peered at her curiously. Kelael scowled, as if she were a mosquito.

"Who?" asked Bob. "Who's coming, Osivia?"

She gripped her sides, breathing heavily, hovering. "Engorians. Armored, mounted. Lighthairs, all of them! They're riding from the keep!"

"Spirits!" cursed Kelael.

"How many?" said Bob.

"Many," said Osivia. "Sixteen men on horses. In heavy armor."

"Well, that's not *that* many," said Bob, but he knew it was a foolish thing to say. They had only a handful of archers, mostly unarmed men, and no weapons for getting through good armor. He didn't *really* know, but he imagined taking down an armored man on horseback would be quite an undertaking with only a shortsword.

Torael shook his head. "This kills our plan to attack now. We must retreat."

"But how do they know?" said Bob. "We've only just—"

"Perhaps the woman you talked to," said Torael. "Ellaria. They catch her doing wrong, they question her. But this does not matter right now. Now, we must go. We cannot face mounted men. Not so many."

"Must we bring *him*?" Kelael asked, waving dismissively at Bob.

Torael was already walking toward the scree. "Sora Kelai? Of course. He is friend. Come."

Kelael glared at Bob for a moment, then turned to follow his brother.

"That one doesn't like you," said Osivia. She had regained her composure and was presently wiping her glasses on the end of her white coat.

"Feeling's mutual," said Bob. "Wouldn't be in this mess if it weren't for him."

"Hm. Failure to take responsibility. A common trait among humans. I thought you were better than that, Bob."

"I'm not sure I share your confidence in me. You coming?" He walked southward toward the green and brown hill. A copse of leafy maples rose in the middle distance, heralding the beginnings of the Essen'aelo. A soft flutter of little wings—almost imperceptible—sounded behind him.

As Bob reached the edge of the tree-line, he saw the slaves had gathered just inside it, waiting for the final stragglers. A dozen yards ahead of Bob, Torael and his brother were being embraced by their fellows. Then Kelael was introducing Torael to someone who apparently had been waiting for them just inside the forest. A few more steps revealed that someone to be a human.

He was a short old man with a wide-brimmed, pointed hat—dyed green to match the forest—and a collared, black cloak made of thin leather. He leaned upon a sanded wooden staff with a crystal affixed at its head. The hat conspired with his small stature to obscure all his features, save for a long, bulbous nose that protruded from his face among a tangle of stark-white hair and whiskers. He finished an introductory conversation with Torael and turned his attention to the approaching Bob.

Without the pointed hat, the stranger's head would only come up to Bob's chest. He peered up at Bob from under the hat's brim, leaning on his staff. "Bernard Heathrow, at your service," he said in a scratchy, nasally voice while nodding politely.

"Bob," said Torael excitedly, "Bernard is a wizard! Bob is also a wizard. Tell him, Sora Kelai."

Nearby, Harold erupted with laughter. "Sora Kelai, aye? That's fresh." He addressed the limping form of Gorrelai, whom he still supported. "He does have a magnificent bush of hair, aye?" He chuckled.

Bernard was studying Bob in silence. Bob cleared his throat nervously.

"Time to go," barked Kelael with authority. Bernard turned to join the procession into the Essen'aelo, and Bob gratefully followed.

They had suffered minimal casualties. Two dead slaves, who had been unfortunate enough to catch swords during the conflict, had been left behind. A few others bore the markings of whips, and of course there was Gorrelai. He limped along through the trees with the rest, supported between Harold and the lithe form of Fan, who struggled under his brother's weight, but carried it anyway. A couple of the resistance fighters, whom Torael had referred to as *Gasheera*, warriors, had suffered minor cuts and scrapes that had already been wrapped. It seems they'd come prepared. All told, it was a major victory in the eyes of the slaves. They'd suffered enough for a lifetime in the mines and were happy to finally be free.

The party, about sixty all together, tromped through the forest as it thickened around them, making haste but also celebrating. Osivia swirled above them near the canopy, darting back and forth, occasionally rising above the branches to scout their rear. A few of the En'harae had broken into a chorus of song. The Hari words were hard for Bob to decipher, but the melody roused his spirits, and he got the gist of it, anyway. It was a song about freedom.

Bob found himself walking between Bernard and the yellow-haired Hirrell. "Too bad Harold has his hands full," said Bernard to Bob. "That man can carry a tune."

"Do you suppose," said Bob to Hirrell, "that it's a good idea for them to be singing? What if the Engorians hear?" He didn't mean to ignore the little wizard. He just found himself unable to carry on small talk with a stranger.

Hirrell was grinning. "Let them have it, Sora Kelai. Your faerie said the men are still many miles off. By the time they arrive, we will be away from their ears. Say, you have your smoke?"

Bernard glance up curiously at the question.

Bob wriggled the pipe and pouch out of his pocket, returning Hirrell's smile. "Sure. Can't say it'll help you walk, though."

"It is for celebrating." He clapped Bob on the back. "You will see the Koreka."

Bob raised an eyebrow. "What's a Koreka? That a city?"

"No, no. We are too far from En'hirin for that. Koreka is…" he struggled to find the words. "It has long been a holy place. One of those who rescues us, he tells me it is now…base. Hideout. Special place for En'harae, guarded by spirits. You will like."

Bob thought back to his first day on Hub, remembered the conflict on the East Road—an engagement, he now knew, instigated by Kelael. He remembered thinking the blue archer might be making his way back to a camp. Then there was Mannix, who'd mentioned finding the body of Willis Bailey but had pointedly left out any mention of bandits.

A picture began to solidify in Bob's mind. The local En'hari resistance had a base of operations hidden somewhere in the Essen'aelo. They'd made it their business to attack travelers on the roads in and out of Swearington—and perhaps other surrounding villages—to harass the Engorians, to weaken their lines of supply, their freedom to travel. Farmer Willis had not been the victim of a random attack by common thieves, he'd been a casualty of war. And Bob, who'd killed two men and an elf, had unwittingly fought for the wrong side.

He felt a pang of guilt at that but swept it away. He hadn't known. Besides, they'd have killed him alongside Willis. He'd had no choice. Best to move forward, knowing where he stood, than to dwell on past mistakes. He only hoped Kelael would see it the same. Bob passed the dragon pipe, now packed, to Hirrell. He was digging in his pocket for a match when Bernard tossed him something.

Bob caught it. It was a pink plastic lighter, like you'd buy at a gas station on Earth. Bob was baffled. He stared at the short man in the pointed hat. Bernard just winked at him.

After a few more hours of walking, talking, and smoking, Bob was brought up short. The crowd of former slaves and their liberators had stopped. Ragged shirts and blue skin were dappled with light as it filtered down through the canopy. Brightly colored hairdos shifted side by side like a displaced coral reef. Muttering and the shuffling of feet was interspersed with the buzz of insects, the rustle of foliage. Osivia flew above the group in lazy circles. Bernard had made his way to the front.

Bob tapped out ashes from the pipe and glanced at Hirrell, who looked a bit greenish, and not from the trees' reflected light. Bob had warned him about smoking too much. "Why'd we stop?"

"I think," began Hirrell, working his mouth. His hands were on his knees. "I think we are here."

"Here…where?" Bob looked around. It looked to him like the middle of a forest. No sign of a building, or a settlement of disgruntled En'hari rebels, or anything. Just trees, bushes, the occasional flower, and a large group of men and elves that could really use a shower.

Just then, Torael pushed his way through the crowd to Bob and Hirrell at the rear. "Bob," he said, smiling. "Come see."

Bemused, Bob followed him through the En'harae, leaving Hirrell breathing deeply through his nose with his eyes closed. Bob received several friendly pats on his elbows and shoulders, and *Sora Kelai*—what he was beginning to think of as his *elf name*—was murmured at him in congratulatory tones.

Osivia fluttered down and settled on his shoulder, notebook in hand. "May I sit?" she asked politely.

"Knock yourself out," muttered Bob.

"I beg your pardon?"

"I mean, go for it, make yourself at home. Whatever floats your boat."

"Does that mean yes?" she whispered.

"Fuckin' A," said Bob softly. He could feel her stare and fought off a smirk. "Yes, it means yes."

The faerie made an exasperated noise and plopped down cross-legged, where she began writing intensely. Her weight was almost imperceptible—it felt like hosting a cricket on his shoulder.

Torael led him to the front of the gathering. Kelael was standing in his patchwork leathers with arms crossed next to Fan, who, like many others, had removed his filthy shirt and tied it around his waist. Beside them both was Bernard, leaning on his sanded staff, gazing into the trees. Nearby, Gorrelai was still supported by the burly Harold, his head down, green dreadlocks dangling in his face.

"What am I supposed to see?" Bob asked Torael. They were standing before a thick copse of trees and dense foliage.

"Be quiet," snapped Kelael.

"Torael may do the honors, of course," said Bernard, eyes still on the trees ahead.

Torael stepped forward and let out an odd, undulating whistle. They waited. The gathered former slaves had grown quiet, and it seemed only the sounds of the forest were audible. Torael whistled again, a sustained, wavering note. The crystal on the end of Bernard's staff began to softly glow.

Then, something happened. There was a kind of ripple in the air above the forest floor, a distortion that pulled itself into the shape of a person. It wasn't a person, though—more like a silhouette. Standing before them was a humanoid outline, barely visible in the light shifting through the canopy. Though it gave the impression of standing, Bob couldn't really see where its feet touched the ground. It walked up to Torael, making no sound as it moved. The light seemed to swivel and crumple around it, vaguely maintaining the impression of a person. It held a transparent hand upward, as if to say 'Hi'.

Torael glanced at Bernard, who nodded in return, the crystal on his staff pulsing steadily with low light. The elf faced the phantom and spoke clearly in Hari. "*We wish to enter, mighty spirit. Your blessing is our guide. We swear to walk with you always, as you walk with us.*"

Bob was amazed. The En'harae had spoken often of spirits, but he'd always thought it was superstition—a religion of nature, or something. But this was a fucking spirit. Holy shit. The apparition bowed to Torael. Its motion was slow and fluid, like it was made of water. In that same languid way, it turned, the light rippling to keep its shape, and stretched out a hand to the trees behind it. It seemed to grab something Bob couldn't see, some invisible handle, and tore away a hole in reality. Then there was a large rectangular doorway glowing with a soft golden light, pulsing minutely in time with Bernard's staff. It was the size of the double doors at Oath Keep, the ones Bob had slammed behind him before he so arrogantly teleported up to Mannix's balcony. Just as suddenly as it appeared, the figure that Torael had called a spirit dissipated, the air ceasing to shape it. The doorway remained. Torael smiled at Bob, turned, and stepped through. Shortly thereafter, Kelael followed, pausing briefly to glare daggers in Bob's direction.

"Not bad, aye?" said Harold as he passed. He carried the kite-shield upon his back and supported Gorrelai in the crook of his arm. "You'll be getting used to it." He winked, and then he and Gorrelai disappeared into the glow.

"Ingenious," muttered Osivia. "Quite ingenious."

Bob could hear the other elves behind him, shuffling their feet and approaching. Then Fan's hand was on his back. The graceful En'hari held out his other hand toward the doorway in invitation.

Bob remembered Kelael's words, speaking of Mannix's efforts to find their location. Words that had seemed so strange, but now made perfect sense.

He does not know how to see us.

Bob took a deep breath and stepped forward into the pulsing, golden light.

M. V. PRINDLE

BOB THE WIZARD

Part Two:
Wizard

"Reality is that which, when you stop believing in it, doesn't go away."
-Philip K. Dick

CHAPTER THIRTEEN:
BATH AND BED STAND

Entering the portal felt like stepping through a curtain of static electricity. It was similar enough to passing through an Astral Gate that Bob half-expected to end up in another world. But when the soft electrical sensation passed, it became clear that the portal hadn't transported him anywhere. He was still in the forest, exactly where he ought to be. The sky was still a pale blue haze, tinged yellow by an impending sunset. Much of the trees and foliage were all still in the places they'd been when he'd stepped through. Only…

Only now there was a huge clearing in front of him. From outside the portal's entrance, the forest had seemed uninterrupted, but it wasn't. There was a community here. Many of the trees had been cut down and turned into structures. Most of them had probably gone to the impressive wooden wall that spanned the long, curved perimeter. The place—the Koreka, as Hirrell had called it—appeared to be almost a quarter mile long and shaped roughly like a pear. Trees dotted the grassy central green, and many footpaths—worn down gradually by tromping feet—wound this way and that across the grounds. Wooden guard towers had been constructed along the wall, spaced with care, connected by catwalks. There was a main path that led from the front gate—where Bob had entered—past a set of stables and up to an impressive three-story, cabin-like structure that sported several wings at ground level. The northern wing seemed to overhang a wide, misty pond of crystal-clear water that stretched along the Koreka's northeastern quadrant, seeping under shallow rock formations just before it reached the walls. The overhanging wing's outer section must have been built upon stilts, for it seemed to hover effortlessly above the gently undulating liquid. A shallow layer of mist silently rolled across the pond, breaking against the building and the rocks to creep back upon itself.

And there were people—mostly of the blue variety, but Bob saw a human or two as well. They all milled about with apparent purpose, tasks to complete, people to see. Laughter and conversation mingled with whinnies and snorts, the calling of birds, creating a pleasant ambience of bustle and activity. Unlike Swearington, which had smelled of shit, rotten vegetables, and burnt metal, this place carried the odors of cooked food, healthy plant life, and polished wood. On Bob's shoulder, Osivia made unintelligible sounds of appreciation and scribbled in her notes.

Trying to take it all in, Bob slowed a bit, letting most of the former slaves file down the pathway ahead of him. He got a sense there was even more behind the big, wooden house he could not yet see. Feeling overwhelmed, he wandered along with the group toward the big central structure. As he got closer, he saw a beautifully carved sign hung expertly above the building's main entrance. It was written in what Bob assumed to be Hari. Having learned only the basics of speaking and nothing of reading, he was unable to decipher it. It made him wish, not for the first time, that he still had the Gatekey.

Bob noticed Torael in a small crowd near the entrance and trotted over. The elf was standing in a tight circle of peers and already deep in conversation. Gorrelai was nowhere to be seen. Fan, also absent, must have taken him to get medical attention. Kelael stood on one side of his brother, the bearded Harold on the other, and across from Torael was Bernard the Wizard. The final member of the circle was an En'hari woman, and Bob's breath caught in his chest as he saw her. His heart beat a little faster, and he was suddenly, absurdly worried about how shabby, dirty, and sweaty he was. She was stunningly beautiful. At least, Bob thought so.

Her skin was azure like Torael's, her hair a shiny, deep black tied back in a tight, complexly braided bun. The leather vest on her torso did nothing, in Bob's eye, to diminish her shapely curvature. She wore no makeup, and her hand rested easily on the pommel of a sheathed sword, fixed on a corded belt about her waist on perfect hips. She wore a kind of chainmail skirt above tight leather pants and boots and comported herself with authority. Her almond-colored eyes displayed concern and interest for whatever was being said.

Bob wasn't sure why he found her so attractive, but as he stood just outside the circle, he found himself fiddling with the clothes Mannix had given him—adjusting his shirt, straightening his pants. He ran fingers through his beard and hair. He glanced around nervously, half expecting Anna to spot him from the crowd and make fun of him with playful jealousy. Then, he remembered she was dead, and was embarrassed to discover that the thought brought not just sadness, but relief. He wasn't glad she was dead, of course not, he loved her, but… He didn't want her to see him like this, struck dumb by another woman. He wondered vaguely—if there was some chance of an afterlife—if Anna was watching, and what she thought of Bob right now, palms sweating like a schoolboy trying to ask his crush to the dance.

"Bob!" Torael's voice cut cheerfully through his thoughts. "Come, join us."

Kelael was glaring at him, as usual, but the others were looking at him curiously. Harold and Bernard stepped back to allow Bob room in the circle. Kelael gave no such courtesy. Bob approached the circle, trying not to stare at the woman, and failing miserably.

Torael, who must have noticed, introduced her. "This is Melanae."

The woman, who stood a few inches taller than Bob, nodded at him. Those brown eyes were hard, but not unkind, like those of a concerned mother.

Bob opened his mouth to reply. "Uh," he said.

"She runs the Koreka," said Torael proudly. "And though we meet here for the first time, I can see she does a very good job." He smiled.

Melanae inclined her head in recognition of the praise.

When Bob just continued to stare, Bernard spoke. Perhaps it was a veiled attempt at mercy. "Torael tells me you are a wizard," he offered.

Bob looked back and forth between Melanae and Bernard. He cleared his throat. "I, uh," he stammered. "Well, the thing is…" The group were staring at him expectantly. "I don't, uh…"

BOB THE WIZARD

Suddenly, Osivia was talking. "Bob is very tired," she said. Everyone looked at her politely, save Kelael, who rolled his eyes. "And dirty. Perhaps we could be directed to a bath and a bed, and could continue introductions at a later time? Perhaps… tomorrow."

Torael suddenly looked guilty. "Yes, of course. The little faerie is right. We have had much trouble today. Harold, would you please?"

"Aye, be happy to," said the burly man. He clapped Bob on the back, making Osivia hop into flight. "Right this way, Face Hair the Wizard!" He trundled up to the building's main entrance.

"Nice, uh, to meet you," said Bob, once again trying not to stare at Melanae, and staring anyway. He tore himself away to follow Harold. Osivia fluttered back down to his shoulder. "Thanks," he muttered to her.

"Bob, what was that?" she hissed in his ear. "At this rate, we'll never find you a mate!"

Bob covered his face in exasperation.

"What's the sign say?" Osivia asked Harold as they caught up to him.

Bob looked up, curious.

Harold glanced at the sign above the entrance. "Oh. Arbor House. The name of the building, follow? Just don't ask me to say it in Hari. I've been told I have terrible pronunciation." He grinned.

The bathhouse turned out to be the wing of Arbor House that sat above the misty pond. It was a large, rectangular room with a high-peaked ceiling, under which ran rows of clerestory windows. The room's interior was partitioned by sliding paper doors partially obscuring rows of wooden tubs inset into the floor. Upon Bob's arrival, each of the oval baths were occupied with former slaves. The place was bustling with attendants carrying water, draining tubs, providing towels, and chit-chatting with each other and those in the baths. Even from the hallway, the air was thick and wet, smelling of soap and perfumes. Laughter and song, splashing and whispers all wound their way to Bob's ears as he arrived behind Harold. Osivia muttered something about research and fluttered off.

There was a line out the door, and Bob sat on the nearby bench to wait, his skin itching with long-preserved grease and newfound anticipation. Harold sat with him. The big man had stowed his shield and armor somewhere, and now he sat shirtless in brown woolen trousers. He looked like a bodybuilder. Could be on a magazine cover, except for all the scars. They'd probably airbrush those out.

"Didn't much expect to find humans here," said Bob, scratching his beard and craning his neck to peer into the inner bathhouse.

"Oh, aye, there's a few," said Harold.

"What reasons do they have for helping the En'harae?"

The big man shrugged his massive shoulders. "Different men got different reasons, follow? Engoria's got few friends these days, and more than a few enemies. Their own people, for one. Men forced into the armies, their crops taken, without payment, for the King. Just angry, they are, fighting against King Flaire more than fighting for the En'harae. And used to be, before the wars, this part of Engoria was run by bandits. Just men out for themselves, follow? Precious few left of that lot, but fuck them anyway. Bastards. Still, what's left of them, they're here. Nowhere else to go, and they get their share of whatever we take, so they don't be complaining much."

Bob once again remembered shooting men on the road, the sprays of gore echoing behind his eyes. He shook it off. "Which are you, then?"

Harold chuckled. "Me? Oh, I'm neither, am I? Got my own reasons."

Bob shifted uncomfortably on the bench. "Don't suppose you want to tell me those reasons." He eyed the other man's scars. Harold looked like he'd seen a few battles and not always come out on top. There was a thick white line running down his chest, crossed by three parallel lines like claw marks. There was more than one round starburst of knotted flesh—probably arrow wounds.

Harold scratched his face and sighed, glancing sidelong at Bob. "Oh, aye. I suppose. Who am I to refuse the mighty Face Hair?"

Bob flushed with minor embarrassment. "Guess you could have that name as much as me."

"Oh, aye, I've got me a beard," Harold said, chuckling. "En'harae find them strange, for all their own strangeness. But your beard, Bob, its magnificent!" He gripped Bob's shoulder and shook him playfully, grinning. Bob couldn't help but smile back. "Bit more gray than mine, though, aye?"

Bob's smile vanished. "What?" He pawed at his beard, lifting its bottom. Sure enough, there were a few tiny gray and white streaks through it. "Fuck me! That wasn't there before!"

Harold burst out laughing, a booming sound that drew a few glances from the former slaves beside them on the bench. "Hard times can do that to a man! Don't you worry, makes you look wise, aye? Gives you the look of experience, follow? Like scars." He slapped his chest.

Despite Harold's joviality, Bob grew sullen. He considered the events of the last week. He had, after years of searching, finally confronted the man—the *thing*—that had murdered his wife and son, only to be tortured by him. He'd been used by Mannix and then thrown back into hard labor. He'd been forced, at the threat of Torael's murder, to whip one of his friends bloody. He'd killed a prone man, nearly been killed by Sonny, and seen more than a few dead bodies. Then, he'd seen a transparent creature in the shape of a person open a glowing door in the middle of a forest. It was no wonder, now that he considered it, his body had manifested signs of stress. But gray hair? He'd never even considered that it could happen to him. He didn't know exactly how old he was. By his estimation, he was still in his late thirties. Seemed too early for this, but here it was. He let out a long breath. "Guess I'll have to live with looking wise." He tried a smile.

"That's the spirit, then."

The line moved, and Bob scooted over on the bench. There were only two elves ahead of him now, and his skin was crying out for him to push past them and dive headfirst into the warm, soapy water. Instead, he turned back to Harold.

"You were about to tell me why you fight with the En'harae."

"Oh, aye. Best start with where I'm from, then. Well, the entire northern strip of the continent is mountains. They go on for miles and miles. So many mountains, no one's mapped them all. Likely never will.

Called the Endless Mountains, they are.

"Anyway, Engoria claims the mountains north of them as their own—a foolish notion. En'hirin has the good sense to know who owns them, which in many cases is no one. Well anyway, that's where my people are. Lots of different tribes, follow? Mine's the Men of Nine Peaks, for the number of mountains we've got to our name. Called the Niners by most. Big tribe, ours, and old. Anyway, our mountains are close to New Tanatha, where them fucking Gez Kar slither all over what used to belong to the En'harae. Cold blooded creatures, they are, and it can get a bit chilly on the Nine Peaks, aye? They have to bring their fire shamans along if they want to attack us, so mostly they leave us alone.

"There's a range stretching from the Endless into New Tanatha and En'hirin called the Still Mountains. Not too far from Nine Peaks. About a decade ago, them Gez Kar came tromping by Nine Peaks on their way there. We fought them, of course. Scaly bastards don't respect anything, excepting maybe that shelled bastard they got for a king."

"Forr Ghaway," said Bob, remembering what Torael and the others had told him in the Cave.

"Aye, the very same. So, these reptilian arseholes came through, and we were having a hard time of it. All three of my brothers died fighting that day. And me, it was a near thing." He tapped absently at the triple-lined scar on his chest. "Then these beautiful blue bastards," he pointed at the En'harae ahead of them in line, "came up from the south and lay into the Gez Kar, drove them away from Nine Peaks. Kelael was there with them. Saved my life, that somber bastard. Pulled me himself back to our castle."

This news caught Bob off guard and he began, unwillingly, to view Torael's dour brother in a new light.

"So, a few days go by, and I'm healed up enough, so I take some Niners southwest with Kelael and the others. Them lizards were heading that way. Well, there's a big fucking battle. Famous, it is. The Battle of the Still Mountains."

Bob nodded, trying to fit Harold's story in with what the elves had told him.

BOB THE WIZARD

"Most of us made it through, my Niners, and the En'harae won, but it was a close thing. The Engorians were supposed to show and help fight the Gez Kar, follow? But they never came. So, after the battle, me and my Niners, we settle at the En'hari camp to rest. Couple days go by, and here come the Engorians. We figure, these bastards are just late, aye? But they come on us and attack. The Gez Kar, their remaining forces rejoin the fight. Our side, we're in trouble, we just fought the lizards for days. It was a massacre. My Niners, they died—every one. We were cut off to the north, and anyway I was all alone from the Nine Peaks, follow? Only blue skin on my side. I find myself falling back, south with the En'harae, and we get away, and there's Kelael, the En'hari who saved my life, still kicking. I tell you, Sora Kelai, I've seen some dirty tricks, but none that ended in so much blood as what them Engorians did under them Still Mountains. Almost the whole of the En'hari army wiped out, the rest clapped in chains and carted off. Don't need to tell you what became of those."

"The mines."

"Aye, some. Others are off doing gods-know-what in other parts of the kingdom." Harold cleared his throat. "Later, we figured out that the lizards and the Engorians made some kind of deal. Them Gez Kar killed my brothers, and them Engorians killed my friends. Meanwhile, the En'harae been nothing but good—good to me, good to each other. When I had the chance to go back to Nine Peaks, I thought, what for, aye? Go back and hide and let those Engorian bastards have their way? Let the lizards have their way? No, not me. Not Harold Whitespring of Nine Peaks. My brothers were dead. What's to go back to? I decided, I'll stay with Kelael and kill some Engorians. Right bastards, they are, and none deserve it more. The lizards, they're mostly stupid, they can't help wanting to kill. But the Engorians and that King Flaire, they're men, and they *chose* to be murdering bastards. Figure I'll pay them back. Can't think of a better way to spend my time."

Bob nodded solemnly, stroking his now-graying beard. A group of former slaves had finished their bath, and Bob stood, ready to follow the two before him into the steamy room of tubs. He wasn't sure how to respond to Harold's story, but the big man didn't seem to need a response.

He rested a meaty hand on Bob's shoulder. "I think you've got it figured, like I did. The En'harae are on the right side of this, aye? Enjoy your bath. I guess you've earned it." And with that, Harold turned and stalked down the hallway, wooden floorboards creaking under his weight.

After his bath, Bob felt like a new man. He hadn't been clean in a couple of months, but it felt like forever, and washing away the dirt and sweat he'd accumulated as a slave had gone some length toward resurrecting the man he was when he'd arrived on Hub. Still, as he brushed at his hair and beard, looking into a small circular mirror, the little streaks of gray remained to remind him he'd changed. He'd arrived alone, after being alone for a long time. Sure, he'd met people along the way, a few of them as different from the people on Earth as the elves were. But he was always passing through—a rolling stone, never gathering moss, as the saying went.

Now, he was surrounded by friends and allies. Though he didn't know Gorrelai, Torael, and the others as well as he could, there was a bond between them, forged in the bowels of the earth and under the whip, that was as strong a connection as he'd ever had.

Aside from his feelings, there was *the deal*—the promise he'd made to help the En'harae win back their country in exchange for help retrieving the Gatekey. Of course, he could always renege on the deal, get the Gatekey and go after Galvidon right away, leave the elves to their own devices. It was a tempting prospect, and one the old Bob might have seriously considered. But the new Bob—the one with gray hairs—didn't think he could do that. Although he no longer felt like Anna was always watching, pushing him on, he felt like the real Anna—not the one he'd imagined demanding vengeance, but the real woman he'd fallen in love with—would be ashamed of him if he betrayed his friends. He finished his brushing and admired his reflection. No, Bob knew now, Anna would rather him do something good than to throw it all away for a chance to kill the Gray Man.

Or maybe he was just telling himself that because, at that moment, he had no idea where Galvidon was. He had to silently admit to his reflection that finding him was still a priority.

And along the lines of priorities—what was the deal with Bernard?

BOB THE WIZARD

Bob took out the pink plastic lighter the wizard had thrown him in the Essen'aelo, turned it in his hand. How did the old wizard get it? Was Bernard from Earth? If he'd gotten to Hub by the same route as Bob—well, that was like lightning striking twice. Maybe he'd come from a different world that was just similar to Bob's earth. After all, the world Bob had been in just before Hub had been flush with technology. Bob had purchased his metal flip lighter—now lost—only days before jumping off that building into the Gate that brought him here. But even if he set aside the mystery of the plastic lighter, there was still plenty to Bernard Heathrow that remained an enigma. What did a wizard on Hub actually do? How did Bernard become a wizard to begin with? How did anyone? Questions worth investigation. Priorities.

He placed the small mirror on the modest oaken bed stand and sat on the bed. Upon leaving Arbor House, he'd been shown through the Koreka's rear sections. By then, Bob had been too fatigued and introspective to notice much. A pleasant En'hari woman guided him to a neighborhood of conical canvas huts. Most of the Koreka's population seemed to live there. There were cookfires and laundry lines. Chattering voices filled the air. Dragonflies buzzed in winding loops. Bob was shown to a hut and told it now belonged to him.

Constructed of canvas and wooden beams, it was shaped like a circus tent, with a wide cylindrical bottom. The hut gained its conical shape from the roof section, which came up to a center point of open air that acted as a chimney. It seemed much bigger from the inside, but Bob figured that was because it had been so long since he'd had an entire room to himself—apart from a cell. The hut's interior was lit by a small, grated firepit, now sporting a modest flame that licked at its iron enclosure and puffed little black streams of smoke toward the ceiling's center opening.

Bob was about to lie down when Osivia's little light entered the tent flap at the hut's entrance, drawing his attention. She hovered around the room for a few moments, admiring the craftsmanship, knocking on the two pieces of furniture—the bed stand, and an empty wooden chest. Then she fluttered down onto the bed beside him.

"Comfy," she said, adjusting her glasses. "How was your bath?"

"Refreshing," said Bob, and ran his fingers through his hair. "Though

I seem to have gone a bit gray."

"Makes you look wise."

"So I've been told."

"You're lucky it didn't fall out. I've observed in humans that extreme stressors often result in deleterious effects on the body. Hair loss or discoloration is one of the most common manifestations." They sat in silence for a moment. "What will you do now?"

Bob cleared his throat. "I imagine we'll figure out a way to get into Oath Keep and steal back my key."

"Are you going to talk to that woman again? You like her."

"Osivia," said Bob, ignoring the question, "why are you helping me?"

She stood up on the bed and began to slowly pace on the sheets, arms crossed. "Helping? I'm not sure I…"

"Don't try to deny it. You did something in the dungeon. It healed me somehow. Then you warned me at the mining grounds about the Engorians. Why?"

"I thought I made that clear. You're interesting."

"There are plenty of humans around here for you to study."

She rubbed lightly at the side of her neck. "You remember when we first spoke, I said I'd been observing you? Well… at first, I'd just come to see the human that'd been thrown in with the En'harae. To see how you would behave around a different species. But, when you were trapped in the mine, I heard your story. About what happened to your mate and offspring. And… how you came here."

She must have seen something on Bob's face—indignation, maybe—because she continued in a rush of words. "It's horrible, what you've been through, and I do want to see how you continue to adapt after suffering a trauma like that. But I'm a scientist Bob, remember that, and you say you came from another world, and that's so fascinating! I want to observe and document how an outsider interacts with our world. But also, I thought, maybe, if you ever were to leave again… I might go with you. Because really, how could I pass up an opportunity like that? To see other worlds? To document the journey! It's a once in a lifetime opportunity!"

"Come with me? Are you crazy? If I leave, I might never come back. You'd never be able to share your… research… with anyone from this world. You could never bring the knowledge back to the other faeries. It would just be you and me, possibly wondering the Astraverse until we're dead!"

Osivia's eyes widened. "Astraverse? What's that?"

Bob rubbed his eyes. "I'm not completely sure. Everything I know I got from this computer lady in a strange place… It's kind of long story. Ask me later. Anyway, far as I can gather, the Astraverse is what they call the network of worlds. You know, like branches on a tree. Each branch leads to a different place in the universe. At least, I think that's what the lady was saying. And the worlds are connected by Astral Gates. The Gatekey lets me open them. And really, that's about all I know. I'm not a scientist—I don't research these things. I just chase Galvidon. And let's be honest, I'm not even very good at it."

She was scribbling in her notebook. "Fascinating, fascinating."

"You can't seriously want to leave your world, your home, with all the people… faeries, whatever… you've ever known, with no guarantee you'd ever come back."

"Why not? They're boring, faeries. Stupid and indolent. They don't approve of me studying humans, and I don't approve of *them*. My research can benefit whoever finds it in whatever world we end up in!" She fluttered excitedly in a circle. "Besides, I'll get to see new worlds! Places other faeries could only dream of!"

"But… You'll get sick of me. I kind of suck, you know."

"Oh, nonsense, Bob. I've been observing humans for a few years now, and I can tell you, you're a good one. You care about others. You stand up for what's right. I like you." Her face flushed pink. "Um, from a scientific perspective, that is."

Bob couldn't help but laugh. "You give me far too much credit. But hey, I won't deny I need your help. So stick around, Tinkerbell."

Her nose scrunched. "What's a Tinkerbell?"

"Never mind," said Bob, smiling. "Now, I'd really like to get some sleep, so if you don't mind…"

Osivia cocked her head. "Someone's coming," she said, and zipped through air and hid behind the bed stand.

"Sora Kelai," said a level voice from just outside the tent flap. "May I enter? I wish to speak with you."

It was Kelael.

BOB THE WIZARD

CHAPTER FOURTEEN:
REST AND RUMMAGE

Despite Bob's yearning for sleep, it was still midafternoon, and daylight spilled briefly into the hut as Kelael, still clad in his patchwork leather armor, entered and the tent flap closed behind him. The elf's short, dark hair revealed a purple sheen in the firelight. He strode into the canvas hut with his arms crossed behind his back, his head lowered. Bob stood nervously, scratching his beard, self-conscious about the gray.

"Sora Kelai," said Torael's brother.

"Kelael," said Bob, his voice scratchy and high pitched. He cleared his throat. "What can I do for you?"

"Have you eaten?" asked the En'hari politely, scanning the room.

"Yes, thanks." He'd found a meal behind Arbor House before Torael had seen him and sent him to the huts with a guide.

"Good. That's good." Kelael picked up the round mirror, gave his reflection a cursory glance, then replaced it on the bed stand. He turned to Bob, looking cautious. "I have spoken to Torael. About… about the time he spent in Engorian hands. It seems…" he hesitated, looking uncomfortable. "It seems there was a cave-in at the mines. At this time, you saved his life." His eyes met Bob's, and for the first time Bob noticed the blue archer's irises were a golden yellow.

"That's right," said Bob, standing erect. "And I'd do it again. Your brother was kind to me when no one else would even look at me. As kind as a man… elf, um, En'hari I mean… could be in that situation."

Kelael's eyes were still on him. "Why were you on that wagon on the East Road?" His voice had an edge to it—not curiosity, but interrogation.

"I'd just arrived in Engoria... On Hub, in fact. Ah, did Torael mention... my story?"

"Yes. Why were you on the wagon on the East Road?"

Bob was unwillingly reminded of Oath Keep's dungeon, of pain shooting through his body. *Where is the Key? Where did you acquire it?*

He flinched and sat on the bed. "I told you, I'd just arrived. I didn't know where I was, or the situation. I was just following Galvidon."

"Galvidon?"

"The being that killed my wife and son. I've been following him ever since it happened."

"Following him why?"

"To kill the bastard! Why else?"

Kelael smirked. "You were seeking vengeance?"

"If you want to say it that way. That farmer was giving me a ride. Seemed nice enough, until you murdered him. Dead farmers aren't nearly as pleasant as live ones."

Kelael was silent for a long moment, staring at Bob, who glanced away, scratching his beard and wanting the conversation to be over.

"I have not seen my brother," said Kelael, "in over eleven years. Even at the Still Mountains, we... fought separately. We have not been close since we were young. Yet, I have always trusted him. He says you are a good man."

Bob looked back at him, but there was no kindness in the golden eyes.

"But I have seen you kill. Effectively and without hesitation. The humans you killed, they do not concern me, but that En'hari was my friend, and a good Gasheera. I will watch you, Sora Kelai, and if your actions displease me, even for a moment, I will end your life and not shed a tear." His gaze was steady and hard.

BOB THE WIZARD

"Don't take this the wrong way, Kelael, you seem like a nice guy and all." Bob stood up again, facing the elf. "But go fuck yourself."

They held each other's gaze. Kelael looked away first with a strained smile. "That weapon you used, on the road. What was it?"

"A gun," said Bob, relaxing his posture.

Kelael turned back, curious. "A what?"

"A gun. A weapon from my world. It's like a crossbow, I suppose, but it fires metal projectiles. Much more deadly." The shotgun had not actually come from Bob's Earth. He'd acquired it in a place called Three Sands, but he decided that he'd rather not get into all that and make this conversation last any longer than it had to.

"And loud," mused Kelael.

"Yes."

"Where is it now? In Mannix's hands?" The questions were softer now, friendlier.

"Afraid so. He took it when he arrested me. I don't know if he's tried to use it yet. If he does, I hope it blows his fucking head off."

Kelael smiled coldly at that. "Perhaps we can recover it."

"Hope so," said Bob. They stared at one another. "Nice seeing you."

"I have more to say."

"What, then?" Bob slid his dragon pipe from the bed stand and fussed over his tobacco. It was running low.

Kelael cleared his throat. "Have you noticed that the En'harae treat Torael differently?"

"I suppose," said Bob, tamping tobacco down into the pipe's bowl. He knew what Kelael meant—the elves deference to Torael, their unspoken respect for his decisions. They had accepted Bob only after Torael had. And there was Ellaria. *I wouldn't help you. But I will do it for Torael.*

"Has Torael spoken to you of his past? Of our family?"

"Not really," said Bob, not looking up from the pipe.

"I will enlighten you. En'hirin has many tribes, and each has many laws and traditions that are their own. But there is a central rulership, to which all tribes submit. It is called the Quaylen. Each tribe sends a representative to its meetings."

Bob was struggling with a match and little sandpaper square.

"Am I boring you?" Kelael arched an eyebrow.

Bob glanced up. "I'm listening," he said, remembering the pink lighter. He set down the match and sandpaper and rummaged in his pocket.

Kelael continued in a curt tone. "Though the tribes are represented, there is one tribe, Ellaren, who founded the original Quaylen. Torael and I are of the Ellaren Tribe. More, our family name is also Ellaren, for we are descendants of the tribe's original leadership. Our father, Terek, was leader of the Quaylen—called the Quaylen Dah—when these most recent wars with Engoria started. As his mother was Quaylen Dah before him. For generations, the oldest member of the Ellaren family has taken this position. It is a symbol to our people, that we are there to lead, as many of our fathers and mothers were before us."

Bob lit the dragon pipe and puffed thoughtfully. "I take it old Terek didn't make it through the wars." He was careful to speak with no trace of mockery.

"He did not. Et tessat sheeram sheral." *May the spirits guide him home.*

"Et tessat sheeram sheral," repeated Bob, staring at the little fire. He could feel the golden eyes on him. With an effort, he met them. "So, who's the oldest living Ellaren now? You?"

Kelael shook his head. "Torael," he said firmly.

"I see," mused Bob, drawing on the pipe. "So Torael's the Quaylen Dah."

Kelael scowled and waved away smoke. "It is more complicated than that. Since Engoria betrayed us, the Quaylen has been destroyed. The tribes are scattered from their territories, fighting the armies of Tanatha and Engoria, or else they have been enslaved, or made into vassals, giving food to the Engorians that occupy En'hirin. The members of the Quaylen are dead.

"His whole life, my brother has trained to replace Terek, learning the ways of governance from him. He and Terek were always close, inseparable. Much closer than I was to either of them. But like so many others, Terek was killed under the Still Mountains. Torael was enslaved. The Quaylen was hunted and murdered by the humans. Now that he is free, Torael is all that remains of our traditional leadership."

Bob continued to puff. "Hmm." He scratched his nose, thinking about the purple-haired Torael—his easy manner, his surety and kindness, but also his deadliness in battle. What Kelael was telling him slotted perfectly into that picture. "Torael is a symbol of hope, then. The last true leader the En'harae recognize."

"Precisely. Sora Kelai, he must be kept alive at all costs, so the people can have hope, but also so the Quaylen may live on."

"And because he's your brother and you love him, don't forget that part," said Bob drily.

Kelael appeared unmoved. "My feelings do not matter. What matters is the future of our people. Torael has told me of your arrangement. He will help you get back this…key. You will join the fight to free our people."

Bob offered him the pipe, but Kelael ignored it.

"Do you intend to honor this agreement?"

Bob coughed. "I do."

"Then listen, Sora Kelai. Soon there will be a meeting of the Koreka's council. Torael has insisted that you be there. Among other matters, we will discuss how to retrieve your key from Oath Keep. I ask that you insist Torael not be on the mission. It will be a great risk, and he is too valuable to lose."

"First you threaten to kill me, then you ask for my help. You need to work on your people skills."

The golden eyes blinked calmly. "Will you help me in this matter?"

"Will you kill me if I don't?" Bob blew smoke at Kelael.

"That would hardly convince Torael to listen."

"Touching."

"Consider my words, Sora Kelai. The future of my people may depend on it."

With that, he turned and strode from the hut. The sunlight made another brief appearance as he exited. After a few seconds, Osivia peeked her head from behind the bed stand. She and Bob regarded each other in silence.

Bob slept. He slept for hours—through the remaining evening and the following night. It was more sleep than he'd gotten in ages, more comfortable than any since the Fool's Rest, and more peaceful besides. It was blissfully free of nightmares, though when he awoke to the sound of birdsong outside the hut, in the early hours, he did have a lingering impression of a dream. He'd been at his old dinner table, in the house that he and Anna had bought together, and she and Daniel were there, and for some reason, Hilda Fields, the old woman from the market, was there too. His mind had made her Daniel's grandmother, and she grouched over all three of them maternally. Then, he remembered upon waking, the form of a transparent person, outline carved out of the light, had torn a hole in the reality of the dining room, and Bob had stepped through to find Torael on an outdoor path. He'd been standing next to two bicycles. Bob and the En'hari, who's purple locks played in the wind, had ridden the path together through a green forest. The sounds of the birds in the trees as they rode had slowly morphed into the chirping outside his hut, and he'd awakened, feeling rested and hungry.

Osivia was nowhere to be seen. Bob made his way from the huts toward Arbor House. As he strode the gravel path, the Koreka's features stood out in the morning light. To his left was a huge garden, cordoned off with some kind of wire fence, already full of busy En'harae. To his right was a long line of equipment sheds set among a copse of trees. Beyond the sheds was a large field with wooden target dummies in front of haybales, and a thick cylindrical pole from which sprouted pegs at various angles. As Arbor House drew closer, Bob noticed several other buildings off to his left along the wall. But his goal, the kitchen, was a bustling wing at Arbor House's rear. It faced Bob as he approached from the Koreka's central green.

Stomach growling, he entered the covered deck area at the kitchen's mouth and approached the food line. He was moderately surprised to see that Hirrell, he of the yellow hair, was behind the counter, hard at work cooking meals.

"Oh, hi Bob," said Hirrell, sounding distracted but happy to see him. "You must try the turkey bacon today. Truly a perfect bird for bacon."

"There're turkeys around here?" asked Bob, accepting a plate.

"Sometimes," said Hirrell, flipping something in a pan.

"Cooking, huh?"

"Oh yes, Sora Kelai. I love to cook. It is my Kafeh."

"My stomach appreciates you," called Bob over his shoulder as he moved away.

After the meal, Bob found a series of benches on the central green behind Arbor House. There he sat, enjoying his pipe, and wondering where he might go to find Bernard. He heard footsteps and looked up to see Torael approaching.

"Bob the Wizard," said Torael good-naturedly. "How do the spirits of the morning treat you?"

"Well, thanks. It's good to be free again. How are *you*, my blue friend?"

Torael smiled and sat next to him. "As you say, it is good to be free. But I fear our troubles are not over. We have a meeting in a few hours, at Arbor House, with the council. We are deciding many things, like how to get your key, so you have magic again."

Bob nodded, and something occurred to him. "Gorrelai. How is he? He was bleeding still when we arrived."

Torael's smile did not waver. "Gorrelai is strong. He recovers. I just come from him." The purple-haired elf nodded toward the group of buildings Bob had not yet explored. "He says your little faerie helps him. He heals faster. Tell me Bob, how did you come to have a faerie friend?"

"Beats the hell out of me."

The elf raised an eyebrow. "This means you do not know?"

"Right. She says she's studying humans. Seems to find me interesting."

"That, I am understanding. The En'harae, we have a saying of faeries. Hard to translate, but basically it says, 'see a faerie once, check your pocket, see a faerie twice, thank the spirits for your luck.' It means, when a faerie stays with you, it is a lucky thing."

"She's saved my ass more than once. Do your people know a lot about faeries?"

Torael shook his head. "Only that they do not like others much. Stay to themselves almost always."

For a moment, they sat in the morning light. The breeze brushed Bob's skin. Bob considered telling Torael about his brother's visit the night before but decided not to ruin the conversation. Also, he hadn't yet decided if he would grant Kelael's request to encourage Torael to stay hidden in the Koreka. Instead, he said, "Say, you think I could get some tobacco around here?"

Torael chuckled. "En'harae, we mostly do not smoke. But they have stolen much on the roads." He pointed to the series of storage sheds, barely visible through the trees on an upward slope of ground. "If we have some, it will be there, in the supplies. It is Harold's job, I think, to keep track. Ask him."

"I'll do that."

Torael stood. "I have things I must do. I will see you at Arbor House at noon."

"Alrighty. See you."

Bob finished his pipe and made his way over to the storage sheds. When he arrived, he found Harold, along with two men and several En'harae, moving crates and boxes. There was a wagon parked nearby, no animals to drive it, and some of the workers were pulling down its contents and sorting through them.

"Ahoy there," said Bob, catching Harold's eye as the big man rearranged a couple of heavy crates just inside one of the sheds.

"Greetings, mighty Face Hair!" called Harold, only glancing up briefly.

"Call me Bob."

"Bob? Well, that's much too ordinary, aye?" said Harold, dusting off his hands and walking over. "But alright, if you like, Bob."

"Listen, you got some tobacco in there somewhere?"

Harold chuckled. "Oh, aye, I reckon. Somewhere. Tell you what, though. Pitch in with this haul, you can take anything you need."

Bob glanced at the wagon. "Really? Anything?"

"You're on the council, aren't you?"

"I am?"

"Oh, sure. Going to the meeting today, aye? It was your effort that tipped us to where to find Torael, aye?" He lowered his voice. "Mighty Quaylen Dah that he is." The big man winked.

"I suppose. Alright then, I'll help out."

He approached the wagon and saw that one of the En'harae working there was Hirrell, his hair exceptionally bright in the sun. "Hi, Bob!" he called, pulling a bulging sack of potatoes off the pile.

"Holy shit, you sure do get around," said Bob.

Hirrell dropped the sack into a cart full of produce. When he spoke, he sounded mildly out of breath. "Just here to resupply the kitchen. Feeding three hundred people is not so easy."

Bob pushed out his lower lip. "Three hundred? That how many are here?"

Hirrell shrugged. "Maybe less, maybe more. This is just what they tell me."

M. V. PRINDLE

One of the humans passed by with a box and ignored them, but one of the other elves glanced up curiously. "*Is this him?*" he asked in Hari.

"*That's right,*" Hirrell replied, grinning. "Sora Kelai."

"*Hey,*" said the unknown elf, swatting a comrade on the shoulder. "*This is Sora Kelai!*"

"Sora Kelai!" said another elf. The name was echoed by the rest of the nearby En'harae.

Bob blushed and held up a hand in greeting. The elves took a moment to stare and then continued to work. "Told Harold I'd help out," said Bob to Hirrell. He made for the big wagon that was being unloaded. Hirrell followed.

"Find any tobacco in here?" Bob asked as he stepped up into the bed of the wagon.

"I am wishing," said Hirrell, climbing up to grab another sack.

Bob began to rummage. He carried a sack of corn for Hirrell. He moved several tins of spices—not tobacco—into the closest shed, where he found a network of partitioned shelves for smaller items. Glancing around, he took some items off the shelves to inspect them and then replace them. After a few minutes, he unrolled a small canvas sack, and the scent of dried tobacco leaves reached his nostrils.

"Jackpot," he said to the empty shed, and pocketed the sack.

He exited and returned to the wagon, which was nearly empty now. The other workers were all off in the sheds arranging things. Hirrell glanced at his cart, now almost overflowing with goods. All that remained in the wagon bed was a long, rectangular wooden crate, wide and deep enough to hold any number of things. It was latched with an iron lock, which Bob pulled and pried at with his hands to no avail.

"Stuck shut?" came Hirrell's voice from behind him.

"Yeah, fucker won't budge."

"Harold!" yelled Hirrell, causing Bob to jump.

The mountain man came lumbering over. "Aye?"

"We need hammer. Have lock," said Hirrell.

Bob stared at the crate while he waited, his curiosity growing. What was in there? Gold coins? Weapons? It was probably weapons. It was the right size to hold a sword or two.

"Stand back, if you please, Bob," said Harold. He now carried a large iron hammer, like a railroad sledge. Bob climbed down, and Harold stepped up into the bed, the wagon groaning under his weight. The hammer arced up high and swung down with considerable force, breaking the lock with a sharp crack and splintering the surrounding wood. Harold stepped back to admire his handiwork. "That's it, then."

Bob eagerly hopped back into the bed. "You mind?"

"By all means, friend Bob." Harold shifted his position to allow Bob to approach the crate.

Bob placed his hands on the wooden lid and could feel the gazes of Hirrell and Harold over his shoulder. He lifted, and the top of the crate—a slab of inch-thick heavy wood—swung upward on iron hinges, producing a robust squeak. At first, Bob was looking at a pile of hay. He grabbed a handful and tossed it over the side of the wagon. Was that…? It couldn't be. He tossed more hay and reached into the crate to pull out the long object within.

"Holy Mary, mother of Jesus," breathed Bob. He stood and held up the object to the sunlight, its brown and black features softly gleaming. It was almost four feet long, thin but heavy.

"What is it?" asked Hirrell nervously.

"A weapon," said Bob, still not believing his eyes.

But it wasn't a sword, as he'd anticipated. It was a rifle.

M. V. PRINDLE

CHAPTER FIFTEEN:
COUNCIL

Bob didn't consider himself a 'gun nut', but he was no slouch when it came to knowledge about Earth's modern weapons. As a boy, he'd gone through a phase in which he'd devoured countless books about war. He'd read about both World Wars, the Korean War, the Vietnam War, Operation: Desert Storm—which had occurred around the time he'd been reading about it—and even some older wars, like the American Revolution and the Civil War. He was a far cry from being a historian, but the time he'd spent poring over military histories had stuck with him, as childhood interests often do. It had helped that his father, a veteran of Vietnam, had encouraged him. Encouragement from his father was rare.

There were many interesting details about the rifle, none of which could be easily explained to Harold or Hirrell, or anyone else in the Koreka. Had there been a different gun in the crate, Bob would probably not be able to recall its specifications. But for anyone with cursory knowledge of First World War weaponry, the model was famous. It was a Short Magazine Lee Enfield, or SMLE: a bolt-action soldier's standard-issue from the middle of the first World War. Since it lacked a magazine cut-out and the long-range sight on its left side, it had to be the Number 1 Mark III, rather than the Mark II, which had been issued earlier in the war but was too expensive to continue manufacturing en masse. The Mark III had an in-built, ten-round magazine that fired 7.7 mm rounds—or 0.303's in England, which was where this gun had come from. There were a few clues that indicated its country of origin, but none so clear as the British flag shallowly engraved into the butt of the weapon's stock. Baffling as it may be, there was no doubt about it—this SMLE mk. III had come from Earth.

BOB THE WIZARD

This realization led Bob to remember the pink lighter, and all at once, wanting to talk to Bernard became a burning desire. He had so many questions, he was practically bursting with them. Yet, he knew he'd see Bernard at the council meeting. He could corner him afterward. He set down the rifle and turned back to the crate.

After further excited digging through straw, Bob found that the wooden crate was a veritable treasure trove. It contained one hundred rounds of 0.303 ammunition in metal boxes, an affixable bayonet, a cannister of gun oil with some soft, clean rags, a compass, a shoulder strap, a pair of combat boots, and at the very bottom of the crate, a folded British flag. He and the two onlookers marveled at the find, stunned. Their silence was broken by questions Bob had trouble answering. How did the weapon get here? What was it doing in this wagon? Did Bob know how to make more of these weapons?

The answer to the final question was a resounding *no*, but for now, one firearm was a godsend. Once they'd uncovered all the accessories and gotten over the initial shock, Bob realized some of his own questions might be answered by his companions.

"Where was the wagon captured?" he asked Harold.

"Road called Southern King," said Harold. "Goes south from Swearington, through the hill country, to Tortellan, Engoria's capitol. Passes through many a village on its way, and there's a particular spot called Ransom Ridge—easy to ambush the road from there, follow? That's where we nabbed it. Had an escort. Lots of trouble for a single wagon, this was. Now I'm seeing why."

"So, it was on its way to Martimus? To the King?"

"Aye."

Something was nagging at Bob—something about language. The Gatekey allowed him to understand languages, yet when the Gatekey had been taken from him, he found he spoke the same language as the Engorians. Either they spoke English, or by some cosmic coincidence, the English and Engorian languages had somehow evolved separately and ended up identical. This latter option seemed incredibly far-fetched. And here was Bob, staring at a British flag. Could there be some connection between Earth and Hub? He remembered something Galvidon had said under Oath Keep.

You speak with an accent foreign to Hub. Which realm are you from?

The Gray Man's focus had been on his accent—not on the fact that he spoke English. Bob realized, still standing in the back of the wagon, that Galvidon saw no mystery in the fact that Bob spoke the same language as the Engorians.

He turned his attention back to the rifle. It was old—early twentieth century—yet well preserved, as if it hadn't been touched since it was manufactured. If it came from Earth, it must have arrived through a Gate. Could Bob find that Gate and return home? If he could, would he? Maybe. Only if he killed Galvidon first. And then there was *the deal*. So much to do before he could return home...

A plan began to form in his mind. He'd retrieve the Gatekey, defeat the Engorians, find and kill Galvidon, locate the Gate, and return home. No sweat. Only about a thousand problems to work out between now and then, a million things that could go wrong. He needed information. Where had the Engorians found the rifle? Where was the Gate to Earth? Did Galvidon know where it was? Was Galvidon planning to go there? Was Galvidon even still here?

Anna's voice rose unbidden from the back of his mind. *Find Galvidon. That's the only thing that matters. Find him and kill him for what he's done. I can't rest until you do, Bob. Daniel and I can't rest.*

Bob shook his head. That wasn't really Anna, she would never be so bloodthirsty.

Kill him, Bob. We can't rest. Find him. Kill him.

Bob rose and moved toward the supply sheds to find a pack, gritting his teeth. A tear pushed its way down his cheek, and he wiped it roughly away. He could feel his friends' stares on his back.

"I will, love," he whispered. "I'll find him."

After packing the British military equipment, he carried it all to his hut and left all but the rifle, which he held onto, slung over his shoulder on its strap. He was nervous about drawing stares. Would people ask, 'wow, what is that futuristic weapon Sora Kelai is carrying?' But of course, none of the inhabitants of the Koreka had the slightest idea what a rifle was, so no one paid him any attention. Kelael might have guessed what it was, since he'd seen Bob wield a shotgun on the East Road, but thankfully Torael's bristly brother was nowhere in sight.

Osivia was waiting for him at the hut. She excitedly peppered him with questions about the rifle. He told her the story as they made their way out onto the central green and proceeded to Arbor House. True to form, she recorded it all in her notebook.

Once they reached Arbor House, it didn't take them long to find the meeting chamber. The kind En'hari woman who'd shown Bob to his hut directed them to the staircase and bid them take it to the third floor.

"Thanks, Chaera!" Osivia called to her as she fluttered after Bob.

"Chaera, huh?" said Bob as they ascended the sturdy staircase. "You learn everybody's name already?"

"Goodness, no," replied the faerie. "I've only learned one hundred and six names. Still two hundred and forty-two names to go."

"Jesus," muttered Bob.

At the apex of the stairs, it became clear that the entire top floor of Arbor House was the meeting chamber. The polished woodgrain floor and walls shone, caught by the daylight falling through rows of arched windows along the eastern and western walls. It was high noon, and the sun's indirect reflections on the wood seemed to bathe the room in an ovular golden aura.

A large map of the continent pinned to the north wall—across from the staircase—was the room's only decoration. It was labeled *Sheral*, the Hari word for *home*, but by the word's style and placement on the map, Bob gathered it was the also the name of the continent. He mentally noted that Robert Caplan, born in Texas, United States, North America, Earth, was currently located at the Koreka, Engoria, Sheral, Hub. Contemplating the distance between the two—both in terms of footsteps traveled and in experience gained—threatened to melt his brain.

M. V. PRINDLE

He turned his attention to the room's center, where a large oval table of thick oak dominated, surrounded by straight-backed wooden chairs without cushions. Some of the chairs were populated by familiar forms. Each of them sat in silence, alone with their own thoughts, awaiting the impending conversation.

Opposite the staircase sat Melanae, still apparently dressed for battle and strikingly beautiful—though Bob refused to let himself be dumbstruck by her again. She sat reviewing a ledger, a stack of loose paper covered in diagrams near at hand. Her fingers traced the pages as she read, and she spared Bob a brief glance as he entered. On one side of her sat Kelael, back straight and arms crossed, in his patchwork leathers. He gave Bob a long look as he entered but said nothing. On her other side was Harold, his chair pushed back on two legs, his feet crossed upon the table.

Next to Harold sat Bernard the Wizard. His shortness was compounded by a slouch, resulting in his head only coming up a foot above the table. He sat cross-legged in his chair, his black, collared cloak drooping over its sides. He no longer wore his hat, and his white hair and beard fanned out in all directions, giving him the appearance of a dwarfish, disheveled, bearded Einstein. But the oddest thing about him was that he appeared to have a duck in his lap. Bob could only see its sleek black feathered head poking out from its wizardly roost. At first Bob thought it might be stuffed, but then it looked at him, gave a perfunctory quack, and went back to ignoring him.

"Is that a duck?" Osivia whispered from his shoulder. "I hate ducks!"

Bob removed the rifle from his shoulder, made sure the chamber was empty for the millionth time, and placed it on the table, where it produced a heavy *thunk* that was loud in the quiet room. Everyone seemed to find their eyes involuntarily drawn to the weapon. Kelael shifted excitedly in his chair. Bernard and the duck eyed the rifle curiously, but neither Harold nor Melanae yielded a reaction.

Bob hesitated for a moment behind an empty chair across from Kelael. He didn't want to be directly across from Melanae, as he was afraid of embarrassing himself by staring, but he didn't want to be looking at that duck either. Who brings a duck to a meeting? He sighed and noisily scraped out the chair next to Bernard. As he sat, Osivia fluttered across to his right shoulder, putting Bob between herself and the duck, which watched her movement closely.

Kelael eyed the Lee Enfield hungrily. "Is that—"

"Sure is," said Bob.

"What?" asked Melanae, looking up from her reading. "What is it?"

"It is a powerful weapon," said Kelael. "It can kill men from several feet away—"

Bob interrupted him again, this time with a chuckle. "This one can kill from much further than that. That gun I had on the East Road was a shotgun, designed for close range. This is a rifle with an effective range of about a third of a mile. At the right angle and distance, it can punch through steel like it was paper."

Kelael, Melanae, and Harold all stared at him in shock. The duck emitted a soft sound that seemed to say, *I'm bored.*

"Damn," muttered Bernard. He then addressed Melanae. "We've closed all the Gates we know about. It could not be Azenbul. The warehouse at the Nexus is guarded by Axiis. We must have missed something, and the Engorians must have found it."

Any reply was preempted by the sound of feet tromping up the stairs. "Hello!" Torael's voice floated into the room. "Apologies for lateness. Gorrelai still is walking a little slow."

Bob turned, and despite everything else, felt a flush of relief at the sight of Gorrelai. The big elf limped over and sat on Bob's right, putting a hand on the table for support as he lowered himself.

"It's good to see you up," said Bob quietly.

"*I cannot wait to kill more humans*," whispered Gorrelai in Hari, and winked.

Bob grinned as Melanae began to speak.

"I officially welcome you, Torael Ellaren, to the heart of the resistance. May the spirits smile upon you." She dipped her head in his direction.

"And you, Melanae Taeno," replied Torael.

"I extend this welcome to our other newcomers. Gorrelai Soe, accomplished Gasheera, welcome."

In reply, Gorrelai saluted her with a closed fist to his forehead.

"Sora Kelai, wizard and ally to Torael, welcome."

"Yeah, thanks," said Bob, trying not to admire her body as she faced him.

Osivia cleared her throat in his ear, but he barely noticed.

"I must confess," continued Melanae, "in all the council's meetings, we've never had this many sitting members."

"Seven is far too many," mumbled Kelael, crossing his arms again.

"Eight," whispered Osivia.

"Eight," repeated Bob reflexively.

"Pardon?" said Melanae.

Bob realized he'd just repeated what Osivia had said and took a moment to decide what she'd meant. "Uh, there are eight of us."

"Correct," said Bernard in his scratchy voice. "Don't forget Quaker."

The waterfowl produced an irritated quack.

"My mistake," said Kelael drily.

"Nine, then," whispered Osivia, sounding defeated.

"Nine, then," said Bob.

They all looked at him. Quaker the duck clapped her bill.

"Keep that duck away from me," Osivia hissed in Bob's ear.

"What do you mean?" asked Melanae politely.

Bob glanced to his shoulder where Osivia stood, arms held protectively around a diminutive notebook. Everyone's gaze shifted slightly, as if noticing the golden-haired faerie for the first time.

"Hi," said Osivia sheepishly.

"Oh, the faerie," said Torael, azure face smiling. "Hello, faerie."

Kelael scowled. "Absurd. You see what you've started, Bernard? Now everyone thinks they can bring a pet to the council!"

"I'm not a pet!" said Osivia indignantly.

"Wak!" said Quaker, shaking her head.

"Quaker," said Bernard, "is a familiar."

"Wak!" said Quaker.

"And are you a familiar?" Melanae asked Osivia, one eyebrow raised.

"No!" protested Osivia. "I'm a scientist!"

Kelael was preparing a retort, but Bob cut him off. "She's my friend," he said. "And she saved your ass." He pointed at Kelael. "Maybe you forgot, she warned us about the cavalry riding on our heels."

"I'm sold, aye?" said Harold, speaking for the first time. "Torael trusts Bob, Bob trusts the pet faerie."

"I'm not a pet!" Osivia stamped her foot.

"*I also trust the Faerie*," snarled Gorrelai in Hari, pointedly not looking at Kelael.

"All in favor of allowing the faerie to stay?" announced Melanae.

Five hands and a duckbill touched the table. Osivia fluttered nervously. Only Bob and Kelael hadn't moved. Bob got the idea, and slowly placed his hand on the table.

"Fine," said Kelael, exasperated.

"Wak," said Quaker.

"Thank you," said Osivia, and curtsied in her white coat. "But my name is Osivia Glenbrook, not, 'the faerie.'"

"Very well," said Melanae, "Osivia Glenbrook, scientist and ally of Torael, I welcome you. Now, if none of you mind, we can move on to the matters at hand."

Kelael scowled and changed the subject. "What has your creature discovered, Bernard?"

The wizard cleared his throat. "Grim news, I'm afraid."

"Wak," Quaker agreed sadly.

"Quaker returned this morning," said Bernard, glancing at Bob, "from her sojourn at Oath Keep. It appears that our contact there has been killed."

The words settled over the table. "Wait," said Bob, dread building in his chest, "what contact?"

"The En'hari woman who contacted us at your behest," said Bernard. "She was caught returning to the keep after making contact. She was then incarcerated, tortured for information, and killed."

"Ellaria?" asked Bob, his voice husky.

"I believe that was her name, yes," said the old wizard. "I'm sorry."

"I promised her we'd free her..." Bob remembered how little either he or Ellaria had believed her escape possible at the time. Now, knowing she was dead, guilt ground at him nonetheless.

Kelael snorted derisively. "This comes as no surprise. Humans are despicable creatures."

Bob glanced at Harold, but the mountain man didn't meet his eyes.

"This is my fault," said Torael softly. "She has died to free me."

"Us," said Gorrelai in heavily accented English. Then, in Hari: "*She died for all of us.*"

"*Et tessat sheeran sheral,*" intoned Melanae.

Six voices repeated the phrase. The sunlight crept along the floorboards.

Bob addressed Bernard. "Your duck..."

"Quaker," said Bernard, smiling apologetically.

"Got it," said Bob. "How were you able to gather information from Quaker? You can speak to animals?"

"Some," said Bernard. "But Quaker is more than an animal. She is my familiar. We share a special bond that allows us to communicate quite effectively. I send her out to spy…"

"Wak!" said Quaker indignantly.

"Excuse me," said Bernard. "I send her out to *gather information*, and she returns to share it."

"Yes, yes, the duck is very impressive," said Kelael. "So the woman is dead. We can attempt to free the remaining keep-slaves when we strike. But before we discuss that matter, we must focus on the Koreka's primary purpose—the disruption of the enemy. The Engorians have been increasing the security on their roads. Shipments are being consolidated and guards more heavily armed. It is only a matter of time before we lose more people. We must change our tactics."

"We could hit the other mines," said Harold. "Free more slaves."

"A tempting prospect," said Melanae, "but difficult for several reasons. Many of the mines have hit dead ends and are now unpopulated. Most of the biggest are located very far from us, flanked on two or more sides by other mines. And even if we managed to strike one and pull out with few casualties, we'd have nowhere to put the slaves. We're full to capacity, after yesterday. This place was designed as a base of operations, not a refugee camp. Frankly, I'm nervous about the current food situation. Freeing more captives would force us to change our priorities. We'd have to focus on smuggling our people back to En'hirin."

Gorrelai said something in Hari, too rapid for Bob to translate.

Torael nodded. "He is right. We will be sending them back to the occupation. Working in the mines is just as dangerous as En'hirin, right now."

"Indeed," said Melanae.

Kelael crossed his arms. "New tactics. Something that will put a dent in the supply lines to our country."

M. V. PRINDLE

Harold sighed. "Swearington's biggest export is iron. If we're not hitting the iron, then what?"

"Is it, though?" asked Bob. The table turned its gaze on him.

"Is what, what?" asked Kelael irritably.

"Is iron their biggest export?"

"What else would it be?" asked Harold.

Bob thought of his first few days in Engoria. "Sheep," he said. "Or, wool, rather."

Torael and Bernard looked thoughtful. Everyone else looked incredulous. Quaker cleaned her chest with her bill.

"He's right," said Osivia. "I've spent a lot of time around Swearington, watching humans. Their clothes are wool, their armor leather. They cover everything with canvas made of sheepskin."

Harold shrugged. "Now that I think of it, the man's got a point. I've pulled plenty of wool off the wagons. Sheds are full of the stuff. I was too focused on their weapons, aye? For them, you need iron. But you need clothes for an army as well, follow? Banners, tents..."

"It could be a devastating blow to their economy," said Osivia. Bernard nodded in agreement.

"Their... eco-what-now?" said Harold.

"Economy. Their money. Swearington exports iron and wool, right? That means someone is paying for iron and wool. If we take one of those away, they'll become solely reliant on the other for income."

Gorrelai asked Torael what Osivia was talking about, and Torael did his best to translate. Gorrelai laughed and slammed the table with his fist. His next words were easy for Bob to understand. *"We take their purse!"*

"Right!" Osivia fluttered happily at being understood.

"Very well," said Kelael. "So we start killing the sheep farmers."

"What?" said Bob, thinking of Hilda Fields. "Hell no! That's not what I meant at all. Those people have done nothing to you. They're innocent!"

169

BOB THE WIZARD

"This is war, Sora Kelai," said Kelael. Gorrelai reluctantly murmured assent.

"Well, I won't help you fucking kill civilians," said Bob flatly.

Torael spoke. "I have an idea." All eyes turned toward him. "There is a way both to do this thing, and to get Bob's key."

"Well," said Harold. "Don't leave us in suspense, Quaylen Dah."

Kelael scowled deeply at Harold's use of his brother's title.

"For now," said Torael, "we will change our attention to taking sheep from the pastures. This may also help us with the food situation. Our thievery of the animals will come to the attention of the Engorians. Then, once they have committed to guarding the pastures, we use this stealing of sheep as a diversion, while Bob and others strike Oath Keep and retake the key."

"That might occupy some guards, but what of those in the city?" demanded Kelael.

Melanae nodded. "We will send a third team into the city. They will pretend an attempted larceny at the ironworks."

"A second diversion, aye?" muttered Harold. "They'll be worried about that iron. Just like I was, aye?"

"Those will have to be some fast runners," said Bernard.

"I know of some," said Melanae.

"Fan," said Gorrelai. "*Runs like the spirits are chasing him.*"

"And who, brother," asked Kelael, "do you plan to send with Sora Kelai to the keep? Send on the most dangerous part of the mission?" There was a warning in his tone. Kelael glared at Bob pointedly. Bob shifted uncomfortably in his chair.

Torael hesitated. "Well, surely our most skilled fighters must go."

Kelael turned his glare on his brother.

Torael momentarily wilted. "Apart from me, of course."

Kelael appeared satisfied.

"I will be on the sheep team," said Torael firmly.

The two brothers' eyes remained locked for a moment, as if in a silent battle of wills. After a moment, Kelael nodded and looked away.

Bernard spoke up. "No need to worry, Kelael. I'll go with him."

"Wak!" said Quaker.

"Oh, no," said Bernard sternly. "You're staying home."

After that, the meeting fell to less interesting matters. While Osivia sat on the table, dutifully taking notes, Melanae, Kelael and Harold did most of the talking. They discussed the Koreka's supplies, food rationing, and there was some point of contention about guarding the walls. They reviewed information gathered by scouts—Bob assumed most of the scouts weren't ducks—discussed Engorian troop movements, and there was something about Engorian internal politics that Melanae felt might end in a change of the kingdom's leadership. It went on for hours. Bob wanted to talk about the rifle again. In fact, he had many burning questions. But his interest began to flag around the turn of the third hour, and soon all he could think about was tobacco.

Before the meeting finally adjourned, they reviewed Torael's plan, agreeing to shift eighty percent of the raids from the roads to the pastures. Kelael and Torael briefly discussed the types of training each team should practice, and Melanae declared they'd be ready to strike in a couple of weeks.

Torael suggested to Bob that he begin training with a sword. "Our most skilled swordsman will teach you," said the purple-haired elf.

"You then?" asked Bob hopefully.

Torael shook his head and offered a wan smile. "No, my friend. Kelael is our best."

Bob and Kelael stared at each other, neither one of them thrilled.

Melanae called the end of the meeting. "*Et tessat sheera morae,*" she said. *May the spirits guide our journeys.*

Bob stood and stretched gratefully. As the others filed out, Bernard remained seated. He seemed to be studying Bob as if searching for something in his face. Bob found himself alone in the meeting chamber with the old wizard and Osivia.

He hefted the rifle and slung it over his shoulder. "What was all that you were saying about a nexus and Gates?" He wanted badly to smoke, but now was his chance to get some answers.

Bernard continued to stare a moment, then seemed to catch himself. "It's quite a lot to explain. Especially since I don't know how much you remember."

Bob narrowed his eyes, bemused. "Remember?"

"Excuse me, I'm old. I meant to say, I don't know how much you already know."

"Pretend I don't know anything."

At this, Bernard seemed unaccountably sad. "I see. Of course, of course. Tell you what." He stirred in his seat and Quaker hopped and fluttered down to the floor, stretching her wings. Then the old wizard stood. "I've a hut two rows down from yours. You can't miss it. Stop by tonight, and I'll try to explain."

"Alright, sure," said Bob. He felt even more questions burgeoning, formless, in his mind.

Bernard retrieved his staff where it had been propped on the table, then made for the door. Quaker waddled just behind him. The stairs produced barely a sound as they descended.

Osivia breathed a sigh of relief. "I hate ducks."

M. V. PRINDLE

CHAPTER SIXTEEN:
UNDER THE TAPESTRIES

Osivia excused herself when they exited Arbor House. As she fluttered into the afternoon air, Bob headed to the kitchen. It being that awkward time of day between lunch and dinner, the covered deck area was empty. Hirrell stood with several other cooks behind the line, preparing to feed hundreds in a few hours. The yellow-haired elf noticed Bob's approach and grinned. Hirrell declared he was on break, grabbed two bowls of steaming vegetable stew, then came around the cook-line to sit with Bob. Bob smoked before he ate. They shared small talk, discussing the weather, complaining to each other about minor things. Bob lamented that Torael was pressuring him into taking lessons from Kelael, and Hirrell bemoaned the constant, thankless work of kitchen life. What neither of them said—what hung over them like a specter—was that they were simply happy to be out of the mines, and all their petty complaints were nothing—*nothing*—compared to the troubles they'd left behind. When the meal was done, Bob lit the pipe anew and shared it with Hirrell. Soon the moment was over, and Hirrell bid Bob farewell to reenter the kitchen.

Bob set off across the central green toward the huts. His belly was full, his need for nicotine fulfilled, and his mind began to wander. The sun was descending, shifting the light to a muted yellow. The sounds of the Koreka filled his ears—the echoes of distant conversation, the buzz of dragonflies, the occasional crack of wood against wood; the sounds of branches swaying, of wind rippling the grass, of the flit and twitter of birds; the sound of the earth deeply humming an endless dirge, the voice of the rocks a resonant melody that reached out to him, reached into him, calling.

BOB THE WIZARD

Wait. The sounds of the rocks and the earth warbled through him, strumming him like a guitar string. Voices. Calling. Singing. Everywhere.

He looked up. He'd made it halfway to the huts and now stood mere yards from the dense foliage and trees surrounding the equipment sheds. A flicker of movement caught his eye within the tangle of plants. He stepped toward it, ivy and twigs crunching underfoot. The deep humming intensified. He stepped again. Something was calling him wordlessly. Beckoning.

"Hello?" Bob called hoarsely into the trees.

The world was awash with sound. A slow melody twined around his insides. What was happening? What…

The movement came again, just ahead of him among the bushes. Was it just a tree branch swaying in the wind? No—something stepped out of the foliage, cast in shadows.

It was a person. Or was it? Was it a trick of the light? Bob stepped closer yet again and the shadows resolved into a small bipedal figure. Bob stared intensely, waiting for movement. Had someone infiltrated the Koreka? Was it something mundane, like an elf pulling weeds? The longer he looked, the more convinced he became he was not looking at a human or an En'hari. It moved again, slow, and he saw it: a human shaped creature, the size of a child, with a round, oversized, hairless head and bumpy, brown skin. It regarded him from the shadows with hollow eyes. The branches of the trees swayed slightly in the wind, temporarily illuminating the thing's face. It appeared to be made of earth. Its eyes were two coal-black pits, but deep within them were two tiny points of purple light for pupils. The creature possessed no nose or mouth, so its expression was unreadable. Bob was frozen, unable to distinguish between fascination and terror. The little earth-person raised a hand as if in greeting, displaying four clumpy fingers.

"Bob, are you alright?"

Fan's voice cut through everything. The humming melody was abruptly gone, the creature with it. Bob turned. Gorrelai's half-brother stood just outside the copse of trees, concern etched across his face. Birdsong and the buzzing of bugs were the only sounds.

Bob had no idea what was going on. The sounds he'd heard—the music—was something he'd told himself was madness. It was just the strain of being a slave twisting his mind. But now he was free, not in the mines but in the Koreka, and this latest experience had been the most vivid yet. He feared the madness that had begun in the mines had followed him, and now had somehow gotten worse. But even more, he feared that what he'd seen and heard was real.

He approached Fan on the green. "Yes, of course I'm all right," he lied. "Just exploring a bit."

Fan studied him in silence.

"Saw Gorrelai. He's much improved." To his relief, the smile he offered Fan was genuine.

The En'hari relaxed and returned the smile. "Yes, the doctor says he will make a full recovery. He will be back to kicking things over in no time."

Bob glanced at the sky, which was transitioning from ochre to orange. "Headed to the huts. Walk with me?"

"I would love to walk with you, Sora Kelai."

They walked.

As they arrived at the huts, Bob saw Osivia swirling between the meager yards, chit-chatting away with two different groups of En'harae. She seemed to be relaying snarky messages from one group to the other. Peals of laughter swelled after a delivery. Bob called out to her. She fluttered silently down to him and Fan, smiling.

When Bob had mentioned that he was en route to visit Bernard, Fan had asked if he could tag along. Seeing no harm in it—and wanting a friendly face along anyway—Bob had agreed.

"We're headed to Bernard's," said Bob now to the faerie. "You want to come?"

"Visit a wizard? Of course!"

"Great," said Bob. "You know which one is his? He said it was a couple of rows down from mine."

Osivia wrinkled her nose. "I could guess. There's one hut in particular that really stands out. That one is probably Bernard's."

"Stands out how?"

She grinned. "You'll see."

Bob and Fan exchanged a look.

When they arrived at the correct row, Bob immediately understood what Osivia had meant. Ahead, past the regular fare of brown and tan canvas, was a multicolored heap of layered cloth, high as a small house. It looked like a giant pile of rugs. As he got closer, Bob saw that it was actually just another hut, but it had been totally covered—all but the entrance—with overlapping tapestries. There were reds and blues, oranges and purples, golds and whites. Bob could make out a few pictures peeking out from underneath the layers, and he could swear one of them was Michelangelo's Sistine Chapel.

Hard to miss indeed.

"Odd sense of home décor," said Bob. "Anna would hate it."

"She didn't like mess, huh?"

Bob shook his head. "She'd straighten the picture frames in the living room almost every day. My sock drawer gave her fits."

"I kind of like it," said Osivia. "It's… different. Different means interesting. Like you, Bob."

Bob grunted in reply.

Fan smiled and glanced at Bob. "I have never met a *Tesera*, but they have a reputation for doing things like this. Odd things. I look forward to hearing his reasons."

The Hari word was familiar, but Bob was drawing a blank. "*Tesera?*" he asked.

"Oh," said Fan. "*Tesera*. Wizard."

M. V. PRINDLE

Bob adjusted the rifle on his shoulder. "Right," he muttered. The sky was reddening. "Well, now or never, I suppose."

But as he turned to enter the tapestried hut, he was stopped short by Bernard standing just outside the tent-flap.

"A fine evening," said the old wizard in his nasally, scratchy voice. He leaned on his sanded, tree-branch staff, the crystal atop it winking in the evening light. The wizard peered at him through his whitish mane, which seemed to cover his whole face while his hat was on. "A fine time for some wine, wouldn't you say?"

Bob cleared his throat. "No thanks to the wine. Got anything to smoke?" Bob still had plenty of tobacco, but if he could smoke someone else's… why wouldn't he?

"Of course," said Bernard with a wry smile. His hazel eyes fell on Osivia, then Fan. "You are all welcome." He looked back to Bob. "But I'm afraid I must ask you to leave the rifle outside the door."

Bob hesitated. Then he remembered the rifle wasn't even loaded. Besides, for some reason, his gut was telling him he could trust Bernard. He shrugged off the rifle and propped it next to the tent flap, where Michelangelo's hand of God aimlessly pointed amid a patchwork of images. Fan had taken an expertly crafted slingshot from his belt and approached the hut, ostensibly to leave the weapon next to the rifle.

"Oh, that's quite alright, you can take that in," said Bernard with a polite smile.

Bob saw understanding bloom on Fan's face and wished he shared it.

"Are any of you carrying any other metal?" asked Bernard. "Other weapons, metal buttons, anything?"

Fan shook his head. Bob patted his pockets, reached in, and brought out the pink lighter Bernard had thrown him in the forest. He proffered it to the wizard.

Bernard's tangle of eyebrows rose in recognition. "Ah, yes. Plenty more where that came from. Just leave it with the gun, if you don't mind."

"Um," Osivia began sheepishly. "My pen has some metal. But I need it to write."

Bernard stroked his mane. "No problem, my dear. I believe I have some faerie pens as well."

Bob was definitely confused.

Osivia flew down and gingerly placed her pen in the grass next to the rifle. Once it left her hand, Bob couldn't even pick it out, it was so small.

"Now," said Bernard, "right this way." He vanished behind the tent flap.

Bob, Fan and Osivia all looked at each other. Bob shrugged, stooped a bit, and stepped through behind the wizard. He was completely unprepared for what followed.

When he was eleven, Bob's mother had taken him to an amusement park. Not a local fair—one of the big ones. He'd managed to revisit the park several times afterward, even taking Danny once for his eighth birthday. But that first visit had made quite an impression on him. It stuck out in his memory as being the first time he'd experienced sheer terror and utter joy simultaneously. He'd been tall for eleven, and gangly. Tall enough to ride the Killer Croc, the biggest, meanest, fastest rollercoaster in the park. It had blown his mind. The feel of the air building pockets on his skin, the thrill of accelerated movement, the world whipping around him in multicolored streaks. He thought he might die at any moment yet felt unaccountably alive.

It was this experience that dominated his thoughts after stepping into Bernard's hut. He suddenly felt as if he were rushing through a tunnel. The world was nothing but streaks of color, rippling and wobbling, almost blinding. He felt no air pressure, but an unmistakable feeling of acceleration weighed on his body as if he were an astronaut leaving the atmosphere. His ears were awash with white noise, like he was standing next to a jet engine. A point of white light directly ahead—the end of the tunnel—rushed up to meet him like a barreling train. He tried to cover his face but found he couldn't move.

Then, as abruptly as it began, the journey was over. He found himself standing in the foyer of a sturdy house, floorboards gently creaking under a welcome mat of woven straw.

"Make way, make way," said Bernard, gesturing him forward. Dazed, Bob moved toward the wizard's voice just before he heard Fan's feet plant on the floor right behind him.

"Oh, my goodness!" exclaimed Osivia from somewhere. "That was exhilarating! What happened? Magic! It was magic, right?"

Bob was getting his bearings. He'd teleported enough times to know that's what'd happened—teleportation. He, Fan, and Osivia had started in the Koreka and ended up just inside the front door of this house. However, using the Gatekey, he'd only ever teleported maybe half a mile, at the most. He got the sense that whatever had just swept him here had taken him much farther than that.

The house was impressive. Its taupe, plaster walls and spacious, open rooms made him nostalgic for Earth. In the living room, a hearth set into the back wall crackled pleasantly behind a black metal curtain. On an adjacent wall, two large rectangular windows looked out upon the night. The sun had been just beginning to set in the Koreka, but here, outside the windows was nothing but velvety black.

"Magic it was, Osivia Glenbrook," said Bernard, placing his hat on a slender rack by the entrance. "Come in, come in. Oh, I don't believe we've been introduced, young man." He held out a hand.

"I am Fan." They shook. "You are Bernard, of course. Pleased to meet you, sir. I have heard many tales of the *Teserae* but have never met one."

"Well," said Bernard, "now you have." He turned and gestured at the walls. "You'll have to excuse the lack of decoration. All my tapestries are in use elsewhere."

"In use," said Bob, "doing what, exactly?"

Bernard gestured for him to sit. A round polished living table, its curved legs carved to resemble paws, sat between a cream-colored plush couch and a crimson, cushioned wing chair. Bob shrugged and plopped down on the couch. He nearly groaned with pleasure at the soft resistance of the cushions. Fan sat down lightly beside him, hands on his knees. Osivia was hovering by a bookshelf to Bob's right.

"The tapestries," said Bernard, making his way to the red chair, "help the air spirits to remember where I want them to take people who step into my hut." He propped his staff against the chair and sat. "Terrible memories, air spirits. The older the spirit, the better they catch on to things. But air spirits are almost always young. It's their nature. Anyway, in order to achieve the magic of teleporting great distances, one must possess at least one object that has been to the intended destination. Preferably an object that was at that location for a long time. Those tapestries were on these walls gathering dust for a decade, most of them, so they are a strong reminder to the spirits. Now, you might be wondering why I put not one, but *all* my tapestries on top of the hut. It's just a safety measure. To really, *really* make sure the spirits take you to the right place. Wouldn't want them to forget where they're taking you halfway through the trip!"

Bob remembered the swirling, high-pressure tunnel of color and thought he understood. Air spirits had somehow been responsible for transporting him. The prospect of being dropped in that tunnel by whatever was carrying him was... unsettling. He turned his mind to a more comforting subject. "So, how about that tobacco?"

"Ah yes," said Bernard, and leaned forward, reaching to a drawer set into the pawed table.

All at once Bob realized the room was lit by an overhead electric lamp. He pointed at it, brow raised, staring at Bernard.

"I have electricity," said Bernard sheepishly. "There's a generator in the basement. I don't use it every day, but when I have guests..." He shrugged.

Bob glanced at the open windows that looked out on the dark. "Aren't you afraid someone will see? Wonder what's up with the house that glows at night?"

"Not at all," said Bernard, waving a dismissive hand. "No one knows how to see us."

There was that phrase again. Perhaps Bernard could hide his house as well as the Koreka.

"These air spirits," said Osivia, "they took us from the Koreka to here?"

"That's right," said Bernard, fiddling with the drawer. It seemed to be stuck.

"Where is here?" asked Fan.

"Just over seven hundred miles east of the Koreka, along Engoria's east coast. We're on the outskirts of Bruster, the kingdom's largest coastal city. It's about half a day's ride to the northeast." He was still struggling with the drawer. "Damn thing."

Bob lifted his foot and brought his heel down on the table. He added no force. Gravity and weight were enough. The drawer popped open.

"Ah, a concerted effort," muttered Bernard, pulling out an ornate pipe.

From the couch Bob could see a mishmash of trinkets in the drawer, including several colorful plastic lighters. Bob drew his own pipe from his pocket and placed it on the table.

"Oh yes," said the old wizard, pausing over a tray of shredded tobacco. "Osivia, look on that desk over there in the corner. I believe I have some faerie implements in that silver cup."

"Why did you make us leave our metal?" asked Bob.

"Help yourself, Bob," said Bernard, setting the tray of tobacco in front of him. The old wizard leaned back, pipe in one hand. With the other, he stroked his tangled, white mane. "I think I'll let Fan answer that one."

Bob looked curiously at his blue friend.

Fan seemed surprised for a moment, but then shrugged. "Well, as a boy, I was taught that the *Tessat*, um, the spirits, are of Life, and that forged metal is of Death. They are opposite. Because of this, many spirits fear metal. Our shamans, the *Tessaeshi*, will not even touch it. It is said… It is said that forged metal can kill the spirits." He looked at Bernard as if hoping this was the explanation the wizard was expecting.

BOB THE WIZARD

"Quite right," said Bernard. "Humans have only been here for about a thousand years, and before then, there was no forged metal on Hub, at least not on Sheral. The humans' arrival marked the beginning of many troubles for the En'harae, the introduction of metal—namely iron, and more recently, steel—being just one of them, but possibly the most significant. Tell me, Fan, do the En'harae now implement metal of their own?" He spoke the question as if he already knew the answer.

"We do," said Fan. "Though, as I said, the Tessaeshi will not touch it. Mostly it is the Gasheera who make use of it."

"I get it," said Osivia from the corner of the room. "We had to leave our metal because the spirits are afraid of it. And the spirits were to bring us here." A moment later she was peering into a silver cup from above. "Oh, nifty!"

"Are you saying," said Bob to Bernard, "that the spirits would refuse to take us if we were carrying metal?"

"Most probably," said Bernard, puffing on his pipe.

Bob grabbed a lighter and sat back. "Then how did you have that lighter you gave me? The pink one. How did you get it from here to the Koreka?"

"Mmm," said Bernard. "Quite observant, aren't you? Well, as it turns out, the longer you have a connection to a particular kind of spirit, the more that kind learns to trust you. The air spirits and I have had a relationship for a long, long time. So, I can get away with little things, like carrying a lighter with a small amount of metal. However, I doubt even I could convince them to carry me across the continent while I was holding that rifle. That would be too much for them, even if it was me. There are ways to shield oneself from the backlash, but it would be a risky endeavor, in any case."

"I thought you said air spirits have a short memory," said Osivia. Her voice had a hollow, echoing quality to it, and Bob realized she was talking from inside the cup. "How can they remember their relationship with you?"

"A fine question!" declared Bernard. "Bunch of detectives, aren't you?" He chuckled. "The answer, my dear faerie, is instinct. They are born with some measure of communal memory. It is individual memory that eludes them."

This didn't really make sense to Bob, but he decided it wasn't important right now. He'd come here seeking answers. "Speaking of the rifle, where did it come from? You spoke of Gates at the meeting. Please, what do you know about them?" He lit the dragon pipe.

Bernard eyed him through the smoke. "Well, you said to pretend that you don't know anything. But if you are interested in Astral Gates, clearly you do know *something*. Tell me, Bob, are you from Earth?"

No use in hiding it. He nodded. "Texas."

Bernard gestured at himself with his pipe stem. "Montana."

Fan looked back and forth between them.

A light like a flashing bulb emanated from the silver cup in the room's corner, then Osivia fluttered out of it happily. "You've got some great stuff in there, Bernard."

Bob was staring at the old wizard. "So, there *is* a Gate to Earth on Hub…"

"That there is. More than one. The one at the Nexus is the most famous among the knowledgeable, but it's been shut down. Besides that, its guarded. But before all that, sometime during the First World War—I'd guess 1917—the British discovered the Gates and attempted to establish a colony. They moved in weapons to supply a small invasion force. Their efforts failed, thanks in large part to the wizards. Until your discovery of that rifle, we'd assumed the Nexus was their only port of entry. But the Engorians could not be getting the weapons from the Nexus. Its guardian is too powerful. They must have stumbled on another Gate. This is troubling news for the resistance. The Engorians are fierce enough without firearms to aid them."

This explained the British flags. "So, this Gate to Earth at this Nexus… it leads to somewhere in England?"

"That it does. I first came through it in 1987, during a brief time in which the wizards were… recruiting."

"What about the guardian?" asked Osivia, fluttering over to the couch. She sneezed in a cloud of smoke. Bob noticed she'd taken out her notebook.

"She'd struck some deal with the wizards at the time," said Bernard. "She was more amenable back then."

Bob glanced at the lighters on the table. "You brought all these lighters with you in 1987?"

Bernard sighed. "Young lady, I'd ask that you not write this part down."

Osivia bookmarked the notebook with her pen and closed it.

"And none of what I'm about to tell you should leave this room. It is imperative that this information not reach the Engorians. Understood?"

Fan nodded respectfully and Bob grunted in assent.

Bernard cleared his throat. "Have you heard of a place called Azenbul?"

"I have," said Osivia. Fan was nodding.

"No," said Bob, coughing slightly.

"The Wizard's Tower," said Osivia. She'd perched on the couch, behind Bob, probably in an effort to avoid the smoke. "That's what the Engorians call it."

"Yes, well," said Bernard, "they know of its existence. It is a mystery to them, a folk tale. And it should stay that way. The truth is, Azenbul contains several Astral Gates of its own, one of them to Earth. They remain sealed most of the time. Sometimes, we open them for various reasons. The first time I returned to Earth, thirteen years had passed on Hub, yet on Earth it was still 1995. And what's more, that would imply that time moves faster on Hub than on Earth, but the years here *feel* longer. There's a mystery for you." He winked. "Anyway, I've returned to Earth three times. Each time, I return with various technological comforts. Only enough for myself, you see? The wizards have strict rules regarding technology. I only get away with what I do because I'm one of them."

M. V. PRINDLE

"This is an amazing story," said Fan quietly.

"Fascinating," agreed Osivia.

Bob's mind was racing, working to absorb this new information. He had so many more questions. Where to begin? He took a long draw on the pipe and let it out slow. Start at the top, of course. "Have you heard of Galvidon?"

Bernard pursed his lips. "Can't say that I have."

Bob racked his brain, tried to dredge up the things Galvidon had said to him. Anything the old wizard knew that might get him closer to the Gray Man would be welcome. "What about… the Galon Var?" This was the race that Galvidon had claimed as his own.

Bernard looked up sharply. "Where did you hear that?"

"From Galvidon. The asshole I'm chasing."

Deep concern cast a shadow over Bernard. "Tell me of this Galvidon. Spare no detail."

Bob told his story again. He kept it as short as he could and managed to avoid crying. Fan and Osivia, who'd both heard the tale before, listened politely in silence. Bob started with coming home to his family's murder, skimmed over most of his travels, and ended with the slaves' rescue at the hands of the resistance. He was particularly careful to convey the things Galvidon had said to him in Oath Keep's dungeon.

For almost a full minute after Bob had finished talking, Bernard stared into space. His pipe was cashed, and he set it down. "A remarkable story if I've ever heard one. This Galvidon spoke shades of the truth, Bob. The Precedentials were real, the Anterior is real. The Electum, the Order of Tag Nah and their Eliminators, all real. As for what God has to do with it… well, I'll leave that for philosophers to decide. But I am greatly concerned by this Galvidon's presence on Hub. We've managed to keep this realm sealed off to the Order for… well, for a long time."

"He usually leaves quickly," said Bob. "He finds his victims, these Electum, and then exits through a Gate to the next 'realm.' He could already be gone from here. Long gone."

BOB THE WIZARD

Bernard scratched at his hairy white chin. "I doubt it. He went to the trouble to get close to Flaire, to become a Councilor. Surely that was for a reason. I believe he is attempting to establish a foothold of control. He may have already contacted the Order." He suddenly stood. "Wait, wait, wait," he muttered, striding to the bookshelf. He selected a large volume the size of a coffee table book and returned to the wing chair.

As the old wizard got comfortable, Bob saw the title of the book was *Astral Cosmology and Interwoven Structure*.

Bernard flipped to the index in the back and then rifled through pages. "Ah, here we are." He peered down at the book. "Ah, just as I thought. The next alignment isn't until a week from now."

"Alignment?" asked Osivia.

"Astral alignment," said Bernard. "The Astraverse moves, like everything else in the universe, in cycles. Communication through the astraplasm is impossible between certain locations until they align properly."

Bob glanced at Fan. "You know what he's talking about?"

Fan shook his head.

"What is, 'astraplasm'?" Bob asked Bernard.

"It's the stuff between the realms. The stuff that holds them in place. Its kind of like jelly. Astral jelly."

Bob stared at him blankly.

"Very well, just one moment." He flipped through several pages, found what he wanted, and set the book down on the table facing Bob, smoothing down the pages. He then got up again, snatching up his staff. He leaned on it as he shuffled back to the bookshelf.

Bob studied the open pages. It was a strange image—like a starburst, only the "rays" coming from the circular center were crooked and angular, like tree branches. In one corner it was labeled, *The Astraverse*. The center of the image—enclosed in the circle—was a mandala-like pattern of circles and squares. Outside the center circle, within the "branches," were thousands of tiny circular dots, much like clusters of stars would look on a star map.

Bernard lay another book next to the first. It was also open to an image. The second book showed a globby starburst shape with tangled branches radiating from the center. "This first picture, as I'm sure you can see from the labeling, is a best-guess map of the Astraverse. Much of it is conjecture. This second picture might help you understand the first a little better. It's a brain cell. More specifically—a multipolar neuron."

Fan and Osivia were quiet.

Bob stared at the images. "Are you saying... the Astraverse is a giant brain cell?"

Bernard chuckled. "Certainly not. No. Maybe. Well... probably not. But the point is, the Astraverse has many things in common with a microscopic cell. Note the nucleus. The branching things are called dendrites on a neuron, so we call them astral dendrites when referring to that part of the Astraverse. In a cell, the various components are held within the cell wall by cytoplasm, a jelly-like substance. The same is so for the Astraverse."

"Astraplasm," said Osivia, sounding unsure.

"Yes," said Bernard. "Which brings me to my original point. The nearest realm to Hub where the Order has a sizeable presence is called Chaysan. Here." His finger rested on a little circle on the map just under the base of an astral dendrite. "We are here." He pointed to a large circle blocking the base of an adjacent dendrite. "On Hub. Because of the way the Astraverse moves, and the relative positions of the two realms, communication between them is impossible for a large part of the Astral Cycle—the Astral Year, if you like. But they will align for communication in about eight days. Therefore, when considering Galvidon the Eliminator and his efforts to consolidate power in Engoria, I predict, with all my wizardly wisdom, that he will be communicating with the Order of Tag Nah through the astraplasm on that very day."

Bob tried not to get excited. "And... what can we do about that?"

Bernard shrugged, then sighed with relief as he lowered himself once again into the chair. "Without further information, there is really only one thing to do. When Galvidon makes the call, we listen in."

BOB THE WIZARD

"How are we supposed to do that?" asked Osivia.

"Oh," mused Bernard, "I know the perfect duck for the job."

… M. V. PRINDLE

CHAPTER SEVENTEEN:
MYSTERY AND METAPHOR

Bob woke the following morning from a dream of deep, resonant songs that vibrated his bones. He did not feel particularly rested. Aside from the strange dream, he'd remained at Bernard's late into the night after a particularly long day. By the time the wizard had returned them to the Koreka—a trick he managed by having everyone touch his sanded wooden staff—it was past midnight. Despite the bizarre truths buzzing around his head, Bob had fallen asleep as soon as he was horizontal.

He drank deeply from a waterskin before packing the dragon pipe's bowl. He coughed and hacked for two minutes straight before lighting it. He ducked out of the tent flap and almost fell on his face.

He stumbled but kept on his feet. Something was piled up in front of the hut's entrance. It was rocks. His fumbling exit had knocked a few of them over. They lay in a haphazard pile directly in front of his tent flap. The dirt around them was formed into swirls and lumps.

"The fuck?" murmured Bob, looking both ways down the row of tents. He saw many En'harae, but they were just going about their own business, nothing suspicious about them. Bob eyed the rocks. What was it? A warning? Maybe it was a show of respect—some kind of En'hari tradition he wasn't aware of. He puffed on the pipe thoughtfully, then left the stones where they lay and walked toward the Koreka's center.

Bob arrived at the kitchen and waited in line. The pile of rocks was already forgotten. He saw Fan leaving the deck and waved him over.

"Going back to Bernard's tonight. You coming?"

"I cannot, Sora Kelai. He is very interesting, but my Kafeh calls."

"Oh yeah? And what's that?"

"I do not know the word. I make clothing."

"Fan, I do believe you're a tailor."

The En'hari smiled. "Yes, this is it. I am a tailor. I have dreamed long of the day I witness the clothing I have made worn by a free people. Though, Melanae has asked me to repair some leather armor." He shrugged. "This will have to do, I suppose."

Bob waited in line for another fifteen minutes before he reached the front. He saw Osivia fly by but let her be. She'd already made it clear she'd be happy to return to Bernard's come evening. Hirrell was too busy to take a break to eat with him, but when Bob was looking for a table, he saw Torael sitting by himself at the deck's corner.

Bob sat across from the Quaylen Dah. "Eating alone, huh? I thought you were popular."

Torael smirked. "They prefer to admire me from a few feet away. It is alright, I am used to being… separate."

Bob nodded, a little dismayed that his jibe may have stung more than he intended. He knew how Torael felt.

"Melanae is teaching me Engorian," said Torael after a moment, "so I may improve in speaking."

"Oh, she a good teacher?"

The En'hari shrugged. "She taught Kelael. He speaks it much better than I. Though, he does many things better than I."

"Shit, that reminds me, I'm supposed to be meeting him about now." Bob jammed a final bite of breakfast in his mouth.

"The spirits help you if you are late," said Torael with a wink.

Bob hurried back toward the Koreka's center. The training field spanned a large swathe of green ahead of him to the left. Coming from the kitchens, the fastest way there was to cut through the equipment sheds. Absently, he was thinking about the things Bernard had said, which led him to think of the dream he'd had, which in turn reminded him of the strange pile of rocks. He realized, as he approached the dense foliage around the sheds, that that damn music was back. A low rumble, constant, like the hum of an industrial machine. A drawn-out melody, like an opera sung by a vast, unknowable giant. It was one voice, ten, a hundred, a thousand voices.

Bob forced himself to stay calm. Sometime the previous night, he'd begun to suspect that these strange experiences—the songs of the earth—were somehow connected with the spirits. After all, Bob had seen a spirit, hadn't he? It had opened a glowing doorway into the Koreka. He'd been transported across a continent by the spirits. The thought that the bizarre music was not madness, and in fact was the spirits somehow trying to communicate with him, was a comfort he didn't yet dare embrace. The thing he'd seen, here by the sheds, was so different from what he generally considered to be possible, he still feared it and what it might mean. Yet, avoiding it would yield no answers. He moved deeper into the trees.

The strength of the voices intensified as he moved toward the center of the copse. Individual voices began to break away from the whole. "Bob," a rumbly voice whispered behind him.

He whirled. No one there.

"Bob," said another, similar voice from off to his right.

"Sora Kelai," said another, from the bushes.

"Robert James Caplan," said another faintly.

"Bob the Wizard," said another.

He realized he'd reached the center of the Koreka. A large, slate-gray boulder sat among the trees. It was fat and squat and round. The loudest, deepest voice emanated from it. Atop it sat the little mud person, its round, clumpy head outlined in the greenish light of the copse. It's tiny purple pupils flashed from the pits of its eyes. "Robert James Caplan," it rumbled heavily. "You are new. Do you remember?"

"Remember?" Bob repeated. Something Bernard had said after the council meeting flashed in his mind.

BOB THE WIZARD

Especially since I don't know how much you remember.

"What am I supposed to remember?" He asked the creature atop the boulder.

A series of heavy crunches tore through his thoughts. He turned to see Kelael approaching in a shaft of daylight. "You are late, Sora Kelai."

The voices had vanished again. Bob swiveled back to the boulder. There the rock remained, yet it now lacked a mud creature.

"Did you…" said Bob, turning back to Kelael. "Did you see that?"

Kelael glanced to where Bob had been staring atop the boulder. "Did I see what?"

It wasn't madness. It couldn't be. The experiences were too consistent. And he had to talk about it, or he might *really* go mad.

"There was a creature. Like a little person, made of mud. It spoke to me."

Kelael, clearly already at the edge of his patience, waved a hand sharply. "It was probably just a spirit."

"Should I be worried?" asked Bob, already deeply worried.

"Of course not," snapped the En'hari. "Now let us begin. I do not have all day to waste on you." He turned and stalked through the underbrush toward the training field. Just like that, they were done discussing spirits.

"Get your sword up."

Bob lifted the practice sword slightly.

"The point directly at my face. *Directly*, I said."

For the next few hours, Bob ducked and sidestepped. He swatted at Kelael with his wooden sword. He rolled and tumbled, jumped and jabbed. He parried, dodged, and thrust. Spun and swung. Danced and clashed. His efforts yielded naught but exhaustion and defeat.

"You move too much," Kelael told him. "Move only when necessary.

In motion, you are off balance."

"If I don't move, you'll just hit me!" panted Bob, clutching bruised ribs.

"I will hit you anyway," said Kelael steadily.

Bob sighed. "Alright, fine. I should just stand still?"

Kelael shook his head. He arranged himself into the basic stance he'd taught Bob at the beginning of the lesson. "Strike me," he said calmly.

Bob made sure his stance was okay, and then made a swift chop for Kelael's shoulder. He felt the wooden blade cleave through empty air and suddenly the dulled edge of Kelael's sword was at his neck.

"You're dead," said Kelael.

The elf was standing mere inches from where he had been at the time of Bob's strike. He had sidestepped the minimum distance to avoid Bob's sword and moved in for the kill.

"You see?" said Kelael, lowering his weapon. "I moved very little, yet you are dead, and I am not. Now, we will add the shield. They are over there. Hurry up, I must meet with Melanae before lunchtime."

———◉———

"This place is amazing! I can fly right out of it, and it all disappears! Then I can fly back in!" Osivia's skin flashed with white light. Conversations drifted across the rows of huts.

"And the craftsmanship of the walls is really first rate. How did they build all this in the middle of the forest? I wonder if it was built slowly over time, or if they had to scramble to build it all as fast as they could. That doesn't seem realistic, they'd make too much noise. Ooh! Maybe the spirits are also blocking sounds! So, the spirits must have been doing their thing when the En'harae started building. And that means Bernard must have been here since the beginning. Unless they had someone else who could do magic. A shaman, maybe. The Tessaeshi."

She seemed to be talking mostly to herself, so Bob just listened as he walked. His back was sore from Kelael's lessons.

BOB THE WIZARD

"And the wildlife!" Osivia went on. "Did you know there are three distinct species of dragonflies in this area? It's a good thing they're small. Dragonflies and faeries don't exactly get along. Sometimes they think we're lunch. Don't even get me started on the time the entire Faerie Commune went to war with this one kind of dragonfly... Let me tell you, it takes a lot to convince a faerie to fight, let alone go to war."

Bob had taken a nap after lunch. It was now a couple of hours before sunset, and the sky was a pale, cloudless blue. They passed by the row his hut was on, jogging his memory.

"Did I tell you about the rocks?" he asked as they approached Bernard's lumpy, colorful hut.

He told her about waking up and finding a pile of rocks outside the tent flap. Then, sensing some connection between the two events, he told her about the creature he'd seen that Kelael had said was a spirit.

"Fascinating," she said. "It seems like this spirit is trying to tell you something."

"I hope Bernard can help me figure it out," said Bob, and ducked under the old wizard's tent flap. This time, he braced for the intense journey.

"Sounds like an earth spirit," said Bernard. His voice floated from the house's small kitchen—where the wizard was rummaging—to where Bob now sat on the cream-colored couch.

"Okay," said Bob, raising his voice so it travelled. "What does it want with me?"

Osivia floated just above the desk in the corner, where, upon her request, Bernard had placed *Astral Cosmology and Interwoven Structure* for her to read. Outside, the sunlight was a deep yellow. The lamp on the ceiling was off, leaving the room in a half-lit twilight.

Bernard rounded a plaster corner and entered the living room carrying a bottle of wine, a wine glass, a frying pan, a saltshaker, and a kitchen sponge. "Well, that depends," answered the old wizard, setting the odd assortment of objects on the pawed living table. "Spirits typically

194

all want the same thing—a partner. A host, if you like. They have trouble affecting the physical world without one."

"Why do they want to? Affect the… physical world, I mean."

Bernard sat in his red wing chair with a sigh. "I'm not sure. Perhaps reproduction." He moved the wine glass to the center of the table.

"What?" Bob wasn't sure he liked where this was going.

"Well, the spirits are born in the astraplasm around a particular realm as reflections of concepts ideated by the conscious entities within that realm."

Bob blinked. "What?" he repeated.

"Never mind," said Bernard. "Their motivations are irrelevant. What matters is the result." He exhaled sharply and the wine glass rose in the air of its own accord, spinning slowly, hovering a few inches above the table.

Bob saw a translucent figure dart across the room behind Bernard. The flash of movement was accompanied by a sound that Bob could swear was a child's giggle.

Bernard sat, relaxed. He exhaled sharply again, like a man firing a blowgun. The wine bottle rose from the table into the air, approached the slowly spinning glass, and then began to pour wine as though gripped by an invisible waiter.

The translucent figure darted up next to the table where it paused. It appeared to be a cherubic child, its outline and form insinuated by slight disturbances in the air. It looked at Bob, and Bob thought it was grinning. He heard that giggle again as it darted away.

"Osivia, did you see that?" called Bob, eying at the floating glass and bottle.

"See what?" she said absently, absorbed in her reading.

"She didn't see it," said Bernard calmly. He sharply inhaled, and the glass and bottle rotated and set themselves down upon the table with no drop of liquid spilled. "But you did. Do you know what that means?"

BOB THE WIZARD

"She wasn't paying attention?" said Bob drily. He was doing okay with the wine staring him in the face, begging him to drink it. He just needed to smoke. That'd be enough. He took out the dragon pipe.

Bernard bore a serious expression. "It means you, Bob, *are* a wizard after all." He didn't sound the least bit surprised.

"It does?" Bob didn't feel any more wizardly than he had as a slave. No Gatekey, no magic.

"Only about half of the En'harae can see the spirits. Of those, only about half can hear them. And of those that can hear them, only about half can command their power. These, the humans call shamans. The En'harae call them Tessaeshi." Bernard inhaled sharply and the wine glass rose again and floated gingerly into his awaiting hand. Bob saw the air-baby dart by again. The old wizard drained the two fingers of wine in the glass, then reached down and set it upon the table himself. "Humans, on the other hand… humans that can interact with the spirits of Hub are rare. *Very* rare. They are called wizards. The Teserae."

Bob, not wanting to be a total mooch, had brought along his own stash this afternoon. He commenced packing the dragon pipe. "At the moment, I don't feel particularly magical." He lit the pipe with a series of rapid draws and spoke with the pipe in his teeth. "Though, I admit, I want to know more. How do I… do that?" He nodded at the wine glass.

"Well, it's different for every wizard, and different for each kind of spirit. In my experience, no magic user—shaman or wizard—is able to control more than one or two kinds of spirits. It's like certain spirits are simply drawn to certain people, and vice versa. For example, I am able to control spirits of air and spirits of light. Other kinds of spirits I can see, but not hear or control. Furthermore, a wizard requires a focus for each type of spirit they command."

Bob puffed thoughtfully. "A focus? What do you mean?"

Bernard nodded as if he'd anticipated the question. "In order to answer that, I'm afraid we must get into another lesson."

Bob spread his hands. "By all means, teach. Lay it on me."

"First I must warn you that the only way to discuss these matters with a layman is through metaphor."

"Like the brain cell thing," said Bob.

"Like the brain cell thing," acknowledged Bernard. He leaned forward and sat upon the edge of the chair. "Okay. As you are well aware, all matter in the universe is constituted in physical bodies. I have one, you have one." He lifted the wine glass in one hand. "The glass has one. Now, the metaphor about the brain cell is helpful to understand the shape of the Astraverse. But to understand its function, we must consider things differently. Think of a subway system. In this metaphor, the physical universe is the 'above ground,' and the Astraverse is the network of tunnels, under the 'ground,' that allow for travel. You with me so far?"

"Sure," said Bob.

"The subway of the Astraverse has entry and exit points all over the universe. Many are in the same observable universe in which Earth resides. Some are in other parts of the universe, parts completely inaccessible by physical travel.

"Now, back to bodies. All physical bodies have a corresponding astral body. Each physical body—and I'm including inanimate objects here—is like this wine glass. It exists perfectly well on its own. Yet it remains empty. Unfulfilled. Its true potential unmet. But if we introduce an astral body…" He lifted the bottle in his free hand and poured another two fingers of red liquid into the glass. He replaced the bottle upon the table, then held up the glass with thumb and forefinger, gazing at it intently. "Ah, perfection."

"Perfection?"

"Well, no. This is rather cheap wine, after all. But you take my meaning. The glass is a container waiting to be filled. Its purpose is to hold wine. Anyway, the point is, the universe is comprised of physical bodies—the glass—and their astral counterparts—the wine."

"Like… like a soul?" Bob wanted to believe the old man, but he learned a long time ago to stop listening when someone started telling him about his soul.

"Perhaps, if that helps you understand. I impart no theological significance to these matters. They simply are. In any case, the astral body is the part of you that can actually travel between realms, through the astraplasm. The Precedentials' Astral Gates store the information about your physical body upon an exit and reconstruct it upon an entry."

"Reconstruct..." This was unsettling. "So, the Gates..."

"Destroy you and rebuild you, yes. I wouldn't worry too much about it. We are destroyed and rebuilt much more often than you'd think. Besides, your astral body makes the journey completely undamaged."

Bob just stared at him through a skein of smoke.

Bernard drained the wineglass again and smacked his lips. "In any case, just as a physical body can exist without an astral body to fill it, so can an astral body exist on its own. That is what the spirits are. They're purely astral creatures, with no toehold on the physical realm... unless they have a conduit."

Bob thought he was getting it. "Like a shaman or a wizard."

"Precisely." The old wizard smiled. "Now, shall I push forward?"

Bob nodded reluctantly.

"Ok then, back to astraplasm. There're some things you have to understand about Hub. It is a unique realm in several respects. For one thing, it's abnormally large and blocks the mouth of an entire dendrite on its own. But more relevant to this discussion—it is one of the only realms where the spirits can get in. Let me explain. One moment."

He turned his head toward the corner of the room where Osivia hovered above the desk. He gave one of those sharp puffs from his lips. A small object leaped off the desk and flew past Osivia, causing her to shriek in alarm.

"So sorry, my dear."

Osivia scowled at the two of them before shaking it off. She resumed reading.

Bernard caught the object as it reached him. It was a small leather pouch drawn at the mouth with string. He poured the contents onto the frying pan. Little round, flat-bottomed beads of blue glass rolled out and scattered across the pan. Bernard then poured a tiny amount of wine over them. The result was that the frying pan became a kind of dull, red ocean around an archipelago of little blue islands.

"While the Astraverse has many things in common with a microscopic cell, it is actually a flat plane, like this pan. The beads represent the realms. The wine represents the astraplasm. Now, as you observe, you may note that, due to the hard shells of the realms, the astraplasm is incapable of getting inside them." He grabbed the saltshaker and shook it liberally over the pan. Little white flecks settled into the thick red liquid. Some of them clung to the outside of the blue beads. "The spirits," he said. "They exist naturally in astraplasm, and cannot exist without it, much like a fish requires water. Now," he grabbed the sponge and tore off a small piece, then dropped the piece into the pan, where it began to soak up the salted wine. "Hub, on the other hand, has a semipermeable barrier. The astraplasm can enter, and with it, the spirits."

Bob hadn't been this fascinated with anything other than finding Galvidon since before he could remember. "Ok, I think I get it."

"Good. Because this was all I could come up with to explain it quickly." He puffed sharply from his mouth and all the objects on the table began to float toward the kitchen. A translucent, cherubic head peeked at Bob from behind the wing chair. Bernard leaned forward and pulled the drawer open, which stuck momentarily but then gave way. "On we go." He cleared his throat.

"Just as physical bodies exert force on one another, astral bodies do as well. When either a physical or astral body is exerted upon, its counterpart is affected. If I push you, your astral body is likewise pushed. On most realms, this is as far as it goes. However, on Hub, when my astral body pushes yours…" He sharply exhaled. Bob felt a nudge on his shoulder as if Bernard had touched him. "…your physical body is also pushed."

Bob's mind worked hard to absorb and integrate all of this. He cashed out the dragon pipe and reached for more tobacco.

"Whereas our astral bodies—yours and mine—are mainly confined within us, the spirits have no confinement on Hub. They are free to exert Astral Friction—the application of force from one astral body to another—freely, within the limits of their ideation."

Bob was unsure about that last sentence. "Limits of their ideation…?"

"Ah, forgive me. The easy way to say it is, 'their element.' So, an air spirit can affect the air, a light spirit light, and so on."

"And an earth spirit could pile rocks outside my hut," said Bob, mostly to himself.

Bernard, having heard the story, nodded sagely. "Just so."

Bob had finished packing the pipe and commenced lighting it again.

Bernard fiddled with his own pipe and tobacco as he continued. "A spirit chooses its bond, and once it does so, it enacts that person's will. It feels the thoughts and intentions of its host and applies Astral Friction to make the changes the shaman or wizard desires. And that brings me around nicely back to foci. As you may be currently experiencing, the human mind is very resistant to the idea that it could have such power. You might as well ask a toddler to ride a bicycle. The task is so monumentally difficult, so beyond what the mind believes itself to be capable of, that it must be tricked. You must give the toddler training wheels."

Bernard puffed at his pipe as it lit. In the corner, the smoke had reached Osivia, and she scowled and tried to wave it away.

"You must give the mind something to latch onto, something it can use to help explain the results of its actions. Additionally, a focus helps to limit those actions. It helps the spirits distinguish between a stray thought and a command. For example, if every time I considered moving an object through the air it happened, the world around me would be a hurricane of flying objects. I use my breath along with the thought as a signal to the air spirits that this particular thought is one for them to act upon. This breathing is my focus. For air spirits anyway. I use a different focus when commanding light spirits."

Bob remembered the crystal atop the wizard's staff, how it had pulsed with light in time with the glowing doorway in the Essen'aelo.

"I know a man," said Bernard, "a wizard, who carries around a magic wand. Uses it for fire magic. That is his focus. Understand?"

Bob thought he did. "Okay, so what's my focus?"

Bernard shrugged. "Beats me. It's different for every wizard." He put his pipe between his teeth and hopped off the wing chair, grabbing his staff.

"Where are you going?" asked Bob.

"*We* are going outside," said Bernard. "We're going to find an earth spirit."

BOB THE WIZARD

CHAPTER EIGHTEEN:
FOCUS

Bernard led Bob out the front door of the house and into the yard. The sun was a shimmering disk in a haze of orange clouds.

The house was at the top of a hill. To the distant north, Bob could just make out the gray line along the horizon he knew to be the Endless Mountains. To the northeast, hundreds of torches and lanterns came alight, one by one, as the nearby city of Bruster prepared for nightfall. In all other directions, the deep green of pine trees stretched as far as Bob could see.

The sloped front yard was not particularly well kept. It smelled faintly of pollen and rotting leaves. The tall, rasping stalks of khaki-grass encroached like weeds. The lawn was patchy and walked over. A fat bumblebee buzzed by Bob's head.

Bernard was leading him down the hill along a slipshod gravel pathway. "There's one more thing you should understand about the spirits," said the old wizard, picking his way carefully and leaning on his staff.

"Shoot," said Bob. He was walking much slower than he was able. Out of habit, he patted the pocket that held his pipe.

"They have somewhat of a hierarchy. The older the spirit, the more influence it has over others of its kind, the more power it can wield over physical bodies."

Bob filed this away, though he wasn't quite sure why Bernard had chosen to tell him at that very moment.

"Ah, here we are," said the old wizard.

They'd arrived at a small outcropping of stone. Here, the face of the hill was a sheer, gray slab. The ground, likewise, was interrupted by slightly elevated slabs of weathered rock. Pebbles and chunks of whitish gray stone were scattered like fallen soldiers.

Bernard turned to Bob. "Alright then, go ahead." He smiled encouragingly.

Bob glanced around. "Go ahead… and do what?"

"Call an earth spirit."

Bob stared. "How?"

"How did you do it before?" Bernard absently tapped his staff on the ground.

"I didn't. It just happened."

Bernard sighed. "Very well. Sit down please, facing the rock wall."

Bob hesitated, then complied.

"Now. Listen."

Bob listened. The grass whispered in the breeze. A bird of prey shrieked in the distance. A faint clatter of someone hammering near Bruster's outer wall floated on the air. Bob waited. "I don't hear any—"

"Listen, I said," interrupted Bernard. He sighed and sat down next to Bob on the uneven rock.

They sat in silence for several minutes. Bob heard more sounds, but none of them were spirits. He began to wonder if this was all a waste of time. Just because he sometimes saw spirits didn't mean he could control them. He should be doing something else, something that would help him get closer to Galvidon. He stared at the gray wall. A bumblebee flew by somewhere, its buzz sweeping through his thoughts. The buzz didn't die away as he expected. It remained steady, vibrating in his head. It stretched and deepened into a growl. The growl grew into a rumble. The rumble grew into a roaring chorus of deep, resonant voices, tones shifting like glaciers. It was all around him then.

BOB THE WIZARD

And there sat the little mud person, cross-legged, its back to the gray slab, its lumpy skin patchy with shadow in the failing light. Empty sockets stared at Bob like abyssal ambassadors.

"Ah, there we are," said Bernard softly. "Wonderful."

"It's so loud," whispered Bob. "It's so loud, but I can hear you just fine."

"You are hearing astral voices," murmured Bernard. "And you hear them with astral ears, so to speak. It is not the same as hearing with physical ears. But quickly, speak to him, before he loses interest."

Bob cleared his throat, eying the spirit. "Um, hello, earth spirit," he said. Stupid. This was so stupid.

"Bob the Wizard," rumbled the mud creature. "Do you remember?"

Bob scowled. Not this again. "It's asking if I remember. It asked me that before. What does it mean? What am I supposed to remember?"

"Mmm," said Bernard noncommittally. "Ask his name."

Bob glared at the old wizard for a moment before addressing the creature. "Spirit," said Bob, "what is your name?"

There was a moment in which Bob thought the spirit would ignore him, but then it answered. Its voice seemed to emanate from the air around it. "I am called Erto," it said.

"Says its name is Erto," muttered Bob.

"Oh, you don't say," said Bernard, as if this name was to be expected. "Now, ask it to do something for you."

"Do something? Do what?" Bob kept his eyes on the creature called Erto. The deep, melodious voices still blared in his astral hearing.

"Ask him to move that rock," Bernard was fidgeting with his empty pipe, and he pointed with the stem at a nearby stone the size of a softball.

"Like, ask him out loud?"

"To begin with, yes, I think that will be fine."

M. V. PRINDLE

Bob cleared his throat, still feeling rather silly. "Erto, pleases bring me that rock."

Nothing happened. Bob repeated the command. Still nothing. Bob became frustrated and told Bernard that he was never really a wizard, that this was stupid. Bernard insisted that, as a human who could see the spirits, Bob was, in fact, a wizard, and that learning magic required patience. They sat at the outcropping until a couple of hours past sundown. The crystal on Bernard's staff glowed like a bulb in the dark. At some point the astral voices began to fade, and Erto disappeared. Before then, Bob tried to add breathing, like Bernard did for air spirits. He tried holding a handful of earth. He tried beseeching the spirit like he'd seen Torael do the first time they'd entered the Koreka. All his efforts yielded the same result, which is to say, no result at all.

Bob returned to Bernard's house irritated and disappointed. Osivia requested a few more minutes to finish a chapter of *Astral Cosmology and Interwoven Structure*, so Bob dejectedly smoked his pipe under Bernard's electric lamp, unable to speak lest he be unduly rude to Bernard. Once Osivia was ready, she and Bob each put a hand on the sanded wood of Bernard's staff. One of the old wizard's sharp breaths and a swirling high-pressure tunnel of color later, they appeared inside the tapestry-covered hut. Bernard had made Bob promise to come back every evening to continue his attempts to get through to Erto. Bob had agreed reluctantly, if for no other reason than he still felt like Bernard was holding back some vital information. Bob mumbled his thanks and went straight to his own hut. He fell asleep to the sound of Osivia's voice as she rattled off the things she'd learned from the wizard's book.

Bob dreamed he was in the back yard of his old house. It was bright and sunny. Anna sat in a lawn chair in a bathing suit and sunglasses, sipping a glass of red wine through a straw and watching him and Danny play. Danny, currently six, was blowing bubbles. The spheres of crystalline soap wafted in clusters through the air.

"Soap bubbles have a semipermeable barrier," said Danny in his small voice.

Suddenly uncomfortable, Bob looked to Anna for an explanation.

She smiled at him. That lovely smile. It always struck him in the heart, even if they were fighting. "You are new," she said. "But you should still remember."

Bob furrowed his brow. That word. Remember. He was tired of hearing it.

"Focus, daddy," said Danny.

Bob looked back at his son. Danny's eyes were missing. In their places were hollow sockets. In their depths, twin points of purple light blinked.

"Focus," said the eyeless child.

Bob clawed through the dream to wakefulness.

The following day was a repetition of the last. He woke, he ate with Torael at the kitchen. He sparred with Kelael at the training field while, behind them, a group of En'harae practiced shooting arrows at the target dummies. At some point, a raiding party had returned with a dozen sheep. Bob saw Harold and two En'harae attempting to herd the animals into one of the structures by the hospital building. Bob ate lunch and then headed back to his hut for a nap, giving the equipment sheds a wide berth. He woke and returned to Bernard's with Osivia. Osivia read while Bob and Bernard spent several hours outside at the rock outcropping. Bernard dodged all of Bob's attempts to wrest from him this *thing* he was supposed to remember. At the end of the day, Bob was just as irritated with the old wizard as he was with Erto and himself. So acute was his frustration that he did not even allow himself to think about spirits or magic or the Astraverse while he was at the Koreka. He figured there was plenty of time for dead ends once he returned to Bernard's.

Again, Bob woke in his hut and walked to the kitchen for breakfast. That morning, he and Torael were joined by Fan and Gorrelai at the tables. None of them talked about their troubles. As they ate, they shared banter and jibes instead. Bob was pleasantly surprised to find that Fan and Gorrelai would be joining him on the training field that day. After the meal, Torael entered Arbor House while Bob and the others set out across the central green.

"Soon, we all will fight," said Fan as they walked. "We need training."

Gorrelai spoke jovially in Hari. "*I must wake up my body. It has grown used to lying down like an old cat.*" He glanced down at himself in disgust, though to Bob, the big elf still looked fit enough to wrestle an angry lion.

"And I have not fought in a long time," said Fan. "I am... without practice."

"Rusty," offered Bob.

Fan appeared to consider. "Rusty. Yes, this word makes sense."

Kelael scowled at them as they approached. He opened a heavy drawstring bag and tossed Bob a practice sword, who caught it much more deftly than he would've just three days ago.

For a few minutes, Bob sparred with Kelael. It went as he expected: badly. However, today Fan and Gorrelai were there, and Bob noticed Fan having a similar experience to his own. Gorrelai, who'd taught his younger brother how to fight in the first place, was clearly dominant. After the fourth time Bob had lost his weapon, he noticed Gorrelai staring at him with an irritated gleam in his eye. Bob thought maybe the big elf was going to criticize his technique, but instead he turned to Kelael.

"*This is pointless,*" said Gorrelai in his native tongue. "*I cannot practice at my strongest against Fan. He is not skilled enough.*" Behind him, Fan was nodding and rubbing at his elbow. "*I require a better opponent. A true Gasheera.*" The big elf stepped toward Kelael, practice sword at the ready.

Kelael kept his eyes on Gorrelai but addressed Bob. "You may spar with Fan. Remember your lessons." Then he strode purposefully to the center of the clearing and faced his new opponent.

Fan slunk behind his brother's back and approached Bob. The slender En'hari kept his practice sword down, so Bob did the same.

"We can practice," said Fan, sidling up to Bob. "But first we watch."

Kelael and Gorrelai began to engage. After only a few seconds, Bob saw that Kelael had not even come close to unleashing the extent of his skill during their practice sessions. Gorrelai came in with a keen thrust, and, quick as lightning, Kelael slid his blade along that of his attacker's and twirled it into an underhand strike that caught Gorrelai under the arm. He did not apply much force—the motion seemed choreographed.

BOB THE WIZARD

Gorrelai nodded, seemingly unperturbed, and they began again.

Again, Kelael bested Gorrelai. Then, once more.

Gorrelai laughed. "Yes!" he exclaimed in English. Then, in Hari: "*A challenge!*"

Bob and Fan exchanged an amused look as another bout began. This time, Gorrelai struck, and Kelael began his smooth counterattack, but suddenly, Gorrelai had dropped his sword and grabbed his opponent's hands. There was a split second in which Kelael's eyes went wide, and then Gorrelai checked him with his whole body. Kelael flew to the ground and Gorrelai was left standing, holding his opponent's weapon. He held it aloft like a trophy and laughed in triumph. Bob and Fan laughed with him.

"Alright," said Kelael crossly, standing up and dusting himself off. "Enough spectating. You two are wasting the day."

Bob and Fan began to square off, still smiling.

Bob ate lunch. Hirrell had been working all that morning, so he took a break to eat with Bob, Gorrelai, and Fan. Neither Torael nor his brother appeared.

Afterward, he returned to his hut for a nap. He woke and returned to Bernard's house, where he spent several hours with the old wizard at the rock outcropping, first relaxing and concentrating on his hearing, then attempting to coax Erto to engage in Astral Friction. Bernard had brought several implements for Bob to try as a focus, including a wand, a staff, an ornate sword, and a burnished copper crown with inset emeralds. None of it worked. Bernard suggested that maybe Bob ought to make something—a staff, perhaps—or better yet, a stone dagger. Bob, having no experience crafting either of those objects, and frustrated to the point of wanting to quit, merely stared sullenly at him in reply.

At this point Bob was wondering why he was spending so much time with Bernard. He'd liked the guy at first, found what he had to say interesting. But the wizard was cagey about some things. Bob felt as if the old wizard and Erto were ganging up on him. As if they both knew something Bob didn't but wouldn't tell him. Something that they thought Bob should remember. This, more than his own failing at magic, was undermining his trust in Bernard and the entire process the wizard was putting him through. The most bizarre aspect of this supposed conspiracy between Bernard and Erto was that Bob didn't see how he could have done something they would remember, when he didn't. Bob had been blackout drunk a few dozen times in his life, but none of those episodes had lasted long enough for him to have come to Hub and forgotten. All other scenarios he could think of—in which he'd somehow have met either Bernard or Erto before—were even more far-fetched. It just didn't make sense. It made him feel as though they were playing a trick on him.

That night, Bob was on the verge of telling Bernard he wouldn't be coming back, of avoiding the equipment sheds, of pretending the whole thing never happened. The only reason he didn't was Galvidon. It wasn't that he thought Bernard could teach him magic that would grant him enough power to finally end his vendetta—all inklings of hope in that regard had been quashed. It was what Bernard had said about the Astral Year. About Galvidon contacting the Order of Tag Nah. That was now five days away. More than anything, he wanted to hear what Galvidon would say. He wanted to know—*needed* to know—what the Gray Man was up to, where he could be found. Until then, Bob decided, he'd just have to play along with Bernard. Besides, another day of failure might just convince the old wizard that Bob would never be able to command a spirit. Bob could only hope.

The next morning arrived, and as he walked to breakfast, Bob repeated to himself that the opportunity to eavesdrop on Galvidon was only four days away.

Only four days away.

This day was much like the last, and the one before that. Practice with Kelael. Breakfast and lunch with friends. Today, he didn't get a nap because Bernard had given him an assignment. He was to find a rock on the Koreka's grounds that could reasonably be shaped into a dagger. Bob of course thought this was stupid, but he did it anyway, telling himself there were only four more days. Only four. He found a chunk of flint along the wall behind the hospital building that fit in one hand nicely and tapered to a dull point. Despite himself, he felt a bit like a boy again, exploring the outdoors and finding rocks and sticks of interesting shapes, pretending they were weapons. Then again, he chided himself as he returned to the huts, there's a line between childlike and childish. That's what this was. A childish fantasy. He wasn't a wizard. He was just a dude who used to have the Gatekey.

At least Bernard had begun to feed him dinner. Bob hadn't even realized he'd skipped the meal the first two nights he'd been there, so intensely had his head been swimming with thoughts of spirits and the Astraverse. The heavy smoking had probably contributed to a lack of appetite as well. But by the third night, Bernard had taken to cooking in preparation for the arrival of his guests. Osivia, oblivious to Bob's disenchantment, eagerly devoured small portions of food and large portions of books. She was only a little disgruntled when they arrived to find Quaker waddling around on the floorboards. Bernard assured Osivia that the duck would not hurt her, but Bob did notice that Quaker had a tendency to stare at the faerie.

Bernard spent most of the evening instructing Bob how to chip away the right sections of the flint so that a reasonable blade and handle resulted. They wrapped the handle in cord and Bernard dug out an old leather sheath from a cardboard box in his closet. By then it was already too late to head to the outcropping, so Bob was spared that humiliation.

Three days remaining. Only three.

Bob was back at the house again. Bernard was talking but Bob barely heard him. He was too busy thinking about how much he'd improved with sword and shield since he'd begun training with Kelael, about what Galvidon might be doing, about anything but whatever the old wizard was going on about. Bob found himself following him outside into the ill-kept yard, down the gravel pathway as it spiraled along the circumference of the hill. Found himself arriving at the outcropping of stone slabs. Found himself sitting cross-legged, staring at the rock face. Listening. Waiting. Hearing the voices, voices that at first had seemed alien, threatening madness, but now were boring, familiar.

And there sat Erto, his little lumpy brown body unmoving, his empty eyes sparkling briefly violet. Bob removed the flint dagger from its sheath inside his woolen coat. He felt its weight in his hand. He thought about the dagger, staring at Erto. He concentrated. The stone in the dagger had an astral voice, pulsing with a thrum of bass. Bob realized that the astral chorus was the combined voices of the rocks and earth in the vicinity. They each sang their own songs, and those songs combined into a greater song.

"Erto," said Bob, flush with newfound excitement at this revelation, "bring me that rock." He pointed with the dagger.

Nothing happened.

"God damnit!" Bob burst out. He dropped the dagger onto the slab. "This is pointless!"

Bernard remained sitting calmly, offering no reply.

Bob began rummaging in his pocket. "If we're going to sit here for fucking hours staring at a lumpy mud-baby, I'm at least going to smoke." He began packing the dragon pipe.

Bernard watched intently.

"Waste of time. This has been such a waste of time. I should be practicing my shooting. Or helping Hirrell in the kitchen. Or taking fucking English lessons from Melanae. Anything but this." Bernard had made sure he carried no metal—which meant no lighters. Bob brought out a match. It popped alight from within a square of sandpaper. He puffed at the pipe in angry little draws. "Move that rock, Erto," he said mockingly.

The rock wobbled.

Bob's heart froze in his chest. He stared at the rock. It was the one Bernard had indicated with his pipe stem four nights previous. Smoke escaped Bob's mouth in a thick gray cloud.

"Erto, please bring me that rock," he said quietly. This time his tone was respectful.

The rock wobbled again. Bob saw Erto cock his round head. The rock began to spin on the ground like a top. Then it skidded over the slab, clattering, and landed in front of Bob, spinning to a stop like a coin.

The rock's voice moved with it. Bob's heart was pounding. He glanced at Bernard.

The old wizard was grinning. "Interesting," he said. "Try another command. More complex."

The astral voices still blared. Bob glanced at Erto, who remained calmly seated, staring at the world through hollow sockets. The dragon pipe smoldered. He placed the old leather sheath on the slab next to the dagger and cleared his throat.

"Erto, re-sheath my dagger." His voice was shaky now.

The dagger wobbled and then rose clumsily, then flopped down on top of the sheath and ceased movement.

"Mmm," said Bernard. "Puff on the pipe a little and try again."

Bemused by the instruction, Bob complied. The smoke plumed around him. He repeated the re-sheathing command. The dagger spun gracefully and tucked itself into the sheath.

Bob met Bernard's eyes and saw some of his own excitement reflected there. "What the fuck?" said Bob.

"What is your pipe made of?" asked Bernard. He pushed himself to standing with his staff.

Bob stared at the beautifully carved dragon pipe. He blinked as a streamer of smoke tried to blind him. "I don't know. Looks like wood and ivory."

The old wizard approached and hunkered down, right next to Bob. He leaned close and inspected the dragon pipe in the evening light. "Carved stone. Bleached. And yes, some wooden components."

"So is the pipe my focus?" asked Bob.

"It seems that way. Try a command while just holding it."

Bob pointed the pipe stem at a little round stone by the base of the slab wall. "Erto, stack that rock on the first rock."

The little round stone appeared to briefly vibrate, then was still.

Bob didn't need Bernard to tell him what to try next. He drew deeply on the pipe and exhaled. "Erto, please stack that rock on the first rock."

The little round stone skipped across the slab floor and became affixed atop the appropriate rock as if drawn and stuck by a magnet.

Erto's voice rumbled in the astral air. "I can hear you very well, Bob."

Bob, his earlier rancor completely forgotten, broke into a huge grin. He turned to Bernard. "I found it! I found my focus!" He started to laugh but fell into a coughing fit instead.

Bernard was also smiling, though his seemed a little forced. "Yes. Quite an unhealthy one, at that."

BOB THE WIZARD

CHAPTER NINETEEN:
THE FAMILIAR'S FOOTAGE

Two more days until the Astral Alignment. Bob had ceased repeating the count to himself, but he was still aware of it. As he woke in his hut, morning light peeking through the crack in the tent flap, he felt invigorated in a way he hadn't been since before arriving on Hub. He could do magic. He was a wizard.

At breakfast, the news bubbled urgently inside him. Holding himself in check, he listened to Gorrelai as the big elf announced that he'd be out hunting the rest of the day. Fan politely asked Bob how things were with him, and he told his friends, with contrived calmness, that he'd found his wizardly focus and could now command an earth spirit. Their reaction was perfect. They cheered and shook him by the shoulder. They laughed and spoke blessings to the spirits. Bob tried to pretend he was nonplussed, like it was no big deal, but failed. He felt a grin splitting his face.

"The spirits know who honors them," said Fan.

"*I always knew you were a real Tesera!*" proclaimed Gorrelai.

"Do not tell Kelael," said Torael. "He cannot see the spirits. He will become annoyed with you, especially since you are a human who sees them."

Torael chewed on a bite of breakfast and studied the wry look Gorrelai was giving him.

"On second thought," said Torael, wrestling with a smirk, "perhaps you *should* tell him."

M. V. PRINDLE

This began a discussion among Bob's companions about the many spirits that had once inhabited the Koreka. While he listened, Bob gathered that the Koreka was a kind of lodestone for the spirits—that for most of its history, it was a place for En'harae pilgrims to commune with the spirits, to seek great truths, to purify mind and body in its waters. The Tessaeshi had kept it hidden, commanding spirits of light to keep it invisible, spirits of mind to bewilder would-be intruders. Many a foolhardy adventurer—explained Torael—had sought the Koreka, only to become hopelessly lost in the Essen'aelo. After the Battle of the Still Mountains, the Engorian's betrayal had first led to many Tessaeshi leaving the Koreka to reinforce the struggling pockets of En'harae resistance, then ultimately to the elimination of most of the Tessaeshi. The Koreka's sole remaining shamanic guardian, Jacaeb Ka'Inslee, had been here to greet Melanae and her Gasheera upon their arrival. Bernard had arrived some weeks later, just after Jacaeb's untimely demise on a mission, to keep the place hidden while the walls were finished. Thus marked the Koreka's full transformation of identity: once a place of communion and prayer, now a wartime base of operations. All in all, a depressing story.

The meal finished, Torael went to join Melanae in the council chamber. Gorrelai left to prepare for the hunt, and Fan, on his way to tailoring at the huts, walked with Bob. The slender En'hari offered his goodbyes as Bob broke off to join Kelael at the practice field. After practice, Bob hit the equipment sheds to re-up on tobacco. He ran into Harold, and Bob told him the wizardly news. There were astral voices, but this no longer disturbed him.

That night, Bob returned to Bernard's in a good mood. He'd skipped his nap. Instead, he'd simply lay in bed staring at the little opening in the ceiling, contemplating seriously for the first time the implications of his newfound power. Bernard had said that the spirits didn't manifest in other realms. Spirits could only enter Hub because of its semipermeable barrier. It stood to reason that, if Bob ever left Hub, his power over the spirits would stay behind. He would still follow Galvidon to the next world if he had to. But if he could confront Galvidon here, on Hub… Well, he liked his chances a lot better in a one-on-one with Erto as his wingman. Maybe that violated the customs of the one-on-one credo, or something, but Bob didn't care. When it came to killing Galvidon, Bob would cheat any custom, any day. At least, that's what he told himself. In any case, he now had even more incentive to find and confront the Gray Man sooner, rather than later.

At Bernard's, Bob listened to Osivia ask questions about astral physics while he ate a rabbit stew thick with celery. Normally, he despised celery. But he remembered the gray liquid he'd been forced to eat daily at the mines. He devoured the crispy green chunks and thanked God for small favors. Not that he'd forgiven God.

He and Bernard spent the evening at the outcropping. Bob practiced asking Erto to do things. Rocks flew around. They stacked in a tower formation. They stacked in the shape of a house. At Bernard's suggestion, Bob got Erto to raise a cloud of dust. Millions of particles of brown earth slowly rose from the ground into a thick plume. All the while, of course, Bob smoked.

With one day remaining, Bob's mood was elevated even higher. It seemed like getting the Gatekey back was only a matter of time. He had another entire week to practice his magic. By the time he got to Oath Keep, Mannix wouldn't stand a chance.

◆

The day finally arrived. Or so Bob thought. He couldn't take his mind off of Galvidon all through breakfast. He felt like a kid before Christmas.

At the practice field, Bob learned some intermediate-level shield techniques. Kelael insisted that he not block but *deflect* an attack.

"Meeting a blow force for force can break your arm," said the En'hari. "You must move the incoming force away from your body."

Bob's left arm was throbbing by the end of the session. After Bob had put away his equipment, he made to walk to Arbor House for lunch.

"Wait, Sora Kelai."

Bob turned. "Yeah?"

"I have orders for you," said Kelael. "From Melanae."

Bob waited.

"Our scouts have noted a heavily guarded caravan approaching

Swearington from the northeast. Melanae and I believe it will continue its journey through the city and be on Southern King shortly. We also believe this caravan may contain another gun. It follows the same path as the one you and Harold found the weapon in. We will know for sure tomorrow. If it continues to Southern King, it will be heading for Tortellan." Kelael's golden eyes studied Bob for a moment before he continued. "The caravan is escorted by men in heavy steel plate. Normally, taking it would be very costly. However, we are now in possession of a weapon that can pierce steel armor from a distance." He gave Bob a pointed look. "And we have someone capable of using it."

Bob took this in. "So… you…" he cleared his throat. "Melanae wants me on the raid? With the rifle?"

"The raid will take place at Ransom Ridge. If it is as we think it is, you will leave morning after next."

That was fine. Bob could barely think that far ahead. All that mattered at that moment was the Astral Alignment. "Aye-aye, captain," said Bob, with a lazy mock-salute.

"I will see you tomorrow, Sora Kelai. We will begin the basics of fighting in a line. Do not be late."

Without waiting for a reply, Kelael walked briskly toward Arbor House. Bob gave him a good head-start before heading the same direction.

That night at Bernard's, Bob was faced with disappointing news.

"What do you mean, we can't listen to Galvidon tonight?" demanded Bob. "It's been eight days! You said we'd listen tonight!"

"Ah, yes, slightly unfortunate phrasing on my part. Quaker must witness the event first. Then it will take her the rest of the night and all morning to return to the Koreka. So, if she succeeds, we will be able to view Galvidon's activities tomorrow evening. Plus, all of this is contingent upon the supposition that Galvidon is in Tortellan with King Flaire. If he is somewhere else, Quaker's efforts will have been in vain."

"Shit," said Bob. Christmas had been postponed. Maybe even cancelled.

BOB THE WIZARD

"How will you do it?" asked Osivia. "Your magic is so intriguing!"

"Magic?" said Bernard, surprised. "Oh my, no! I'm using a camera."

Bob frowned. "Don't you have some magical connection to Quaker? You said something like that at the council meeting."

Bernard smiled sheepishly. "We *do* have a connection. Our astral forms are mildly intertwined. It allows us some benefits. For example, I always know where she is. We can share minor thoughts. But I cannot see through her eyes. For that, I require a camera."

"Huh." Bob shrugged. "Magic, technology. Whatever works."

"What's a camera?" asked Osivia curiously.

They told her.

Later, something good happened to offset Bob's disappointment. At the outcropping, he managed to command Erto without the use of his voice. By holding the thought of what he wanted at the forefront of his mind, he found Erto could understand and comply. Bernard explained that thoughts have a kind of astral form of their own. He told Bob that his connection to Erto was growing stronger. Bob had trouble grasping these things intellectually, but in his mind, he could feel what Bernard was talking about. It was strange. Like hearing with "astral ears," there were some things that could only be understood through experience.

The entire next day, Bob was a nervous wreck. He felt like a rug had been pulled from under him. He thought constantly about Quaker. Had she made it to Galvidon? Had she been caught? Had she returned yet? How far could a duck fly in a day, anyway? What if she dropped dead of exhaustion and the footage was lost? What if Galvidon wasn't even in Tortellan? What if he *was*, but Quaker took hours to find him, and she returned late, after Bob left for Ransom Ridge? He'd have to wait several more days to see the footage!

He was sullen at breakfast and lunch. He was clumsy at the practice field. Instead of his nap, he went to the boulder by the supply sheds and listened for the astral voices of the rocks. He smoked and practiced moving his stone dagger around without touching it. He repeatedly launched it blade-first into a tree, picturing the tree as Galvidon.

Then the moment finally arrived. The swirling high-pressure tunnel of color seemed particularly harsh that evening. Bob was shaking with nerves as he sat down on the cream-colored couch. It was still early evening, and yellow sunlight poured liberally through the two rectangular windows, creating slanted blocks of bright gold on the floor's reflective wooden panels.

Anticipating the footage almost as much as Bob, Osivia sat on his shoulder with a fresh notebook. It turned out Bernard had all kinds of faerie-sized objects in that silver cup, including a tiny bookbag that Osivia could wear like a belt so that it hung against her hip, nicely concealed by her long, white coat.

Quaker lay in the corner on a fluffy dog-bed. She was asleep. Snores in the form of rhythmic little quacks puffed from her nostrils.

"Is she okay?" asked Bob, eying the duck.

"Oh, fine, fine," called Bernard from a room down the hallway. "Ducks can fly almost a thousand miles in a day, you know."

"That answers that question," mumbled Bob to himself. Then, to Bernard, he said, "Did she do it? Did she find Galvidon?"

"Oh yes," called Bernard. "Haven't watched the whole thing yet, but there's definitely at least one Galon Var on it."

Bob felt a rush of cool relief wash through him. On his shoulder, Osivia let out a held breath.

"Here we are," announced Bernard, appearing at the mouth of the hallway.

He was wheeling an old CRT television across the hardwood. It was mounted on a rusted, black rolling stand. The sight of it washed Bob's insides with nostalgia. The television was a dusty old box from 1990's Earth, complete with bunny ear antennae and a built-in VCR. It was the kind of thing Bob would spend a Saturday glued in front of as a kid, watching cartoons and Bruce Lee movies. The stand it was mounted on was just like the ones his teachers would wheel into the classroom in order to show a film. It made him think of Earth, which made him think of Anna and Daniel. They'd all watched plenty of television. She liked scary movies, and Danny had still been stuck on dinosaur shows.

As the old wizard rolled the set to a position in front of the windows, Bob saw it was trailing a procession of orange extension cords that led back down the hall. There was a little black box on one of the stand's shelves, and it was in turn plugged into another box—probably an adapter. The probably-an-adapter was then plugged into the back of the television. Bernard had positioned it so that it was perpendicular to the couch and chair. He glanced briefly around the room, then hissed out a sharp breath. Shutters drew themselves closed over the windows. The gold bars on the floor disappeared as gloom descended.

Another breath and the wing chair lifted into the air and rotated to face the television, then fell steadily back down. "Stay still now," said Bernard to Bob and Osivia. He exhaled sharply a third time, and Bob felt the couch lift off the ground under him, rotate ninety degrees, and settle back down to the floor with a thud. He caught a glimpse of the air-baby in the low light. A brief astral giggle emanated in the room and then faded.

Bob recovered from the experience quickly. It was becoming harder and harder to surprise him. He was thinking about Galvidon. "There's something I've been wondering."

"Oh?" Bernard was fiddling with all the wires and connections. It appeared all the devices were plugged into a power-strip. The power-strip was plugged into the first of a line of extension cords, which carried power to it from whatever the final cord was plugged into.

"The Order of Tag Nah," said Bob. "This group Galvidon belongs to. All I know about them is what Galvidon said. Seems to me they want to control Precedential tech by controlling who gets to use it. By controlling these Electum, these people whose genes allow them to use the technology. But other than that… who is the Order of Tag Nah? *What* are they?"

Bernard sighed and waddled to his staff near the front door. "Dangerous, is what they are." He grabbed the staff and leaned on it, brow furrowed. "It'll take a bit of explaining…"

Bob glanced at the television in the dim light. "Some explanation might help me understand what I'm about to watch."

"I agree," said Osivia. "I'm interested in all pertinent data."

"Very well," said Bernard, ambling with the staff over to his chair. "They began as a small cult in the Anterior."

"Remind me what that is again," said Bob.

"The Anterior," piped Osivia, "or the Urdis Varin, is the original realm in the Astraverse. It's located at the center of the nucleus, and its where the Precedentials came from, and also where humans and Galon Var first evolved."

Bob gave her a sidelong stare.

"Really, Bob, I told you all this in your hut. Don't you remember?"

"Sure," lied Bob. Osivia talked a lot. He had a tendency to tune her out. "Just needed a refresher."

Bernard, now in the chair, smiled at the faerie. "I see you have no trouble remembering what you read."

Osivia flashed white light at the compliment.

"A skill I seem to lose more and more as time goes on," said the old wizard. "Anyway, the Order of Tag Nah was first the Cult of Tag Nah, eons ago. This was shortly after the Cataclysm—the event that mostly wiped out the Precedentials. The Cult was founded by a group of the Electum's descendants who believed that God had created the Cataclysm in order for the Electum to ascend to great power. These were a minority among the Electum. Most Electum in the Anterior followed the wishes of the Precedentials—that the Electum use their technology to protect and feed the people. Some Electum in other realms, outside the Anterior, were already forgetting about the Precedentials. It had been several generations since the Cataclysm, after all.

"And the Cult of Tag Nah was strong in their belief. Single minded. On the other hand, the other members of the Anterior's Electum couldn't agree on anything. They held committees and everything was bogged down by politics and bureaucracy. One by one, the Cult of Tag Nah had them killed. Eventually, the Cult became the sole proprietors of the Precedentials' legacy. They consolidated all power in the Anterior for themselves. They became the Order of Tag Nah, and immediately made it their business to seek out the other realms, to dominate them. To find the other descendants of the Electum, and to either turn them to their own purposes or kill them. The first Eliminators were trained and sent out to scout realms, assess them, and eliminate threats. Soon after, the armies of the Order would arrive to claim the realm and all its resources. The Order, once a cult with thirty members, was now an Astraversal Empire."

Osivia softly glowed yellow while scribbling furiously in her notebook. Bernard glanced at Bob, who gave him no indication he should stop talking.

The old wizard took the cue. "After a few dozen realms were conquered, the consequences of the Order's actions began to catch up with them. Across the Astraverse, there were still descendants of the Electum who remembered the Precedentials. The knowledge and technology had been passed down, in certain places. When word of the Order's conquests reached them, these Electum began to coordinate, first within their own realms, then with those in other realms as well. They created an organization called the Astraversal Protectorate." Bernard eyed Bob hesitantly. "I believe your friend Rashindon mentioned it the night your family was killed."

Bob nodded, staring at the blank television. In the gleam of the low light, he could see a reflection of the room, contorted in odd places by the screen's curvature. "That he did."

Bernard tapped his staff on the floor and cleared his throat. "The Protectorate have a force of people much like police. They attempt to intercept Eliminators, or undo the damage they've done, when such a thing is possible. It seems clear that this Rashindon was one of them.

"Anyway, aside from the advent of the Protectorate, the other consequence the Order now faced was that they'd spread themselves too thin. Even with trillions of citizens across multiple realms, they could not distribute resources and manpower fast enough to keep expanding. This, in addition to the new opposition from the Protectorate, was enough to create a very long lull in their activities. Both the Order and the Protectorate spent centuries of Earth-time building up weapons and gathering Precedential technology when they could find it.

"But finally, the Order became strong again, sure of itself. And again, the Eliminators were sent out. The Tag Nah Order has been at it ever since. They don't expand to just any realm anymore. They are more careful to target realms that will provide maximum benefit. Which is why the wizards on Hub have worked to block their entry for so long…" He trailed away, propping his staff on the arm of the chair.

Bob was troubled by the story. It all seemed vaguely familiar somehow, and not because of what Galvidon had said in the dungeon. It was like he remembered it in a different way than he normally remembered things—like how hearing astral voices was different than normal hearing. Astral memory—was that a thing?

"Sunset has arrived," announced Bernard.

Bob realized they were sitting in near-darkness. Osivia's glow produced more light than the cracks in the shutters. "Oh," he said hoarsely. "Let's do it."

Bernard must have been holding a remote because the television turned on. The hum and crackle of static electricity from the screen was palpable. At first the display was a blank gray square. Slanted white bars rolled over the screen. Then, there was color and sound, and the room became illuminated in the comforting, cool glow of televisual technology.

The old screen displayed an evening sky from a duck's-eye-view. Well, it wasn't exactly through Quaker's eyes—the camera seemed to be mounted at the base of her neck, so occasionally neck-feathers or her bill would encroach at the top of the screen. The wind rushed against the microphone as the duck flew, creating a crackling static hiss from the speakers. Bernard—holding a remote after all—fast forwarded through footage of the sky, the ground rolling at the bottom of the screen.

"Already queued past several hours of this," said Bernard. "This should be about right." The footage resumed normal speed.

BOB THE WIZARD

The sky had darkened to night, and the screen was grainy black. Slowly a tiny light came into focus, and then another, then another. As the Quaker-cam began to descend, Bob saw she approached a walled city. Bob could see thousands of lanterns sparkling from the streets like an army of fireflies, illuminating the angular shapes of the buildings.

"Ah, here we are," said Bernard. "Tortellan."

Bob couldn't help but compare Tortellan to Swearington, the only other Engorian city he'd seen. The capital city seemed smaller in circumference, but its buildings were taller. Leading up to the gates were rows and rows of vineyards. Beyond the gates were swathes of tall, squarish, stone structures, buttressed and adorned with fluttering pennants and carved stone replicas of turtles. Quaker dove within shitting distance of street level, and Bob saw a large fountain in the shape of a turtle. There were turtles on the pennants, turtles painted on signs for restaurants and inns. It was turtles, all the way down.

Quaker caught a gust, rising in the air, and over the sparkling lanterns in the city's sprawl appeared the massive central keep. It was not as tall as Oath Keep, but much wider, built as an enormous oblong dome. The keep was, of course, made in the shape of a turtle. The dome was at its center, blocky and irregular. There were four guard towers spaced apart on the keep's perimeter to resemble flippers or legs. The head of the inanimate reptile was a stone wall built around a gigantic granary. The granary's conical roof gave the turtle the appearance of wearing a party hat. The great stone beast was lit on all sides by ensconced lanterns and torches held by the tower guards, so that it resembled a huge, turtle-shaped birthday cake.

Quaker swooped right by one of the flipper-towers, passing mere feet from the guards. Bob caught a glimpse of them looking bored, and they gave no reaction to the sight of a duck flying to the keep. The camera hovered and wavered as Quaker changed trajectory, and a moment later she came to a rest on the peak of the granary's roof. She produced a few soft quacks as she settled, peering down onto the keep's grounds—a space between the high outer walls and the main, dome-like structure. The grounds were little more than a narrow pathway of cobblestones, its walls bedecked with decorative ivy. A guard strode by going one way, and another man—some kind of scribe, by the scrolls he carried—came from the other, and the two passed each other without words. Quaker, so silent Bob wondered if there was something wrong with the audio quality, floated down onto the cobbles. She looked one way, and then the other, then scuttled in the direction the scribe had gone. The camera jiggled as her little duck feet ran.

She came round the curve of the path in time to see a doorway into the castle begin to swing shut. She honked softly with effort and scrambled for it, propping it with her bill just before it was able to latch. The camera wiggled for a moment and Bob could see nothing but blurry door, and then Quaker was inside the keep.

The corridor was dark, but light shone from around the bend. She made for it, but then the scribe she'd followed came back the way he'd come. Bob was startled in sympathy. He sat up straighter on the couch. Quaker just softly stepped aside, and the man strode past her in the shadowy corridor, muttering to himself, not even glancing at the little duck spy. Bob was beginning to be very impressed with how good Quaker was at this. No doubt she'd done things like this before. Bob heard the door swing shut behind the camera, and Quaker slid along the wall, around the bend and towards the light.

She made her way through a noisy kitchen, weaving and scuttling under legs and around equipment, and then through another hallway. The interior of the castle was heavy, mortared stone lit with ensconced lanterns and decorated with turtle banners of black, green, and gold. Once Quaker was through the kitchen, the floors were lined with plush, deep green rugs that reminded Bob of the red carpets rolled out for celebrities on Earth.

The lanterns were placed conservatively enough that they created little oases of light between long stretches of shadow. Quaker moved more swiftly when she passed one, staying in the murk when possible. The keep at night seemed labyrinthine, endlessly confusing. Quaker stopped a few times at an intersection, craning her neck around corners and softly honking under her breath. She passed a few more guards, a serving woman, a turtle-themed mosaic. The only true threat she encountered was a big tabby cat. There was a flash of feline tail, and Bernard's wonderous waterfowl shrank into the shadows. The cat's ears twitched as it looked in her direction, its eyes glimmering in the lanternlight. Next to Bob on the couch, Osivia gave a little gasp. The tabby seemed to grow bored and padded silently away. Quaker waited for several minutes, glancing around nervously.

"I hate cats," Osivia whispered. "Even more than ducks, I hate cats."

"Relax, young lady," said Bernard softly. "We know she gets home safe."

Bob glanced to the dog-bed in the corner where Quaker lay, now silent but softly breathing, her sleek, little head resting on her chest. In just the last few minutes, he'd gained enormous respect for the bird.

The Quaker in the keep was on the move again. She scuttled through the shadowed corridors until finally she came upon her target—the monster, the myth, the legend—the demonic-looking Gray Man, Bob's own quarry: Galvidon.

It took Bob a moment to realize that he was looking at a throne room, its size and color muted by the dim. Around one of the chamber's central columns bent an unnatural light—a cold urban glow that no torch could replicate. Bob could tell it was technology—a computer monitor, maybe, or a television. Quaker silently crept toward the glow. Galvidon's horned silhouette was clearly defined as he stood facing a gleaming screen, back blessedly turned to the web-footed intruder. Bob let out an involuntary snort, like an irritated bull.

"Is that him?" asked Osivia.

"Fuckin' A," growled Bob.

As Quaker approached further, a face resolved itself on the glowing screen. It was another of Galvidon's race, a Galan-Var. The tech Galvidon was using looked unfamiliar, but Bob recognized a video chat when he saw one. Galvidon spoke in low tones, his voice a smooth rumble. There was a response from the glowing screen, a woman's voice. Bob realized he couldn't understand what either of them were saying.

"Shit!"

The video paused. Bernard cleared his throat. "They seem to be speaking Varantian."

"Shit!" repeated Bob.

"Not to worry," said the old wizard. He clicked the remote and a menu popped up on the screen. He selected a box that said 'subtitles.' "I actually acquired the conversion box on Galon Innis. It has a handy translation feature." He clicked through the menu, which displayed options for at least a dozen languages Bob had never heard of. Bernard found 'English' somewhere near the bottom and selected it. He began to rewind the footage, then paused it just as Quaker was entering the throne room.

"What's 'English'?" asked Osivia. "Shouldn't you pick 'Engorian?'"

"Not an option, my dear," said Bernard patiently. "Engorians speak English. They have just forgotten their true roots."

"How is English even an option if you didn't get the box on Earth?" asked Bob.

"The British made it here to Hub, didn't they?" said Bernard. "They really get around."

"You're kidding," said Bob.

"I'm afraid not. Now, shall we?" He clicked on the remote and the video resumed.

Quaker silently crept toward the glow. Galvidon's horned silhouette was clearly defined as he stood facing the screen. Bob watched in relief and fascination as English subtitles appeared in white block letters at the screen's bottom. Galvidon spoke in low tones, his voice a smooth rumble.

"...can hardly abide this King Flaire's idiocy much longer. The man is an incompetent buffoon."

The horned, gray, feminine face on the screen chuckled. "Do away with him," she purred. "If he is as you say, I'm sure the Triad wouldn't miss him."

"Unfortunately," said Galvidon, "for the time being, I still require him to be alive. Forgive me, Iona, I complain uselessly. Tell me, how goes the inquest on Chaysan?"

BOB THE WIZARD

"Slowly," said Iona distastefully. "I envy you Galvidon, finding an interesting realm in which to play. I find I am dreadfully unsuited to this kind of work."

"My efforts are indeed fruitful thus far. The levels of astraplasm in the atmosphere are higher in this realm than anywhere I've seen outside the Urdis Varin. And I have discovered a people here, the Blueskins Flaire's people use as slaves. I have seen signs among them of Astraversal Communion."

"Really? Among the slaves? How odd."

"But you know what this means. They could be—"

"Yes, yes, let me think," snapped Iona, scowling. Galvidon remained silent.

Bob was suddenly certain that he hated this Iona woman. She was probably another Eliminator, and that made her just as much of a murderer as Galvidon.

Galvidon tapped a few buttons on the device attached to the monitor. "I am sending you the continental telemetry I've been able to gather. Unfortunately, the Astral Gate by which I entered is one-way, and bears out from a convoluted path an army could never follow. I have been unable to detect any other active Gates in my vicinity, though I know they are there somewhere. I have seen evidence of inter-astral technology, and it is very unlikely it arrived here by the same Gate that I did."

Iona's eyes moved like she was reading something. "Inputting telemetry." She tapped on some keys that were off screen. "Analyzing." She sighed impatiently and there was a lull. Then, she straightened her posture. "There. I'm sending you coordinates now. There is a deactivated cluster of Gates a few dozen clicks northwest of your current position. It looks like one of them should lead to Kedris, which has a Gate that leads here, to Chaysan. You will locate and reactivate this Gate while I prepare a sufficient force for invasion." Her brow rose. "Finally, something interesting to do."

Galvidon took a moment to read the information as it began to scroll along the bottom of the screen. "I have heard of this place. The humans here call it the Nexus. It being inactive explains why it wouldn't show up on my scans. There are rumors it is guarded by a powerful creature."

"I'm sure you'll figure it out." Iona smiled, reminding Bob of a grinning shark.

"An interesting coincidence," murmured the Gray Man.

"Oh? What's that?"

"My intelligence indicates a large cache of inter-astral weapons at this Nexus. I had already intended to send a contingent to that location. Now it seems I must go myself."

"To what purpose would you put these weapons?" asked Iona. "They cannot be superior to those the Order has provided you with."

"Indeed, they are not. Yet they are far superior to the weapons available to our Engorian allies. Though many of the Blueskins have been successfully pacified, there remains a rogue element in their country of origin. I wish to aid King Flaire's efforts in eliminating them. That is, unless you think the Triad would object."

Iona appeared contemplative. "Probably not. I can ask them, but it will take weeks to hear back. By the time I get back to you… Well, it's probably best for you to proceed."

Galvidon nodded. "There is one more thing."

"Yes?"

"There is a man here," said Galvidon. "He claims I eliminated his family on a different world."

Bob was sure Galvidon was talking about him. His guts felt suddenly drenched in ice water.

Galvidon continued. "He seems to have arrived here using Precedential technology—an Astral Key. Yet my scans indicate he does not possess the markers of the Electum. In all my service to the Order, I have never encountered such a person."

Iona's hand rested lightly on her chin. "Troubling. Perhaps he is from the Alphabet. An Immortal."

"I have indeed heard whispers of the Vigilantum here. In their ignorance, the Engorians believe them to be magical. Yet this man seemed completely unaware of who I was, of everything, really. If he is Vigilantum, his memories have not returned as they should."

"A fascinating puzzle indeed. Capture him and prepare him for transport and debriefing. If this is impossible, eliminate him. Clear?"

"Perfectly," said Galvidon.

"God is knowledge, God is power," said Iona.

"God is knowledge, God is power," echoed Galvidon.

The glowing screen winked out, leaving the room—and Bob's tumbling thoughts—in darkness.

CHAPTER TWENTY:
RANSOM RIDGE

Despite so many of his questions being answered, Bob's head was spinning with them. He didn't know where to start, and in any case, he was probably leaving in the morning for Ransom Ridge. He and Osivia touched Bernard's sanded staff, travelled through the high-pressure tunnel, and arrived back in the tapestried hut in the Koreka. Once in Bob's hut, Osivia fell asleep at the foot of his bed. He thought he might stay awake all night going over what Bernard had said about the Order, over what Quaker's footage had revealed. But he was exhausted, so fell asleep quickly.

The next morning, he had no time to think. It was all hustle and bustle. Fan arrived at his tent and woke him apologetically, saying he was needed at the front gate. For the first time since Bob had met her, he'd had to wake Osivia. She woke cheerful enough but expressed no interest in accompanying Bob on the raid.

"Violence is the language of the ignorant," she said.

He wasn't sure about that, but he understood not wanting to go. *He* didn't want to go. As he packed ammunition and checked the rifle's action, he considered asking her to come along just because he enjoyed her company. But he decided against it. That would be selfish, to ask her to endanger herself and to witness violence, just so he could feel a little better. She wished him good luck and fluttered away as he strode out into the cool morning air, toward Arbor House and the front gate.

He grabbed a quick bite at the kitchen, and Hirrell, his yellow hair grown so long it was up in a ponytail, also wished him luck. All Bob's other friends seemed to be elsewhere. After breakfast he rounded Arbor House on the stable-side to find Harold Whitespring of Nine Peaks waiting for him with a pair of horses. Bob greeted the chestnut mare Harold offered him, then awkwardly stepped into a stirrup and swung himself up onto the saddle. He'd ridden animals before, but he was still very much a novice. The mare seemed patient and good-natured, though, and Bob was grateful for that.

Harold mounted the other horse—an enormous black and white destrier—and then he and Bob were cantering past a stand of trees toward the front gate. When the gate came into view, Bob's heart sank a little. The raiding party was mounted and ready, awaiting Bob and Harold's arrival. It was about a dozen En'harae, all equipped with longbows, shortswords, and bucklers. Among them, six inches taller than his fellows, sat Gorrelai. He held no bow, but he wore a vicious-looking curved blade on his back and an impressive suit of gambeson, chain, and studded leather. At the group's head, sitting easily in the saddle atop a beautiful gray horse, was Kelael. He was the party leader, of course. Bob silently cursed. For the next few days, Kelael was his boss.

Bernard, bleary eyed, stood next to Melanae by the gate, neither of them mounted. Bob figured they were here to see the party off.

"My eyes rest easy on you, Whitespring," said Kelael to Harold. It was the nicest thing Bob had ever heard Kelael say. "Sora Kelai," said the En'hari with a curt nod, then turned to trot his horse the few remaining yards to Bernard and Melanae. A few of the other En'harae glanced at Bob curiously at Kelael's use of his name. From within the group, Gorrelai shot Bob a friendly grin.

When the mare brought Bob within speaking distance of Melanae, his heart skipped a beat. She was as beautiful as ever. She looked at him in a flat, knowing way that was not entirely uninviting. In other circumstances, he might consider pursuing her, chasing his feelings to see where they led. But now, embroiled as they both were in war, obsessed as he was with finding the Gray Man, he knew it would never work, even if by some miracle she was interested in him. He pushed his attraction away, denying it purchase in his thoughts. He wondered, if Anna might be watching, what she thought of that decision. Would she be jealous? Or would she want him to move on? It didn't matter, he decided, what she would think.

M. V. PRINDLE

Anna was dead. That's why he was here.

"Don't forget what you've learned," said Bernard. The old wizard had walked up next to him. "It could be useful. But remember, Erto will not help you if you are holding metal." The old wizard eyed the rifle slung over Bob's shoulder. Bob nodded. Bernard gave him a worried look that only lasted a moment, then ambled back to Melanae beside the gate, his staff leaving divots in the dirt path.

Melanae gave a short speech, mostly about how long it would take them to travel to the ridge and then return. Bob was only half-listening. He did notice that she mentioned Bernard would, "reseal the Koreka," as soon as the party departed. At the end, she said, "*Et tessat sheerat morae.*" May the spirits guide our journeys.

Everyone echoed the phrase, even Bob.

They left through the gate into the thick of the Essen'aelo with Kelael in the lead. Bob and Harold brought up the rear. After exiting the gate, Bob turned to see the glowing doorway in the forest—the only sign they'd just left an outpost. Shortly, the party's advance obscured even that.

Harold and Bob shared some small talk, but soon the pace set by Kelael and his gray horse allowed them no breath for conversation. The trees floated by like signposts on a highway. Bob finally began to reflect on the previous evening.

There was a lot of Galvidon and Iona's conversation that Bob did not understand, despite the subtitles. Galvidon said he'd seen evidence in the En'harae of something called Astral Communion. Bob wasn't exactly sure, but he had a good idea that meant magic. Galvidon had been talking about the Tessaeshi, the shamans of the En'harae. But what did shamans matter to the Order? Why would the presence of Tessaeshi convince Galvidon to stay on Hub for so long? It seemed he wanted to wipe them all out. But why?

The Gray Man had also mentioned astraplasm. *The levels of astraplasm in the atmosphere are higher in this realm than anywhere I've seen outside the Urdis Varin.* Bob remembered Osivia saying that the Urdis Varin and the Anterior were two names for the same thing—the original realm, the center of the Astraverse. Maybe… maybe the spirits could enter the

BOB THE WIZARD

Anterior like they entered Hub. Maybe the Order of Tag Nah feared that, if people like the Tessaeshi reached the Anterior, their magic would pose a real threat. That might explain why Galvidon and Iona thought that the Order would approve of eliminating the En'harae. *The Triad*, they'd said. The Order's leadership?

Then there was the Nexus. Bernard had said that the wizards had shut it down, a story seemingly confirmed by the two Galon Var. Galvidon had been concerned about a weapons cache there. He wanted the weapons to give to Flaire, to aid the king in the extermination of the En'harae. He'd used the term "inter-astral weapons." Bob had a hunch that there was currently an inter-astral weapon slung over his own shoulder. That meant there were guns at the Nexus. If so, this was great news for Bob. He knew Galvidon was going to the Nexus. He could head there himself, meet and kill the Gray Man, and have a bunch of guns to give to the En'harae—thereby fulfilling his end of the deal he'd made with Torael. Two birds, one stone. After he got the Gatekey back in a week or so, he felt confident he could convince Torael to help him get to the Nexus. Ironically, Bob felt that, with a stash of firearms on the line, Kelael would probably back the plan. If they succeeded... If they got the Gatekey, made it to the Nexus, killed Galvidon and got the guns, there they'd be at the Nexus, where there was supposedly a Gate to Earth. Maybe Bob could go home. It was a possibility that was hard to wrap his head around.

But of all the things the Galon Var had discussed, none nagged at Bob more than what they'd said about *him*. They'd used strange words like *Alphabet*, *Immortal*, and *Vigilantum*. What did they mean? One of the words kept floating up to the forefront of his mind. *Immortal*. Bob could remember growing up, getting sick sometimes, getting hurt sometimes. Just like everyone else. Nothing had ever given him the impression that he couldn't die. They had to be wrong. But the one thing that bothered him the most hadn't come until the end. *If he is Vigilantum*, Galvidon had said, *his memories have not returned as they should.*

There it was again—someone behaving as though Bob had forgotten something. First Bernard, then Erto, and now even Galvidon believed that Bob was suffering some kind of memory loss. But he could remember his life, damn it. He could. Maybe it was a case of mistaken identity. Maybe he looked like someone... But that didn't fit. It wasn't that Galvidon thought he looked familiar, it was that Bob could use the

Gatekey but he wasn't Electum. And Bob had no explanation for that. It all left him feeling lost, a stranger in his own life. Before the last week, he'd never had reason to question his own identity. Now, nothing was certain. All he could do was keep going, to see where it all led. As he rode, the Essen'aelo seemed to bear down around him from all sides.

After a little over an hour of hard riding, Kelael called for the party to walk their mounts. At this slower pace, chores were attended to, water was passed around for the horses and their riders. Bob found himself in the thick of the En'harae. Harold strode next to him, kite shield strapped to his back, a straight blade at his side, a small crossbow tied to his saddle. Gorrelai was just ahead. Midmorning light filtered through the lush canopy to wink off his armor. Bob looked around for anyone else he knew. He spotted Titchell, a nondescript elf with feathery, lime colored hair. Titchell had been a fellow slave at the mines, had been assigned to the dousing crew with Bob and Gorrelai the day Gorrelai had lost his shit on the slavers. Bob didn't really know Titchell, but they had a shared trauma, so there was an unspoken kinship between them. As Titchell didn't say much, Bob figured it would probably remain unspoken.

The journey to Ransom Ridge was to take just over a day and a half. Scout reports indicated that, if they kept to the designated schedule, they'd intercept the target caravan on Southern King as it moved under the ridge on the afternoon of the second day.

Bob spent the next few hours chatting with Harold. They talked about the war, and eventually wound their way into a conversation about their homes and families. Bob found himself recounting the story about Galvidon killing Anna and Daniel. Bob remembered Harold's story about how he'd watched his brothers die in battle, so did his best to not get emotional. Feeling sorry for yourself was not an admirable quality to begin with, and Bob knew Harold had also experienced great loss. Gorrelai walked nearby, listening. Occasionally he would ask for clarification, and Bob or Harold would do their best to translate for him. More than once, Bob turned his head to say something to Osivia, only to remember that she wasn't with them. As they ploughed steadily through the foliage, he thought of things he wanted to tell her, wishing she was there.

BOB THE WIZARD

The Essen'aelo was beautiful. The lush forest was brimming with wildlife. Bob saw a bird colored like a rainbow, and Gorrelai shot a huge, antlered buck near the day's end, causing Kelael to call a halt to set up camp. As Gorrelai began the process of preparing his kill, Bob, Harold and Kelael unfurled pup tents and built a fire, while Titchell and the other En'harae foraged the surrounding area for edible plants. They had an evening of good food, a warm fire, and fine company. Even Kelael could be seen smiling occasionally, though his face hardened when he caught Bob looking at him.

"Kelael fucking hates me," said Bob conversationally to Harold as they posted tent stakes.

Harold was silent for a moment. "There is a saying in the mountains," he said. "If a man has a stick up his arse, don't let him near the trees."

Bob snorted. "And what is that supposed to mean?"

Harold shrugged. "It means it's his own fault he can't get along. Follow?"

Bob struggled to rid himself of the image of Kelael shoving tree branches up his own ass. "Yeah," said Bob, grinning. "I follow."

As the party lay down to sleep, Bob wandered off to take a leak. The night was thick, and the forest buzzed and clicked with insects. Bob's footfalls crunched heavily in the underbrush. He finished his business and turned to head back to the fire.

He suddenly realized he could hear the astral music. The rumbling chorus floated around him in the night, the astral sounds overlapping with the noise of the insects. Erto stood in the underbrush, barely visible in the deep shadows.

"Ahoy there," said Bob, no longer disturbed by the little mud-person.

"I hear you, Bob," rumbled Erto.

Bob cleared his throat. "Um… good?"

Erto cocked his lumpy brown head. "Do you remember?"

Bob scowled. "No," he said crossly, and stomped back to the campsite.

M. V. PRINDLE

The following day, the trees began to grow farther apart. The terrain became uneven as rocks began to appear, jutting from the earth. The ground began to swell into hills and hillocks, and the buzzing of insects receded along with the vegetation, replaced by distant birdsong. The canopy gone, the sky bore down on the group, brilliant azure punctuated by crisp white clouds.

At just after midday, the sun at its hottest, Kelael called a rest to prepare for the ambush. He informed Bob that now was his last chance to smoke for several hours, as the gray plumes from his pipe would give away their position. Bob saw the wisdom in this and relished a large bowl of tobacco as he helped to unpack the weapons and secure the camping gear to the horses. After the pipe was cashed, he repacked it with fresh tobacco and put it in his pocket in case of an emergency. Before long, mounts tied in a grassy clearing, the party made their way on foot across the final stretch of rocky hills. They were taciturn and grim, moving quietly, their minds set on the battle to come.

Anxiety built in Bob's chest as they approached the top of Ransom Ridge. It was a long stretch of plateau that overhung the road below for at least a mile. Kelael began to position the team with hand signals. Everyone moved in a half-crouch, not speaking. Bob was beckoned and placed atop a large boulder that oversaw the entire area. It was atop of a crop of rocks, overlooking the ridge: the perfect position for a sniper.

Bob settled on his haunches, unslung the SMLE and checked the chamber for what might have been the hundredth time since he'd loaded it the previous morning. A cool breeze wound its way across him, but even so, bullets of sweat shot down his face, his chest, his armpits. His hair felt heavy; his beard itched. Despite the metal weapon in his hands, a dull, deep astral hum emanated from the boulder upon which he sat. That was okay; he'd grown accustomed to astral hearing.

From his position, he could see the party had settled into their assigned places along the ridge. Gorrelai and Harold were hidden in a small alcove by the road, closest to where the caravan would arrive. Along the road atop the ridge were the rest of the En'harae, positioned in a dotted line with Kelael at their center. Their bows were ready, arrows nocked, shortswords at their belts. Bob watched the north for the arrival of the wagons. Any time now, a shadow would appear at the horizon and resolve into an Engorian caravan.

Doubt began to creep its way into his thoughts. Was he really doing this? It had all seemed so reasonable, so necessary, when he'd agreed to do it, when he'd prepared to go. Now, though, he was hesitant. Wasn't this murder? Sure, he'd killed before, more than a few times. But lying in wait to kill an unsuspecting enemy was beyond his experience. It felt wrong, somehow, dishonorable.

You have to, said Anna from somewhere. *This is how you get him. This is part of it. Don't forget us.*

"I won't forget," whispered Bob, as dark specks appeared on the northern horizon. He rested the rifle on the rocks, the stock cradled at his shoulder. The specks grew into the forms of humans on horses, into open-topped wagons. The wind carried the sounds of clopping hooves and creaking wheels, an occasional voice, muffled by distance. He waited, watching for the glint of plate armor. He knew the plan: he would deal with the heavy hitters first. Then he would move on to removing the enemy's archers, if any were left after Kelael's team was through. Harold and Gorrelai would assault the caravan at its flank.

The seconds crawled by like sleepy snails. The Engorians continued their approach along the road. Soon the full caravan was in view, two wagons, preceded by riders ahead and behind. One wagon traveled in the center, flanked by two mounted knights. There they were. Bob emptied his mind and positioned one of the armored men in the rifle's sights. He had to wait a few more seconds. He had to make sure Kelael's archers were in range to complete the ambush in one brutal strike. Bob took a deep breath.

The moment arrived. Bob exhaled and pulled the trigger. He was rewarded with the image of his target's face erupting into a red smear of gore. After so much quiet, the report of the rifle was almost deafening, a rolling thunder across the hills. As if through thick water, Bob heard Kelael order his archers to loose.

Heart pounding, huffing like a buffalo, Bob pivoted, reset the rifle's bolt, found the second knight in his sights. The wagons and riders were peppered with arrows from Kelael's archers. Both of the lead riders fell instantly. There were cries of alarm from the men, and shrieks from the horses under fire. Bob's target was wheeling his horse, trying to locate his attackers. Bob couldn't get a bead on his head, so he fired at his center of mass. The rifle boomed again, but Bob was rushing. Adrenaline washed across his nerves; blood pounded in his ears. As the knight righted his horse, Bob's bullet struck his shoulder and bounced off, denting the pauldron.

"Shit!" hissed Bob. A crossbow quarrel flew from the alcove where Gorrelai and Harold lay, but the knight raised his steel shield and it struck there harmlessly. Bob retracted the bolt once again. As he prepared to fire, a thunderous bang erupted from the rear wagon. One of the En'hari archers collapsed with a puff of red mist. Bob swiveled to see an Engorian Darkhair retracting the bolt on his own rifle.

"Shit," Bob repeated like a mantra. "Shit, shit, shit." The Engorians were using the guns. Definitely not part of the plan.

Bob shot the rifleman in the shoulder, turning the guy's arm into a shredded mess, causing him to drop his firearm. A second man rose from the bed of the wagon and fired at Bob, who felt the bullet whistle by his head and tug lightly on his hair before he even heard the report.

Gorrelai, wielding his curved sword, and Harold with shortsword and kite shield, were attempting to unhorse the knight, who was keeping them at bay with practiced sweeps of his blade. Bob saw Kelael rise from behind cover and put an arrow in the second gunman, so Bob shot at the knight. The bullet struck the same shoulder it had previously, and this time the weakened pauldron shattered like a clay pigeon. Bob's bullet bit into flesh, knocking the armored rider askew. Shortly, the knight was stabbed in the throat by Gorrelai and pulled off the horse, which bolted to safety.

There were still men in the wagons, pinned down by the archers. In the center wagon, an Engorian rose with one of the rifles while Bob was resetting the bolt on his own weapon. The man in the wagon fired at Harold as he ran to approach their flank. Bob saw the bullet strike the raised kite shield, no doubt passing right through it, but Harold didn't stop. He bellowed, reached the center wagon, and bounded over the side like a wildcat, Gorrelai close behind.

The other gun rose from the rear wagon, wielded by the only blond Bob had seen in the battle—no doubt this man was in charge of the caravan. Anyway, Bob shot him. At least, he tried to. Bob's rifle jammed.

The mantra returned: "Shit, shit, shit."

Bob's erstwhile target, meanwhile, fired a shot in the general direction of the attackers. It may have been meant for Gorrelai, who was fighting nearby on the center wagon and a perfect target, but the Lighthair was clearly a novice at gunplay, and the shot went wild, whizzing past Gorrelai and Harold and the entire center wagon, striking one of the En'hari archers. Bob didn't see if it was Kelael that got hit—he was too busy trying to clear the jam. It wasn't working. His hands shook. His heart felt like it might explode. The rifle fell from his grip, seesawed off the boulder, and clattered to the ground. He placed his hands on the boulder to steady himself. Closed his eyes. Breathed. Tried to focus. The deep thrum of the boulder's astral voice vibrated his body.

He reached into his pocket and drew out the dragon pipe. He tossed an extra clip of ammo over the side of the boulder. With hands that might impress a stage magician, he popped a match to light and drew a solid hit of gray smoke into his lungs, concentrating. Concentrating. He reached out and placed his free hand back on the boulder.

The earth began to vibrate under him. The boulder hummed beneath his hand like an electric generator. Bob looked up, seeing the battle again in full focus. The Lighthair rose from his cover and took aim, more calmly this time. From his adrenaline-soaked vantage, Bob saw the enemy's features in in crisp detail: the stubble on his chin, the sweat on his brow. He was aiming at Gorrelai again, who was turning to face him but still too far to engage. There was a rumble and an earsplitting crack, and for a second Bob thought the man had shot Gorrelai. But no—the sound was not a gunshot. The earth beneath the rear wagon had erupted like a dirt volcano, like someone had thrown a grenade under the vehicle. The wagon flipped like a pancake, catapulting the blond Engorian into the rocks with lethal force.

The only remaining enemy threw up his hands and took off screaming. It seemed Kelael had not been hit after all: Bob saw him rise and steadily aim, his shot striking home in the back of the man's neck as he ran, causing him to collapse on the grassy hillock, gurgling. The battle was over.

Bob took a shaky draw on the dragon pipe, then slowly climbed down from his perch atop the rock formation. He reached the ground and turned and nearly jumped out of his skin. Erto the earth spirit was standing there.

"Jesus Christ, would you stop doing that?" yelled Bob, clutching his chest.

"Sora Kelai!" Kelael's voice carried to him from around the rock formation. "Are you alive?" called the elf.

Bob inclined his head toward the noise out of reflex. "Fuck yeah, I'm alive!" he called back. He was beginning to feel giddy. He turned back to Erto, but of course the damn spirit was gone. "Be right there!"

"Are you... *smoking*?" Kelael sounded furious.

Bob coughed. "Maybe," he called, and rounded the boulder.

BOB THE WIZARD

CHAPTER TWENTY-ONE:
THE SAME FOR OURSELVES

It occurred to Bob that he was a bandit now. When he'd first arrived on Hub, he'd killed two men and an En'hari for attacking Farmer Willis's wagon. Now here he was, having just killed several men, staring at *their* wagon. It was the one that had brought up the rear, just behind the center one that had flipped. As he climbed up into its bed, he was struck by a feeling of having come full circle. Kelael, the adversary he'd faced that day, now stood beside him as a close ally. Right and wrong, Bob reflected, looked different depending on where you were standing.

Presently, he caught a huge whiff of dead bodies. "Whew!" He waved away the already gathering flies.

"Sora Kelai!" yelled Gorrelai as he approached. "Was you?" He pointed with his sword at the flipped wagon, grinning. The remaining En'harae had just cut two jittery horses free from its wreckage. Gorrelai made a *boosh* sound and lifted his hands to indicate an explosion.

Bob absently patted the dragon pipe inside his pocket. "Yes, I do believe that was me doing magic."

He'd wanted Erto to end the battle, but he'd been too flustered for a specific command. Erto had come through well enough, that was for sure. The spirit must have exerted astral force on the earth underneath the wagon, blasting it upward.

"Not bad, huh?" He tried to make it sound like he totally knew what he was doing, even though he felt the opposite. He bent over in the wagon bed and grabbed a corpse by a pantleg. It was a young man, maybe twenty, full of arrows.

"Bob the Wizard!" yelled Gorrelai triumphantly in his heavy accent. His sword now sheathed, he threw both fists in the air, slowly rotating as if for an invisible audience. He bellowed laughter.

Kelael was nearby, and he turned to stare daggers at Gorrelai. "Show some respect," he said. "Titchell and Guanum are dead."

Bob flinched at the mention of Titchell's name. Looks like he'd never get a chance to really know the guy.

Gorrelai's face and arms fell. "*Et tessat sheera sheral*," he said, suddenly serious. May the spirits guide them home.

"*Et tessat sheera sheral*," repeated Kelael, and surprised Bob by pulling Gorrelai into a stiff, fraternal embrace. Bob shoved the body he was holding over the wagon's side panel.

Harold approached. He was quite a sight. While Gorrelai wore a few signs of the close fighting the two had engaged in, Harold was absolutely covered in blood—his face, his clothing, his shield.

"Brother, are you ok?" asked Bob from the wagon bed.

Harold looked confused. Then he glanced down at himself. "Oh, aye. You should see the other guy." He spat a red gob into the dirt.

"Did you get shot? I saw them fire at you." Bob eyed the kite shield, and sure enough, there was a hole, almost perfectly round, punched through it. Harold calmly propped the shield against the side of the wagon and shifted so Bob could see his massive right arm, where there was a long gash, still oozing blood. "Holy shit!" said Bob. "You got to wrap a shirt around that or something."

"Give it time," said Harold, shrugging. "Just another scar, aye?"

"If you say so," said Bob, and grabbed another corpse from the floor of the bed. "Hey, could you give me a hand? We got to move these bodies if we're going to get to the good shit."

He was telling himself the bodies didn't bother him, but it was only kind of working. The sight of flesh ruined by blades and arrows, the putrid stench of the freshly dead, and the buzzing of the flies might have each been bearable on their own, but together they conspired to induce in him a dizzy nausea. So, he pretended that he was eager to find the guns. But he was just eager to get away from this place.

They commenced with the bloody business of getting to the supplies. It turned out that the two rifles, both Short Magazine Lee Enfield mark threes, were the extent of the caravan's firearms. The Engorians had simply opened the crates and used their cargo to repel the ambush. And though they'd seemed pretty inept in their use, the Engorians knew how to load them, knew which end to point at the enemy. This led Bob to believe they'd already begun the process of learning to wield the weapons. All said and done, Kelael's party dug out both the rifles, two fresh crates still mostly full of ammo, and a handful of other commodities: bars of soap, a trunk of freshly spun linen clothing, and a crate of iron furniture parts. They also salvaged several swords, shields, and various other personal gear from the corpses.

Kelael and his archers went to retrieve the horses they'd arrived with. They'd captured two horses from the Engorians. The rest of the beasts had fled or been killed in the battle, leaving the group with four riderless horses. By the time they'd managed to figure out how to carry all of the heavy equipment back to the Koreka, the sun was dipping toward the horizon. They'd settled on leaving the furniture parts and setting the rest in the surviving wagon, which they stripped of everything extraneous. The two Engorian horses were set to pull the wagon through the Essen'aelo—a task that would slow the party's progress significantly—while the riderless En'hari horses were saddled with the unpleasant duty of carrying home the corpses of Titchell and Guanum. The bodies were placed in canvas as respectfully as possible and draped over the backs of their former mounts. The final task before departure was to drag what evidence of the battle they could eastward across the low hills. They left the crate of furniture parts by the side of the road, a lone monument to their victory. If all went well, by the time some other hapless riders came down Southern King, the elements would have taken care of all the blood and tracks.

They'd packed some food for the journey, and still had venison left over from Gorrelai's kill the previous evening. It was a good thing, too, because, despite their victory, the deaths of their comrades had left the party despondent. By the time they reached a safe distance from the site of the battle, it was well past sundown, and everyone—human, En'hari, and horse—was exhausted. Bob helped to set up the tents while others built a fire, prepared dinner, and tended to the horses. He kept thinking about Titchell—about all the chances he'd had to talk to him, and how he hadn't taken them. How many others would die and leave Bob to regret not saying something to them when he'd had the chance? What if he'd been faster, if he'd been a better sniper, if he'd anticipated that the Engorians might try to use the guns they were carrying? Why didn't he think of that? Kelael and the others had no experience with modern weapons, but Bob did. So why couldn't he see it sooner? He remembered being in a rattling box on the way to the mines, captured by the Engorians, realizing what a fool he'd been. Hadn't he learned anything since then? Hadn't he learned to look before he leapt? Until this night—ears still ringing from gunfire and thighs sore from riding—he thought he'd learned to be more careful, to think things through. Now, he felt like he was in the box again, unable to escape the anguish of knowing he fucked up and knowing there was nothing to do but live with it.

And as he ate by the fire, as he crawled into a pup tent, he couldn't escape the feeling he was being watched. Maybe it was Erto, peering at him from the forest, thinking unfathomable spirit-thoughts. Maybe it was Anna, watching, waiting, judging. Maybe it was God, considered Bob, drifting into sleep. Maybe it was God watching him, disappointed.

He dreamt of his old home, the house on Earth where he'd built a life with Anna. Built one, and almost destroyed it himself with his drinking. But the dream was calming. He sat at the dining room table. The tablecloth was immaculate white. Through the window to the backyard, he could see Daniel as a young man, an age he'd never reached. His son was clashing practice swords with Kelael. The *clip-clop* of wood striking wood was muffled by walls.

"He's a good man," said Anna. She was sitting across the table from him. She was beautiful, her features perfect in the soft light. She looked at ease, happy.

"I know," Bob heard himself say. They sat for a moment in

companionable silence. "I love you," said Bob.

She smiled. "It's not me," she said softly.

"Who?" said Bob, suddenly feeling uncomfortable. Outside, the sounds of sparring had ceased. Daniel and Kelael were gone, replaced by the shambles of an overturned wagon covered in the bloody, flyblown bodies of brown-haired young men. Frightened, he focused on Anna. She was still calm and happy, oblivious to the change of scenery in the yard.

"The version of me you've made up. It's not me. I don't care about revenge, Bob. I care about you."

"Okay," said Bob, unable to ignore the nightmare outside.

"And that feeling? It isn't God."

The scene outside changed again. Light dropped out of the sky until the world outside was utterly black. A flare of unnatural light illuminated Galvidon, staring at him through the window, smiling. He was covered from head to toe in blood. His gray mouth formed words, and though Bob could not hear them, white subtitles appeared in the window. They said: *You should see the other guy.*

"Watch the skies, Robert," said Anna.

He woke.

By the time they'd eaten breakfast, doused the smoldering remains of the fire, packed the equipment, and resumed travel, the dream was forgotten. Around midday, they came to a stream the size of a small river. Bob vaguely remembered crossing it over a rickety bridge on the trip out. Harold advised Kelael to stop, ostensibly to water the horses. Everyone knew the horses were carrying their own water, but no one objected. Harold, still caked in dried blood from the battle over twelve hours ago, stripped to nakedness and cannonballed into the stream, producing an impressive splash.

Gorrelai and the remaining archers joined him. After a long day of traveling in near silence, everyone alone with their own thoughts, the water was a boon. Their worries temporarily forgotten, the En'harae were soon talking, laughing, splashing. Gorrelai wore a smile, his green dreadlocks dripping like leaves. The big elf had changed so much in the short time they'd been at the Koreka. Bob remembered how angry he'd been while a slave, angrier than all of them. Now he was boisterous, friendly. It was amazing what a difference freedom could make. Harold swung his arms together and caught a couple of the En'harae with a giant wave. They retaliated by trying to dogpile him and pull him under.

Bob had to admit, he was in dire need of a bath himself. His skin felt like a layer of wax. He glanced at Kelael.

The En'hari shrugged. "Someone must watch the shores. I am fine here. Join them, Sora Kelai. You smell like a hog." He turned and began to pace slowly down the shoreline to the horses.

"Ah, what the hell," mused Bob, and undressed. As he approached the stream, he thought he saw a flash of silvery metal in the sky. When he looked upward, there was nothing but the blue expanse, white clouds, and an occasional bird. He dismissed it as a trick of the light and eased into the water. Gorrelai splashed him in the face, then demanded he use magic to defend himself.

Just as they'd all predicted, the party made slower time on the return than they had on the journey out. They camped a second time, now deep in the Essen'aelo. The following morning, Kelael sent a pair of archers ahead to bring the news of their victory and to assure Melanae and Torael they were still going to make it home.

They came to the Koreka's gates at sunset. Only a familiar configuration of vegetation indicated they'd arrived. Kelael produced a low, warbling whistle, and the shimmering, transparent, humanoid form appeared. From his time with Bernard, Bob now knew it was a light spirit.

Kelael glanced at him. "Is it here?" he asked, clearly irritated.

Bob stared at the spirit as it stood, waiting, barely visible. "Yeah, boss, it's right there," he said, gesturing.

Kelael twisted in the saddle toward where Bob had indicated. To Bob's silent amusement, the En'hari was off by a couple of feet, and therefore, when he next spoke Hari in a respectful tone, he was addressing a tree. *"We wish to enter, mighty spirit. Your blessing is our guide. We swear to walk with you always, as you walk with us."*

There was a long moment in which Bob began to wonder if the spirit was going to comply. Maybe he'd have to talk to the spirit for Kelael. And Kelael would hate that, so Bob partly hoped that's what'd happen. But then, the glowing rectangular doorway appeared, and the spirit evaporated from sight. Kelael's gray horse cantered through the gate without so much as a glance from its rider.

The party slowly made its way through the luminant passage. Bob waited for the wagon to disappear ahead of him, then gently urged the chestnut mare into the light.

■━━◊ ◉ ◊━━■

The next few hours passed by in a flurry of activity. Despite the late hour, there was much work to be done before bedtime. The horses, including the two they'd just acquired, were taken to the stables to be rubbed down, watered and fed, and to take a well-deserved rest. The wrapped bodies of the fallen archers were taken away on converted mining carts. Bob, Harold and Gorrelai shared a meal with Torael on the covered deck. Torael told Bob that Melanae wanted him to start teaching some of the archers to fire the rifles they'd acquired. After they'd eaten, Bob lit a large bowl of tobacco and followed Harold to the supply sheds, where a handful of freshly rested En'harae were hauling in the crates two of their fellows had just died for. The deep astral hum of the nearby boulder overlapped everything. Bob had learned to tune it in and out, like turning the bass up and down on a stereo.

Osivia fluttered from the night sky and lit on Bob's shoulder. "I heard what happened," she said. "I'm so sorry Bob. I spoke to Guanam a few times, he was nice. Oh, Bob, I could have saved him." She buried her little head in her little hands.

"It's not your fault, Tinkerbell. You're a scientist, not a soldier. It's my fault. I should have warned Kelael the Engorians might have figured out how to use the guns."

She hopped into the air, hovering. "But Bob, you saved the day! I've heard what happened; the En'harae are already talking about it. Is it true? Did you use magic? They're saying you made the earth open up and swallow the Engorians!"

Bob snorted. He suspected Gorrelai might have something to do with the exaggerated tale. "Hardly. I was desperate and afraid. I asked Erto for help, but I couldn't even give him a clear command. And nobody got swallowed by anything. It was just a little eruption that flipped a wagon."

She flew in a tight circle. "Fascinating. Did you use your focus?"

"That I did."

She frowned. "Huh. I was hoping that was only temporary."

"Osivia, it's been less than a week since I figured out my focus."

She gave him a maternal look. "It's never too early to quit smoking."

"Okay, I see what's going on here."

Harold called to him from the doorway to one of the sheds. "Hey! Bob the Wizard! He, whose enemies are swallowed by the earth! This stuff is heavy, aye? You going to help?"

Bob tapped out his pipe against the bottom of his shoe. "Got to get to work," he said to Osivia. "Want to hang out while we move some shit around?"

Osivia appeared to contemplate her response. Finally, she struck a dramatic pose, and affected a bad imitation of Bob's voice. "Fuckin' A!" she exclaimed, giggling.

"Oh, so funny," said Bob, crunching across the dimly lit grounds toward Harold, hiding a smile. Just then, like a sunrise in his mind, he realized how much he'd missed her.

<hr />

The next morning, Bob arrived at the field for practice, but Kelael wasn't there. He found Gorrelai and Fan throwing knives at a target made from a tree stump. Fan was not bad, making the most basic throw successfully over and over, while Gorrelai practiced difficult throws, varying his distance and stance, his angle of approach, his grip on the weapon. Gorrelai told him that Kelael was busy coordinating for the attack on Oath Keep, which was only a few days away. Fan mentioned that there would be a funeral ceremony for Titchell and Guanam that very evening.

Bob thought back to when he'd been trapped with the En'harae in the mines, to saving Torael from the crumbling ceiling of rock, to Paulsin's death. He remembered sitting in a circle, a kind of prayer. "Like in the Cave?" he asked now.

Fan nodded. "Like in the Cave, but nicer," he said, hinging his arm around his neck and letting a black knife spin toward the target. He missed the bullseye, but the knife sunk nicely into the wood.

Bob joined them. He'd always liked knives, even as a boy, and so he'd thrown them before, but he was long out of practice. The first one he threw struck the stump hilt-first and bounced off. Gorrelai threw two knives, one in each hand, from twice the distance Bob had thrown from. Both blades sank into the target, perfectly spaced, one on either side of its center. They had crossed in midair.

"Well, shit," said Bob. "Got some catching up to do."

After lunch, Bob headed for the huts. The funeral was in a few hours, and Bob wanted to talk to Bernard before it began. The day was warm and bright, the sky a deep blue infinity. The grass swished lightly underfoot. Birds sang and flitted from treetops, insects chirped and scuttled. Bob passed numerous En'harae as they moved about their business. They seemed subdued. Usually they were shouting and laughing, sometimes calling to him by his given name, Sora Kelai. Today, Bob received little more than a nod or two, and the En'harae walked quietly, reticent, staring at the ground. Their friends were dead, Bob realized. People they knew and cared about, people who they'd known, some of them, their entire lives. Bob understood. That feeling of loss, he carried it with him. Now, his negligence had led them to carry it as well. His guilt grew, tightening in his chest.

He crested a grassy knoll, and the neighborhood of huts came into view. Bernard's own eccentric hut, covered in overlapping tapestries, was clearly visible from one of the center rows. Bob made his way through the grass, the sun baking sweat off his forehead. The linen he wore felt heavy and scratchy. Snippets of conversation, mostly in Hari, floated on the breeze. The ground turned earthy and brown as he crossed into the rows.

He arrived at the tapestried hut and looked around. No sign of Bernard out here. Bob ducked through the tent flap and entered the empty hut. No fire was lit within and only the opening in the roof let in light. The air was dusty and still. Bob's eyes began to adjust, and he could see with certainty that no one and nothing was here. No swirling high-pressure tunnel. No air spirits. No furniture, even. Nothing.

"Bernard?" he yelled into the hut. "Bernard!" He didn't know what he expected. For Bernard to hear him all the way at his house, maybe. What was going on here? "Well, shit," he muttered, and exited the hut.

He encountered Fan in the rows. He was sitting in a canvas chair outside one of the huts, pulling leather cord through the stitches of some kind of brown garment. Bob asked him if he'd seen Bernard or knew where he might be. Fan apologized and replied in the negative. Bob thanked him and headed toward Arbor House.

He arrived at the covered deck to find Hirrell already on break, eating and reading a large cookbook that was open in front of him on the table. Bob asked after Bernard. As he expected, Hirrell had not seen the old wizard. Feeling put out, Bob had a small snack and then lit his pipe. He shared it with Hirrell, who said he was trying to come up with creative ways to serve mutton. Soon, Hirrell excused himself, and Bob, only becoming more irritable, found himself walking to the bath house on Arbor House's ground floor. He intended to wash away the sweat of the day. If he was lucky, he mused, he'd wash some guilt away with it.

At the cusp of sunset, Bob arrived at the training field. Soon after Bob, Fan, and Gorrelai had left it, En'harae workers had begun transforming the field into a ceremonial site. Torches were planted and lit, wooden bleacher seats were carried from the supply sheds, assembled, and set up in concentric rings. Mosaic stones had been carried from God-knows-where and placed at the center of the field in a circular pattern, creating a slightly elevated stage of many colors. When Bob arrived, the last sliver of sunlight announcing its departure with a flicker at the horizon, the training field had become something like an outdoor theater.

En'harae milled about, talking in low tones, finding seats in the bleachers. Bob saw a couple of humans he didn't recognize, grizzled Darkhairs looking uncomfortably out of place. Newly recruited supply-line harassers, no doubt. As they sat, one of them caught Bob's eye and gestured for him to join them. Bob ignored them, scanning the crowd for someone he knew. Mostly he was looking for Bernard. He wanted to report the old wizard's absence, but both Torael and Melanae, preparing to lead the ceremony, were inaccessible. He hadn't seen Kelael all day, either. Not that Bob was particularly thrilled with the idea of talking to him. *Yes, hello asshole, have you seen my wizard?*

He managed to spot Hirrell's distinctive yellow hair and milled his way through the crowd toward him. "Bob!" a little, familiar feminine voice called to him from above. Osivia swirled out of the sky. She hadn't seen Bernard either. Soon Bob sat in the stands between Hirrell and an En'hari woman he didn't know, Osivia perched on his shoulder with her notebook. The sun had bidden farewell, and tonight was a new moon. The sky was a black swathe perforated by faintly glimmering stars—allies with the dancing torchlight against the darkness.

Bob tried to absorb the murmuring crowd. He realized it must be the Koreka's entire population, some three hundred and fifty individuals, all here to fight for En'hirin, or at least against Engoria. Soon everyone quieted as a mournful note rang out. From the shadows outside the torchlight came a procession of En'harae. Each wore robes of animal skins adorned with polished bones and teeth, and they walked with reverential calm, heads lowered, hands folded. Leading them was Melanae, the light glimmering off her onyx hair. Just behind her was Torael, and it was from him the doleful melody arose. He held a wind instrument, like a flute, cradling it as though it were glass, and he gently blew a series of notes that pierced the night with their melancholy. Osivia scribbled furiously in her notebook.

The ceremony lasted about an hour. Melanae spoke, and then Torael. They seemed to be retelling a creation myth, which Bob found interesting at first. After about ten minutes, however, Bob began to wish he could light the dragon pipe, and his ass started getting sore from the bench. At some point, he realized he must have missed at least one of these ceremonies while he'd been at Bernard's. After all, Titchell and Guanam were not the Koreka's first casualties.

The story told, the rest of the adorned En'harae in the procession took turns speaking. It turned out they were the friends and relatives of Titchell and Guanam, and each in turn told a story about them. Bob was only half listening. He'd begun to worry very seriously about Bernard. The old wizard was supposed to help Torael's team when they stormed Oath Keep, so his absence was a blow to Bob's hopes of reclaiming the Gatekey. The ceremony concluded with a familiar prayer: the same one Bob had participated in while trapped in the Cave. Collectively, the voices of the En'harae beseeched the spirits.

We ask for your aid, we ask for Titchell and Guanam. Earth, embrace them, air, carry them, sun, warm them, mind, think them. We pray the same for ourselves. May the spirits guide them home.

Afterwards, the crowd's silence regrew into whispers, then chatter. Everyone began to stand and file out of the bleachers. Hirrell gave Bob a friendly slap on the shoulder and vanished into the milling sea of blue skin. Osivia was babbling about the details of the ceremony, describing everything as, "fascinating." Bob stood on tiptoe, trying to catch a glimpse of the Koreka's leaders. After a minute or two, he resolved to wait until the crowd dispersed, nudging his way to the outskirts. It took him a few tries to light his pipe, but once he succeeded, he took a mighty draw on its stem and gazed up at the stars. They were beautiful—crisp and clear spheres of perfect white light arrayed in incomprehensible patterns. Osivia was still talking. Bob wasn't paying attention, but he liked the sound of her voice. Liked that she was there.

There was a soft flutter and a crunch of grass in the darkness to his right. Osivia went quiet. "What was that?" she asked nervously, putting Bob between herself and the noise. The crowd had mostly thinned out, and several of the torches had been carried away by homeward travelers. The Koreka's grounds seemed lonely, dark, and uninviting. The fluttering sound came again, closer this time. It sounded familiar, but Bob couldn't quite place it.

BOB THE WIZARD

"Erto?" he called into the darkness.

"Wak!" replied the night.

"My goodness!" cried Osivia with relief.

Quaker scuttled out of the darkness. The duck was clearly exhausted, breathing hard, walking in a halting fashion, like a prize fighter after a bout. Her feathers were ruffled and dirty. She scuttled up to Bob and plopped down at his feet, panting through her nostrils. "Wak," she said tiredly.

She was wearing a little polyester harness. Attached to the harness, snugly against Quaker's feathery chest, was a little black bag with a zipper. Bob bent down and reached out.

"May I?" he said to the duck.

Quaker replied by turning her head to the side, further exposing the bag. Bob unzipped it and pulled out the note inside. It was hastily scrawled in pencil on the back of a page torn from an encyclopedia. It said:

Bob,

I have been called to Azenbul. Some crisis is afoot. No time to explain. However, this much I know: You MUST retake the Gatekey. You MUST go to the Nexus. I'll meet you there, I hope.

-B

P.S.

Please feed Quaker. She likes peas.

CHAPTER TWENTY-TWO:
CONTINGENCY

Less than an hour later, Bob was in the council chamber for an emergency meeting. Bernard's note sat on the table atop scattered maps and lists. Bob looked around at the council members. Bernard and Quaker were absent—the wizard for somewhat mysterious reasons, the duck because Bob had dropped her off at the kitchen, instructing Hirrell to find her some peas.

Melanae stood behind her chair, arms crossed, looking worried. Next to her was Torael, who sat forward, huddled in his furry coat, eyes agleam with interest. They both still wore their ceremonial outfits, so now and then bones and teeth would click and clack with their movement. Harold had his feet on the table and chewed on a toothpick. Gorrelai sat quietly, his familiar scowl returned, while Kelael paced incessantly along one side of the room. Osivia was standing on the table, hand to chin, studying Bernard's note intently.

"*I have been called to Azenbul*," she read aloud. "Why would he need to go to the Wizard's Tower on such short notice?"

"It does not bode well," said Melanae. "A crisis at Azenbul is unheard of. It is a tower of wizards. What could possibly befall them that they could not handle alone?"

"Maybe Bernard is the most powerful of them," suggested Harold. "Maybe there's something only he can do, follow?"

Melanae looked doubtful. "Bernard is powerful, yes, but not the most powerful. There are others who wield greater magics even than he. He has spoken of them. They refuse to directly interfere with the conflicts on Sheral, or so they claim. They have their own priorities, and their own reasons."

"If we are going to continue with this foolish plan to assault Oath Keep," interrupted Kelael, still pacing, "we must go *now*."

"What about the Nexus?" asked Bob.

"What about it?" snapped Kelael.

"There are guns there," said Bob, hoping his hunch was right.

"What?" Kelael ceased pacing to stare at him. "What guns?"

"Yes, Bob," said Torael calmly, "please tell us. What do you mean, there are guns at the Nexus?"

"Quaker… that is to say, Bernard and I, spied on Galvidon a few days ago. He was in Tortellan, at the keep shaped like a turtle. He spoke to someone far away. Someone from his kingdom, I guess you'd say. Long story short, we learned there's a stash of weapons at the Nexus. The way he talked about them… well, I'm almost certain its guns." As he spoke, Bob noticed Melanae seemed to grow uncomfortable. He was struck by a realization—she already knew about the guns at the Nexus.

Kelael looked around at each of them, as if he couldn't believe they were all still sitting there. "Well, let's go! Let's go get the guns!"

Nobody moved.

"Kel," said Torael, "we must first complete the attack on Oath Keep. This is the deal we… the deal *I* have made."

"Spirits damn your deal! We don't need this key! We need weapons!"

Bob had never seen Kelael so agitated. Gorrelai was silently watching the exchange, seemingly uncertain of who to back.

Torael remained impassive. "We will help Bob get his magic key back. He has already helped to get us two of the weapons, and now he has given us valuable information about the location of more. We will repay him. I will keep my promise."

Kelael turned away angrily. He huffed for a moment, then leaned his hands against the wall as if suddenly tired. "Very well, if this is your wish. But as I said, if we are to go, we must go. Now."

"Unfortunately," said Melanae, "Kelael is right. We have only a day or two."

"What?" said Bob. "A day or two until what?"

Kelael turned back around to face Bob. "We lost our wizard." He spoke as if explaining something obvious to a child. "The good one, anyway."

Melanae cleared her throat. "Bernard maintains the magical protections around the Koreka with daily rituals. Without him, the light and air spirits will forget why they are here and wander off. Our enemies will be able to see and hear us."

Harold spoke. "Ah, forgive me, aye? But can we even proceed with the plan without Bernard?"

Torael glanced at Bob. "Of course," said the En'hari. "Osivia and I can lead the Wranglers without him."

Osivia briefly flashed like a bulb.

Kelael kicked an unoccupied chair. "You cannot still think to come along on this fool's errand! You must return to our people before we are discovered, and you are thrown back in chains!"

"Calm yourself, Kel. I will leave just as soon as we have the magic key."

Osivia spoke as if addressing the group, though her eyes were on Kelael. "There is a chance the Gatekey will be necessary to obtain the guns. If we don't get it, and travel to the Nexus first, we may discover we must turn around and travel back to Swearington."

"Bernard says to get the Gatekey," said Harold around his toothpick. "We trust he has your people at heart, aye? We've always listened to him before."

Melanae finally pulled out her chair and perched on its edge. Her outfit lightly jangled. "What say you, Gorrelai?"

BOB THE WIZARD

Gorrelai was back to glowering into space. His eyes found Melanae, and his scowl softened. *"I agree with Kelael that we must retrieve these weapons. I have seen what they can do. We would be fools not to acquire them."* Kelael's eyes gleamed and Bob's heart sank a little. *"But,"* continued Gorrelai, *"I also agree with Torael. We must help Bob. He has helped us. It would be dishonorable to do otherwise."* This statement settled over the table. Before anyone could respond, Gorrelai added, *"Also, I look forward to killing many humans at the keep."*

"Okay," said Melanae, nodding.

"Fuckin' A," muttered Bob.

"It is too late for us to leave tomorrow." said Torael. "No one will be rested. Day after tomorrow, we proceed with the plan."

"I will begin evacuation procedures," said Melanae. "The entire Koreka will be ready to depart upon your return from Oath Keep, Quaylen Dah."

Kelael pointed an accusing finger at Torael. "Brother," he said, "if you die on this idiot mission, I will kill you."

⚊◯⚊

When the meeting adjourned, Torael asked Bob to stay for a moment. Melanae's gaze lingered on Bob as the others filed out before her. She looked poised to speak, but instead just smiled thinly before exiting. Bob watched her go reluctantly, wanting to follow her but not knowing what he'd say. Osivia strolled along the tabletop, hands planted on her hips, studying the various maps, notes, and diagrams beneath her like a tourist at a gallery. Bob cleared his throat, and she looked up, noticing only she, Bob, and Torael remained.

"Oh," she said, glancing at Torael and beginning to hover, "I'll just be going, then."

"It's alright, little faerie, you can stay," said Torael lightly. Osivia fluttered to Bob's shoulder. The En'hari sat in silence for a moment, studying Bob with kind eyes. "Bob," he said. "How are you doing?"

Bob looked back at him and saw nothing but earnest concern. He scratched his beard and took a long, deep breath through his nose. "I'm so afraid, I might shit myself," he said honestly.

Torael looked at him, his concern softening to amusement. He chuckled. "It is the same for me, Bob," he said. "I will shit all over these sacred animal skins."

Bob snorted. Osivia giggled. Then they were all laughing. For a few minutes, they gossiped and joked. Bob told Torael about Erto the earth spirit, and Torael countered with a story about how he'd bonded with a water spirit as a boy.

"The water spirits are mostly gone from this land. They are especially afraid of the humans' metal. But when I was a boy in En'hirin, we lived on the coast. I met a water spirit while fishing with my mother. Her name was Myno, and she helped me catch many fish for many years."

"What did Myno sound like?" asked Bob, thinking of the astral chorus of the earth and rocks, the childlike giggle of the air spirit in Bernard's house, the total silence of the light spirit at the gate.

Torael considered. "No one has ever asked me that before. I suppose she sounded like… bubbles. It is hard to describe."

"I understand." Something occurred to him. "So, are you Tessaeshi?"

"Not precisely," said Torael. "I am of the Ketra. The Ketra are like… we are like generals, I think. We learn to make decisions, to command others. Most Ketra would otherwise be Gasheera. I suppose, had I not been the eldest child of the Ellaren family, I would have been Tessaeshi. In this case, I would probably have been killed when Flaire cleansed En'hirin of our shamans."

Bob cleared his throat, dodging around that last part. "Do you have any advice for me? On commanding the spirits?"

Osivia had been sitting quietly on the table, copying the big map of the continent on the wall into her journal. At Bob's question, she paused and looked up expectantly at Torael.

The En'hari shrugged. "At first, I had to ask out loud. Later, I began to feel the connection to the spirits. The Tessaeshi talk much of this connection. It is a central concern in En'hari belief. Anyway, all I know for sure is, when you ask a spirit for help, what you want must be true."

Bob stared. "True… how?"

"It must be truly what you want," said Torael. "You can lie to other people, but no one can lie to the spirits. They know us better than we know ourselves."

Bob was silent, thoughtful. Osivia was taking notes. Bob realized he could hear astral voices, even now, floating in the background of his hearing.

"There is something I wished to talk to you about, Sora Kelai," said Torael, straightening in his seat.

Bob looked up. "What's on your mind?"

"Kelael says that if I die, he will kill me." Torael smirked. "Though once I am dead, it is not his wrath, but something else my soul may fear." He looked Bob in the eye. "If I do fall, Kelael will inherit the title of Quaylen Dah. He will be the eldest remaining Ellaren, and the people will accept him." He sighed. "Though he will not share their acceptance. Not at first. He will be angry and sorrowful over my death, yes, but also, he has rejected leadership all our lives. His position here in the Koreka is the most power he has ever held."

"But you aren't going to die," said Bob, suddenly wanting to smoke.

"But if I do," insisted Torael, "You must help him accept the title. I fear for my people if they cannot name a single living member of the Quaylen, cannot name a Quaylen Dah. I fear for them anyway, yet—this is the last thing we have left of our unified nation. Please Bob, promise me you will convince him if the time comes."

"Okay, okay, I promise, I'll help him figure it out if—and that's a big fucking if—the time comes. But what makes you think he'll listen to me? I mean, the guy hates me."

Torael smiled. "He does not hate you, Bob. You see the way he speaks to me, yes? His brother and his ruler!" He laughed. "He is prickly, I think. But anyway, it doesn't matter if he likes you. He will know I asked you to help him accept the title, and he will do it in the end, I think, for me, and for his sense of duty to our people."

Bob stood, increasingly distracted by the urge to smoke. "If you say so, brother." He shook Torael's hand and gave it a pat. "I will hypothetically help you."

They had one day to prepare. Bob was packed and ready to go less than two hours after breakfast, so he spent much of the day wandering the Koreka, looking for people to help out. During his time under the sun, he began to notice a subtle shift in color had occurred. Some of the trees displayed leaves that were brittle and brown, their branches stiff like knotted skeletons. The grass was yellowing and patchy. Bob glanced at the sky, realizing it hadn't rained since he'd arrived at the Koreka. The En'harae who tended the garden must have their hands full. No matter, he supposed, with plans for evacuation underway. He headed to the supply sheds to help Harold pack everything into the wagons. His ulterior motive—finding some tobacco from a recent run—was fulfilled nicely.

Later, Bob had dinner at the covered deck. While Arbor House itself was not being deconstructed, Hirrell and the other cooks were under pressure to use all the perishables, so there was a bit of a party going down on the central green. Bob eyed an En'hari waltzing by with a wineskin, briefly considered having some wine, and dismissed the idea. Instead, he ate a generous helping of food and headed to his hut. He realized he'd begun to think of the little conical dwelling as home—the place he hung his hat, as they might say where he came from. And this was his final night. He allowed himself to feel the regret of losing a comfortable place, because the alternative was to admit how afraid he was, as he had to Torael—afraid of failing, afraid of paying a price for the Gatekey he was unprepared to pay.

Osivia was waiting in the hut. Seeming to sense his mood, she began to make an excuse to leave.

"Don't go," said Bob, reaching for the rifle, preparing to clean it for the second time that day. "It's fine, really. I probably won't say much, but..." he shrugged. "I don't know, tell me about your research."

For almost an hour, that's what she did. She told Bob about the three distinct varieties of dragonflies in the area, the mating behavior of local finches, the specifics of the En'hari funeral ceremony, and her hypothesis about the dominance of specific hair colors in En'harae reproduction.

Eventually, she said no more, and minutes passed with silence between them.

"Bob?" she said after a while.

Bob, having finished cleaning the gun and oiling its barrels, now lay on his back in bed, staring at the little opening at the hut's vertex. "Yeah?"

"I've been thinking about tomorrow."

"Same," said Bob, pushing a hand to his eyes.

"Are you going to kill him?"

"Who?"

"Mannix."

Bob hadn't really considered that. He thought of the Lord of Swearington—his smarmy manner, his perfectly cropped blond beard. He remembered staring through iron bars at Mannix's smug face, hating him. The man had thrown him into slavery. Shouldn't that alone give Bob all the reason he needed? Yet, Osivia's question had him thinking. Why had Mannix put Bob in the clattering box and sent him to the mines? Because there was evidence—perhaps circumstantial, but still evidence—that Bob had committed several murders. Bob had broken into Mannix's room, threatened the lord's safety, demanded information. Bob had taken Farmer Willis's wagon and all his goods and tried to pass them off as his own. Bob, while not actually guilty of the murders, was technically a killer, literally a trespasser and a thief.

Then Mannix had, admittedly through his own greed, inadvertently helped Bob by keeping the Gatekey from Galvidon's clutches. He'd used bribery to bring Bob around, rather than more brutal or invasive means. The Lord of Swearington was an asshole, Bob couldn't deny that, but was he a monster? Bob didn't think so.

Then again, Mannix was a prejudiced slaver, talking down to people because of their hair color, treating the En'harae—who Bob was beginning to think of as family—as subhuman. Fulton Mannix might not have been an unrepentant sadist like Scarface, but he was certainly complicit in the dehumanization of an entire race. Could Mannix be blamed for that? For taking part in a system that had been established completely beyond his control?

All of this ran through Bob's head in a few seconds. He glanced at Osivia. "I don't know. If you'd asked me in that dungeon, I would have said yes. Now? I'm not sure."

Osivia nodded. "You've killed before. Does it... affect you?"

Bob thought of the bandits he'd shot that day on the road, remembered giving two of them a chance to run off. Why had he done that? Because he didn't want to kill any more people than he had to. That was still true. "Of course it does. I don't enjoy killing—I enjoy living. Sometimes, you just can't have the one without the other."

"I don't think you should kill Mannix," she said, not meeting Bob's eye. "Not because he's good. He's vile. Because *you're* good."

Bob smiled despite himself. He thought of Mannix again, and anger and fear pushed the smile away as quickly as it'd come. "I don't know about that, Osivia. But I'll keep it in mind."

The assault on Swearington was to consist of three teams: The Infiltrators, the Runners, and the Wranglers. The Runners were composed of a dozen fleet-footed elves led by Fan. They were to enter Swearington first, climbing over the wall at a point chosen for its lax security. Once inside, they would rush the ironworks closest to Oath Keep, grab something valuable, and run throughout the city, pulling the attention of the guards. As soon as possible, they were to drop whatever they were pretending to steal and escape. The Wranglers, led by Torael and Osivia, were to make a show of stealing a herd or two near the outer gates, creating further distraction and confusion among the forces of Swearington. Torael had initially entertained the idea of actually bringing back sheep to the Koreka, but with the evacuation planned for his return, the mission had been amended so that no sheep need actually be stolen. As long as they had the attention of Swearington's armed and armored, they'd consider their job well done. The final and most vital team, the Infiltrators, would be comprised of Bob, Gorrelai, Harold, and Kelael. They'd fight their way inside the keep, retrieve the Gatekey, and retreat before Engorian reinforcements could arrive from the city.

BOB THE WIZARD

The Wranglers departed the Koreka first, as they had the most ground to cover. They set out even before dawn, leaving Bob harboring a secret fear that he'd spoken to Torael for the last time. As he and the chestnut mare trotted away from the outer gate and into the Essen'aelo, Bob turned and looked back. The outer walls of the Koreka, previously invisible from the outside, now appeared as a dim outline. It had already started; the spirits were beginning to leave.

The journey to the walls was to take just over a full day of riding. They were to camp just inside the tree-line at the end of the first day, leaving only a brief dash to the walls the following morning. Sharing an initial destination, the Infiltrators and the Runners rode together. A bit of luck would see them back at the Koreka on the evening of the third day. Upon their return, they'd decide who was to accompany Bob to the Nexus, and everyone else would accompany Melanae and the rest of the Koreka west into En'hirin.

As Bob's mount cantered through the sun-dappled underbrush, he found himself abreast of Fan. The slender En'hari had recently cut his hair to military shortness, turning his dark blue head into a turquoise ball accentuated by sharply pointed ears. He wore tightly fitted black linen and buckled leather on his joints—a design that would make it easier to climb and tumble against rough stone. A shortsword was strapped tightly to his back. Bob had to admit, the slender En'hari looked pretty awesome. It made him consider his own appearance.

Bob hadn't gotten his hair cut since the mines, and it had become so long that he now wore it tied back atop his head like a homeless samurai. His beard, now a salt-and-pepper gray and black, puffed out from his face, falling all the way to the center of his chest. Before they'd departed, Fan had presented him with a gift. Bob recognized it as the brown garment he'd been working on the day Bernard had gone missing. It was a brown leather jerkin with hardened shoulder pads and several pockets clasped with bone buttons in the chest and waist areas. It was clear Fan had had Bob in mind as he made it—it bore no metal, the pockets were the perfect size to hold a pipe and tobacco, and there was a scratchy strip of fabric over the right breast that was perfect for striking matches. When Fan had given it to him that morning, Bob had surprised them both by pulling the guy into a hug, giving his thanks.

"Please, Bob," said Fan, "it is the least I could do for a friend."

Under the gifted jerkin, Bob wore loose-fitting linen designed to baffle incoming arrows. He'd pulled a respectably heavy pair of leather boots out of the sheds which laced up almost to his knees. Like Fan, he carried a shortsword, though he preferred to wear it on a belt, which he'd removed and tied to the saddle for riding. His back was burdened with the SMLE, its safety snugly engaged, loaded with a single ten-round clip. Needing to travel light, he'd brought only a single replacement clip tucked away in his saddlebag.

As they rode side by side in the Essen'aelo, Bob turned to Fan. "Your father was Gasheera, you said," said Bob. "A great warrior."

Fan glanced at him with a smile. "That is true, Bob. Gaeren Soe won many battles against the Gez Kar. He is a hero to the En'harae, a name they still speak nearly a decade after his death."

Bob nodded—a gesture made easier by the movements of the chestnut mare beneath him. "If he were here," asked Bob, "and we asked him for advice... what would he say?"

Fan took a moment to consider. "He'd tell us not to underestimate the enemy. And he would tell us that we must be prepared for the possibility of defeat." He ran a hand across his fuzzy head. "He was never much of an optimist."

"Don't have much of a contingency, do we?" said Bob, mostly to himself.

Fan glanced at him with a raised eyebrow. Bob had learned that look. "Oh," he said, "I mean, we have no back-up plan."

Fan shrugged his bony shoulders. "Our back up plan is to retreat."

For a while longer, they rode in a quiet punctuated by hooves clomping through underbrush. Bob noticed Harold directly ahead of him, looking mountainous on his black and white destrier. The party entered a clearing, bathing them all in warm sunlight. Butterflies danced in patches of tall grass. Bob heard an eagle shriek in the distance.

Fan cleared his throat. "Tell me Bob. If *your* father were here, what would *he* say?"

"Get me a beer," said Bob without hesitation.

Fan opened his mouth to reply when a deep shadow fell across the clearing. Everyone craned their necks to look skyward. A silhouette was carved against the sky—a long, snake-like body held aloft my massive, bat-like wings. Its head was triangular, the tip of its tail finned. Bob instinctively reached for the rifle, but the creature glided on, and its shadow passed from the clearing.

"Was that..." murmured Bob.

"A dragon, aye." said Harold, swiveled in his saddle. "Nothing to worry about."

"Nothing to..." Bob trailed off, narrowing his eyes at the mountain man.

"Oh, aye. That was Axiis. This far from home, she rarely attacks people. Loves sheep, though." Harold chuckled.

"The dragon has a name?" asked Bob, bewildered.

"All things have a name, Bob," said Fan.

"Aye, that's right," said Harold. "Anyway, she won't be a problem for a while. Come on, then." He spurred his horse forward.

Bob turned to Fan. "What does that mean? 'Won't be a problem for a while?'"

Fan looked uncomfortable. "I am sorry Bob, it is common knowledge here. I thought you knew."

Bob's mouth felt suddenly dry. "Knew what, exactly?"

Fan began to trot his mount after Harold. "Axiis is a famous dragon, Bob," he called over his shoulder. "She lives at the Nexus."

Bob and his horse stood motionless, watching Fan and the rest of the party fade into the trees. He heard the eagle shriek again, closer this time.

"Great," said Bob. "That's just fucking great." He pressed his legs together and cantered across the remainder of the clearing.

M. V. PRINDLE

It seemed Erto had joined the party. Bob saw him standing stock-still in shady underbrush as their horses carved a path among the maples and birches. He saw him behind a boulder. Saw him at the mouth of an overhanging rock. Each time, the spirit simply stood, watching him. Once, Bob held up a hand in greeting only to be met with a passive stare from those deep, hollow eyes. The next time Erto appeared, he remained still, as before, but this time held up one spindly, lumpy hand—a stoic imitation of Bob's gesture. All the while, Bob heard a great number of astral voices calling and singing all around him.

The party risked a small fire as the sun began to set. After taking care of the horses, unpacking their minimal camping gear, and consuming a prepacked meal of salted meat and raw vegetables, Bob was too exhausted even to be afraid of what might happen the following day. As he lay upon a rough pallet of canvas sheets by the fire, the last thing he saw before sleep took him was the earth spirit standing just beyond the edge of the firelight, watching him. Rather than causing alarm, the sight of Erto brought him comfort, and he was out like a light.

He awoke to smoldering embers and the sound of Harold singing some song about warriors and a mountain. Bob was a little surprised to see Erto standing there in the middle of camp, exactly where he'd been as Bob fell asleep.

"What, you've been there all night?" he muttered.

The spirit did not reply.

The party ate a quick breakfast, packed their gear, and buried the remains of the fire. No one said anything beyond what was necessary. The game was on now, deadly serious, and a silent but insistent determination permeated the air. Only Harold seemed immune. The mountain man carried on singing his folk songs in a deep baritone as the morning unfolded, and only fell to silence once the horses had been secured. When they reached the edge of the forest, Fan and Bob exchanged a long look before the En'hari and his team of Runners ducked away and began the journey across the grassy plain.

Beyond the whispering field of khaki-grass, the walls of Swearington were clearly visible, their thick gray masonry a stark monument to ugliness. The horizon was muddied by the smoke and fumes that rose from the city. Bob's pulse quickened. Something in his guts tightened. A shard of ice seemed to burgeon in his chest. He removed the dragon pipe from its pocket in his jerkin. These days, he always made sure it was packed before it was stowed. He lit a match with shaking hands and drew deeply on the pipe.

"I hear you, Bob," rumbled Erto. "Can you hear us?"

The spirit was standing between him and Kelael, who didn't notice. The En'hari was, however, giving Bob a sharp look.

"I can hear you," said Bob.

Kelael continued to glare but said nothing.

"Listen, Bob," said Erto. "Listen. Can you hear us?"

Bob listened harder as he stared toward Swearington's walls. He heard the clanking of metal on metal carried by the wind, the distant song of birds, the chirps and buzz of insects. He felt himself tune into the astral voices. They carried in a bass so thick and full it seemed below the human threshold of hearing. It was a constant, eternal hum, like an endless generator beating at the heart of the world, a chorus of voices, deep and resonant, coming from the earth underfoot, from the stones scattered across the plain, from the massive layers of sediment miles below. It came from the city. Like a breaking dawn, the astral music washed over Bob. He could hear the voices in the stones of the wall, from the bricks in the buildings beyond—the houses, the shops and inns… from the keep. Erto was there, in all of it, inside it. The stones and the earth were Erto, and Erto was them.

"Yes, Bob," said Erto from beside him. "You hear us very well."

Bob grinned in a cloud of smoke.

CHAPTER TWENTY-THREE:
OATH

On a hunch, Bob had left his rifle and sword tied to his horse. He was a little nervous about going into battle without the weapons but was unsure if he could command Erto while carrying them. Despite his training, he still couldn't bring himself to trust a sword to save his life. The SMLE had jammed at the ridge, though he knew that should be a rare occurrence. But still, the purpose of the Runners and Wranglers was to distract attention away from Oath Keep. If Bob went in there, guns literally blazing, he'd probably alert the nearby guards, negating the efforts of the two teams. If he could use Astral Friction as his weapon, all the better.

"Our turn," said Kelael. "Stay low." He, Harold, and Gorrelai moved into the field in a high crouch.

Bob hesitated. He wanted to be sure. His eyes fell on a nearby stone about the size of a softball. He could feel Erto's chorus reaching to him, as if he were connected to it. Not that it was part of him, exactly—more that it fit him like clothing. One hand gripping the dragon pipe, he reached out with the other toward the stone, trying to find its singular voice. It wobbled on the ground.

"Sora Kelai!" There came a harsh whisper from the grass. He looked up. Kelael was crouched there, scowling. "Are you coming or not?"

Bob nodded but turned back to the stone, puffing on the pipe. He thought he could hear its individual song in the sea of voices. Somewhere in a place he couldn't describe, he pulled. The stone rose in the air and flopped toward him, landing with a thud in the dirt at his feet. Pleased but

BOB THE WIZARD

not satisfied, he glanced at Kelael.

The En'hari's expression had softened to interest. "Try again."

Bob turned to another, similarly sized stone and concentrated. He listened, found its voice, and pulled. The stone flew toward him and he caught it easily. He chuckled.

Kelael was scowling again. "Yes, very nice, Bob the Wizard. Now let's go." He ducked into the grass. The astral voices all around him, Bob followed.

The khaki stalks rasped like angry snakes as the wind flowed across them. Bob's heavy boots crunched noisily as he tromped behind Kelael in a stooped jog. The journey to the high city wall took almost half an hour. Bob held a palm over the pipe's bowl to extinguish it. Finally, he and Kelael came upon Gorrelai and Harold just in time to see the last of Fan's Runners slip over the wall. There was a guard tower nearby, just behind the wall, that seemed unmanned.

"Nobody working today?" said Bob softly, pointing at the tower.

"This is the western edge of Shadow Quarter," answered Harold. "The slums, follow? The guards mostly avoid the whole borough."

"*Arrogant fools,*" said Gorrelai in Hari.

Bob could hardly disagree. If his memory of Jenna's map was right, Shadow Quarter was actually more than a fourth of Swearington proper—it was closer to half. For the guards to ignore almost half the city... they must either be confident in the Darkhairs' good behavior, or completely indifferent to their suffering. Bob glanced at the remnants of the moat, now little more than a dipping impression of crumbled earth and dead grass. It was clear that Mannix was not concerned with preventing this kind of infiltration. Like Gorrelai said—arrogant.

Kelael opened a small pack at his belt and produced a grappling hook attached to a long cord. He began to swing it.

"Wait," said Bob. "I've got a better idea." He looked up at the wall. Erto was standing atop it, hollow eyes studying them. The astral voices warbled in Bob's ears. He withdrew a match from his brown jerkin and relit the pipe.

Kelael glared at him. "What are you doing?" he demanded. "This is no time to—"

"*Let him smoke,*" broke in Gorrelai in a harsh Hari whisper. "*It helps him do magic.*"

Kelael rolled his eyes and mumbled something.

Puffing away and smirking at Kelael's annoyance, Bob looked back at the wall. He concentrated. A few seconds later, a vertical line of stones slipped their mortar and began jutting outward from the wall, forming a makeshift ladder up to the edge of the guard tower. Harold produced a low, impressed whistle. Gorrelai chuckled and clapped Bob on the back before grabbing a handhold and pulling himself up. Kelael nodded silently, replaced the hook in its pack, and avoided eye contact with Bob as he followed Gorrelai.

"After you, Bob the Wizard." Harold grinned.

They came down the guard tower's true ladder on the city-side of the wall, landing behind a dilapidated tenement. There were scorch marks along the cobbles at its base, indicating it had been built atop the burned-down ruins of a previous building. Its slanted roof and sagging walls blocked the sun, keeping the four of them in shadow. Bob closed his eyes and flexed with Erto's chorus, barely hearing the gentle grind of the wall's stones shifting back to their original positions. He cashed out the pipe and began repacking it.

"To the keep," whispered Kelael. "We must be in place when Fan gives the signal."

The Infiltrators stayed low as they swung around the tenement, keeping to the city shadows. Bob stowed the loaded pipe back into the jerkin.

If it were just Bob and Harold, the two of them could have easily waltzed through Swearington all the way to Oath Keep. After all, they were just a couple of Darkhairs. Due to Harold's size and armament, they'd easily pass as mercenaries. With two blue-skinned En'harae along— both of whom were just as dangerous as they appeared—remaining undetected was paramount.

BOB THE WIZARD

The four of them slunk along dripping alleyways and shambled corridors. It was the part of all cities that most people never see or think about, but that Bob knew well. It was the back alleys, where people put their trash. In his home city of Austin, it was where businesses kept dumpsters and recycling bins, old crates and bags full of refuse. Even in broad daylight, Bob recalled, almost no one would be back there. The garbage truck would roll up, shrieking and roaring like a territorial monster, to claim its prey—the previous week's rubbish. And almost always, the metal beast consumed its meal away from prying eyes. The men and women driving the truck were the sole witnesses. People didn't like to think about trash. They tucked it away, pretending it didn't exist, allowing it to be someone else's problem. And that behavior seemed to hold true in Engoria. There were trash bins, barrels of filthy oil that smelled like they were foul even before they were discarded, rusted metal scraps, rotting shreds of parchment. Most importantly—no people.

The sounds of the slum reached them through thin walls: prostitutes already on corners, calling to customers; junk collectors tossing their findings into carts, advertisers from wealthier boroughs yelling about their latest deals on buckles, mutton, or fabrics; the clop of horse-hooves and screech of unoiled wagon wheels. Bob could detect the earthy, metallic smell of melting iron on the wind, the robust presence of horse manure, and the stench of human urine. Once, they came upon a derelict sitting in a pile of filth. They simply passed him in silence as he muttered to himself.

After minutes that stretched on long enough for Bob to acclimate to the smells, he and the other Infiltrators reached a shadowed nook between the keep's outer wall and the back end of a church adorned with cloudy, stained-glass windows. The wall around the grounds of Oath Keep was only about ten feet high—low enough to climb over with a boost from nearby empty crates. But it was not yet the right time. They rested, crouched against the side of the church, looking to the sky, awaiting the signal from the Runners.

Erto stood at the mouth of the alley. Bob was tuned-in to the astral voices, but he was careful not to listen too hard. They were so loud here, where there was so much stone. He had a feeling that, if he were careless with his astral hearing, the voices would blow out everything else, effectively rendering him deaf. It was just a matter of listening the right way, of balancing the physical and the astral. Not much different from riding a bike, considered Bob as he watched Erto's little mud-avatar. You knew you could fall, but with experience, the fear melted away and only the illusion of control remained.

At the mouth of the alley, slowly, like a branch in the breeze, Erto extended an arm upward, pointing a clumpy finger to the sky. Bob looked up to see a brief explosion of blue smoke erupt like a firework over the city to the north.

"That's it," said Kelael. "Here we go." He may have opposed the mission, but now that it was underway, he was focused on the task with a fierce intensity. He deftly launched himself from a crate, grabbed the lip of the stone wall, and vaulted over it. Harold was right behind him, eschewing the crate for a simple hop, then a flex of his massive arms. Gorrelai gave Bob a nod, flashing a rigid grimace, and soon vanished over the lip of the wall behind the others. Heart hammering, the tower of Oath Keep taunting him from the courtyard beyond, Bob moved to join his allies.

The courtyard was just as he remembered it. A small sea of polished cobblestones surrounded the seven-story keep like a shining moat, the recently cut grass at its edges a healthy emerald green. From the squat foundation rose the impressive tower of white and gray stone, decorated with large panes of stained glass before displaying its impressive crenelated balconies and luxurious balustrades. Atop the keep flew the white and black flag of Swearington—an encircled fist—and the green, black and gold turtle-banner of Tortellan. The banners rumpled and popped in the wind. The building's wings stretched to the north and south, and on the southward side Bob noticed a series of tiny rectangular windows mere inches from the ground. It was the top floor of the dungeon, he realized. One of those windows had been his.

Aside from Bob and his cohort, the courtyard of Oath Keep was empty. "Where is everyone?" asked Harold, glancing around. "I guess the Runners proved their mettle, aye?"

Bob eyed the keep. "It's even bigger than it looks," he said, remembering his time there. "At least two guards just inside the door. Probably at least a dozen more in there, not to mention Mannix. There's a dungeon, for one, and it's manned." He glanced at Oath Keep's south wing.

Gorrelai's head snapped around. *"The En'hari prisoners! I had forgotten."* He shot a hard look at Kelael. "Slaves," he spat the word in English, a dangerous gleam in his eyes.

"Yes," said Bob carefully. "There were slaves, last time I was here."

Gorrelai's curved sword rasped against its scabbard as he drew it with an impressive flourish. *"We will free them."* His tone brooked no argument. He strode purposefully toward the keep's double-doored entrance, and Kelael followed silently. Bob and Harold exchanged a glance, then fell into lockstep behind them.

Bob took his waterskin from his belt and took a long swallow, feeling it wash down a film of nicotine in his throat. He replaced the skin and withdrew the dragon pipe.

Gorrelai reached the doors first. Instead of walking through them, he pressed his back against the wall beside them and nodded to Kelael, who nocked an arrow and drew back his bow, levelling it at the crack where the doors met.

"Bob, stand back," ordered Kelael. "Harold, get the door."

Bob popped a match to light, positioning himself opposite the door and behind Kelael. Harold approached the wall beside the doors, across from Gorrelai. Bob drew on the pipestem, producing a gray plume in the still air. Harold reached a scarred and muscled arm to the doorhandle and pushed the door open a few inches.

Immediately, Kelael loosed the arrow. "Go!" he shouted, reaching for his quiver. Gorrelai kicked the door closest to him and it crashed inward. He and Harold charged in. Bob moved after them and saw the raised dais where Archlector Carosel usually sat scratching away with a quill. Today it was empty. As before, only two guards had been stationed here in the atrium. Now, both lay dead—one with an arrow protruding from his eye, the other cleanly decapitated.

M. V. PRINDLE

Gorrelai shook blood from his blade, splattering the marble floor. He glared at the two corpses as if daring them to move. "*Where is the dungeon?*" he demanded of Bob.

Bob gestured to an alcove to the south of the entrance. "Down those stairs."

The big elf strode purposefully in that direction and disappeared down the staircase.

Kelael started after him. "*Gorrelai, sifah! Sifah!*" Wait.

Harold sighed. "Best to not split up, then. Come on, Bob." He turned and followed the other two Infiltrators down the stairs.

Bob intended to follow, but he glanced up through wisps of smoke at the atrium's inner balconies, and a flash of movement caught his eye. He craned his neck. There, behind one of the highest balconies on the north side, a surprised face stared down at him—hard, calculating eyes set in handsome features, framed by well-kept blond hair and beard. It was Fulton Mannix. Bob's heart gave a hard thump. He started for the stairs to the north of the entrance, but as he reached them, a creak of the double doors caused him to pause and look around.

"Bob? It's just me." Fan stood in the doorway, the daylight behind him cutting out his figure in the comparative gloom of the atrium. He waved at stale smoke. "I can smell you from outside."

"Fan? What the fuck are you doing here?"

"I came to report," said Fan, stepping into the atrium and softly closing the doors behind him. "There is something strange going on here."

Bob glanced up at the balconies, but he couldn't see much from where he stood by the stairs. He had to get to Mannix. What if there was some way to escape? What if Mannix had a way to call an army down on them? He swung around to look at the stairs to the dungeon. But what if his friends needed him? No, they could take care of themselves. The Gatekey was so close! He turned to Fan. "Great, you can tell me on the way up."

"Up?" said Fan, clearly confused. Bob was already ascending the stairs.

BOB THE WIZARD

"Bob! Where is my brother?"

"He's busy!" called Bob, not turning around. He couldn't slow down, couldn't stop to talk. He was closing in on Mannix, closing in on the Gatekey… and that meant he was closer to finding Galvidon, to killing that ugly son of a bitch once and for all.

Yes, Bob, said Anna, egging him on. *Yes, Bob, get him!*

His teeth gripped the pipe. As he climbed, he could hear Fan's soft footfalls following.

Soon Fan was right behind him, mildly panting. "The Runners," he said, "our job was easy. Very easy. There were hardly any guards or troops at all."

"Good," said Bob curtly, smoke drifting from his nose. He reached a landing and a sword blade thrust toward him from the corridor, barely missing his neck. "Shit!" He leaned away and, finding Erto to still be with him, yanked on a stone in the wall with Astral Friction. There was a grind and a shiver as the chunk of masonry ripped from its mortar before flying through the air to slam into his assailant's crotch. The man, who wore the black and white half-plate of the Swearington Guard, doubled over. Bob set a foot on his shoulder and kicked the guy into the approaching guard behind him. Fan had drawn his shortsword but hesitated to attack the fallen men. Bob wrestled with the desire to kill them. Instead, he waved a hand, and with Erto's blessing, the stones along the inside of the doorway grew and stretched, forming a newly made wall to block the corridor.

Fan blinked. "Very impressive, Sora Kelai. The spirits smile upon you." Bob grunted in reply and resumed his ascent up the switchbacks of the staircase. "Bob," called Fan, continuing to follow. "Why do you think there were so few armed men in the city? Where do you think they went?"

Bob cashed out the pipe and began to refill it as he climbed. He dully recognized that he was wheezing. At Fan's question, Bob recalled the Engorian army he'd seen from the hill by the mines—the thousands of people and animals carving a dusty path across the landscape. "They probably got called away. Maybe to En'hirin. Maybe your brothers and sisters are putting up more of a fight than they thought. We got lucky."

Take the win." They reached another landing. Bob risked a swig of water before relighting the pipe.

As they rounded the switchback they were confronted by another group of guards. One of them held a long pike with a serrated tip, and the other two had drawn swords. With the quickness of a gunslinger, Fan withdrew the bone slingshot from his belt and launched a spherical projectile. A plume of thick blue smoke erupted in the stairwell, mixing with the tobacco smoke, obscuring everything in swirls of aqua and marine. The guards cried out in alarm, the pikeman making a desperate thrust at Bob. His muscles well trained by the hours with Kelael, Bob sidestepped, grabbed the shaft of the pike, and yanked hard. The guard stumbled over his coughing comrades, crashed into a guiderail, and plummeted noisily onto the landing below. Still clutching the pike, Bob jabbed its dull end into one of the remaining men's plated chest. The guard slashed wildly with his blade, ineffectually chipping the pike's shaft. The guy tripped backward over his own feet, colliding with the final guard. The two of them clattered to the floor of the approaching corridor in a tangle. Bob waved away a cloud of smoke, coughing heavily. He and Erto sealed the corridor.

"Bob, what is going on?" asked Fan. A scowl had settled across his face, and in that moment, he looked much like Gorrelai. "Where are the others?"

"Dungeon," said Bob, pushing past his friend and mounting the stairs. "They're looking to free some En'hari prisoners. But I saw Mannix, God damn it. He's up there. I won't let him figure a way to weasel out of this." He clambered upward. "Come on."

On the top floor, the staircase ended in the mouth of an archway, where the path split into two. Continuing straight through the archway would lead down a new set of stairs into an antechamber, while a left turn just past it led to a shallow balcony that overlooked the antechamber and wound to a new corridor. There was a loud crack from the antechamber's gloom and a crossbow quarrel whizzed past Bob's head.

"Down!" he barked, and dove left, taking cover behind the lip of the shallow balcony. Two cracks came in quick succession, followed by quarrels snapping against stone as they struck the balcony railing.

BOB THE WIZARD

"I am out of smoke bombs," said Fan, crouched next to Bob.

"Here!" yelled a voice from the antechamber. "Bandits in the keep! Here!"

There was another crack and another snap as the man fired again. Bob and Erto gripped the ceiling above the guards and yanked. There was an enormous crash as the section collapsed, raining deadly rubble down upon Bob's assailants. He peeked over the balcony railing. The two guards had been partially buried. One of them lay next to his dropped crossbow. Bob rose and made his way down into the antechamber. He stood above the fallen guards, blood boiling. Fan stood behind him, glancing around uncomfortably.

There came a scuff of boots on stone and Bob turned to see Mannix glaring at him from the gloom of the balcony's second corridor. Eyes wide, the Lord of Swearington receded back into the shadowy hallway. Bob bolted for the stairs.

"Spirits!" cursed Fan in frustration, but then followed.

Bob rounded the top of the stairs and peeked around the corridor after Mannix. He saw nothing but rows of doorways down a darkened hallway. He cashed out the still-smoldering pipe and refilled it yet again, hardly noticing as he burned his thumb on the embers.

"Bob," said Fan, catching up with him.

Bob popped a match to light and sucked in smoke. It was becoming harsh and foul-tasting, and his tongue felt swollen—sure signs his body had had enough.

"Bob," said Fan again.

Ignoring both his body and his friend, he continued pursuit. The corridor was familiar. There, that door on the right—the balcony he'd teleported to with the Gatekey was beyond it. Mannix's private chambers were at the end of the hall to the left.

Get him, said Anna. *Get that slaver bastard.*

"Are you sure this is a good idea?" demanded Fan in a harsh whisper. "I think we should wait for the others."

M. V. PRINDLE

Blood pounded in Bob's temples. Somewhere at the back of his mind, he knew Fan was right. But that understanding was buried under a mountain of fury: his anger at Galvidon, at Mannix, at himself.

No, do it now, said Anna. *Don't listen to him. Do it now.*

Bob strode down the hallway. His teeth creaked as they pressed into the pipestem.

"Bob!" pleaded Fan. "Bob!"

Bob reached Mannix's door, and when he brought up a leather boot, it was covered in a layer of stone. He slammed his foot into the doorhandle, which cracked as the door exploded inward.

"That's quite far enough, Bob!" Mannix ordered from across the bedchamber. In his hands, pointed squarely at Bob's chest, was the sawed-off shotgun.

Bob sneered. "Figure it out, did you? Good for you. You want a cookie?" He took a step forward.

Mannix raised the gun higher. "Approach no further, Bob! I don't want to kill you, but I will."

This gave Bob pause. Mannix didn't want to kill him? He could sense Fan behind him, just outside the door.

"Throw down your weapons," ordered Mannix.

"Fan, stay back," muttered Bob. He drew in a breath of smoke, then removed the pipe from his mouth and slowly raised his hands. "I have no weapons," he said to Mannix, and dared another step forward.

"You're here for the key, yes?" said Mannix. Though he held the gun, there was a tremble of fear in his voice. Bob narrowed his eyes. Right hand still gripping the sawed-off, Mannix used his left to reach to his neck and tease out a chain he wore there. Upon the end of it swung the Gatekey, its ornate surface winking in the soft light. Bob's anger flared. "I'll give it to you," said Mannix. "Here, take it." He swiftly pulled the chain from his neck and tossed the Gatekey to Bob, who caught it in his free hand.

BOB THE WIZARD

Bob briefly inspected the little green meter, which was dark. No charge. Completely baffled by Mannix's actions, he set the Gatekey around his neck. His confusion ate away at his anger. "Why?" he asked, his voice hoarse. He felt the fury that had clouded everything else begin to melt.

Something in Bob's tone seemed to relax Mannix some small amount. The twin barrels of the shotgun dipped slightly. "It has been brought to my attention, Bob," he said, "that you might be the only person in the world who can use that thing. It opens special doors, yes? Well, being a man of knowledge, I'd very much like to see what's on the other side of those doors. If you died, I might never know."

Bob laughed derisively. "You still think I'm going to help you? After everything you've done to me? After what you've done to the En'harae?" He inched forward.

Mannix's grip on the gun loosened further. A look of frustration crumpled his face. "You don't understand—"

Bob launched himself at Mannix, grabbed the gun barrels with both hands, his shoulder connecting with Mannix's chin, the dragon pipe clattering to the floor. The Lord of Swearington bucked backward but didn't relinquish his hold on the gun. The two men struggled, wrestling for control of the weapon. There was a clap of thunder as one of the shells fired into the ceiling, raining debris down upon them as they continued to twist and pull. Mannix cracked Bob in the nose with an elbow. Bob bellowed and slammed his forehead into Mannix's face. The gun went off a second time, blasting a nearby table and showering pieces of carved wood and crockery all over the room. His grip finally superior, Bob wrenched the now unloaded shotgun from Mannix and cracked the stock across his face. Mannix sunk to the floor against the wall, battered and bloody. Bob's nose and forehead throbbed with pain, and every pump of his heart was accompanied by a memory.

He remembered Mannix taking the Gatekey from him at the market, remembered how helpless he'd been. He remembered the endless days at the mines, being whipped and beaten, being worked nearly to death; remembered Scarface tossing him a whip.

"I'll fucking kill you!" screamed Bob, dropping the gun. The astral voices blared in his hearing. Nicotine raced through his bloodstream. Astral Friction pulled a stone from the far wall and flung it at Mannix's head with all the force Bob could muster.

Something happened. The stone inexplicably shifted into a horseshoe shape and clunked against the wall, trapping Mannix by the neck. Bob yelled incoherently and pulled two more stones, willing them to punch through Mannix's vital organs and end him once and for all. The stones flew at Mannix with lethal velocity, but they twisted into a new shape in midair, clapping Mannix's wrists against the wall. The Lord of Swearington, his eyes wide with astonishment and terror, remained alive, shackled like a thief in the stocks. Bob bellowed again, this time in frustration, and kicked over a wardrobe, which crashed to the floor and spilled its contents. Among the various clothing items, Bob saw his black trench coat. Somehow, the sight of it calmed him. He inhaled deeply and turned to Mannix.

"Why can't I kill you?" he whispered.

Unbidden, Torael's voice bubbled up from somewhere in his memory. *What you want must be true.* Then, Osivia: *I don't think you should kill Mannix.* Bob realized he was crying and wiped at his tears with his palms.

"Shit," he muttered.

Fan spoke shakily from the doorway. "Bob, we should go. You have the Gatekey. Let's go."

"Wait," croaked Mannix. He looked almost comical, shackled to the wall with horseshoes of stone, blood oozing from his nostrils into his mouth. "I want you to understand, Bob. When my people came here over a thousand years ago, the elves and the lizards controlled the entire continent. We had to fight for every square inch of this land, because they fought us every step of the way! We were at war for centuries. Centuries, Bob! Do you know how this city got its name? Do you know why this castle is called Oath Keep?"

Bob bent down to retrieve the pipe, then the trench coat, shaking the latter free of debris. "Can't say that I do."

"This is where the first treaty between Engoria and the elves was signed. Where we swore to have peace! I didn't break that peace. It was

BOB THE WIZARD

Flaire. Flaire and Forr Ghaway, that Sun-cursed lizard warlord! Not all Engorians wanted this war, Bob. Not all of us want what Flaire wants."

Bob finished pulling on the trench coat. Since last wearing it, he'd lost fat and gained muscle, so it didn't fit exactly as it had before. "You think any of that excuses your actions?" He walked over to Mannix and squatted down to look him in the eye. "Let me tell you something, Fulton. When I got here, I'd lost my way. I'd forgotten how important every life was. I only thought of myself—what I wanted. If I'm a better man than I was then, even a little, it's because of the En'harae. And what do you do? Sit here in your comfy tower, fucking slave girls while the men you own pull iron out of the ground so you can make weapons. You are a stain, Mannix. The only reason I can't kill you now is because of them, you understand? They are better than you. And so am I." He rose and crossed to the shotgun, retrieving it off the floor. "Where's the rest of the ammo?"

Mannix pointed a shaky finger at a desk in the corner, where, for the first time, Bob noticed his own brown backpack sitting atop it. He strode to it, briefly checked the pack's contents, stuffed a few slugs into his pockets, made sure he had his pipe, and crossed to the door where Fan waited impatiently.

"Alright," said Fan with a forced smile, "let us tell the others of our victory." He padded down the corridor ahead of Bob, toward the antechamber.

Bob followed, awhirl with contrasting emotions. Victory, Fan had said. So why did he feel so hollow? Fan rounded the corner onto the antechamber's balcony. Bob opened his mouth to apologize to him for being so brusque on the way up the stairs, but he never spoke. There was a crack from the floor of the antechamber and a whistle in the air. Fan fell sideways as a quarrel pierced his neck. Terror trumpeted in Bob's chest. He cracked the shotgun's breach, stepped back behind the wall for cover, quickly found a slug in his breast pocket, loaded it, swung the breach closed and pulled the hammer back. He waited. Fan twitched on floor beside him.

"Here!" the guard shouted weakly. "Bandits! He—"

Bob stepped out from the corridor and shot him in the chest. The slug passed through the guard's plate like it wasn't there. The man, still half buried in rubble, coughed a spray of blood and fell still. It was the guard that had shot at them earlier. Bob had collapsed part of the ceiling on top of him just before spotting Mannix. He'd left the unconscious guard beside a loaded crossbow.

"Fan," said Bob. "Fan!" He gripped his friend's shoulder and rolled him over. "Oh, no," groaned Bob. He felt his tears returning. "Oh, no, no, no."

Fan was dead.

BOB THE WIZARD

CHAPTER TWENTY-FOUR:
FALLEN HEROES

Bob stood for a moment, wiping his eyes, trying to decide what to do. He couldn't leave Fan. If he did, Gorrelai would undoubtedly insist on returning here to retrieve the body.

Gorrelai.

Just thinking about him turned Bob's stomach. How would he react? The big elf had been through enough already. Well, there was nothing for it. Bob secured the sawed-off in its rightful place inside the trench coat and bent down. He struggled with Fan's body and hoisted it onto his shoulders. His friend's blood pattered onto the floor from the neck wound.

Bob descended. On his way up the staircase and in Mannix's room, his mind had been racing. Now his thoughts were sluggish. By the time he approached the bottom landing, he was unsure if he'd had a single cogent thought along the way. He could hear the voices of his friends in the atrium. Would they still be his friends when they saw the burden he carried? Doubt gnawed at him like an infestation of rats.

As Bob rounded the final switchback, Harold called to him. "Bob! There you are! Where'd you go? You missed quite a scene. Kelael almost got himself impaled. Distracted by a woman, aye?" Following this was a feminine laugh, a voice Bob didn't recognize.

"Shut your mouth, human, or you'll get impaled yourself," said Kelael, sounding uncharacteristically cheerful. "We won, yes? All safe and sound. Proof we don't need a wizard."

Gorrelai began to laugh but cut short as Bob stepped out of the shadowy stairwell. The En'hari's eyes narrowed. Bob leaned down and gently lay the body on the stone tiles. Six pairs of eyes fell upon him— three En'hari women, all wearing those brown, sack-like dresses, stood with the party. Gorrelai crossed the space between himself and his brother's body with but a few strides. He looked down at Fan's slack face, the quarrel still protruding from beneath his mouth. Gorrelai dropped to his knees, hands pressed to his forehead.

"Is that..." began Harold.

"What is he doing here?" snapped Kelael, all trace of cheer erased. He moved to just behind Gorrelai. "What did you do?" He drew his sword.

Numbness crawled out of Bob's heart and washed across his body. "He came in to tell us something," he said tonelessly. "I got the Gatekey, and we were doing fine, but then..." he trailed off, staring at the floor.

Gorrelai's knee popped as he stood. He carefully stepped around Fan toward Bob and then stood to face him. Bob's gaze came up to meet his. The En'hari's eyes shone with welling tears. Bob remembered Gorrelai's angry fits, how he destroyed mining equipment and threw around a dozen slavers before they could subdue him. The big elf might kill him. At that moment, Bob felt like he deserved it. He held Gorrelai's gaze, awaiting judgement. Gorrelai moved, and despite Bob willing himself to submit, he flinched. But two muscular blue arms drew him into a hug. Bob's eyes went wide, then he tentatively returned the embrace.

Gorrelai released his grip and stepped back. "*I will carry him,*" he said softly in Hari.

Kelael sheathed his blade, scowling. The three blue women huddled together, confusion on their faces.

"Right then," said Harold with forced authority. "We freed the prisoners and got the Gatekey. Time to go, aye?"

When pressed by Harold, Bob relayed what Fan had said about the city being empty of forces. The mountain man and Kelael conferred for a moment in the courtyard of Oath Keep. Bob and Gorrelai stood in silence with the women. After a moment, Kelael declared that, now with a party of seven and Fan's information, expedience should prevail over secrecy. They would not bother to hide their escape—they would simply exit the city as swiftly as possible. Harold asked Bob if he could get them through the city wall without a gate. Still hearing the astral voices emanating from the earth and masonry, Bob nodded.

The party exited the courtyard's front gate and plunged openly into Shadow Quarter. Something in the trench coat knocked Bob's hand as he walked. He investigated the corresponding pocket, pulling out a sleek, black object.

"Well, I'll be damned," he murmured, staring dumbly at the pair of sunglasses in his hand. He opened the tines and placed the glasses on his face.

"What is that?" asked one of the blue women. She had striking hair of purple and red shocks. "Can you even see?"

"See just fine," Bob replied, smirking despite his despondent mood. She left it at that.

It was midafternoon and Swearington was in full swing. They walked down the major thoroughfare they'd skirted in back alleys on the way to the keep. According to the street signs it was called Shady Way, and Bob had rarely seen a worse misnomer. Shady Way was anything but shady—it baked in the sun, only the eaves providing shelter. Bob was uncomfortably hot under the linen, the jerkin, and the trench coat. Beads of sweat gathered in his beard.

The road was a filthy skein of dried mud and pebbles, lined with tenements on one side and saloons and shops on the other. Carts rattled and squeaked, criers and merchants called. Bob saw a woman beating a rug on her porch. People stopped and stared at the seven strangers as they passed. Some shook their heads and returned to their business, while others dropped what they were doing and, curiosity and shock warring on their faces, followed the party at a respectable distance. Harold strode with arms crossed and head high, while Kelael glanced around nervously, occasionally brushing the bow on his back with one hand. Gorrelai walked with Fan across his shoulders, head down, green dreadlocks obscuring his face. The three women kept close to the other

En'harae, leaving Bob at the rear. By the time they approached the high city wall, the party had gathered a crowd behind them like sharks leading a school of remoras.

"They've freed slaves from the keep!" someone loudly observed.

"Hey, I know you! You're that wizard!"

Bob craned his neck to the crowd and saw the source of this last comment. It took him a moment, but he recognized a dirty face. It was the beggar that had seen him teleport from Oath Keep the day he'd first met Mannix. Bob noticed Harold had stopped, looking at him with knitted eyebrows.

"Keep walking," Bob muttered to him.

The crowd was chattering. Bob distinctly heard the word "wizard" several times.

"Cast a spell and make us some food!" someone yelled.

"Look at the elves, mommy! They don't look like monsters to me..."

"What's that on his eyes? Can he even see?"

A woman in rags carrying an infant reached out and touched Bob's arm as he walked. "Save us, too!" she pleaded. "Save my baby!" The crowd erupted further, everyone seeming to shout at once. Harold and Kelael had reached the wall. The En'harae women clustered around them as Gorrelai approached.

Bob slipped the trench coat and backpack off and calmly handed them to Harold, who accepted the items wordlessly, eying the crowd. The coat and pack held all of Bob's metal, except... His hand reached to his neck and caressed the Gatekey. He was unsure if he could bring himself to remove it. He thought he remembered employing Astral Friction while wearing it in Mannix's room, but his head was still feeling cloudy.

Erto was standing next to him. "You may keep it," rumbled the spirit in a voice only he could hear. "It is even older than I, and I fear it not." Bob's hand fell to his side and he turned to face the wall. He removed the dragon pipe and began to pack it. The crowd was murmuring and shifting, seemingly not wanting to get any closer to the strangers.

The rest of Bob's party scooted along the wall to give him space. He lit the pipe. The smoke was acrid and unpleasant. He fought back a gag and his head swam. Too much nicotine, in too short a time. He pushed through it, concentrating on what he wanted Erto to accomplish.

The crowd chattering behind him, Bob raised a hand, and next to him, Erto did the same. A section of the wall began to break apart, the stones rearranging like a puzzle solving itself. In a few seconds, the stones stilled, and there was a gap in the wall large enough to walk through.

The crowd emitted a collective sigh of amazement. Bob turned to face them, unsure of what to say. They looked at him expectantly. He glanced at the woman with the baby, then surveyed the other faces: dirty, sweaty, hungry faces. He cleared his throat.

"I don't need to save you. You can save yourselves. Anybody know where the Lighthairs keep their food?" There was a collective murmur of assent. "Well," continued Bob, "today, you might not find too many guards on duty." The people exchanged looks. "Or any guards at all."

The crowd was silent for a moment, then it erupted again as everyone started talking at once. Attention fell from Bob and turned to what he'd said. He stepped toward the gap in the wall, holding up a hand in farewell.

"Wait," a woman said to him. "What is your name, Wizard?"

"Oh, uh, I'm Bob." He offered a tired smile.

"Bob the Wizard," the woman mused.

The party slid out of Swearington and into the tall grass beyond. Bob followed his friends and closed the gap, the crowd still babbling behind him.

Bob's face had begun to swell. He was pretty sure he was developing two black eyes, and he could feel a fresh egg protruding from his forehead. His lungs were sore. His throat felt scratchy and raw. His hands and arms bore bruises and scrapes from his scuffle with Mannix. His back hurt. In short, he was miserable. Still, all the physical pain felt far away. As he crunched through clumps of khaki-grass, his eyes remained locked on Gorrelai ahead of him, and the burden the En'hari carried. The sight of Fan's limp form hurt in a way all the rest couldn't touch. *I have dreamed long of the day*, Fan had said, *I witness the clothing I have made worn by a free people.* A dream that would never be realized.

The party moved wordlessly across the grassy plain and into the tree-line. Bob reached his mare, the beast serenely cropping grass along the base of her tree. He gave her a friendly pat on the rump and tied the shotgun and his backpack to the saddle. He removed the trench coat and draped it over the horse's back and loosened his jerkin. He gulped down the rest of the water in his waterskin, grabbed another from the saddlebag, and drank that one too. The gentle breeze under the shade of the Essen'aelo caressed the sweat on his forehead.

Slowly, as if he emerged from a dark tunnel, the world opened up around him. He became more keenly aware of his companions—Gorrelai hitching Fan's blanket-wrapped body over his horse, Kelael softly speaking Hari to the three former slave-women, Harold stroking the black and white destrier's neck, humming under his breath. Bob turned back to the chestnut mare who gamely bore all his equipment. He stared at the rifle and sword, then at the shotgun, the backpack, the trench coat. He lightly touched the sunglasses on his face, felt the Gatekey swing against his chest. He was struck by a sense of overlapping identities. At this moment, he realized, the man he was when he first arrived on Hub met the man he had become. Who was he now—still the man chasing Galvidon, or someone else?

Kelael ordered the party to mount up. Gorrelai's horse carried Fan, so each of the other three Infiltrators had one of the women ride behind them in the saddle. Bob ended up with the woman who'd commented on his sunglasses, her arms around his waist, her red and purple hair brushing against his back in the breeze. Her name was Keea. The party made its way southwest.

━━◉━━

Just before nightfall, Bob's party encountered the Runners at the designated rendezvous location. Fan's team was dismayed at what had become of their group leader. They whispered blessings over his body and muttered resentful curses. Their chagrin was interrupted by the sound of bleating animals.

Soon a cluster of lights approached through the darkening forest. One, brighter and more consistent than the rest, resolved into Osivia. The others, orange and flickering, turned out to be lanterns mounted upon a horse-drawn wagon. Atop it in the driver's position sat Torael, festooned with sheepskins. There was yet another wagon behind him, and it appeared the En'harae Wranglers were all accounted for. Torael's team—some sitting in the wagons, others walking their horses alongside—came with dozens of sheep. The animals seemed excited to be on such an adventure. They waggled their behinds and scuttled about in the foliage, munching on leaves and bleating happily.

Torael raised his arms expansively. Bob glanced at the wagons, which seemed chock-full of supplies. "My first thievery!" declared Torael, grinning. "How did I do?"

Bob approached the wagon. "We lost Fan."

Torael's arms lowered, and his face fell. "Fan? Oh, no. This is most terrible. What happened?" Before Bob could answer, the Quaylen Dah yelled for Gorrelai.

Bob told Torael the events of Oath Keep. Gorrelai arrived and listened. Bob left out the part about not killing Mannix, glossing over those few minutes as best he could. He just couldn't bring himself to admit it in front of Gorrelai. Bob himself was unsure if he'd done the right thing. Was it wrong to let a man like Mannix live to potentially hurt more people? Bob only had a feeling to defend his actions, an intuition that told him Mannix might change for the better. But in the face of his brother's death, surely Gorrelai would see such justifications as weak and unfair.

After Bob's account, Torael thanked him and fell into a quiet discussion with Gorrelai. Bob saw the pained look on the big elf's face as they spoke, as if he were barely keeping his feelings in check. Struggling with guilt, Bob worked his way into the crowd of En'harae toward the recently built campfire. The sounds of voices, the rustle of hooves upon leaves, and the bleating calls of sheep almost drowned out the crackle of the fire.

He sat down on a log next to Harold, where the mountain man stared into the flames. Bob could see Osivia's dancing light weaving among the En'harae. Across from Bob, a wall of licking fire between them, sat Keea, matching Harold's thousand-mile stare. He realized she was the first female En'hari he'd ever seen. She'd been the one bringing scrolls to Carosel the first time Bob had entered Oath Keep.

Harold placed a hand on Bob's back, and as the camp broke into a minor victory celebration, the two of them sat in silence. Bob smoked, letting other people's conversations wash over him. From snippets here and there, he learned that the Wranglers had encountered even less resistance than the Runners. The sight of a dozen En'harae swarming out of the forest had set the only two guards in the vicinity running from them, rather than after them. Torael's team had simply approached the nearest farm and had—through the power of sheer mob intimidation—taken everything. Bob thought of the old woman from the market, Hilda Fields, and of Farmer Willis, and felt a new pang of regret blossom among his thoughts of Fan. Torael's Wranglers had taken someone's livelihood. Bob had stolen things before. Out of necessity, he'd told himself at the time. That's what this was, wasn't it? Necessity?

Word got around that, among the supplies the Wranglers had taken, were two barrels of wine. Someone tried to hand Bob a wooden tankard of the deep red liquid, but he ignored them, continuing to stare into the popping fire. After his own tankard, Harold began singing a song about fallen heroes. For such a big, hairy, bull of a man, he had a beautiful voice. Soon, everyone was listening.

The sun cracked over the horizon, stirring the camp. Bob came out of troubled dreams in which Fan was chasing him, asking him for help, but Bob kept running away. He woke with a hard, palpable taste in his mouth. Maybe it was nicotine. Maybe regret.

Bob got up and poked the embers of the smoldering fire, contemplating breakfast. Around him, the campsite slowly came to life. It seemed that despite Fan's death, a buoyant mood had gripped the En'harae. They'd technically achieved a victory—food and supplies taken from the humans, the Gatekey in Bob's possession. They seemed to have a vague understanding, based on rumor, that Bob was to use it to procure them weapons. They mourned the loss of one of their own, but, Bob knew, they'd grown accustomed to losing people. Besides, only one casualty was a better outcome than most of them had expected.

It was well into the morning before the camp was fully stricken and the large party, now numbering over thirty people and dozens of accompanying animals, was ready to depart. At Torael's request the previous night, Bob and Erto had erected a shallow earthen wall around the perimeter in order to prevent any sheep from wandering too far. Once everyone was organized, the horses accounted for, the sheep incentivized to gather, Bob lowered the barrier and the bandit caravan set off west through the forest.

Bob decided to walk and let someone else ride on the mare. Once they were underway, Osivia found Bob and began talking immediately. First, she expressed her condolences for Fan.

"He was the only En'hari who ever asked me about myself," she said. "He was such a good listener. Patient and kind. It's such a shame." Then she was talking about her experience with the Wranglers, confirming the story Bob had heard in snippets the night before. "You should have seen those guards run," she giggled. Then she seemed to notice the swelling on Bob's face for the first time. "I can take care of that," she offered. Bob didn't object, so she had him remove the sunglasses. "Oh, geez, you run into a wall?" She lit upon his forehead and Bob was momentarily dazzled by a profusion of white light. Afterward, the deep aches faded, leaving his face tender but otherwise healthy. Bob mumbled his thanks. Finally, she asked Bob what he thought would happen next.

"I'm going to the Nexus, soon as we get these people back to the Koreka for evac," he said.

"Who's going with you?" she asked, spinning in a circle around his head.

"Don't know, but someone'd better. I got no fucking idea where the Nexus even is."

"It's north of here, in the mountains," she said. "And a little west, I think."

"You've been there?" asked Bob, crunching through underbrush.

"Goodness, no. But I copied the maps in the council room." She patted the bookbag on her belt. "Remember?"

Bob nodded. "Right." The horses snorted around them. The sheep seemed agitated.

She scrunched her nose. "That one is almost full. Going to need a new one soon. Say, do you smell that?"

Bob's face tightened as he looked up at her. He sniffed the air, then shook his head. "Tobacco has a way of fucking up your sense of smell. What is it?" Nearby, a horse brayed and twitched, nostrils flaring.

Osivia took a few investigative sniffs. "Smells like… something's burning. Hold on, I'll be right back." She zipped upward through the canopy. A pair of sheep zig-zagged toward him, bleating nervously, nearly tripping him. A minute later, Osivia pierced the canopy like a little glowing meteor.

"Smoke!" she yelled. "Smoke on the horizon!"

Bob was surprised by how upset she was. Around him, the horses tossed their heads. The sheep were going crazy, running in circles and yelling at everyone in sheep-language.

"Where?" called Kelael from somewhere ahead.

"The Koreka!" exclaimed Osivia. "It's burning! The Koreka is burning!"

Kelael's commands rang throughout the forest. "Bob, Gorrelai, Harold, with me!"

As Bob reclaimed his mare, Torael hopped down from where he rode on a wagon and jogged toward the front of the caravan. "I'm coming!" he declared.

"Don't be stupid, Quaylen Dah," snapped Kelael. "You will stay here in safety."

Torael scowled and crossed his arms but did not argue.

BOB THE WIZARD

Bob plunged through the Essen'aelo, abreast of the other Infiltrators, galloping around trees, whipped by branches. The smell of burning wood reached his nostrils, gaining potency with every hoofbeat. Soon the blaze was apparent, partially masked by a pall of smoke. The Koreka, now fully visible from the outside, was consumed in fire. Bob's mare whinnied and pulled up short, refusing to approach further. Gorrelai, Harold, and Kelael reined in their protesting mounts, and soon the four of them sat in their saddles, jaws open in dismay. Even at their current distance of two dozen yards, the heat was intense, warming the skin on Bob's face and hands, evaporating his sweat.

Many of the trees around the Koreka's perimeter had fallen. The grass around the outer walls was tromped into clumpy mud. Bodies of En'harae, humans, and horses were strewn around the gate. The human corpses were garbed in the black and white of the Swearington Guard. A swathe of churned earth seemed to cut across the ground from the north toward the En'hari base and continue south through the forest. Vegetation had been stomped and crushed, as if a massive procession of heavy hooves had ground it all to dust. The Koreka's guard towers shot tongues of flame to lick at the sky. Through the shambles of the front gate, Bob could just make out Arbor House on the central green—an incinerated skeleton on the verge of collapse. The mist over the pond was evaporated, the pond itself shallow and muddied with blackened debris, choked with bloated corpses. Bodies were visible on the grounds as well. Nothing living stirred. So much for the ancient holy place of spirits. It was now nothing but a burning grave.

Not all the surviving trees were far enough from the gates, and the branches of a nearby birch flared alight before their eyes. "*The whole forest will burn if we do not act,*" said Gorrelai in Hari.

"*We don't have nearly enough water with us,*" said Kelael bitterly, also in his native tongue. Then, in English, he spoke to Harold. "Return to Torael and have him send everyone to Lake Azer, just under four miles southwest of here. Use anything we have to carry water—bags, helmets, barrels, anything."

Harold nodded sharply and the black and white destrier pulled around to gallop back through the forest. Kelael began speaking to Gorrelai again, telling him to begin cutting down the trees closest to the fire.

Hands shaking, Bob removed the dragon pipe from the jerkin. Lighting a match seemed morbidly ironic, but he did it anyway. He closed his eyes, searching for a way to calm himself. Unbidden, Danny's face swam into his mind's eye. Daniel had liked firefighters. Liked their big red trucks, their slick coats and helmets. If Daniel were at the Koreka just then, Bob knew what he'd say. *Time to be a firefighter, dad.*

Bob exhaled slowly and opened his eyes. He tuned into the astral voices. Erto was here, somewhere. Bob couldn't see him, but he knew he was there. He took a draw on the pipe and tried to think like a firefighter.

First, he tried to smother the fire with balls of earth. He succeeded in a few places along the ruins of the fence, but often the flames were too high to be effectively covered by the amount of dirt he was able to command at once. After a moment of consideration, he attuned to the voices in the earth, felt the roots of the trees snaking their way through the planet's body like veins. He and Erto found the right trees and pushed them out of the ground. There were creaks as they fell, crashes as they plummeted into their fellows and away from the fire. Gorrelai, lacking an axe, had been attempting to chop down a birch with his sword. He looked up in relief as the earth pushed out the tree like an unwanted hair. The Koreka's perimeter was cleared, and the forest was safe. Yet, the fire still burned.

There was little to do but wait. They tied their horses safely inside the fresh tree-line and returned to a spot opposite the destroyed gate.

Gorrelai gestured northward at the path of churned mud and broken trees. "*They came from this direction.*" Then he swung his hand to the south, where, from the edge of the burning Koreka, the jagged swathe resumed. "*And have continued southward.*"

"How many?" asked Bob hoarsely.

"Hundreds," said Kelael, and Gorrelai nodded. He pointed to the distant central green. "I only see a few dozen of our brothers and sisters inside. Perhaps the rest were able to escape."

"Melanae was already preparing to leave," agreed Bob. They watched as a guard tower crumbled under its remaining weight, toppling onto the dry mud with a pathetic thump. "I guess we know why Swearington was so easy." The others nodded darkly. "But what gets me is, why south? They didn't go west to pursue the En'harae. East would've put them on the fastest way back to the city, the way they were ploughing through the forest. Would've put them in our path, as well. Coming from the north I understand. They probably left by North Gate and came west along Horizon until they were directly north of us." He'd noticed Horizon on the map of Engoria in the council chamber because it was the road he'd ridden down while inside a box, on his way to becoming a slave. "So, they could bee-line south through the forest and hit the Koreka. But why *keep* going south? Anything south of here that's important?"

Kelael shrugged. "This far west? Just Tortellan. But this is not what concerns me."

"*How did they find us?*" said Gorrelai.

Kelael grunted. "*Por'chei.*" Exactly.

None of them had the answer. They stood in long silence, watching the rest of the Koreka collapse, the trees within like great candles. Only the fact that almost no grass remained in the area prevented the conflagration from flourishing further. By the time Harold returned with the others, the blaze was petering of its own accord. The En'harae brought water from the lake to dump on the flames, and Bob and Erto's smothering earth joined them in their efforts.

By the time the fire was mostly under control, the sun had begun to set. Some cheeky En'hari archer grabbed a flaming chunk of wood by the cool end and carried it like a torch to the section of rough ground Kelael had designated as the night's camping location. The archer used it to light the evening's campfire.

Bob was exhausted, but there was still work to be done. They had to do something about the bodies. Most were nothing more than blackened skeletons, some in scorched shells of armor, others naked burnt bone. But still others were only partly burned or miraculously untouched by flames. The caravan couldn't sleep with so many corpses around; the smell would simply not allow it. And they all knew, but didn't say, that they wanted to identify their dead. Was their leader Melanae among them? Their friends and family members?

Ditches were dug on the far end of the Koreka, away from camp—one for the humans, another for the En'harae. Bob joined the effort to displace the corpses, first hauling away the fallen Engorians outside the ring where the walls had stood, then moving into the ruined Koreka itself.

A strange numbness had set in. Bob moved mechanically through the husk of what had briefly been his home. He hefted blue-skinned bodies with the help of blue-skinned companions. Something told him that Melanae had made it out. As Kelael had said, there weren't nearly enough corpses to account for all the remaining En'harae, and the few humans, that had been here when the Koreka was attacked.

Just outside the ruins of Arbor House, Bob bent to collect a half-burned corpse. The fellow seemed to be clutching a frying pan in his remaining hand. Had he been rushing to attack the invaders with it? Arrows protruded from the corpse's shoulder. Bob sighed and lifted its foot, and the body flopped into a new position. Along a singed skull were the stringy remains of yellow hair.

Bob's breath caught in his throat as he released Hirrell's foot. Too much. It was too much. He turned and marched into the flickering night, toward camp. His boots trampled the brittle remains of the fence. Someone called out to him, but he kept walking until he reached Torael's wagons.

"You look awful, Bob," said Osivia from nearby. "Maybe you should go to bed."

Bob reached the back of first wagon and yanked the tarp off the supplies. He grabbed a wooden mug and tapped the wine barrel.

"Thirsty, huh?" said the faerie, hovering by his head. Her smile died when she looked him in the eye. "Are you okay?"

"No," said Bob. He took a long swig of wine. It washed warmly into his body. He tilted back the mug, swallowing the rest in two gulps. He immediately began to refill it.

"Wait a minute, Bob," said Osivia. She was clearly concerned, and for some reason that made Bob angry. "I thought you didn't drink. Didn't you say drinking almost ruined your life?"

BOB THE WIZARD

"Fuck off," growled Bob, and chugged the second helping.

Osivia scoffed and fluttered away.

Bob belched and began to refill the mug.

M. V. PRINDLE

Part Three:
Vigilant

"We feel and know that we are eternal."
-Benedict de Spinoza

CHAPTER TWENTY-FIVE:
SICK AND TIRED

The walls of jagged rock cast a sickly green hue. Bob's head felt like an overfilled water-balloon, and as he shifted his weight to looked around, it lolled on his shoulder. He seemed to be underground. The smells of fresh earth and burnt oil tingled his nostrils, and he heaved as if to vomit, but nothing came out. The earthen walls glistened as if covered in snot. Bob didn't know where he was or what was happening, but it was all he could do to concentrate on breathing. In through the nose, out through the mouth... he heaved again.

"You have consumed poison," said a deep, gravelly voice. Bob forced his eyeballs in the direction it had come from, and there, sitting cross-legged upon a boulder, was one of Erto's little mud avatars, its hollow eyes fixed on him. Bob gave no reply, sitting back against the hard rocks and wiping sweat from his brow. "I have been able to hear you quite well, until now," said Erto. "This poison blocks our connection. Is this why you have chosen to poison yourself? Do you wish our link severed?"

Bob belched, feeling liquid bubble up in his throat. "You don't usually talk this much," he said thickly. The world seemed to tilt on a hidden axis, spinning around Bob of its own accord.

"Why have you consumed poison, Bob?"

"Oh Jesus, I don't need a lecture."

"I merely wish to understand. I see many of your memories. I know you have traveled this path before. The activity you have chosen to focus our connection is also damaging to your body. I do not understand these things. This capacity for self-destruction… I have witnessed it in many human souls but have never understood. I see your pain. Perhaps you wish to distract from your pain by suffering a greater pain."

Bob felt the world settle a bit. He took a steadying breath. "What're you, my therapist?"

Erto sat in silence, regarding him with hollow eyes. Somewhere in their depths flashed two tiny points of purple light.

Bob's head throbbed at the temples. "Look man—uh, Erto," he mumbled. "I don't even know where I am right now. How did we get here?"

"You brought us here, Bob," said the spirit. "It is your dream."

Bemused, Bob glanced around. He realized they were in the Cave, where he'd saved Torael's life and first met Gorrelai, Fan, and Hirrell. The place had been changed by the dream, however—its walls oozed with luminescent slime.

"So it is," sighed Bob. "Are you a dream, too?"

The little avatar shrugged. "I am as much a dream as you."

Bob just stared, feeling like his guts were made of angry snakes.

Erto waited a moment, then repeated his question. "Why have you consumed poison, Bob?"

Bob struggled to sit up straight, groaning in frustration. "It was a mistake. Just another dumb fucking mistake in a long history of dumb fucking mistakes."

"So, you do not wish to sever our connection?"

"What? No. No, I… I think I need you, Erto. I need your help if I'm going to…" His train of thought hit a brick wall. The world started to spin again. What was it again? What did he need to do? A furious sense of urgency rushed upward from the depths of his mind. Galvidon's impassive face flashed at him from the shadows. "I need your help," Bob croaked at Erto. He cried out in pain as his sides seized and he doubled over, vomiting bright green sludge onto the rocky floor.

"I suggest you ingest no further poison."

Bob spat. There was a war being fought inside of him. On one side, there was his hatred of Galvidon, his respect for the En'harae, his budding friendships with Torael, Gorrelai, Osivia, and Harold, his determination to defeat the Engorians, to enact vengeance for Anna and Daniel, to finally return home. On the other side was just a singular voice, but it was loud, so loud.

Fuck it, said the voice. *Why fight when it only leads to more suffering?*

The first faction of this internal war completely agreed with Erto. This part of Bob was disgusted with himself.

Getting drunk, now? Pathetic. You didn't even drink when your family was murdered. You were strong, then. Now you are weak.

The second faction was ready with its reply: *Fuck you*. Inelegant, yet somehow equal in strength to its opposition.

"So much anger," rumbled Erto, as if to himself.

Bob was breathing too hard. "Got a lot to be mad about," he said, and a cramp gripped his abdomen. Grimacing, he struggled to his feet, holding out his arms for balance. "Oh, nope, shit. Nope." He plopped back down with a minor belch. Erto sat staring, unmoving. Bob heard the green goop on the walls trickling like thin jelly. He sighed. "I'm just tired of death. It follows me. I can't run fast enough."

"Death does not follow you. You follow Death."

"The fuck I do."

The spirit cocked his head. "Do you not seek the death of Galvidon?"

"Yes," said Bob at once. "I think so." He remembered being unable to kill Mannix, despite being furious at him. "I don't know." Bob hesitated. "No, you know what? Fuck that slimy gray shitbag. God damn right I seek his death."

"Curious," said the spirit.

"Shit," said Bob, not wanting to get Erto's point, but getting it anyway.

BOB THE WIZARD

"Do you know what I see, Robert James Caplan? You hate Death. Yet, you do not fear It, so you seek It out. You wish to enact punishment upon It."

Bob was silent.

Erto continued. "Do you see, Bob, that Death is not your enemy?"

Bob caught a wave of dizziness and steadied himself, scowling. "Oh yeah? Then who is?"

"You tell me."

"Galvidon," said Bob, exasperated.

"Who else?"

"What?"

"Who else is your enemy?"

Bob didn't understand what the point of all this was, but he didn't seem to be waking up, so he considered Erto's question. Engoria? Was Engoria his enemy? Before Bob could voice his thoughts, Erto spoke again.

"Who is responsible for the deaths of Daniel and Annabeth Caplan?"

The world gave a small lurch and then settled. Bob struggled to think straight. An image flashed from memory: seeing Galvidon on a television screen talking to a female Galon Var named Iona.

"The Order. You're saying the Order is my enemy?"

"No, Bob," replied Erto. "You are saying it."

Bob got the impression that Erto was smirking behind his featureless stare. His words carried a kind of triumph, as though confident he'd imparted wisdom. Erto's meaning wormed through Bob's brain. Killing Galvidon was not enough. Not only would the act not fully avenge his family, it wouldn't prevent the Order from perpetrating further acts of murder. It would be like taking a single bullet out of the enemy's gun.

His mind's use of a gun-analogy jogged loose another thought, and suddenly he altered course. "Erto, can I ask you something?"

The spirit produced a gravelly rumble. "What do you wish to know, Bob?"

Bob's chest fluttered. He belched again. "What's up with you and metal? I'm still not clear on the rules."

Erto rumbled again, contemplative. "Human metal is inimical to my kind. It has no voice and is not one of my brethren. For this reason, it is known among us as the Voiceless. Some among my family—those of water and wind—are short lived, transient. They are born and pass quickly back to integration. I, Erto, am old—so old I can remember the first souls arriving on Hub. In addition, metal untainted by humans carries my voice. I know it closely, as it sings my own songs. Of all my family, I am the most efficacious at facing the Voiceless. I have a singular tolerance to its proximity, though it is still beyond my ability to control."

Bob struggled to make sense of this. "Ok, but why can't I hold it? You don't need to control it if I'm controlling it."

The spirit tilted his overlarge head. "Such propinquity interferes with my ability to hear you."

Before Bob could reply, a bright point of sunlight erupted at the apex of the Cave. Dazzled, Bob shielded his eyes as the light intensified.

"He's waking," said a woman's voice.

White light blazed around him until it blotted out Erto, the Cave, everything.

Bob was vomiting before he was awake. He came to on his side, retching onto the grass. His head throbbed as though caught in a vise, and a sheen of sweat covered his skin. Everything hurt. A damp cloth wiped his forehead, bringing a modicum of relief, and Bob realized he was not alone. His eyes squinted open and were greeted by the sight of Keea crouched over him, red and purple shocks framing her face, concern etched across her mousy features. Behind her, the silhouette of Harold Whitespring blotted the sun.

"Bob?" Keea tentatively uttered. "Bob, can you hear me?"

BOB THE WIZARD

Bob rolled onto his back. "Loud and clear, mission control," he muttered, covering his eyes.

There was a pause, then Keea's voice. "What does this mean?"

Harold grunted. "Means he's going to live, aye? Let's get him up."

The next few hours were a hellish blur. Bob could not remember who or where he was during most of it. He kept looking for Erto, wanting to talk to the spirit, to apologize for something, yet he was unsure of what. Whenever Bob craned his rubbery neck to peer around, the spirit was nowhere to be seen. At some point he was aware of being stripped naked, and that was cold. He was ripped into consciousness when someone tossed him into a body of water, and that was colder. Bob gasped and yelled a stream of curses before Harold's voice reached him.

"Hey now, you're alright," said the mountain man. "Just getting you clean, Bob. I've seen outhouse rats less filthy."

Fully aware now, Bob realized with dismay that he was being washed in Lake Azer. All he wore was the Gatekey. Harold held him upright in the water, and Keea stood at the water's edge, hands on her hips, eying them. It must have taken them at least an hour to haul him here.

Embarrassed and ashamed, he snatched the washrag from Harold's hand. "Okay, okay, I got it, thanks," he said thickly, fully turning his back to Keea.

Harold laughed without rancor. "Too late, my friend. She helped me strip you."

Bob considered drowning himself. "Hope you brought me some damn clothes."

While he washed the filth from his body—a caked mess of vomit and shit mixed with dirt and sweat—he tried to remember how he'd ended up here. There was the burning Koreka, and finding Hirrell, walking to the wine as if in a trance, no decision having been consciously made, slave to a deeply seated rejection of what life entailed. He remembered snapping at Osivia, drinking sharply flavored wine by the gulp, wondering into the forest...

Then nothing. It was a good old fashioned black out—a tradition handed down to Bob by his father, a family legacy ingrained in his DNA. The sensation of knowing he'd lost time was a familiar one, in the same way that failure was familiar, and loss. It was a comforting disaster in that at least it was something he knew how to live with. Maybe that's why he'd done it—latching onto a familiar pain was better than being subsumed by a bevy of unknowns. He remembered the Cave dream vividly, and now recalled Erto's words: *Perhaps you wish to distract from your pain by suffering a greater pain.*

In the lake, Bob spat angrily. Something about being psychoanalyzed by a bunch of rocks made him feel obvious, inadequate, naked. "Well, I *am* literally naked," Bob mumbled to himself.

Harold and Keea had, in fact, brought him some damn clothes. He dressed himself in the spun wool gratefully after toweling off. Keea politely turned her back, and Bob was grateful for that too. His humiliation had been complete enough as it was. The three of them set off back toward the campsite by the demolished Koreka. The sun was high, its light streaming through the canopy in bars. Keea handed Bob some sheep jerky, and he gnawed on it absently as they crunched along the underbrush. Bob's headache had subsided but not vanished, and his stomach had settled down. He'd probably come close to death in a number of ways: alcohol poisoning, vomit asphyxiation, wild animal attack. Would have been easier if one of those things had happened. Still, easy or hard, now digesting fresh protein and wearing clean clothes on a beautiful day, he was glad he'd made it through. All he'd accomplished, he realized, was making everyone else's life a little harder. He glanced at his companions and cleared his throat.

"Thanks," he said. "I guess I might be dead if you hadn't helped me."

Harold flashed him a tight, knowing smile. "Probably not dead, aye? But who wants to wake up covered in puke and shit?"

Bob made an embarrassed noise and bit a chunk of jerky. "Maybe you should've left me to it."

"Nonsense," said Harold. "I've been there before. Not since I was a very young man, I admit. Sometimes we do not know our limits. As long as we learn, aye?" He winked.

BOB THE WIZARD

Bob barked a laugh. "I might not be so great at learning, Harold. I knew what would happen, but I did it anyway. Where I'm from, that's called being a fool."

Keea turned her head. "Then plenty of men in this world are fools."

Bob eyed her. "What's that supposed to mean?"

She smiled without humor. "There were several guards at the keep who drank themselves stupid all the time. There was one in particular, a short man, and stupid even before the drink. Lem was his name."

Bob immediately recognized the description. She was talking about Short, one of the guards he'd given the sunglasses to the day he'd arrived on Hub.

"He was sweet, though," continued Keea. "Sweet for a human, anyway. The number of times I've cleaned him up, well… I'll just say that cleaning one of my drunken rescuers was a welcome change from cleaning one of my drunken captors."

Harold elbowed Bob in the ribs. "She's the one that came to get me, follow? You'd still be lying in your own filth if it wasn't for her."

She chuckled. "Oh, tell him the truth, Whitespring."

"Right, then," said Harold, rubbing the back of his neck. "Well, sun had just come up and she found you on her way to fill the waterskins. First she went to Kelael…"

Bob felt a smile bloom across his face at the thought.

"He said to leave you there," said Keea, "that it served you right for being useless, and a danger to his brother's safety."

"Then Torael started yelling at him," said Harold. "And Gorrelai was still pretty drunk himself, follow?"

"Osivia was crying," said Keea.

"Gorrelai poured a mug of wine on Kelael's head," said Harold.

"And someone threw bread at him," said Keea, now struggling to keep a straight face.

"So Kelael threw a punch at Gorrelai," said Harold.

"Right in the face!" giggled Keea.

"Aye, and Gorrelai just laughed at him and said he hit like a faerie. So, he stormed off. And Torael ran after him."

"So, Harold volunteered to help me," finished Keea with a grin.

Amused as he was, Bob felt incredibly stupid. They were fighting about him. He'd been so wrapped up in himself he hadn't considered how much the En'harae might need him—if only for the fact that he possessed the Gatekey. Torael and Gorrelai had stood up for him, and he'd been ready to drink himself to death, because of what? Pain and loss? The En'harae had suffered enough pain and loss for a hundred lifetimes. Ever since he'd arrived on Hub, he kept finding himself having regrets, realizing how selfish and shortsighted he'd been. What he'd said to Harold about not learning anything seemed truer at that moment than it ever had before. Would he ever change? Learn from his mistakes? Or was he doomed to keep repeating them?

No. Bob believed in a future that was not set. He could change—he had to. No more pure self-interest, he told himself. No more making others pay for his own predictable mistakes. He'd think things through, act with deliberation.

Or would he? He remembered his self-righteous speech to Mannix. He'd claimed to be better than the Lord of Swearington. He didn't really believe that. Even when he'd said it, he didn't believe it. Thinking of it now made him want to crawl into a hole and hide.

No matter what, though, he had to get better. He had to learn to see when he was about to repeat a mistake. If he didn't owe it to himself, he at least owed it to Anna and Daniel. He wanted to be the person they'd want him to be.

"I owe you both a debt," said Bob. "I'm really very sorry. It won't..." Did he dare to make the promise? "It won't happen again."

"Well, that's fantastic, aye?" said Harold, a twinkle in his eye. "But just to be safe, we poured out the rest of the wine."

BOB THE WIZARD

When they arrived at camp, Keea excused herself to retrieve Bob's soiled trench coat. Despite Bob's protests, she insisted on taking it back to Lake Azer herself for a wash, explaining that she and the other two women they'd rescued from Oath Keep—Rae and Laia—had already planned to do a load of laundry for the entire group.

"We are capable of more than laundry, of course" Keea said, "but we are so used to it, doing this will help us forget what danger we are now in. Besides, Bob, we look forward to a lone walk through the trees in freedom."

He made her promise to take along at least one armed escort. This turned out not to be a problem, as Laia had become close to an archer named Forell and was already planning to make him come along. Bob saw them all talking and gathering clothes and got the distinct impression that no one had to twist Forell's arm. The young En'hari seemed infatuated—he stared at Laia, smiling stupidly through it all. Well, good for them. At least someone was having a good day.

Bob began to get anxious about staying by the destroyed Koreka. Their enemies knew they were here—at least, they'd known the Koreka was here. Shouldn't they all leave? Bob realized that his drunken episode may have cost everyone an entire day. It was well into the afternoon now; soon there'd be no daylight left to travel by. He guessed Torael would risk one more night of camping here. But something else nagged at Bob.

He scanned the camp for Osivia's hovering glow. He looked in nearby trees, bushes, tents. He asked around. No one had seen her since morning. His guilt morphing into concern, Bob began to circle the camp's perimeter, widening the path of his search with each rotation. Finally, the sun an orange disk in a low haze of clouds, he found her at the scorched rubble of Arbor House.

Like the final tooth in a rotted mouth, a single beam jutted out of the blackened foundation. Atop it lay a small open book bound in sheepskin. Atop the book Osivia sat cross-legged, golden hair down and fluttering mildly in the breeze. Her skin pulsed a dull orange color that matched the sunset. Debris crunched with Bob's approach, but she gave no sign she'd heard.

He stood a yard away in sullen silence, studying her as she pretended to read. He thought he saw her pulsing skin flare briefly to red.

"I'm sorry, Osivia," he said. "I shouldn't've pushed you away like that. You didn't deserve it, and I knew that, but I did it anyway because I was angry. That's not an excuse, just a reason. Listen, I tried to warn you—I suck. Kelael's right, I am useless. Plus, I'm an idiot. I'm a useless fucking idiot."

She turned her head and her luminescent skin changed to yellow. He couldn't read her expression.

Desperate, he kept talking. "And I probably wouldn't be here if it wasn't for you. Alive, I mean. And you're way smarter than me. Did I mention that I'm an idiot?" Bob realized he was literally wringing his hands and forced them to his sides. She arched an eyebrow and threatened a smirk. "A big, hairy, useless, fucking idiot," he continued. Her other eyebrow rose and the light from her skin dimmed. "You were right and I was wrong," said Bob. "So very, completely wrong."

"And I will never do it again," she said, crossing her arms.

Bob sighed. "What?" he asked tentatively.

She cocked her head. "I'm waiting for you to say, 'and I will never do it again, Osivia.'"

"Do what again? Drink?" asked Bob. He knew how it went. You fucked up and drank too much, you promised never to do it again. For a while, you kept your promise. For a while. "I already promised Harold..."

"No, dummy. You yelled at me for something that wasn't my fault. I was trying to help you, Bob, and you treated me like... like... like I didn't matter!" She thrust her arms at her sides and leaned toward him. "You were an asshole!"

Bob placed his right hand on his heart and raised his left. "I. Robert Caplan, asshole extraordinaire, hereby promise that I will never be an asshole to Osivia again. If I break this promise, may I be bathed in honey and fed to fire ants."

She was smiling now. "Fire ants? What're they?"

"Horrible creatures from the faraway land of Texas," said Bob, feeling the tension between them finally dissolve. He stepped closer. "What're you reading?"

She glanced down at the book. "Oh, just a book I found in that stuff we took. *The Common History of Engoria*. It's actually pretty interesting. It says that two thousand years ago, the Gez Kar and the En'harae lived in peace."

"Huh," said Bob, patting his pockets and realizing he didn't have his pipe. "What happened?"

She scrunched her nose. "Well, it also says that humans came from the sun, so I can't be sure of its accuracy. But it says once the humans arrived, everyone was fighting for land and resources."

Bob considered. "Sounds about right. But you're from here, didn't you already know this stuff?" He glanced toward camp.

"Most faeries aren't very interested in history," she said, making a face. "The records we do have are spotty and inaccurate." She fluttered upward and began closing the book. "Would you mind carrying it back? It's heavy."

Bob picked up the book. It weighed about two pounds. "Well, what *are* most faeries interested in?" They started back to camp through the rubble.

"Oh, you know, being left alone, mostly, and…" she trailed off.

"And what?" asked Bob.

"Mating," she said with some disdain.

Bob chuckled. "Not too different from humans, then."

CHAPTER TWENTY-SIX:
FIRESIDE

As Bob and Osivia approached the campsite, it became apparent that Torael had made up with his brother. The two En'harae stood side-by-side near the fire, which had been built up with shaven branches into a flaming pillar that warmed the whole area. Torael's arm rested around Kelael's shoulders. Bob stepped into the circle of warmth among the rest of the En'harae, glancing at faces. The crowd was roughly arranged in a half-circle, everyone facing the Quaylen Dah at the fire. As they chatted amongst themselves, Bob could sense their anticipation.

"What's going on?" Bob asked Osivia.

"Wouldn't you like to know?" she chided, tipping her glasses to glare at him.

"Yes, please," said Bob, patting his pockets yet again, hoping he'd somehow missed the pipe the first several times. "In just a second." He pushed through a knot of En'harae, making his way toward the wagons. Torael saw him and waved him over. Bob nodded but kept walking, holding up an index finger.

Horses snorted at him from nearby as he approached the exact spot he'd told Osivia to fuck off. The sheep scuttled underfoot, hemmed in by hastily erected makeshift fences. Bob placed *The Common History of Engoria* atop the supplies, then scanned the ground. He followed a rough trail of disturbed earth that may or may not have been left by a drunken wizard stumbling into the forest. Behind him, the sun was flickering its goodbye.

BOB THE WIZARD

He heard footsteps approaching from the dark, but they were mercifully followed by the sound of laughter. He looked up from the trail—it was dying off anyway—to see four blue forms approach through the trees. It was Keea, of course, with Rae and Laia and Forell, returning from Lake Azer. Their conversation abruptly concluded as they spotted him. He saw in each of them a moment of tension that swiftly passed as their recognition dawned.

"Bob," said Keea, smiling. "What brings you away from the fire as the sun sets?" Her three companions silently eyed her.

Bob cleared his throat. "I'm looking for, uh—say, you haven't seen…" He scratched his head. All four of the En'harae stared at him like parents waiting for a toddler to form a coherent sentence. "A pipe," he said finally, "shaped like a dragon?"

"Oh, yes," said Keea, nodding. "I am sorry, I had forgotten. It was in your jerkin." She rustled inside the canvas bag she carried and handed him the dragon pipe, his pouch of tobacco, and the bundle of his remaining matches. "Speaking of your clothing, you'll have to get it tomorrow. I left it all on the rack. It's still pretty soaked, especially that big black coat."

Bob was humbled by how helpful she was. "Thank you," he said honestly, and began packing the pipe.

She offered a wan smile and the four En'harae continued their stroll back to camp. The dragon pipe intermittently glowed as Bob puffed on it. Nicotine washing across his nerves, he recalled the dream he'd had while blacked out.

"Erto, you still out there?" he softly asked the night.

He listened, straining for the sound of the astral voices. There was nothing but the gentle swaying of branches, the soft bleat of gathered sheep, the babble of the nearby En'harae filtered by foliage and distance. He realized he was standing alone in the dark and made his way back to the fire.

He arrived puffing away and returned to Osivia, who now hovered by the two towering forms of Harold and Gorrelai. The big elf slapped Bob on the back when he found them. Bob saw that Gorrelai's left cheek was bruised and swelling. He didn't seem bothered.

Osivia scowled. "You *just* promised not be an asshole," she said.

Bob, suddenly wary, narrowed his eyes. "Yeah…"

"And then you immediately ditch me to go find your stupid pipe!"

Bob thrust his head back in surprise. "What? No, I didn't ditch you, I just left for a minute."

"Save it," she snapped, and fluttered onto Harold's shoulder—the one opposite Bob so his view of her was blocked by Harold's head. The mountain man shot Bob a guilty look, offering an almost imperceptible shrug.

Bob sighed in frustration. Looks like Osivia was still upset with him, after all. And Bob found himself unable to tune into the astral voices. He'd managed to piss off both Erto and Osivia. He wondered if anyone else was mad at him. Why did he have to go and drink that wine?

At the fire, Torael released Kelael and stepped forward. Backlit by flickering flames, his purple hair seemed to glow from within. He spoke Hari in a loud, authoritative voice. "*Brothers and sisters!*" he called. The crowd's chatter died away as faces turned. "*And friends,*" he added, nodding to where Bob and Harold stood. "*We have achieved a great victory only to suffer a greater loss. Moreover, our nation has been brought to its knees—our people slaughtered or enslaved by the Engorians. Melanae Taeno, leader and guardian to many of you, and my dear brother Kelael, have told me of the Quaylen's destruction at the hands of our enemies. The tribal leaders are dead, the tribes scattered, disbanded, or extinct. Yet the spirits still walk with us. They join their voices with ours. There is a future for En'hirin. Though we have fought with every stride, we must continue to fight for this future.*"

The crowd stood in hushed reverence, hanging on his words. Behind his brother, Kelael shifted his weight impatiently.

"Here, we are vulnerable," continued Torael. "*Our food dwindles, the enemy may know we are here, and we are but small in number. So, we leave with the dawn. We return to the heart of En'hirin. I return as Quaylen Dah in name only, but that shall soon be remedied. Kelael and I believe Melanae escaped the attack on the Koreka. There was a rendezvous location agreed upon in case of such an attack. I am confident we will find her there. Once we have regrouped, the spirits shall consecrate the birth of a new Quaylen.*"

A sudden cheer erupted from the gathered En'harae. Torael raised his voice to speak over them. "*I plan to name Melanae of Tribe Taeno as my Second.*"

The cheers increased in volume. The excitement was infectious, and Bob found himself sharing a smiling glance with Harold as Gorrelai whooped beside them. Torael waited for the crowd to simmer. Behind him, Kelael's expression remained impassive.

After a moment, Torael continued. "*As you know, most of the Quaylen's members are traditionally selected independently by each tribe. However, current circumstances make that impossible. I therefore take it upon myself to appoint new members, until such time as the tribes are well enough to take up the task.*"

He paused, studying the silent crowd, waiting. He seemed to sense no objections, and so continued. "*Gorrelai of Tribe Soe, please step forward.*"

Gorrelai's head twitched in surprise. Slowly, he stepped forward to face Torael. Excited whispers broke out among the En'harae.

"*Tribe Soe is an ancient and respected tribe,*" declared Torael. "*They are known for producing fearsome Gasheera and Ketra, as well as capable hunters and craftsman. This reputation is well earned, for many Soe have perished in battle against our enemies, and many enemies have perished at their hands. Few of their leaders remain.*" Bob saw that Gorrelai was watching Torael carefully. "*Yet in the time I have known him, Gorrelai has proven his strength and resolve time and again. Though, some may say his ferocity is too easily unleashed.*" The Quaylen Dah smirked as the crowd produced a light chuckle. He faced Gorrelai. "*Gorrelai of Tribe Soe, as acting Quaylen Dah, I officially invite you to sit upon the Quaylen as head of your tribe.*" The crowd went wild with cheers. Harold erupted into a belly laugh.

Gorrelai seemed blindsided. For a moment, his eyes darted amongst the crowd under a deep scowl, as if he were sure a joke was being played on him. Then, seeing the genuine joy in their faces, he softened, and then lit up with a huge grin. He looked back at Torael, who matched his smile.

"*When I first met Torael, under the human's chains,*" began Gorrelai, and the crowd settled to hear him. "*I thought, this En'hari is not so impressive. He scampers to stay under his father's shadow.*"

At these words the crowd became dead-silent. The fire seemed extraordinarily loud. Gorrelai scanned their faces, seeming to absorb their discomfort. Then, he burst out laughing.

"*I was a fool!*" he declared. There was a collective sigh of relief and amusement. He returned to addressing Torael. "*Torael Ellaren, the spirits must truly love you. You endure suffering yet maintain a giving heart. You witness death, yet you smile in its face, knowing it will come to your enemies. You see the strength and goodness in others despite their failings. You are a true leader. I gladly sit beneath you, and I accept your offer.*"

He embraced Torael and the snapping fire seemed to join in the applause. Then, the big elf slapped the Quaylen Dah on the back and returned to his spot by Harold. The mountain man shook him playfully by the shoulders.

"Congratulations," said Bob. He noticed that Osivia had returned to his own shoulder. Silently relieved, his smile began to feel genuine.

Torael's commanding tenor broke through the chatter. "*And there is one other,*" he said, "*who I invite to En'hirin's leadership. Ellaren is the largest and most numerous tribe, and though it is my own, the seat of Quaylen Dah supersedes all other concerns. A Quaylen Dah no longer belongs to their tribe, they belong to the En'harae. Therefore, Tribe Ellaren still requires a representative. For this position, I nominate the most capable En'hari I know.*" He turned to face the fire and his brother. "*Kelael of Tribe Ellaren, do you accept?*"

The crowd's reaction was subdued. Kelael, despite being at the Koreka for much longer, seemed less popular than Gorrelai. This didn't surprise Bob in the least.

All eyes were on Kelael as he stepped forward. "*As Torael said, seats on the Quaylen are usually nominated by tribal elders,*" he shot Torael a sharp look, "*not the Quaylen Dah. In addition, my brother is not technically the Quaylen Dah yet. He must first perform the ritual and receive the blessing of the spirits. In my opinion, he should not be doing anything until then, least of all appointing members of the Quaylen. However, I will play along with his little game. I accept the position until such time as an adequate replacement can be found. Assuming of course, Torael is not rejected by the spirits during the ritual.*"

There were no applause. Everyone but Torael stood in awkward silence. For his part, the erstwhile Quaylen Dah seemed to expect all this. He stood, smiling sagely at the crowd's discomfort. "*It is decided*," he declared. "*Et tessat sheerat morae*." May the spirits guide our journeys.

"*Et tessat sheerat morae*," said Bob along with the crowd.

"*Now*," continued Torael, "*we must prepare*."

With this declaration came a distant rumble in the sky—an approaching storm. Too late to quench the fire by a day, it now threatened to drench them in their sleep. A few heads craned in its direction.

"Quickly, it seems," added Torael, reverting to English. "Or soon we will be swimming."

The crowd parted as everyone rushed to tend the horses and sheep, pack away all unnecessary items, make sure everything was well-covered, make sure the tents were firmly erected. Shortly, Bob stood next to Harold and Gorrelai, Osivia upon his shoulder, facing the fire and the En'harae brothers. The way the group's leadership had all remained stationary almost seemed rehearsed. Perhaps it *was*—plenty of discussion could have occurred while Bob was… indisposed. He was unsure of what made him more uncomfortable: having blacked out while the others planned without him, or that he was considered part of the inner circle. He felt undeserving of the position, and by the way Kelael was currently studying him, Bob had a pretty good idea the En'hari felt the same.

"We must discuss the journey to the Nexus," said Torael, once the six of them were alone by the fire.

Everyone was quiet. They knew what he was going to say, Bob realized. And if he'd been sober the night before, he'd know too.

Torael looked Bob in the eye. "I cannot send anyone with you," he said quietly. "This is not an army. Most of these people have only learned to fight recently. Gorrelai and Kelael are the only true Gasheera among them. Also, there aren't enough supplies to provide for a large party travelling all the way into the Endless Mountains."

Bob nodded, staring at a swirl of leaves on the ground. In the distance, thunder boomed again.

"You do not have to go," said Torael. "I know we made a promise to each other, but I believe it has been fulfilled by both of us. You have the Gatekey once again. We have knowledge we did not before. I release you from further obligation. To travel overland, through the territories of Engoria and New Tanatha, into the mountains where Axiis nests—it is simply too dangerous. Instead, come with us to En'hirin. We will find Melanae, gather the Gasheera. Then we can march to the Nexus and retrieve the weapons. This way is much safer." Torael studied him intensely. "What say you, Sora Kelai?"

Bob should have seen this coming. Torael had his people to think about. He couldn't risk their lives on a dangerous mission based on reconnaissance from a duck, regardless of what Bernard's note had said. Torael had been gung-ho about the mission to Swearington, but that was before the Koreka's destruction and the disappearance of Melanae, before the death of so many of his charges, before Bob had revealed his true nature at the bottom of a wine barrel. Bob could almost see himself from the Quaylen Dah's perspective—an unpredictable and unreliable failure. A man thrown into captivity with the En'harae because of his own arrogance, a man who only had one purpose—to catch and kill Galvidon—yet had, by his own admission, failed at that purpose for years. Bob remembered what Keea had said Kelael had called him. Useless. Maybe he was. He lifted his head and saw Kelael watching him, but in his eyes, what Bob saw surprised him. Bob expected loathing, a reflection of his own self-doubt, yet in Kelael's gaze he saw a kind of defiant hope, as if the En'hari were willing him to resist despair. The sky in the north crackled with lightning.

Bob opened his mouth to speak—though he did not know what to say—but was interrupted by a keening gust of wind. The pillar at the firepit rippled with disturbed flames. The group turned as one to see a shadowy figure approaching from the ruins of the Koreka. Whoever it was, they were short. For a stupid, ecstatic moment Bob thought it was Danny—his son approaching from beyond the rim of death as though he'd only taken a wrong turn somewhere.

But of course, it wasn't Daniel Caplan. Leaves crunched under the figure's feet as he stepped into the firelight. Osivia zipped up in alarm. Harold gasped, and Kelael loosed a bitter laugh.

It was Bernard. He stood lit by the undulating orange glow, leaning on his sanded staff, his great, puffy white beard dancing in the breeze.

"Jumping jackrabbits!" he exclaimed with a scowl. "What are you people still doing here?"

Just before the rain began, Bernard performed a strange breathing exercise, and there was a palpable ripple of air. When sheets of rain began to fall, they splashed against something above the camp and slipped along the air as if the water struck an invisible dome. Throughout the following conversation, Bob could see a group of En'harae—including the archer Forrell with an arm around Laia—standing at the edge of Bernard's barrier, watching the torrent of raindrops slip down the air as if it were glass.

"You have much explaining to do, Wizard," said Kelael.

"What happened at Azenbul?" asked Osivia.

Bernard leaned on his staff, eyeing the group as if trying to decide where to start. Finally, he said, "what happened to the Koreka?"

"What happened?" burst out Kelael. "You left!"

"The spirits forgot us," said Torael. "Your magical protections faded. We left in haste to retrieve the Gatekey—"

"*Which we retrieved*," broke in Gorrelai.

"Yes," continued Torael, "as you say, Gorrelai. When we returned, the Koreka was burning. The assailants left a trail that is hard to miss. We believe they came from Swearington, struck from the north, and then continued south. We still do not know how they discovered us. Even with the spirits gone, they would have had to already know our location to organize such an attack."

Bernard nodded, glanced around, and lowered himself onto a log by the fire. "I believe I know the answer to that mystery." He shot a look at Bob. "I'm afraid it may be my fault."

Harold sighed as he sat down next to Bernard. "Right, then. What are you meaning by that?"

The others began to sit around the fire, one by one. Bob sat last, between Torael and Gorrelai. Osivia remained on his shoulder.

"Well," said the old wizard, "I sent Quaker to Tortellan to spy on Galvidon."

At the mention of the Gray Man, Gorrelai spat over his shoulder.

Bernard scratched his large nose. "I believe she was followed back to the Koreka."

"Followed… by whom?" asked Torael. "Does Galvidon also possess a familiar?"

"Something like that," said Bernard. "At Azenbul, I believe I saw… Tell me, have any of you seen a metal object in the sky?"

At the question, something in Bob's mind struggled to shake loose. For some reason, he thought of bathing in a stream. The other members of the group exchanged puzzled looks and shook their heads. Bernard was about to speak again when Bob suddenly stood. Startled, Osivia swirled into the air. The stream—that was it. The barest flicker of memory surfaced, just a snippet of a dream he'd had. It was Anna's voice. *Watch the skies, Robert.* Then, that very day at the stream, Bob had thought he'd seen a flash of metal in the sky.

"I saw it," he said. "I think I saw it, I…" He clenched his fists. "I didn't know what it was. I thought it was nothing. I thought…"

Kelael was staring at him flatly. "What, Sora Kelai? You saw what?"

"A drone," said Bernard. "A metal machine that can fly, that can show its owner what it sees from a great distance."

Bob realized he was the only one standing and sat back down. Osivia flew in a lazy orbit around the group.

"So," said the faerie, "Quaker returned to the Koreka from Tortellan, and got to your house through your hut. The drone followed her to the Koreka, where it saw her vanish when she passed through the light-barrier. Galvidon realized what happened and told Mannix our location. Mannix sent out a large force, that for some reason kept marching toward Tortellan when they were finished with us."

"Aye, that fits," muttered Harold.

"But what I don't get," said Osivia, "is why the drone would be at Azenbul."

Torael rubbed his face as if to wake himself. "Yes, Bernard. This is a good question. What does Galvidon want with the Wizard's Tower?"

Bernard's face darkened. "Many things, my young Ellaren. And I'm afraid he has received them. I was called to Azenbul because a powerful item had disappeared—the Hub Keystone."

Kelael let out a sharp breath. Everyone else looked confused.

"What is—" began Torael.

"It is the thing that opens the Gates at the Nexus," said Kelael. Everyone stared at him. "What? I pay attention at council meetings."

"Correct," said Bernard. "I shudder to think of what Galvidon plans to do with it. Bob, Osivia and I have witnessed him speaking of opening the Gates to make way for the Order of Tag Nah."

Bob suddenly felt panic attempt to gain purchase within him. He fought it away. "But that means... We're too late. He's already on his way to the Nexus with the Hub Keystone. We're fucked."

Bernard stroked his unruly beard. "Perhaps, perhaps not. There is still Axiis to consider. He must get past her. That is no easy feat, even for one as capable as Galvidon. I believe there is hope. We can still stop him from opening the Gates. We simply must be swift."

"But how?" asked Kelael. "How can we possibly make it to the Nexus before Galvidon finds a way to best the dragon?"

Osivia fluttered down onto the crystal atop Bernard's staff. "Magic!" she declared. She turned to face the old wizard. "I'm right, aren't I? We're going to use magic!"

Bernard nodded. "That would be ideal. But there is yet another obstacle in our path. As I have explained to some of you—the lovely young faerie included—in order to command the air spirits to take us a great distance, I must first have an object that has been to the intended destination. Like my staff, you see? I made it from a piece of a tree on the Koreka's grounds, so I can use it to return here whenever I wish. I have a stone from the Nexus at my house, but I left it in my haste when I headed to Azenbul. Now, the tapestries are destroyed, and I have no way to return home… other than the old-fashioned way. If we could find another object that has been to the Nexus…"

Everyone sat in silence for a few moments, staring into the snapping fire. Bob racked his brain for an answer to the puzzle but came up with nothing. Only Bernard had been to the Nexus. How could any of the rest of them have an object that had been there? His earlier statement floated up to taunt him. *We're fucked.*

Harold looked up suddenly. "Nine Peaks is only about a hundred miles southwest of the Nexus, follow? Niners never go there, but that's because we all know to avoid it, aye?"

Everyone was looking at him. He cleared his throat uncomfortably and continued.

"Just so happens, I've got a cousin who lives in Torful, a nearby fishing village. Only a few dozen miles northeast of here, aye? And she so happens to carry a spear. Her favorite weapon, that spear. Never goes anywhere without it, follow? And this spear, it was made from a tree right outside of Ninth Castle, aye? Right outside my home." He turned to Bernard. "Would that work? We'd have to walk a good ways…"

Bernard was smiling. "Wonderful. Stupendous. Spectacular."

Torael looked uncomfortable. "This is good news, but… I still cannot sanction this mission. I will not order anyone to face a dragon. And I still must return to En'hirin. Melanae is waiting for me."

"Well, I'm going," said Bob, shooting an apologetic look at Torael.

"Me too," said Osivia. She returned to her place on Bob's shoulder. "I'm going to hide from the dragon, though…" she added sheepishly.

"I suppose I have to go, aye?" said Harold. "No disrespect, Quaylen Dah, but they need me."

Kelael scoffed. "Harold, spirits curse you for volunteering before me. Now I cannot accuse you of following me around," he met Torael's eyes, "for I am also going."

"Kel…" began Torael.

"No, brother, I will go. As you say, you must return to En'hirin to meet Melanae, to complete the ritual, to recreate the Quaylen. You do not need me for that. And I *will* have those guns."

"Don't forget," added Bernard, "that we will be attempting to stop an inter-astral invasion."

Kelael shrugged. "Yes, that too."

"Very well," said Torael.

Bob heard sadness in his voice. There was another stretch of silence among them. Bob realized everyone had begun staring at Gorrelai. He joined them. The big elf had been quiet thus far. Would he accompany Bob, or Torael?

Gorrelai shifted under the weight of stares. He looked to Bob, then to Torael. In the flicker of the flames, his features were thrown into relief—his swelling cheek, the exhausted caste of his eyes. In that moment, he looked older to Bob than he ever had before.

"*I burn with desire to accompany Bob,*" said Gorrelai. "*To face Galvidon, to face a dragon, these are great deeds that most Gasheera will never know. To retrieve these weapons with Kelael, to bring them to our people, would be remembered for generations.*" His face crumpled as if he endured a great pain. "*But I cannot. I must follow the Quaylen Dah. I must protect him, make sure the ritual is complete. I am sorry, Sora Kelai.*"

Bob set a hand on Gorrelai's shoulder. "*Et tessat sheerat morae.*"

They all echoed the phrase.

"It is settled," said Torael. "We go separate ways at dawn."

The rain pummeled the invisible barrier above the camp. The sky clapped with thunder. Bob looked at the group gathered at the barrier's edge. Laia rested her head on Forell's shoulder as they watched the water cascade before them—the same water that now washed away the broken remains of the Koreka, the blood of the dead, and the past.

CHAPTER TWENTY-SEVEN:
WHO WE ARE WHEN WE WAKE

Bob dreamed he was underground again. He wound his way through earthen corridors in near-darkness. Around each corner, the astral voices called to him. When he rounded a bend, the voices had receded to around the next corner. It happened over and over. He called out to Erto, but the spirit never showed itself. Finally, he turned in the maze and was confronted by Galvidon. The Gray Man was facing away from him in the dark. Ahead, great, heavy breaths emanated from the blackness. Bob stepped forward next to Galvidon, and they stood side by side, staring into the breathing shadows. Galvidon turned to him.

"She will not let us pass," he said to Bob. He put a hand on Bob's shoulder. "She guards what we seek."

In the darkness, an orange gleam began to blossom. It swelled into a blaze of fire and shot toward Bob and Galvidon, enveloping them. Bob began to burn.

"Sora Kelai," said Kelael, from somewhere. "You must wake. It is time."

Bob's eyes fluttered open. Kelael was looking down at him. The astral voices were blaring in his ears. It was like waking up to a radio that was too loud. His head pounded. Still hungover, even now. With an effort, he sat up, rubbed at his face, and concentrated on tuning out the astral music. Kelael had already walked away.

The horizon shimmered with the waking sun. The rain had quit sometime in the night. Outside Bernard's invisible dome, the trees of the Essen'aelo dripped onto the muddy ground. Birds sang happily somewhere out of sight.

Bob chugged some water and lit the dragon pipe. He spotted Keea and asked after the laundry. She confirmed his fears—the laundry that had been left to dry at the lake had received an extra wash from the rain. His clothes were definitely not dry. He accompanied her to Lake Azer, along with a few other En'harae, to retrieve the soaked laundry.

According to Harold, it would take them about two days to walk to Torful through forest and hill country. Once there, they had no need for horses. However, Kelael and Harold also had articles of clothing that had been left at the lake, so Kelael convinced his brother to give up one of the wagons and two horses. This would not only make a portion of their journey more comfortable, it would give them something upon which to hang their still-drying clothes.

Bob found the chestnut mare being saddled among the mounts. He rubbed her neck and thanked her for being such a good horse. She stood placidly, absently swishing her tail. Bob said goodbye, found his backpack, the rifle, and the shotgun where they'd been piled with various other items the horses had been burdened with, and went to find the wagon where he'd placed *A Common History of Engoria*. He was afraid Osivia would be irritated if he left the book, and irritating Osivia was high on his list of things to avoid.

When he opened the brown backpack, he looked in to find an item he hadn't thought about since his arrival on Hub. He reached in and took it out, inspecting it in the morning light. It was a stuffed, toy llama, about the size of a kitten. Looking at it made his heart hurt. It was Daniel's. When Bob had gone after Galvidon the night of Anna and Daniel's murder, he'd swiftly stuffed the backpack full of supplies, only half-aware of what he was doing. It wasn't until later, already worlds away from home, that he realized the toy had been in the pack all along. Now, he considered tossing the thing to make room for other items. He'd considered this before. And, just as before, he replaced the stuffed llama in the backpack. *The Common History of Engoria* squished the little toy as he stowed it.

Bob sat with Torael and Gorrelai as they all ate a small breakfast. All three of them made an effort at conversation, but too often they lapsed to silence, none of them able to find words that felt worthwhile. Soon, the meal was finished, and it was time to depart.

Torael gave Bob a long hug. "I am grateful to have known you, Bob," he said.

"Oh, don't say that. Neither one of us is dying. I'll see you again." He wanted to believe it, but he didn't. He said it anyway.

Gorrelai hugged him too. It was a bit like being caught by a boa constrictor. "*Sora Kelai*," he said, holding Bob at arm's length. "*Your enemy is my enemy. Always.*" Then, he strode away without a backward glance.

Bob arrived at the designated wagon. Bernard sat in the cab, in the driver's position. Kelael sat next to him in his patchwork leathers, bow close at hand. Osivia was resting on the tip of the old wizard's green, wide-brimmed hat. The wagon was adorned with dripping articles of clothing. Bernard had lowered the invisible barrier, so now and then a drop of water pelted Bob's scalp from an overhanging tree.

He'd wrapped his guns in canvas, and now placed them in the wagon bed in a position he hoped moisture would not reach. Harold strode up behind him from the stricken camp. He was shirtless and carried the kite shield strapped to his back with wide leather bands. He tossed his own canvas-wrapped weapons atop Bob's.

"Right then," he said. "Off we go, aye?"

For the first few hours of travel, Bob and Harold walked alongside the wagon as it trundled slowly through the Essen'aelo. Occasionally, Harold would withdraw a shortsword from the wagon bed and chop at a tangle of brambles to make way. Osivia flew ahead, and doubled back along their perimeter, searching for danger. Bob and Harold passed the time with conversation. Bob told Harold about the Order of Tag Nah and recounted the conversation between Galvidon and Iona. Harold told Bob about the cousin they were off to find. Her name was Brumhilde, and she and Harold had been childhood friends. Harold's father had taught them both how to fight and hunt, and apparently Brumhilde was a fierce opponent.

BOB THE WIZARD

"Bit of a rivalry, we have, aye? She always managed to get the bigger kill, but I could usually beat her in a scrap, follow? Not always, mind. Brumhilde is quite a woman."

Anyone that could stand up to Harold in a fight was someone Bob didn't want to mess with. It was a good thing, he mused, that Harold spoke as though the two of them were on good terms.

Around midday they halted the wagon for lunch, letting the horses graze while they ate sheep jerky and some berries Kelael said were edible. They tasted like grass but settled nicely in Bob's stomach. Osivia seemed to like them. She asked after Quaker. Bob had also been wondering what had happened to the little feathery spy. Had she been caught in the fire? But Bernard informed them that Quaker was fine. After the meal of peas provided by Hirrell, she'd rested a day and then flown back to Bernard. She'd been happily floating in a lake near Azenbul since before Bob had retaken the Gatekey.

"When I returned to the Koreka," said Bernard, "I'd thought I'd have to catch up with you. I thought Torael would've insisted on going to the Nexus. So, I thought I'd be walking a good way, alone, possibly all the way to the Nexus. I had to leave Quaker behind. That sort of travel is too hard on her."

Soon, they reattached the horses and were off again. Kelael volunteered to walk, and Harold said he didn't need to rest, so Bob found himself atop the wagon next to Bernard.

The ride was full of jolts and shudders. Bob tried to begin a conversation with Bernard several times but kept getting interrupted by small things. They had to stop for Harold to clear a path. They had to stop because a small log had jammed itself under the wagon carriage. They passed over a rocky outcrop that rattled the wagon and made hearing anything else impossible. Before he knew it, the sun was dipping, the light was paling, and it was time to camp for the night.

"The forest's edge is just beyond this next rise," said Kelael as Harold and Bob were building the fire. "We could make it farther today, but we would be out in the open. Better to stay here and lose a few hours, than to risk discovery."

Bob was exhausted and could hardly argue. His ab-muscles were sore from unconsciously clenching them atop the wagon. However, the day had grown hot, even under the canopy of the Essen'aelo, and the clothes were dry. Beneath the descending chill of evening, Bob wrapped himself in the trench coat, made toasty warm by a day exposed to air and sunlight. Likewise, Kelael donned a green, fur-lined, hooded cloak, and Harold put on a woolen shirt. Bernard, who'd probably been uncomfortable during the day, was already dressed for cooler weather in a cloak of his own. Bob asked Osivia if she was cold, and she said that faeries didn't get cold. Something about their own light shielded them from temperature change.

Another piece of good news was that Bob had seen Erto several times throughout the day. The spirit was back to his usual tricks, showing up every so often along the path, watching from the shadows. Once, Bob waved to him. The next time the spirit showed up, he waved at Bob. By the end of the day, Bob found that the astral voices were just as easy to tune into as they'd been at Oath Keep.

There was very little in the way of food, so Harold and Kelael wandered off in the failing light to hunt. Osivia said she was going to explore a little before bed. Bob found himself sitting by the crackling campfire alone with Bernard.

They smoked. They talked about the journey, about how long it would take to reach Torful the following day, about how long it would take to get to the Nexus from Nine Peaks. The conversation died away as they ran out of comfortable things to talk about. Eventually, sometime after sunset, Bob looked up at Bernard across the fire.

"What is this important thing I'm supposed to remember?" he asked. He'd been thinking about Galvidon, which led him back to the mysteries in the Gray Man's conversation.

"Mmm?" said Bernard, pretending not to hear.

"Don't pull that shit with me, Bernard. I have a right to know." Bob didn't know if he had the right or not but asserting that he did couldn't hurt anything.

The old wizard studied him for a long moment. "I'm afraid you wouldn't believe me if I told you."

Bob glared at him. "Bernard, a few years ago, I was a garbage man. The strangest things that I saw all involved the things people would throw away. Entire computers, sometimes. Perfectly good bicycles with a flat tire. Entire cooked meals. Books, photographs, films and albums of music. People think that, because they don't value something, it has no value. Anyway, that was strange to me. That was the limit of how weird the universe could get.

"Since I got to Hub, I've met a race of pointy-eared people with blue skin. I've made friends with a faerie, met a duck that can spy, bonded to an earth spirit, and now I can make rocks fly around with my mind. And right now, I'm talking to a wizard around a campfire, on a mission to a place with doorways to other worlds guarded by a dragon. What, in the name of all things holy, gives you the impression that *anything* would be too fucking strange for me to believe?"

Bernard stared at him. The hard-set concern etched across his face slowly melted. He produced a chuckle. "Very well, Bob, very well. I suppose you're right. Now is as good a time as any." He cleared his throat. "You already know of the Precedentials, the first race in the Astraverse. They evolved on the First World, what we now commonly call the Anterior. Eventually, they developed technology so advanced, it could alter the very fabric of reality. They used this technology to create the Astraverse. They made that key around your neck, and the Gates it opens. They made many things with many purposes, and some with no particular purpose at all, simply because they could."

Bernard began to pack his pipe with tobacco. "This was long after the humans and the Galon Var in the Anterior had evolved to their current state. Anyway, the Precedentials seeded various realms with genetic material and transported willing colonies of humans and Galon Var to many of these places. With these colonists came some Precedential tech. However, the Precedentials were concerned that, if the technology should fall into the wrong hands, it could produce disastrous results. So, they selected certain traits that they felt were conducive to responsibility. Those who had these traits were genetically modified to be able to operate Precedential technology, while all others would be unable to do so. This genetic modification is passed down through reproduction."

"The Electum," said Bob. "you're talking about the Electum. Anna and Daniel, they had this… genetic modification, and that's why Galvidon killed them."

"As you say. The Electum." Bernard seemed uncomfortable, unable to look Bob in the eye. He puffed on his pipe and stared at the fire. "As I've explained before, the Precedentials were not perfect in their selection. After all, a subset of the Electum became the Order of Tag Nah. But the Precedentials had anticipated this. To them, the Order, or something like it, would be an unpleasant but inevitable byproduct of the Electum's creation. And so, they created the Vigilantum."

Now, Bernard's eyes were on him. Bob's heart beat a little faster at the word *Vigilantum*—one of those mysterious words from Galvidon's conversation.

"This is its official name, though it has other names in common parlance. Members of the Vigilantum are often referred to as Vigilants, or Immortals, and the group itself is sometimes called the Alphabet, for reasons I hope will become clear shortly. The purpose of the Vigilantum is to act as guardians of the Electum and to uphold the Mandates. That is, the Vigilantum is to protect those members of the Electum that seek to better the Astraverse, to make life more comfortable for its inhabitants. But the Vigilants are also to eliminate threats from within the Electum— to make sure something like the Order does not gain dominance."

"Haven't really done their job, then, have they?" injected Bob.

Bernard scowled. "No, we have not. It doesn't help that, for all their foresight, the Precedentials made one glaring error. The Vigilantum is the highest order of their creations—we are the watchers, you see? Yet no one watches *us*. And there is at least one among our number who does not follow the Mandates."

Bob had become completely distracted by Bernard's use of the word *we*. *There is at least one among our number*, said the old wizard.

"Bernard, are you in this Vigilantum? Is it passed down, like the Blood of the Electum?"

Bernard stared at him for a long moment. "Yes, Bob, I am of the Vigilantum. All the wizards of Hub are. All of them, Bob. Even you."

Bob's head twitched in surprise. Before he could respond, Bernard was talking again.

"But it is not passed down from generation to generation. It is passed from life to life, within an immortal astral body."

"How…" Bob's mind was racing, but he couldn't seem to finish a line of thinking. "What…?"

"I have said all things possess an astral body, yes? Even and especially you and I? When most living things die, their astral body is broken down, its fundamental components recycled by the Astraverse. Memory is sometimes preserved, but rarely, and imperfectly when it is. However, the members of the Vigilantum are different. When one of us dies a physical death, our astral body is recalled to the Anterior in its entirety, where its memories are stored. The astral body—our astral body—is then reborn into a new physical body—an infant—somewhere in the Astraverse. Upon reaching adolescence, our memories begin to return—the important ones, anyway. The Mandates. Our first life. Sometimes, memories of various other lives we've endured surface as well—often very strong memories that were important to one of our incarnations. We never remember everything, of course. The mind, even the mind of a Vigilant, can only hold so much before it falls to madness or simply ceases to function. But we always remember the Mandates, and we always remember our first life. It has always been so.

"That is, until now. Your name is **R**. My name is **B**. I have known you for so long, it is impossible to calculate. I sensed that it was you as soon as we met in this forest. Yet, *you* did not know *me*. You were born as Robert James Caplan, the latest life in a long series of lives, yet your memories did not return as they should have. I did not know why. I still don't. There is only one explanation that makes any sense to me. Someone—a very powerful and knowledgeable someone—*did not want you to remember*."

Bob stared at Bernard, stared through him, trying to fit it all in his mind, trying to reconcile it with everything that had happened. "I'm… I'm that old? I didn't… I don't feel that old. Do I?" He was talking to himself. Bernard didn't respond. As he thought about it, Bob realized he did feel old—much older that his late thirties. He'd always felt that way, even as a kid, like he was waiting for everyone else to catch up to him in some abstract, indescribable way. He stared off into the darkness, and there was Erto, just beyond the ring of firelight, watching the conversation. Bob turned back to Bernard, opened his mouth, desperate for something to say—anything to put the brakes on his racing thoughts. He felt like he was being transported by air spirits—rushing down a tunnel, completely out of control.

The underbrush crunched behind Bernard. From the shadows, Harold's bulk approached, followed by Kelael moving in lithe silence.

"Right then," announced Harold, grinning. "Who wants rabbit?"

It took over an hour to prepare and cook the two animals Harold and Kelael had killed. While they worked, Bob stared at the fire, trying to get a handle on what Bernard had told him. Despite his speech about how he'd become accustomed to strangeness, Bob's first instinct was to unilaterally reject what Bernard had said. *Bullshit*, his mind told him. *It sounds like bullshit*. Yet, he knew it wasn't. For one thing, everything Bernard had told him since they'd met had turned out to be true. Bob had rejected the idea that he would ever be able to command spirits, had convinced himself at one point that Bernard was just a crazy old man and that there was some hidden, mundane explanation for the things he could do. But Bob had been proven wrong. Doubting Bernard now would just be baseless, stubborn denial. And then there was that feeling. That feeling deep in his core. He remembered a flash of recognition at Bernard's story about the Order—how the tale had felt familiar, like he knew it already. He remembered wandering if there was such a thing as astral memory. Everything Bernard said tonight fit snugly into the gaps in his information. And more, it *felt* true. By the time Bob consciously decided to believe the Vigilantum was real, he realized he'd already unconsciously accepted it.

Kelael handed Bob a roasted rabbit haunch. As he began to eat, his mind simmered and finally settled down. He decided that being a Vigilant didn't change anything. At least, not right now. He was still Bob. He still loved Anna and Daniel. Still planned to kill Galvidon. If anything, this new information gave him a future. Ever since he'd stepped into his first

BOB THE WIZARD

Astral Gate, he'd been unable to see beyond killing Galvidon. He always saw that as the end for him. He even thought, on those nights when he was awake and alone with his thoughts, that after he killed Galvidon, he might as well just kill himself. After his revenge, there was nothing left for him. No reason to keep going. More recently, he'd thought—with renewed hope—he might be able to kill Galvidon and then use the Nexus to return to Earth. But now… Now, he could see a strange, new future gathering like storm clouds. Maybe there *was* something for him after Galvidon, after all.

Harold and Kelael were having a conversation, and Osivia was hovering nearby over *A Common History of Engoria*. She had a tiny sliver of cooked rabbit in one hand. Bernard ate in silence, seeming to contemplate the fire.

"The letters," Bob said to him. "Our names, **R** and **B**, what do they mean?"

Osivia looked up from her book. Kelael and Harold fell to silence and looked over as well.

Bernard glanced at their companions. His eyes asked a silent question of Bob. *Are you sure?*

Bob offered a single nod.

"Those are not our real names," said Bernard. "They are nicknames. Our real names are lost to time. There are twenty Vigilants. Each was named for a letter of the Precedentials' alphabet, of which there are twenty. I was the second Vigilant. You were the eighteenth. In each of our incarnations, our first name always begins with the appropriate letter. For example, each time I am born, my name begins with the second letter of the alphabet appropriate to the culture I have been born into. This time, I was born in Montana, where they speak English, and the second letter is B."

Bob was nodding. He bit a chunk of roasted haunch.

"What are you two talking about?" asked Osivia curiously.

"Bernard says I'm an ancient, immortal guardian created by the original race in the Astraverse," said Bob nonchalantly around a mouthful of rabbit.

Kelael, Harold, and Osivia stared at him with their mouths open.

Bob pointed the haunch at Bernard. "He's one too," he said, wagging his eyebrows.

Osivia coughed like she was choking on something. Kelael scoffed dismissively, and Harold barked a great, booming laugh. A few seconds passed, then all three of them looked back at Bob, who kept his face still.

"Really?" demanded Osivia.

"You can't be serious," said Kelael.

Harold just continued to stare.

Bob turned back to Bernard. "Can I get my memories back? I was supposed to get them back, right? Isn't there a failsafe, or something? Some way I can fix whatever was done to me?"

Bernard glanced nervously at their audience, then nodded his head slowly. "I believe so, yes. I believe there is a way to reclaim the memories." He looked up at the night sky. "But we must rest. We have tarried too long as it is. Let's discuss it…" he glanced again at Kelael, Harold and Osivia, "another time."

"Well," said Bob, shrugging. "I guess it's bed-time."

"No, wait!" said Osivia.

"They are having a joke," said Kelael.

Harold stared at Bob like he was trying to decide if he could fit him into a suitcase.

Bob had trouble sleeping. He lay on his back and stared at the stars.

He thought about Rashindon.

You are special, Bob. Galvidon cannot see it.

And Erto.

BOB THE WIZARD

Robert James Caplan. You are new. Do you remember?

And Bernard.

It's quite a lot to explain. Especially since I don't know how much you remember.

Remember?

Excuse me, I'm old. I meant to say, I don't know how much you already know.

He remembered something Anna had said to him only a few months after they'd first met. It was on a date—one of those obligatory dates after you'd both committed, but still wanted to go out and be seen together, simply to share proximity out in the world. They were getting ice cream. They took pictures in the photobooth. A silly one, a sexy one, a serious one.

You are so confusing, Anna said, stirring a cup of rocky road. *Sometimes I feel like you're just a kid, and other times I feel like you're a million years old. Like you know secrets.*

My mom used to tell me I was born with the world on my shoulders. It's not wisdom. It's stress.

Ice cream helps with stress. Are you going to finish that?

How did Rashindon know he was a Vigilant, but Galvidon didn't? How many times—how many versions of Bob—had met Erto, met Bernard? How many times had he been in love like he'd been with Anna? A hundred? A thousand? A million?

Did Robert James Caplan even really exist? Or was he just a shell, a fresh coat of paint? If he got **R**'s memory's back, would he still be the same man? Would Bob, and all the things he'd accomplished, suffered through, wished, feared, learned… would it all disappear, swallowed by the new person, the stranger, sleeping inside him?

We are destroyed and rebuilt much more often than you'd think.

Something Bernard had said.

Bob closed his eyes. As he drifted into sleep, he wondered, not for the first time, if he would be someone else when he woke.

M. V. PRINDLE

They ate the last of the sheep jerky for breakfast. No one talked about the previous night's conversation. If it weren't for the fact that he kept catching Bernard worriedly staring at him, Bob might have thought he'd imagined the whole thing.

Anyway, as travel commenced and the day wore on, questions about identity became academic. They left the Essen'aelo behind, meaning they were exposed on all sides in open country. The khaki-grass grew thickly, painting the horizon in a swishing blur. Dozens of grasshoppers launched away from every step they took. Harold and Kelael took turns chopping down particularly dense knots of grass in the wagon's path. They were leaving an obvious trail, but once they got to Torful and found Brumhilde, that wouldn't matter. No one could follow them after they'd teleported to Nine Peaks.

After a couple of hours, they reached Horizon Road. They were several miles west of the mine Bob, Torael, and the others had been rescued from. Even so, the proximity to a major road made them all nervous. They waited several minutes in a nearby copse of trees while Osivia made sure the coast was clear. Then, they quickly crossed Horizon and reentered the sea of grass. The horses were clearly confounded that no one else wanted to stay on the smooth pebbles of the road.

Several more hours passed, and Bob came to the conclusion that, if he never saw another grasshopper, he could die a happy man. Eventually, the tall grass began to lessen, leaving the shorter, bright-green grass to dominate. The hills became more pronounced, and crags and boulders became more commonplace. Trees started appearing again. The party passed under the occasional birch, maple, or pine. The grasshoppers became smaller and less densely populated. Bushes of little round leaves began to dot their path. Bob saw squirrels.

Soon, the smell of the air became humid and fresh, the odor of fish hinted at its edges. The bushes and foliage grew thicker. Trees began to appear more frequently. They were passing through a dense clump of brambly weeds when Kelael hissed a warning from ahead.

Bob didn't hear what he said, but the others acted instantly. Bernard pulled the horses to a stop. Harold drew his sword and strapped his shield to his arm, padding his way over to Kelael. Bob could see him trying to be quiet, but he was simply too big. His footfalls produced loud crunches. Osivia dimmed her glow and zipped to Kelael to investigate.

Bob, sitting next to Bernard on the wagon, withdrew the dragon pipe. He was trying to conserve his tobacco. He only had enough for three or four more bowls, and he knew he had to save it for his magic. He'd barely smoked all day, and presently struggled not to simply light the pipe and begin smoking. He exchanged a look with Bernard, and then the two wizards clambered down from the cab to join the others.

Bob and Bernard were quieter than Harold, but not by much. As they approached, Bob saw Kelael and Harold crouched behind a thicket, Osivia hovering nervously between them. Kelael had his bow out and an arrow nocked. Before Bob could ask what was happening, Kelael rose swiftly to standing and loosed the arrow. There was a dull thump and an animalistic screeching noise. Harold darted from cover, and Kelael nocked another arrow.

"It's still alive," said Osivia.

Kelael loosed the second arrow. This time there was a wet squishing sound, a gurgling chirp, and then a heavy thump.

"Never mind," said Osivia, sounding a little sick.

Bob pushed aside some brambles to see what this was all about. He saw Harold standing over a dark shape on the ground. Kelael motioned for them to move forward, so Bob followed the En'hari, scanning the landscape for anything out of the ordinary. They met up with Harold, who stood frowning down at the corpse of one of the strangest creatures Bob had ever encountered.

It was small, about the size of a Labrador, and covered in deep green scales that caught the daylight with a dull shimmer. Its head was almost as large as its body, and its alligator-like jaws lay open on the ground, a slimy pink tongue lolling onto the bloody grass. Sharp fins ran along its head and back. It had four clawed limbs, but its shape indicated a bipedal creature—its legs were thick and muscled, its arms thinner and ending in hands with opposable thumbs. One arrow protruded from its bony shoulder, another from its soft throat. Its dead eyes were open, and though they were yellowish with slitted pupils, they were set into its face in a disturbingly humanlike fashion.

"What the ever-loving fuck is that?" whispered Bob.

Kelael was scanning the area intensely. "Osivia, see if you can find the rest of them."

"Oh. Okay." Her voice shook. She zipped into the air.

Kelael turned to Bob. "It is a sherka. There are many kinds of Gez Kar. The sherka are the smallest. Mostly they are used as skirmishers and scouts."

"Gez Kar?" said Bob. "I thought they were in New Tanatha, or something. What is it doing here?"

"This is most concerning," said Bernard. "Bob is right, it has been decades since the Gez Kar have dared to come this far southeast. This should not be here."

Kelael nodded. "Yet, it is here." He shared a meaningful look with Harold.

"What?" asked Bob. "What is it?"

Harold cleared his throat. "The sherka are scouts, follow? They always belong to a brood. Never very far away, aye? If this sherka is here, that means more Gez Kar are nearby."

"It means," said Kelael, "the armies of the Gez Kar have entered Engoria."

CHAPTER TWENTY-EIGHT:
TORFUL

They waited tensely for Osivia to return. The two horses cropped the grass at their feet. Bob wondered idly how Torael and Gorrelai were doing, and whether they'd yet caught up to Melanae. Harold stared silently, arms crossed, at the corpse of the sherka, a seething hatred in his eyes Bob hadn't seen from him before. Kelael scanned their surroundings like a sentry. Bernard had his eyes closed, his hands around his staff, and seemed to be whispering to himself. Bob watched him for a moment and then almost fell over backward.

A giggling, translucent cherub swirled out of the air above Bernard's hat and shot into the trees, where there was a brash disturbance of leaves that earned a glance from Harold and Kelael. After a time that felt much longer than the few minutes it was, Osivia floated down through the canopy.

"I didn't find any Gez Kar," she said, "but I can see Torful. It's only a couple of miles away."

Kelael nodded. "Bernard and Bob, get the wagon moving. Harold, on the left flank. I'm on the right. Osivia, cover our rear. Everyone, keep your eyes open." He walked into the grass.

Harold complied with his instructions immediately. Osivia shared a look with Bob. Bob shrugged at her and returned to the wagon with Bernard.

"Does it bother you he thinks he's in charge?" Bob mumbled to the old wizard.

M. V. PRINDLE

Bernard scoffed. "He *is* in charge." He gave Bob a sidelong smirk. "Can't you tell?"

They got the wagon moving. Bob jerked his head around at every swaying branch, every snapped twig. He patted at the pipe in his pocket and tuned into the astral voices a bit more than usual. Their serene songs did nothing to settle his nerves.

The smells of fish and fresh water had become pronounced in the air. Bob began to hear the steady rush of a river. Soon they reached a point where the brambles and weeds vanished, and the land opened up on all sides. They stood at the crest of a rise, overlooking Horizon River and the village of Torful beyond. The river ran east to west at a slow but implacable pace. Across from the party on the north bank were rows of wooden piers with inbuilt docks, where a score of dinghies and fishing vessels were tied. Bob could see a few boats on the river as well. A group of villagers sat on one of the piers, casting lines.

Torful itself was only a dozen or so structures, mostly constructed of wood and plaster. Bob could make out a windmill, a steeple, and a granary. Just beyond the village to the north, the land sloped sharply upward to a high ridge, atop which pine trees grew in a thick forest. Aside from the steady slosh and churn of the running water, the village of Torful was a quiet place.

There was no good way to get the wagon down the rise. In any case, the vehicle—now barely functional after its trip through the forest—had fulfilled its purpose. The party went about retrieving all of their supplies from the wagon bed.

In a few minutes, Bob wore the brown jerkin Fan had made, his matches, pipe, and tobacco stowed within. He wore the trench coat, sunglasses, and backpack. The sawed-off was tied inside the coat, the rifle slung over his shoulder next to the pack. The earth and rocks sang to him as he watched Harold unhitch the horses.

Bernard and Bob led the party down the slope at an angle. Behind them was Kelael. After a short argument with Harold, he'd slung his bow so as to not terrify the villagers. The sight of an En'hari would trouble them enough without him waving a weapon around. Behind Kelael, Harold brought up the rear, leading the horses carefully down the incline.

BOB THE WIZARD

Bob didn't see Osivia, but he knew she was around. Erto sat watching them from the top of the rise, little lumpy legs dangling over the edge.

When they reached the bottom and the edge of the water, they saw there was a bridge about a quarter mile downriver, to the west. There was just enough room along the root-choked shoreline to reach it without getting wet. One of the horses had to wade into the shallows but didn't seem to mind. As the party advanced, the villagers on the pier watched them with interest.

Finally, they made their way into a bridge of sturdy wooden planks. Bob saw a sign proclaiming that they were on West Pine Way. The party must have been travelling parallel to the road for the last few hours. As they approached the end of the bridge, a slim, sandy-haired man ambled toward them from the villagers on the pier. He wore a crisp, white, button-down shirt and beige breeches. His shaven face was framed in thick sideburns. He held up a hand in greeting but bore a distinctly uninviting expression.

"Hello," he called to them. "Name's Nathaniel. I'm the mayor." He glanced warily at Kelael. "What brings you to Torful?"

"Why, I'm pleased to meet you, Nathaniel. Please excuse my elf. He will not harm you. I am Bernard. My retinue and I are simple travelers from Borgamash. We have horses to sell, if you would be so kind as to accommodate us."

Nathaniel's eyes moved over them. "Very well," he said with forced cheer, "please follow me."

The villagers on the pier were still staring at them. Bernard allowed Nathaniel several steps before following.

"That was an obvious lie," Kelael hissed at the old wizard. "None of us look like we are from Borgamash."

Bernard shrugged. "*He's* never been to Borgamash."

When they were only a few paces away from the village proper, Bernard's air spirit suddenly returned. It dove out of the air like a kamikaze and abruptly stopped right next to the old wizard, where it whispered something in his ear, then vanished in the blink of an eye.

Bernard whirled. "They are here!"

Bob saw two balls of fire arc through the air from the ridge to the north like flaming arrows. He watched them plummet, unable to decide what he was looking at. The fiery spheres struck atop one of Torful's largest wooden structures—the granary—where they exploded into a conflagration.

Kelael and Harold had drawn their weapons and were wildly looking around for something to attack. The horses bolted downriver.

"What..." began Bob, but then he saw. A swarm of Gez Kar had begun pouring over the ridge in the north. There must have been over fifty of those sherka. They hopped and skittered down the ridge, nimble as mountain goats, snapping their slavering jaws. Among them were a few larger, humanlike Gez Kar, with bulging, scaly muscles and sharklike teeth. They wore armor made of jagged bone and leathery hides. Their hands ended in talons, and thick green tails protruded from their backsides. They climbed down the sheer face of the ridge like lizards down a stone wall. But they were not the worst.

The source of the fireballs came last, trundling the long way around to the village, deliberate and heavy. Maybe twelve feet tall, it's scaled legs were like pistons, its arms ropey with muscle. Its entire torso was encased in a plated shell that dovetailed to spikes along the edges. Its head was long and round, its nostrils flaring pits. Its eyes were slitted and gleamed with malevolence. It wore a headdress of dangling teeth and bones—some of which were obviously human. Strapped to its shell with hide were two torches that rose above its head like banners. The twin flames fluttered in the wind.

Bob had no time for questions. A wave of sherka approached at staggering speed. Next to him, Bernard hissed out a sharp breath, and a gust of wind blasted the nearest group of sherka, sending them toppling like bowling pins. An arrow from Kelael pierced one of the creatures in the eye.

Bob unslung the rifle, disengaged the safety, retracted the bolt. Harold bellowed and flung himself into a group of snapping sherka, cracking the huge shield against one and cleaving the skull of another with his sword. Bob shot one of the beasts just behind the mountain man as it began to pounce. He shot two more that were attempting to flank Kelael. One of the man-sized Gez Kar approached between two buildings and Bob shot it in the head. Its brains splatter-painted the wooden planks behind it.

The village was in full panic. People screamed and ran in the streets. A group of men were attempting to put out the flaming granary, but the fire had already spread to the adjacent structures. That Nathaniel guy was nowhere to be seen.

Bob backed up, shooting sherka until the rifle produced a dull *thunk*. He tossed it aside and untied the shotgun. He stayed a few feet behind Kelael and Harold, covering their flanks while they battled sword and shield to tooth and claw. Bestial shrieks, grunts, and chirps filled his ears. Soon, the shotgun was empty and discarded as well, and he, Kelael and Harold had been gradually herded to the center of town. The torn corpses of villagers littered the ground.

"Mommy?"

Bob heard the small cry behind him. He turned. A little boy, maybe six, was standing alone, paralyzed with fear.

"Mommy!"

Facing the boy was a hissing sherka, rearing back to pounce. Suddenly Osivia was fluttering in its face, flashing wildly. It shrieked and snapped at her to no avail. Harold appeared in a bullrush and swiftly smashed it between his shield and the side of the nearby building. The creature burst with red goo.

Bob realized they were in front of a saloon—the kind with swinging double-doors. He thrust the little boy through the entrance. Dodging some claws, he withdrew the dragon pipe. Bernard hissed and slammed his staff into the ground, creating a burst of air in a half-radius that swept several sherka off their feet and brought a man-sized Gez Kar to its knees. As he popped a match to light, Bob heard some astral voices that were particularly loud and turned to see a well, rung with thick white bricks, only a few feet away in the central courtyard. He ducked as a fist of razor-sharp talons swung at him from a huge, scaly arm. He drew on the pipe and concentrated. One of the white stones around the well shot from its mortar, reshaped into a thin stone spear in midair, and impaled

Bob's assailant in its scaly chest. It's bone armor cracked, and a spray of blood misted over Bob. The creature roared and swiped at him again.

The huge, shelled Gez Kar with the torches had arrived at the fray. It matched the roar of its fellow, and twin beams of white-hot energy shot from the torches, burning two thick furrows in the earth as they swung toward Bob and his friends, who all dove aside. The searing wake of the beams left the well in three smoldering sections.

Kelael and Harold were still holding their own, blocking, slicing, and smashing through the sherka. Harold was currently engaged with one of the larger Gez Kar, and Bob saw Kelael kill three sherka at once in a series of deft slices as they attempted a coordinated attack. Both of Bob's companions were covered in splatters of blood, dirt, and viscera.

Suddenly, the double doors to the saloon burst open. A spear as big around as Bob's arm was thrust out from just inside. It pierced the skull of a big Gez Kar with a crunch, then retracted. A huge woman stepped out of the saloon. She was at least seven feet tall and had muscles to rival the Gez Kar. She wore a sleeveless jerkin and a long skirt of dyed-blue wool. She spun into combat, batting away sherka with the thick shaft of the spear, slicing and impaling with its blade. With a single thrust, she punctured the throat of a large Gez Kar, easily pulling out into a spin that flattened the skulls of two more sherka. Her long, straight, reddish brown hair whipped and flowed with her movements.

Bob took a pull on the pipe. He had a creative idea, inspired by Osivia's intervention. Erto heard him, and obliged. Clouds of dirt rose into the air like swarms of bees, congealed into blobs, and flew into the faces of the remaining Gez Kar. Blinded, they roared and shrieked, clawing at their own eyes. Harold, Kelael, and the big woman—probably Brumhilde—dispatched them swiftly.

Bernard was battling the shelled creature singlehandedly. They faced each other from a distance of six feet. Bursts of flame and focused energy flashed and lanced toward Bernard in a fusillade. Each gust of heat and fire was batted aside by the wind. The creature tried to swipe at him with its huge claws, but it seemed the air would not allow it. Bob saw the cherubic spirit swoop behind the Gez Kar, taunting the creature with a poke of the tongue and a waggle of the fingers. Bob and the others slowly approached from behind Bernard. Kelael shot an arrow that bounced harmlessly off the monster's carapace. The shelled creature roared and increased the ferocity of its fiery attacks. Bernard's wind blocked it all. Finally, the old wizard slammed his staff on the ground again, and this time the crystal atop it flared like a flash grenade toward the Gez Kar. Bob nodded. It was basically the same trick he'd stolen from Osivia.

Dazzled, the creature wailed with frustration, blinking rapidly. Bob noticed that it blinked... sideways. Bernard stepped forward, hissing loudly with his breath, and the air around the massive creature pressed on it from all sides. The monster writhed and released an earsplitting roar that buckled into a shriek as its shell cracked with an enormous *crunch*. Before everyone's eyes, blood and ichor burst from the Gez Kar's skin as it was mercilessly crushed. The thing collapsed in a gory heap, dead.

"Jesus Christ," muttered Bob. "Remind me not to piss you off, Bernard."

Bernard's eyes met Bob's and bore nothing but sullen sadness. The old wizard looked away, and Bob realized that almost the entire village was on fire. In the heat of battle, he hadn't noticed the true heat of the flames. The granary had fully collapsed and was naught but a pyre. The manor next door—possibly Nathaniel's house—was half-burned down, while several other buildings had met the flames but not yet been engulfed. There was a lone pair of burly Darkhairs still battling the fires with buckets of earth. The rest of the living villagers had fled the streets. Bob could now make out a long line of hovels stretching east along the riverbank, blessedly untouched by flames. Faces peered nervously at him from small, rectangular windows.

Bernard closed his eyes and breathed deep and slow for several seconds. Then he released his breath in a protracted sigh. The air pressure shifted. Bob's ears popped like he was descending in an airplane. For a moment, it was hard to breathe. Then the world seemed to right itself, and the next thing Bob knew, all the fires had gone out. Wisps of black smoke danced skyward.

"Wow," said Bob, impressed yet again. "Could have used that trick at the Koreka."

"I cannot be everywhere at once!" snapped Bernard, not looking at him.

The saloon was the only structure untouched by the fire. Presently, there was a creak as someone exited its doors. Nathaniel now stood on the building's porch, wide eyed and shaky. "That…" he tried again, "you…" his voice cracked. "Magic is illegal in Engoria! By order of the King! You… you're under arrest!"

Kelael spat derisively. Harold burst out laughing. Bob drew a breath of tobacco smoke, narrowing his eyes at the mayor of Torful.

"Nathaniel!" boomed the big woman with the spear. "Get your skinny arse back inside before I be coming over there!"

Nathaniel flinched like an abused dog, glared at the woman, then backed up through the saloon's entrance. She turned to Harold and a huge grin broke across her face.

"Harold, you wee lad! Where've you been hiding yourself?" She planted her spear in the ground and opened her arms wide, striding to Harold. They spun as they embraced, and Harold chuckled.

Wee lad? Bob noticed with amusement that Brumhilde was a foot taller than her cousin. She was easily taller than all of them but being bigger than Harold was impressive in its own right. When Bob glanced around at his surroundings, the giddiness of victory paled away to sadness. Suddenly he understood Bernard's foul mood. There were bodies everywhere, human and Gez Kar alike, tangled in bloody messes all around. Torful was a smoking ruin. The earth was churned into gooey mud.

Osivia landed on Bob's shoulder. "Oh, your jacket," she said softly.

Bob looked down at himself. On the breast of the trench coat, just above his heart, the top layer of leather was cleanly sheared in three perfectly parallel lines. It reminded Bob of the scar on Harold's chest. He let out a slow breath.

"So!" said Brumhilde. "Aren't you going to introduce me?"

"Oh, aye, aye," said Harold from beside her. "Brumhilde, this is Kelael, an En'hari Gasheera, and my best friend." Kelael inclined his head. "And

BOB THE WIZARD

that's Bob and Bernard, aye? Couple of wizards, follow?"

"Two wizards in one place!" exclaimed Brumhilde. "What unlucky mess have I stumbled into now, aye?" Her smile was large and infectious. Her eyes fell on Osivia. "Oh, and a faerie! Perhaps I spoke too soon about luck, aye? And what is your name, little faerie?"

Osivia fluttered up and affected a curtsy. "Osivia Glenbrook, ma'am. Pleased to meet you."

"Well, that's lovely. I'm Brumhilde. I suppose you're all here for a reason. But I might as well hear it over a drink, follow? What do you say?"

Bob exchanged a look with Bernard, and then the party followed Brumhilde into the saloon.

As they entered through the swinging double doors, Brumhilde propped her ten-foot spear in a nearby nook, where its blade fit perfectly into a worn divot in the rafters. The common room was full of round wooden tables covered in notches and scratches, each surrounded by rickety, hollow-backed chairs. To the right of the entrance ran a messy bar lined with worn stools. To the left, in the corner, a curved banister traced a stairway to the second floor. There were stuffed fish, and the head of a large buck with impressive antlers, mounted on the wall.

The tables and stools had been abandoned. The saloon's occupants—no doubt mostly refugees from the battle—now huddled together against the back wall. Bob counted six women, three men, and four children—one of whom was the little boy he'd shoved through the entrance. One of the men was Nathaniel. The group quivered and cried as the party entered, their boots heavily scuffling on the worn floorboards. With each step taken by Brumhilde or Harold, the floor groaned and creaked.

Bob tucked the dragon pipe away in the brown jerkin and studied the villagers. One of the men—a burly Darkhair with broad shoulders and a goatee—Stood behind the little boy, a hand laid protectively on his shoulder. None of the women behaved that way toward the boy. None of them were his mother. Bob glanced down at himself, at his companions. All of them were covered in blood. The boy's mother was most likely one of the corpses outside. Maybe not. Maybe she was one of the lucky ones that made it to the hovels. Bob grabbed a greasy rag from the nearest table and wiped his face. The rag came away stained with the brown of drying blood. Brumhilde was casually poking around behind the bar like she owned the place. Bernard, Kelael, and Harold sat nervously at one of the tables. Osivia fluttered around the room, studying the decorations. Bob approached the goateed man and the little boy, bringing his backpack around under one arm to unzip its largest compartment.

He faced the man, who inhaled sharply but unflinchingly met Bob's eyes.

"We don't want you here," hissed Nathaniel from nearby. "The King will here of this!"

Bob ignored him. "Your wife," he said to the goateed man. "You know where she is?"

The man shook his head. The little boy looked up at Bob with eyes like sparkling saucers.

Bob nodded and slowly lowered himself to one knee in front of the boy. The father watched him carefully. "I had a little boy once," said Bob softly. He glanced to the father. "And a wife. They're gone now." The boy began to breathe more heavily. "But I'm not," said Bob. "And neither is this," he slowly reached into the backpack and pulled out the stuffed llama.

The boy's eyes lit with curiosity. He spoke in a small voice. "What... what is it supposed to be?"

Bob looked at the toy, putting on a show of consideration. "Well, it's a llama. A magical creature that protects its owner. It belonged to my son, but I want you to have it."

The boy glanced up at his father questioningly. The man looked from Bob to the llama and back and offered a shrug. The little boy smiled and took the stuffed animal from Bob's hand.

"Don't take that from him!" exclaimed Nathaniel. "It could be dangerous!"

The boy scowled at Nathaniel and hugged the toy possessively to his chest. A nearby little girl glared at the boy with jealousy.

"Nathaniel," Brumhilde called sharply from where she now sat at the table with the others. "Get outside and help the other men deal with the damage."

Nathaniel glared at her with unmasked hatred.

"Now," said Brumhilde, crossing her arms.

Nathaniel stormed across the room, noisily disturbing the chairs as he made his way to the double doors.

"Useless man," muttered Brumhilde.

Bob gave the boy's father a nod and then crossed to the table to join his friends. Harold patted the table in front of the chair next to his own. Bob sat, and in front of him was a mug of deep red liquid. "Oh," he said, "I don't—"

"Sweetberry juice," said Harold. "It's sweetberry juice. Sweetberries only grow up here in the north, follow? A favorite of mine as a lad."

Bob tasted the drink tentatively. A sweet warmth rolled over his tongue and down his throat. "Mmm." He nodded to Harold and took a long swallow.

Osivia settled on his shoulder. "That was a nice thing you did, Bob," she whispered in his ear. "I knew you weren't always an asshole."

Bob suppressed a chuckle.

"Alright then, lovelies," said Brumhilde pleasantly to the villagers, "shows over, follow? Lizards are dead. Time to be picking up the pieces, aye?" She watched them, smiling, until they began to shuffle their feet. Most of them left the saloon in a daze. One of the women went up the stairs, and the man who was neither Nathaniel nor the boy's father—a grizzled, balding man with a long white apron— moved behind the bar and began cleaning.

"Looks like this place would fall apart without you," said Bob between sips of sweetberry juice.

Brumhilde gulped down her mug and belched. Bob caught the distinct odor of beer-breath. "Why, thank you. What was your name again? Ben?

You both had B names." She turned her head to the bald man behind the bar. "Bring me another, please, Jacky."

"Yes'm," mumbled the man called Jacky.

"I'm Bob. That's Bernard."

Bernard's big green hat dipped as he inclined his head.

"Ah, Bob is it then?" said Brumhilde. "Look at all of us, with B names." She grinned.

"Bernard," said Bob. "Why didn't your spirit warn us about the Gez Kar sooner? Air spirits are supposed to be swift."

Bernard sniffed. He hadn't touched the mug in front of him. "Indeed, they are swift. Yet, as I have mentioned before, air spirits are incredibly forgetful. Faffle probably watched the Gez Kar for several minutes before he remembered he was supposed to come tell me about them."

"The spirit's name is Faffle?" asked Brumhilde. "How adorable."

Kelael took a small sip from his mug, watching the exchange in silence. Now and then, he glanced at the entrance.

Harold cleared his throat. "Speaking of late arrivals, what took you so long to join the fight, Brum?"

Brumhilde arched an eyebrow. "I was asleep, follow? Damn lizards attacked during my nap time, the rude bastards." She took a swig from her mug. "Anyway, my turn for questions, aye? What're the beautiful lot of you doing here in my town?"

Harold cleared his throat. "Well… Brum, the thing is… we need to borrow your spear."

She glanced at her spear where it was propped in its nook in the corner. "My spear? Why, you little hairy bastard! What for?"

"You need not part with it," said Bernard. "As long as you are willing to come along."

Brumhilde set down her mug. "Come along… where?"

"Home, Brum," said Harold. "We've got to get to Nine Peaks, follow?"

BOB THE WIZARD

She rolled her eyes. "Have you lost your mind, cousin? Your father will have you training teenagers for war in five minutes flat! Why do think I left? The bastard only got meaner with the years, after Junior, Sam, and Meryl died. Why would you want to go back?" She glanced around the table. "And why would you all want to go to Nine Peaks? Maximus Whitespring will have you fighting Gez Kar before you know which way is up, you mark my words."

"We're not going to Nine Peaks," said Bob. "That is, it's not our final destination. We need to get to the Nexus. As you saw, Bernard has command of air spirits. Like Faffle. He can get us anywhere in an instant, but only if we have an object that has been to the place we're going. We don't have anything that's been to the Nexus. So, we figured we could use your spear to get to Nine Peaks, then walk the rest of the way."

"The Nexus?" Brumhilde glanced at Osivia. "Maybe this is all an unlucky event, after all, aye? Why, in the name of the peaks, would you want to go *there*?"

"To stop a devastating invasion," said Bernard.

"To kill the man that murdered my family," said Bob.

"To acquire weapons for my people," said Kelael.

Brumhilde looked around at them, eyes wide. "Well now. Seems you've got some good reasons, then." She sighed and looked again at the spear. "Well, much as I don't want to go to Ninth Castle, I couldn't bear to part with her. I've carried her since I was a wee lass." She drained the dregs from her mug and set it down loudly. "Right then. When do we leave?"

Osivia fluttered up and softly pulsed with light. "Are we ever going to talk about the fact that the Gez Kar seem to be invading Engoria?"

"There is nothing we can do," said Kelael softly but firmly. "It is Flaire's problem, not ours."

Harold nodded. "Aye. One thing at a time."

"Now," said Bernard, addressing Brumhilde's question and ignoring the rest. "We leave now." He scraped back his chair and stood. After a moment, everyone else did the same.

Brumhilde walked to the nook in the corner and removed the spear. "We need to go outside for this magic, or…?"

"This will be fine," said Bernard, moving a few chairs to make a small clearing. "Hold it straight up, please, so we can all get a firm grip."

Brumhilde stepped into the center of the cleared floor, the boards underneath her protesting loudly. She placed the butt of the spear on the floorboards and held it straight. The tip of the blade almost touched the peaked ceiling. From behind the bar, Jacky watched this all impassively, wiping a glass with a rag.

"Alright, everyone, now's the time," said Bernard, placing a hand on the shaft of the spear. Everyone followed suit. Osivia hugged the shaft above their heads. Kelael crouched down and gripped the spear near the floor.

"Ready?" asked Bernard. Everyone's grip tightened.

"This had better be worth it, follow?" said Brumhilde. "Jacky, don't be letting Nathaniel do anything foolish while I'm gone."

"Yes'm," said Jacky.

Bernard hissed out a sharp breath, and the world became a swirling tunnel of color that pressed down on Bob, pushing him inexorably northwest, away from Torful, and closer—ever closer—to whatever awaited him at the Nexus.

CHAPTER TWENTY-NINE:
NINTH CASTLE

The colors coalesced and hardened around them. Bob became aware of standing in a grassy clearing full of blue flowers, holding onto Brumhilde's spear. The moment after the party arrived, Bernard collapsed onto the ground.

"Bernard?" Bob darted to the old wizard's side. "Bernard?" He bent over in the grass and fumbled for a pulse—something he'd never been very good at. As he struggled, he noticed Bernard was breathing. Bob let out a relieved sigh. "He's just out," said Bob, glancing up at the concerned faces of his companions. "Probably from the strain of so much magic."

The tip of Brumhilde's spear glinted in the afternoon light. Bob realized the wizard had transported them all a couple hundred miles while they were all holding an object that contained forged metal. Maybe that was why he'd collapsed.

Osivia fluttered over Bernard's face and rubbed her hands together, producing a large droplet of blazing light that fell over him like a powdery shroud. His breathing deepened but he did not wake.

"He's not in immediate danger, as far as I can tell," said the faerie. She glanced worriedly at Bob. "I could be wrong, though. I read something in one of his books about magical backlashes sometimes causing comas."

"Should I carry the man?" asked Brumhilde helpfully. She was almost twice as tall as Bernard. He'd look like a child in her arms.

"No, no, I'll do it," said Harold. He bent over and gingerly lifted Bernard, cradling him in the nooks of his elbows.

The wide-brimmed hat see-sawed to the ground, where Bob picked it up, beat it against his leg to knock off the dust, and folded it up to put away in the backpack. When he opened the pack, a wink of coppery metal caught his eye. It was the spare ammo clip he'd stowed for the assault on Oath Keep. The metal lighter he'd brought to Hub was probably somewhere in the pack as well. He glanced up at Harold and Kelael, both of whom wore metal weapons and armor. He realized that, not only had Bernard just teleported them despite the metal in the spear, he'd done it despite the ammo and lighter, the armor, the swords, the shields. Bob looked again at Bernard's unconscious form in Harold's arms. "This might be serious. He needs a doctor."

"Bound to be a healer at the castle, aye?" said Brumhilde.

Kelael was standing with his back to the party, arms crossed, gazing across the huge bowl-shaped valley of flowers. Harold stepped up next to him.

"I do not like this place," Bob heard Kelael mutter.

"Aye, I remember that day as well as you," said Harold. "Lot less pretty at the time, aye?"

"What is he on about, then?" Brumhilde asked Bob in a low voice.

"Not sure," said Bob, matching her whisper. "Harold once told me Kelael dragged him to Ninth Castle after a battle. Maybe he's remembering that. I think he said it was the same day his brothers... well, you know."

"Aye, too well," she said softly. She raised the spear with one hand and pointed it toward a group of hazy gray shapes cut against the southwestern horizon. "The Still Mountains," she said. Bob gazed at them—jagged, massive, and blurred, like teeth in the lower jaw of some unfathomably large monster.

Harold and Kelael started walking east. Osivia, worrying over Bernard, went with them. Bob picked up Bernard's staff and brought up the rear with Brumhilde. As he walked, Bob tried not to trample too many of the wide, open-faced, blue flowers.

"So, Brumhilde," said Bob, adjusting the sunglasses. "What brought you to Torful?"

BOB THE WIZARD

"Well, a couple of years ago I was passing through the wee spot. We were set upon by an unruly group of fellows that fancied themselves bandits, follow? They'd been harassing the villagers for weeks, apparently. Well, me and my Lady tossed them on their arse for their trouble." She patted the spear with her free hand. "By popular demand, Nathaniel offered me a contract, follow? I was just wondering around anyhow. I thought, why not, aye? Haven't had barely a spot of trouble since that day. Until this afternoon, of course."

"Aye," said Harold, from just ahead. "I'm betting you didn't. How do you think I knew you were there? Word gets around about a huge woman, skewering a whole gang of thieves, protecting Torful—well, I tend to hear about that sort of thing."

"You been hanging out with rabble, then, cousin?"

"Aye, more than I'd like."

"Why'd you not come visit me sooner?"

"He was busy," said Kelael without turning around.

The land sloped upwards. The field of blue flowers began to be replaced by tree-lined thickets and rock outcroppings. They trudged along a gravelly earthen path as it wound a shallow curve up a gradual incline. Soon pines and elms enclosed them on all sides. The blue flowers still grew in clusters in the underbrush, but more sparsely.

Sweat beaded on Bob's forehead. His upper legs began to grow sore from climbing the slope. "Fuck me," he said absently, "how'd you carry Harold all the way up this thing, Kelael?"

Kelael glanced at him sharply. "A friend of mine made a litter. I strapped Harold to it and drug it behind me."

"That was you?" muttered Brumhilde, as if to herself.

"They tell me I was bleeding like a skewered sherka the whole way," said Harold, breath puffing with effort. He readjusted Bernard in his arms. "Was a near thing, me pulling through."

Osivia appeared through the canopy. "Almost there," she announced. "Bob, you've got to see it, it's beautiful!"

M. V. PRINDLE

The party trudged in silence along the curving slope for several more minutes. The world faded around Bob and became nothing but the patch of ground directly beneath him. His leg muscles burned with every stride. Finally, the daylight brightened, and the earth flattened out as they came to a clearing.

Before them was a stretch of ground only a few yards long that ended in a sheer cliff which dropped off into a bottomless chasm. A wide, stone bridge stretched across the chasm toward a towering mountainside. Carved into the mountainside was a series of crenelated towers—bound by a massive, central structure—half-hidden by a thick white wall. It had to be Ninth Castle. The mountain's icy peak loomed in the sky above, its summit obscured by clouds. Here, on the party's side of the bridge, was an impressive gate of wrought iron and gold, barring their entrance. On either side of the gate stood a sentry.

One male and one female, the sentries wore minimal armor of leather and fur. In their hands, each held a spear as large as Brumhilde's. As the party approached them, Bob realized with bemusement that the sentries were gigantic for humans. They were both even taller than Brumhilde—eight feet tall if they were an inch. Their muscles were heavy and round, their brows a bit thicker than Bob was used to.

"Harold Whitespring!" the male sentry barked. He strode forward with massive, fur-clad legs, a scowl bending his exaggerated brow. He had shaggy, reddish-brown hair but his face was shaven. Harold carefully handed Bernard to Brumhilde. For a moment, Bob thought they might have another fight on their hands. But the huge stranger threw down his spear as he approached.

"Harold, you bastard! I've missed you like my own, I have!" He slapped his forearm onto Harold's in a violent semblance of handshake, then pulled him into a rough embrace. The guy was two feet taller than Harold, easy. "You been hiding with the elves, I heard!" His big brown eyes found Kelael. "Oh, uh—no offense, aye?"

Harold was grinning. "Bennet Cliffard, you ugly son of a goat. If I've been hiding, it was to get away from that face of yours!"

Suddenly the two men were booming laughter and patting each other on the back. The female sentry looked on curiously. Her posture indicated she detected no threats.

"Aye, aye, you're both uglier than a Gez Kar's arse," said Brumhilde. "We need the healer, you buffoons. Let us in the castle."

The man Harold called Bennet moved his eyes toward her. "Oh, hi Brum," he said. He glanced at Bernard. "Got a wee injured fellow there, aye? Alright then, follow me, I'll set you right." He approached the gate. "You alright for a few, Gina?"

"Aye," said Gina indifferently.

Bennet produced a ring of keys that jangled noisily as he selected the correct one. A moment later, they were on the stone bridge. Ninth Castle loomed ahead, and a depthless, cloudy infinity seemed to broil beneath them in the chasm. A vaporous film of mist hung over everything. Rainbows bent in odd places in the air.

Kelael walked with Lady, Brumhilde's spear. It was almost double his height and he was forced to carry it with two hands. He looked something like a blue man oaring in a kayak. Ahead, from out of the mist, the archway of the central entrance faded into view.

"It is good to see you, Whitespring," said Bennet. "But a lot has changed since you left, follow? Some things I ought to say before you go inside."

"Out with it, then," said Harold.

Bennet cleared his throat, uncomfortable. "Well, for one thing, them Gez Kar are on the move. Seems that northern En'hirin wasn't enough for them. Scaly bastards are all over the mountains, moving further east all the time."

"Aye," said Harold. "I feared as much. We just came from northwestern Engoria, follow? The Gez Kar are poking their snouts in, that's for sure."

Bennet's eyes widened. "That far south? We didn't know. Terrible news, that. Still, we've got our mitts full up here, don't we? The green fuckers keep poring over them mountains like they were born to it. The Gurdun have moved, mostly, to get away. You know how most of them are, don't like nobody or nothing hanging around. Only Skinner is still around, far as I know, aye? Anyway, let me get the other thing over with."

He sighed. "Sorry to be the one to have to tell you, Harold, but your father is dying. Mary says he could go any day now."

"What?" said Brumhilde. "That's ridiculous. Nothing can kill Uncle Max. He's too stubborn, the bastard."

Bennet nodded sadly. "Aye, that's what we all thought, Brum. But it's not so. The man is a hundred and forty-three, after all. Not one bastard in the world stubborn enough to defeat the ailments of age, I reckon. Anyway," he turned back to Harold. "I thought you should know. Now, let's get your friend to Mary before he meets his maker on the doorstep, aye?"

As Bob entered under the archway, his vision dimmed to black, and he realized he was still wearing the sunglasses. He removed them and his eyes slowly adjusted from blindness. Bennet led them down a long, stone corridor, lit only by a large window above the archway. It was wide enough for them all to walk abreast, and tall enough that Brumhilde couldn't poke the ceiling with Lady if she tried. They passed a few enormous stone doors set into the walls, and then the corridor ended in an indoor courtyard. It became apparent immediately that the majority of Ninth Castle was within the mountain itself. The walls were carved stone, unpolished and jagged. Central columns of fluted marble rose to meet heavy overhanging shelves of rock. Wooden beams lined the corners of walls and intersections. Bob could smell raw fish and something like beef, the dry odor of dust and the tangy must of sweat.

Lanterns hung from hooks and sat on tables. There were alcoves—about the size Bob's garage had been—carved along the courtyard's perimeter. Three more high corridors broke from the courtyard in each of its quadrants. The place reminded Bob of an indoor shopping mall. There were even people milling about—walking out from one corridor and down another, from one alcove to another. Bob realized the alcoves were merchant stalls. Now and then a passerby would turn to stare at Kelael as they walked. They didn't seem like hostile stares to Bob—just curious stares.

"You'll want to check in with Max, of course," said Bennet. He accepted Lady from Kelael and the sanded wooden staff from Bob, then ushered Brumhilde—Bernard in her arms—down the corridor to the right of where the party had entered. Osivia fluttered after them. Bob saw Bennet do a double take when he saw her, presumably for the first time.

Bob was left in the courtyard with Harold and Kelael. Harold stared at the corridor opposite the entrance, rubbing the back of his neck. "You two… you two don't have to come along…"

"Nonsense," said Kelael with a crooked smile. "Your father hates my kind. I saved your life. I love to rub his nose in it."

"Well, Bob, I guess you ought to come too, then, aye? In case we have to protect Kelael."

Bob chuckled uncomfortably. "Wait… you're joking right?"

Harold gave him a sidelong glance. "Aye," he said without a trace of a smile. "Joking."

The corridor led to a succession of smaller corridors that branched off in either direction. Harold led Bob and Kelael along the main path. People strode by—huge people, every one. Bob noted a distinct lack of clothing. Not that the denizens of Ninth Castle were nudists, exactly—more that they just wore whatever was comfortable without thoughts of propriety. One guy was nine feet tall and wore nothing but a thong. A huge blonde woman walked by in a sparse leather bikini.

"Well, they'd worship *her* in Engoria," muttered Bob, staring after her.

Kelael snorted.

"Why is everyone so big, anyway?"

"The Blood of the Gurdun," said Harold. In response to Bob's puzzled look, he added, "I'll explain later, aye?"

The corridor ended in a huge throne room. The fluted columns Bob had noted in the courtyard lined either side of the high-ceilinged chamber. A thick carpet of wooly, brown fur stretched from the entrance all the way to the impressive throne.

A raised slab of stone supported a hefty dais, upon which an ornate stone chair was built. Above it, the likenesses of various animals and creatures were carved. There was something like an elephant. A deer. A mountain lion. A snake. A sinuous, winged reptile that was probably a dragon. There were other, stranger things that Bob did not want to guess at. Bob realized the astral voices were blaring in his ears and had to tune them way down. He saw Erto standing in a shadowed corner, apparently admiring the carvings above.

Upon the throne sat the largest man Bob had ever laid eyes on. He was slouched, gray and wrinkled, sunk into the massive fur robe he wore like a skeleton swaddled in fabric. His brow was wide, his lips thick. Wispy white whiskers lined his squarish jaw. Bob thought if the man stood, he would tower to eleven or twelve feet tall.

"Harold," rumbled the enormous, robed figure. "My smallest son." His eyes and lips were all that moved. He seemed paralyzed, cursed to perpetually remain in his slouch. "Your shame has plagued me for these years. Have you returned in some desperate attempt to erase it? Attempt naught! I shall never forgive your failure. Begone again, before my capacity for mercy diminishes further."

Well, that was enough for Bob. He did not like Maximus Whitespring.

"Hello, father," said Harold, looking at the floor. "I've not come for forgiveness, follow? I have yet to forgive myself. I'd never ask that of you."

"There is nothing to be forgiven for," said Kelael loudly, glaring at Maximus. "Do you blame Harold for the Gez Kar? What a mighty man he is then, to have birthed such a savage race on his own. Perhaps you should tremble in fear at his presence, for fear he may vomit lizards all over your robe."

Bob pushed out his lower lip in appreciation. He was beginning to see why Harold had followed Kelael around for so long. The En'hari's ire could be quite amusing when directed at someone else.

"Silence!" boomed Maximus. "Such insolence could only come from an elf. You speak of savage races. You should know. I did not become the King of the Nine Peaks by listening to the drivel that falls from blue mouths."

BOB THE WIZARD

Kelael prepared a retort but Harold cut him off hastily. "Father, I apologize, aye? I've not come to ask of you anything. I am only escorting my friends to the Nexus. I stand before you only to pay respects."

Kelael scoffed audibly.

"What would you know of respect, tiny one? You who could not save your brothers, those who were better than you, all three. Now I will die, and Nine Peaks will pass to your hands. Your weakness will undo all that I have built. I lament that you were born, that your mother did not birth a greater man. Better it would have been for you to stay gone, so that rulership would remain with Gethras."

Bob couldn't help himself. "Wait a minute, I'm confused."

Maximus's big, rheumy eyes found him and narrowed.

"First you told him to 'begone,' but now you're telling him he's going to rule Nine Peaks. Which is it?"

Maximus looked back at Harold. "I see your capacity to befriend impertinent morons has not declined."

"Good question, though," said Kelael.

"Ah…" Harold shifted from foot to foot. Bob got the feeling he was regretting bringing Kelael and himself along.

"Very well," said Maximus. "Since you all seem to have the intellectual capability of dung, allow me to elucidate. I wish Harold was never born. Furthermore, I wish he had never returned. My first instinct upon seeing him this day was to kill him. Yet instinct is often anathema to reason—and law is reason in its most honorable incarnation. I will obey the laws of our people, if only because not doing so would be to lower myself to the unfathomable depths upon which the three of you stride."

"You're quite the poet when you want to be," said Bob, scratching his beard.

"You—" Maximus's words morphed into a fit of wheezing coughs that wracked his huge body. An attendant rushed from a corridor near the back wall and approached the throne with a goblet, holding it to the lips of the King. Maximus coughed gobs of bloody phlegm into it. The coughing fit continued.

"I'll... I'll be back, father," said Harold, and then quickly ushered Bob and Kelael back into the tall corridor.

"I think that went well," commented Kelael.

"You never mentioned your father was the King," muttered Bob.

"He is losing his mind," said Harold softly. "That man he mentioned, Gethras, was dead even before I left, follow? It's no wonder he can't decide if he wants to kill me or make me King. He doesn't even know what year it is."

"Seemed like the old Maximus to me," offered Kelael.

"Aye, well, we're all three lucky that posturing and insults are the way of things on Nine Peaks." Harold changed the subject. "Anyway, Bennet and Brum have likely already told every soul they've come across that I'm here, follow? There'll be a surprise feast, you mark my words."

"You're not surprised," observed Bob.

Harold ignored the comment. "Might as well get ourselves presentable first, follow? I'll show you to the baths." He glanced at Bob and affected a weak smile. "Just like old times, aye?"

The baths were private affairs in cubical stone rooms. From his tub, Bob noticed a series of slanted depressions lining the edge of the ceiling on two sides of the room. The steam from the bath slowly escaped through the depressions, and Bob gathered they were part of some kind of ventilation system.

While soaking the splattered blood, dirt, and sweat from his skin, his thoughts turned to Bernard. The strangeness of Ninth Castle had thus far distracted him from anything else, but now, with a moment to think, a mountain of worries reappeared from the mists in his mind. Would Bernard wake in time to leave for the Nexus? Would he ever wake? The thought of the old wizard dying hurt his heart more deeply than he wanted to admit. Bernard's death would certainly complicate things—make facing Galvidon and Axiis more difficult, make finding the supposed lost memories of **R** the Vigilant a near-impossibility. But more than that, Bob felt a fraternal affection for the man that had been slowly emerging ever since they'd first met in the Essen'aelo. Putting aside Bob's more ethereal feelings, Bernard had taken it upon himself to help the En'harae while the other wizards of Hub apparently hid in a tower, indifferent. He was very patient with Bob, even when Bob was being an asshole. Bob wanted the old wizard to wake up.

He wore the Gatekey while he bathed. He removed its chain from around his neck and held it up in the lanternlight. The little green meter was full, the little dials and buttons undamaged and perfectly in place. The Gatekey—he'd felt so helpless without it. He was so close to his goal now. So close to Galvidon. What prices yet remained to be paid? Thoughts of Fan bubbled unbidden from the depths of his mind.

Bob, we should go. You have the Gatekey. Let's go.

Bob shut his eyes tightly and pressed the Gatekey to his forehead, letting out a long breath. In his mind's eye, the jagged jaws of a Gez Kar snapped at his face. His eyes shot open again. He stared at the ceiling, hearing the astral voices sing their endless songs.

He remembered the Koreka on fire. Remembered the bodies. Lifting a foot, realizing who it was. A small cry of frustration escaped his throat.

Erto watched him from the corner of the room. Within his hollow stare—if there was anything at all—there might have been pity.

In the cooling tub, naked, alone but for the spirit, Bob wept.

He discovered on the way to the feast hall that Ninth Castle was the size of a small city. The mountain must be nearly hollowed out to fit so many corridors, rooms, and people. It took Bob, Harold, and Kelael over twenty minutes to walk from the baths to where the dinner was being held.

The event was impressive. The hall was high and wide, the tables long and sturdy. The food and drink were plentiful, and the towering Niners were boisterous and friendly. It became apparent after only a few minutes that everyone was downright thrilled to see Harold. Bob heard several people eagerly ask him when he would take over for his father. People brought him drinks and plates of food. They crowded around his seat at the table. Women flirted with him. Men loudly offered him their allegiance. They told him stories of battle with the Gez Kar and lamented their problems to him. All the while, Harold nodded and forced a smile, shaking hands and patting arms, listening and laughing at jokes, and eating, eating, eating. Bob could hardly begrudge him this last. He himself devoured so much food he could hardly move in his seat. Someone sitting across from him lit a pipe. Seeing it wasn't a breach of etiquette, Bob withdrew the dragon pipe, lit it, and drew upon it with relish. He spent the next few minutes digesting, smoking, and staring glumly at his empty tobacco pouch.

Kelael was almost as popular as Harold. He was beset with visitors at his seat. The huge people asked him questions. Was he really the one that saved Harold Whitespring? What exactly happened at the Battle of the Still Mountains? Why weren't there any more elves with him? Was it offensive to be called an elf? Would he like to try the pudding? Kelael was much less adept at handling attention than Harold. Bob watched with amusement as the En'hari became more irritated—his answers becoming shorter and terser—as the night wore on.

Bennet and Brumhilde were present. Brumhilde visited Bob and drank a beer in front of him, saying Bernard was still asleep but that Mary, the healer, said he ought to recover fully when he woke. Then she belched and wondered off. Bennet raised a tankard in salute from across the table but didn't approach. Aside from that, Bob received no attention. He enjoyed being ignored. In Engoria, the people had stared openly at him, balking at his long hair, his huge beard, his strange clothes. Many of them had stared at him like he was an alien. At the Koreka, Bob was famous—the man who'd saved Torael Ellaren. The En'harae looked at him often, expecting something grand Bob did not think he could live up to. But here in Ninth Castle, Bob seemed to blend right in. Sure, he was two and half feet shorter than everyone, but they didn't seem to mind. People were polite to him but disinterested in who he was. It was a welcome change.

Eventually, Kelael's admirers finally seemed to get their fill of him. He stood quietly and made his way over to where Bob sat. "Let us go check on Bernard," he said, eying the Niners warily, visibly hoping none would come up and ask him another question.

Bob glanced over at Harold, who was in the midst of telling a group of Niners about the day's battle at Torful.

"...and that's when the dirt rose up and flew into their eyes!" he was saying. Several curious glances were cast in Bob's direction.

"Uh," said Bob, standing up quickly, "yes, of course, you're right. Let's go."

Bob and Kelael walked briskly, side by side, to the room's exit.

Kelael claimed he knew how to get to the infirmary. After wondering down stone hallways for about fifteen minutes, Bob began to doubt the veracity of this claim.

"You sure you know where you're going? Weren't you here like, a decade ago?"

"Of course," snapped Kelael. "This way, I think."

"We came from that way."

They continued to wander, and at some point, Osivia must have heard them bickering, because she appeared above them in the corridors, softly glowing.

"I'm telling you," said Bob, "that way leads back to the feast hall! Oh, Osivia, thank fucking God."

"What are you two doing? I heard you pass by the infirmary ten minutes ago!"

"Sight-seeing," growled Bob.

Kelael crossed his arms in silence.

Osivia led them on a short walk to the infirmary, where they passed a few curtained alcoves before finding Bernard sitting up in bed, reading a book. His white hair looked like he'd stuck his finger in an electrical socket. "Ah, hello there my young friends," he said, looking up from his reading. "I trust the feast went well?"

"Did they feed you?" asked Kelael. "I can get you something."

"Fat chance," said Bob. "You'd never find your way back to the feast hall. They'd find your skeleton in a century."

"At least *my* skeleton has a backbone," retorted Kelael.

"I see you two have become fast friends," remarked Bernard with a smile.

Bob and Kelael glared at each other.

"To answer your question, young Gasheera—and a kind question it was—yes, Osivia and I have received adequate sustenance."

"Are you alright?" asked Bob. "I mean… what happened? Was it the metal?"

"The metal…?" mumbled Osivia. "Oh!" She slapped her own forehead.

Bernard nodded. "That was part of it. I thought I could handle it. I've done similar things before. You see, the spirits' displeasure with metal is not voluntary. There is a kind of natural reaction when spirits and forged metal interact. A destructive reaction, to nearby astral bodies. If one knows how, one can protect oneself from such a reaction. Alas, I fear I may have overdone it a bit against the tortum—overworked my astral body, as it were. I was able to shield you all from the negative effects of the journey. Myself, however…" He shrugged.

"Is that what that big, shelled thing was called?" asked Bob. "A tortum?"

"Yes."

"Are all tortum so… fiery?"

Bernard considered. "They are not the only kind of Gez Kar that can be born to shamanhood, and though fire shamans are the most valued among their kind—for the heat they provide, you see—they are not the only kind of shamans Gez Kar genes can produce. So, I suppose the answer to your question is: generally, yes; technically, no."

"But… you're okay? You'll be able to leave for the Nexus tomorrow?"

Bernard slowly nodded. "I'm a bit weaker than I was this morning, I'm afraid. But yes, I will be able to continue the journey."

Bob let out a relieved sigh. Kelael was nodding silently.

"Anyway," said Bernard, eying Bob and Kelael. "I'm glad you two are here. There is something I've been meaning to tell you, Bob. And Kelael, you might as well hear it too. The other wizards....the other *Vigilants*—" he gave Bob a sharp look, "would not appreciate me sharing this information with an En'hari. But recent events have, shall we say, colored my perceptions of my fellow wizards' opinions."

"You are being vague," said Kelael, not unkindly.

Bernard nodded. "So I am. Comes with the job. Well, allow me to be more clear, then." His eyes hardened. "There is a significant reason why Galvidon—and by extension, the Order of Tag Nah—is interested in the extermination of the En'harae."

Bob, Kelael, and Osivia stared at the old wizard. To Bob it seemed that none of them drew breath.

"The En'harae," said Bernard, "are the direct descendants of the Precedentials."

This statement simmered in the air.

"What?" said Kelael softly.

"Holy fucking shit," said Bob, suddenly unable to stop looking at Kelael.

"Makes sense, though, doesn't it?" said Osivia reasonably. "That's why the Order wants them dead. They can all use Precedential tech."

"They can?" asked Bob. With great effort he pulled his gaze from Kelael and centered it on Bernard. "I mean… can they?" Unconsciously, he reached up to cradle the Gatekey around his neck.

Bernard nodded. "I don't see why not. Long ago, the Precedentials were dwindling in the Anterior, and finally, the remainder of them disappeared. Most scholars— those who know anything about it at all— just think they all died. But they didn't. They saw their world being taken over by the Order, a monster of their own creation, and they fled. They fled, in secret, to Hub. Over the millennia, the knowledge of their own history was lost. They began to eschew technology to embrace nature and its spirits. Slowly, over eons, they became the En'harae. Yet, the genes that allow control of their ancestral technology are still alive and well within them."

Kelael ran a hand across his dark-purple scalp. Bob gripped the Gatekey tightly in his hand.

"Well, what are you standing there for?" demanded Osivia. "Try it out! See if the evidence supports the claim!"

Bob and Kelael stared at her.

"My goodness. Give Kelael the Gatekey, Bob."

Bob clutched the Gatekey possessively.

"Just for a minute, Bob. For science."

Kelael met Bob's eyes and shrugged. He held out his hand, palm up.

Bob lifted the key from around his neck and raised a warning forefinger. "Don't push *any* of these buttons unless I tell you to. I don't know what all of them do."

Wariness bloomed in Kelael's eyes, but he nonetheless reached out and accepted the Gatekey. He held it up and stared at it like an archeologist examining an artifact.

"Okay, so…" Bob gathered his thoughts. He'd never had to explain this before. "Picture the opposite side of the room. Picture yourself standing there. Want yourself to be there. Don't look away from where you are trying to go. Then push this button." He indicated a tiny black bump on the Gatekey's rounded end.

"That's it?" asked Kelael dubiously.

"That's it," confirmed Bob, shrugging.

"Very well." Kelael faced the opposite wall—about three yards from where he stood next to Bernard's bed. He stood motionless for a moment and scowled with concentration. He vanished and reappeared across the room in an instant.

"Woo!" Osivia flew in an excited circle.

"Fuckin' A," said Bob, shaking his head.

"Amazing!" said Kelael, grinning. He cleared his throat and affected a neutral expression. "This is a very interesting revelation. I cannot wait to tell Torael." Reluctantly, he held out the Gatekey to Bob, who snatched it away a little more jealously than he meant to.

CHAPTER THIRTY:
BRIDGES

Bob half-registered that Bernard opened his mouth as if he had more to say. But as Bob and Kelael lapsed into private contemplation, the old wizard returned to his reading. Bob, head swimming with thoughts of ancient races and immortal astral bodies, wondered over into the next alcove and sat down.

The next thing he knew, he was being awakened by Osivia the following morning. He sat up stiffly in the infirmary bed. He'd slept wearing the trench coat. The brown backpack lay on the floor next to the bed. He stood and stretched. He was hungry and thirsty and needed to pee. Above all, he wanted to smoke. He remembered his empty pouch and swept past the curtain blocking the alcove. So much to do before he could leave for the Nexus.

Osivia passed along from Bernard that they were all to meet at the eastern gate, then she flew off. It took Bob almost two hours to find and use the latrine, follow a train of giant strangers through the maze of corridors to the feast hall, eat breakfast, figure out where Ninth Castle's eastern gate was, and make his way to it. The meal in the feast hall was a fast and lonely affair. He sat and ate by himself. From the nearby chatter of Niners, he gleaned that Maximus Whitespring had not yet died.

At the eastern gate he found Bennet and another large man—this one with a beard the color of shoe-leather—waiting for him just inside the exit corridor. Bennet raised an arm in greeting and opened the inner gate. Daylight lanced Bob's eyes from the wide, half-circle window above the exit's archway. He fumbled in the trench coat, pulled out the sunglasses, and placed them on his face.

BOB THE WIZARD

"All waiting for you, aye?" said the shaggy-haired Niner. "Right this way, Bob the Wizard."

Bob didn't remember introducing himself to Bennet. He had a feeling the anonymity he'd enjoyed the previous night would soon expire. Just as well he was moving on.

Bennet opened the outer gate for Bob and then—accompanied by the bearded man—followed Bob outside. It was midmorning, and the sunlight was bright and even. The eastern gate let out onto a wide plateau of curated grass and pine trees. The blue flowers grew in neat clumps. A variety of Niners were milling about in fur and leather. Harold and Brumhilde stood among their fellows, talking casually. Beyond them, Bob saw the eastern edge of the plateau led onto another wide stone bridge—this one sloping downward at a slightly northward angle—attached to an adjoining cliff below.

To Bob's right, on the grassy plateau's southern edge, Bob saw Bernard, Kelael, and Osivia. Bernard leaned against the mountainside, his hands on the crystal top of his staff, head lowered in thought. Next to him—no doubt courtesy of the Niners—was a traveling pack as large as he was. His white mane fanned and whipped in the breeze as he stared at the ground. Bob realized he still had the old wizard's hat in his own pack.

Kelael stood at a guard rail, facing the drop-off, back to Bob and everyone else, arms crossed as he gazed over the landscape below. Osivia sat lightly on Kelael's shoulder, also looking out at the stretching horizon. Bob ambled toward the three of them, unzipping the backpack.

"Your wizardly garb, sir," said Bob to Bernard, proffering the hat with an obsequious flourish.

"Quite right," muttered Bernard, and placed the hat atop his head.

Bob walked to Kelael's side at the guard rail. His breath caught in his throat. A mile or more beneath them was a vast swathe of plains that seemed to stretch on forever. The khaki-grass caught the wind and rolled in waves like an ocean of pale gold. The brilliant azure sky was streaked with runnels of white clouds. But the landscape, though beautiful, was not the main attraction. There was a heard of massive beasts slowly tromping across the plains. The distance made them tiny, but by the way they moved in relation to the grass, Bob judged them to be about the size of garbage trucks. Their shaggy, round, brown bodies trotted steadily with heavy footfalls. One of the creatures inclined its head, and Bob caught the outline of two massive, ivory tusks and a thick, sinuous trunk. The animal trumpeted a call to its brethren—a deep, mournful sound.

"Chess'no baka," said Kelael, glancing at Bob. "The great wanderers of the grass."

"Chess'no…" Bob repeated in a mumble. He was reminded of the Cave, of his first real conversation with the En'harae. Fan, Gorrelai, Hirrell, and Torael had spoken of large animals hunted on the plains of En'hirin. Bob remembered thinking they were talking about bison.

"Mammoths," he said now to himself. Then, to Kelael, he said, "they're *mammoths?*"

Kelael shrugged, causing Osivia to flutter into the air. "If you say so, Bob," said the En'hari. "I have not heard them referred to this way."

Bob thought that might have been the first time Kelael had called him 'Bob,' and not, 'Sora Kelai.' "Whatever they're called, they're beautiful."

Kelael nodded, turning to face the plateau. "And quite delicious, assuming you are alive to eat one after the hunt."

"I believe," said Bernard, "Harold wishes to speak with us before we depart." He pried himself from the mountainside and hefted the traveling pack, sagging under its weight. He huffed.

"You sure you're up to this?" asked Bob.

"If Galvidon defeats Axiis and the Order of Tag Nah come through a Gate, my health will be the least of our concerns." The old wizard tottered off under the overlarge pack, utilizing the support of his staff.

Bob shrugged and followed with Kelael, glancing curiously at Harold, who now stood with a group of Niners by the gate to the bridge. He made his way over to them with the others, studying Harold. The mountain man stood erect and proud, the other Niners clustered behind him deferentially.

"You're not coming, are you?" said Bob knowingly, as he reached them.

Harold shook his head. "I'm sorry Bob, but I cannot, aye? My father will die soon, and the Gez Kar are crawling all over the Nine Peaks. The Niners need a king, follow?"

Bob offered a crooked smile. "Least they'll get a good one this time." Then, for good measure, he added, "aye?"

Harold grinned. "You're an honorable man, Bob the Wizard." He offered a hand.

Honorable. Bob had some doubts about that. He thought of all the times he'd lied to people, manipulated them, in order to get closer to Galvidon. The times he'd stolen. He thought of Galvidon, waiting somewhere to the northeast, and knew that he'd stab the Gray Man in the back at the first opportunity. If he could, Bob would murder the motherfucker in his sleep. No, not honorable. But he voiced none of this. He reached out and shook Harold's hand.

"And you, Harold Whitespring."

Behind Harold, the other Niners seemed to approve of this exchange. They nodded to each other sagely as if this was all as it should be.

"There is one more favor I'd ask of you, though."

"Ask away, aye?"

"I'm out of tobacco. I wouldn't ask, it's just that—"

Harold held up a meaty hand. "Say no more, say no more." He turned his head. "Bennet!"

Bennet stepped forward. "Aye?"

"Go grab our friends four ounces of our finest tobacco. Not that cheap garbage, follow?"

"Aye, right away," said Bennet without a trace of chagrin. He jogged toward the entrance to Ninth Castle.

"And matches, please!" Bob called after him.

Bennet held up a hand in acknowledgement.

"Listen, Bob," said Harold. "I'm not intending to leave you out to dry, follow? I'll try to rustle you up some support. Might take a day or two, but you'll have some Niners at your heels. Just make sure you're still around when they arrive, aye?"

"That's more than I could hope for, Harold. Thanks."

"Oh, aye." Harold glanced at Kelael, then turned to address the Niners. "Alright, you lot, I'd have a word with my friends, follow? Off you go."

The small contingent of Niners broke apart and began to mill away. Brumhilde walked past Bob and his companions on her way back to the castle. "Was a pleasure, my lovelies! I'd tell you to stay out of trouble, but I know you be running to it on purpose. Stay beautiful!" She grinned at them as Bob offered her a wave.

"I like her," pronounced Osivia, watching the big woman stride away.

Bob turned to see Harold and Kelael staring at each other in silence. Their eyes were unashamedly locked. It seemed for a moment that they might go on like that forever. "Oh, come here, you bastard!" burst out Harold, and swept Kelael into a bear hug.

The En'hari's arms were pinned to his sides and he left the ground as Harold shook him. He accepted it all placidly and without protest.

"Going to miss you," said Harold more reasonably, as he set Kelael down.

"Alas, I lose my shadow," said Kelael drily. "Your days of following are over. Now, others follow you."

"Dour to the last," said Harold appreciatively. "You're always welcome in Nine Peaks. If any Niner gives you trouble, just tell them Harold Whitespring said they were a lizard-bellied, air-brained coward with a noodle for a spine!"

"I shall probably do better than that."

"Aye, that you shall, you condescending bastard. That you shall."

Bennet came trotting up with a handful of tobacco. Of course, what

BOB THE WIZARD

was a handful to him took Bob two hands to carry. There were four individually wrapped pouches smelling strongly of Bob's favorite plant, and a bundle of matches. Bob passed two of the pouches to Bernard, stuffed one pouch and the matches in the backpack, then immediately took out the dragon pipe to begin packing it.

"One more thing, before you go," said Harold, looking at Bernard. "You may run into a Gurdun by the name of Skinner, follow? They tell me he's been all up and down these parts, hunting Gez Kar."

Bob looked up curiously as he lit his pipe. Bennet was grinning.

Harold was clearly speaking to Bernard now. "Do you, uh, know how…"

"Do I know," finished Bernard, "how to introduce myself to a Gurdun? I do indeed, Mr. Whitespring. You needn't worry."

"Anyone going to tell me what a Gurdun is?" asked Bob.

"Don't ask me," muttered Osivia, waving at a streamer of smoke.

"Well, Bob," said Harold, "the thing is—"

"I shall explain on the journey," said Bernard. "There will be plenty of time."

"Aye," said Harold, looking relieved. Bennet chuckled and slapped him on the back.

"Well then," said Bernard, eying the stone bridge. "We've got a realm to save. Let's get this show on the road, shall we?"

As the party descended the bridge, Harold began to sing behind them. Bob couldn't make out the words, but he recognized the melody as one Harold had sung before. Soon, Bennet's less talented but still passable voice joined Harold's. As the voices of the two men faded behind him, Bob noticed the astral voices shift their pitch and tone to match the song of the two men. For a moment, Harold and Bennet sang, and the world sang right along with them.

The bridge led to another plateau, which in turn led to a series of other stone bridges—these ungated—which branched off in several directions. Bernard led the party down one of them. Bob realized the bridges were a weblike roadway connecting several mountains together. Bob had a strong suspicion that, if he were to count each mountain included in the web, they'd be nine in number.

The mist churned in the chasm below, its ethereal tendrils reaching up onto the bridges. It seemed to thicken with every dozen steps the party took. They passed over a rocky, gray plateau and near one bridge that clearly led to a gated entrance like the ones at Ninth Castle. A pair of towering Niners stood in misty silence outside the gate. If they saw Bob, Bernard, Kelael, and Osivia pass them by in the middle distance, they gave no sign. As the party advanced further, Bob noticed the journey had a distinctly downward trend. The mist gradually became denser around them. Bob stowed the sunglasses.

"Soon," said Bernard, "we will pass out of central Nine Peaks and into its fringes. After that, it will become much more likely that we encounter Gez Kar, and potentially other unpleasantries."

"What other unpleasantries?" asked Kelael.

Bernard just shrugged.

"So, what's a Gurdun?" asked Bob, readjusting the straps on his pack.

"Seconded," said Osivia. If it wasn't for her dull yellow glow, Bob would've lost her in the mist.

"Mountain giants," said Kelael. "The Gurdun are mountain giants."

The party walked in silence for several footfalls.

"Well," said Osivia, blinking white light, "go on…"

"That is pretty much all I know," said Kelael.

"That's more than most," said Bernard. "The Gurdun are a peculiar race of large humanoids. They have very strict social practices and endeavor to stay away from other races, as they consider them all to be unaccountably rude. Several centuries ago, a small tribe of humans—in an attempt to extricate themselves from ancient Engoria—made contact with the Gurdun. Those who survived, having no wish to return to Engoria, learned the ways of the Gurdun. Eventually there was… interbreeding."

"The Niners," said Bob. "No wonder they're all so big. They're part mountain giant!"

"Something I have long wondered," said Kelael. "A human and a Gurdun. Exactly how…" He let the question finish itself in their minds.

"A large human and a small Gurdun, I imagine," said Bernard.

Osivia giggled.

"Anyway," said Bernard. "Bob has come to an accurate conclusion. The Niners all have Gurdun in their ancestry. And it's not just the Niners. There are many tribes of human-Gurdun hybrids. Like the Gurdun, they tend to stay away from outsiders, preferring others like themselves. Harold was the first human carrying the Blood of the Gurdun to show any interest in outside affairs in over a century. His interest resulted in others sharing that interest. If not for Harold, the Niners would not have intervened in the wars of the En'harae."

"And his brothers would not have died," said Kelael.

"Not under the Still Mountains, anyway," conceded Bernard.

This shed some light on Maximus Whitespring's resentment of Harold. It wasn't as Max had said—that Harold had been too weak to save his brothers—it was that Harold was the reason they were there in the first place. Time, and Maximus's own, sick mind had twisted it all up in his head. Even so, this understanding did not give Bob any sympathy for Maximus. Harold had been trying to help. His intentions had to count for something.

"So," said Osivia, "what are these rules of introduction you and Harold were talking about?"

The mist was so thick now, Bob could barely see two feet in front of his nose. Bernard and Kelael were just dark shapes.

Bernard cleared his throat. "Well, first you must understand that the Gurdun value strength above all else. But physical power plays only one part—and often a small one—in how they measure that strength. To them, deeds are strength. Experience. Unique situations. Now, additionally, the Gurdun consider modesty to be immoral. Why would one hide one's strength? This is what a liar would do. When one Gurdun meets another for the first time, they must take the measure of each other. During this exchange, holding back in listing one's accomplishments is considered a grave insult."

The party walked in silence. They seemed to be moving upward again. The bridge underneath them produced a faint creak.

"Bragging," said Bob. "You're saying they brag to each other? And that's considered polite?"

"Correct," said Bernard. "And they brook no social slight. If a Gurdun feels you are hiding something impressive from them, they will kill you."

Bob produced a low whistle.

"What if," asked Osivia, "you haven't done anything impressive?"

"Then they will gloat at you in an irritating fashion, and then be on their way."

"Oh," said Osivia, sounding relieved, "well, that's good."

"Don't sell yourself short, Tinkerbell," said Bob.

Osivia said nothing but was suddenly glowing a dull pink.

"So," declared Bernard, "all of you need to think about what impressive things you've done and how to go about bragging about them. Because if you don't, you may just find yourselves squashed flat."

Conversation waned as the journey across the upward slopes sapped their concentration. Eventually the mist began to recede. They stopped for lunch on a semi-flat stretch of ground lined with some of those blue flowers. The sun was high, but the air was crisp and cool. Bernard and Kelael had packed food. There was some trail mix made by the Niners that Bob couldn't get enough of. He crunched happily on handfuls of the nuts, dried berries and bits of salted bread. Now flush with tobacco, he and Bernard lit their pipes after the meal before resuming the trek.

BOB THE WIZARD

About an hour later they came to a scree sloping upward to a hillcrest. Erto stood patiently waiting for them, regarding Bob with his hollow stare. Once the party was atop the scree, the mist was completely clear, and they could see northward for miles. All was a forested valley. Pines and elms and firs grew thickly across uneven, rolling hillocks. Now and then a hillock would swell into a small mountain. It seemed that the Nine Peaks were the largest mountains for miles. Yet, in the northern distance, massive, snowy-peaked monsters of rock and earth opacified the entire horizon. It came to Bob then that the mountains each produced a unique chorus of astral sounds, like an aural fingerprint.

Bernard leveled his staff at the giant mountains to the north. "The Nexus lies directly north, between that cluster of mountains. About two days on foot through the valley, I'd say."

"Then let us put one foot in front of another," said Kelael.

"You are close now," remarked Erto. When Bob turned to look at him, he was gone.

The party made its way down the opposite side of the scree, leaving Nine Peaks behind, and entering the forested valley. Absently, Bob reached up to clutch the Gatekey.

They pushed their way through heavy underbrush and tangled shrubbery. Bernard muttered to one of his spirits and an invisible shroud descended around the party, preventing the passage of sound through the air in a radius around them. Osivia was already silent, but Kelael, whose footfalls were almost undetectable, smiled gratefully and said, "Good idea, wizard. You and Bob walking through this forest has likely already woken everything in the valley."

Bob, who considered himself pretty good at sneaking, scowled and said nothing. He had to admit, it was a relief to not have to worry about garnering the attention of any of those *unpleasantries* Bernard had mentioned.

There was an almost comical moment when the party stumbled upon a doe and her young. Startled, the mother deer snorted and leaped six feet in the air before bolting into the trees, her three fauns close behind.

M. V. PRINDLE

It was dim under the canopy and began to darken further as the journey wore on. Bob saw a disturbingly large snake resting lazily in a tree above them. They came upon a small herd of wild boar, who were just as startled as the deer had been. The largest boar remained behind after its brethren fled, staring at the party with ire in its eyes. It tossed its head, grunting, and ate some berries off a thorny bush casually, before ambling away as if nothing had happened. Its message was clear. *I am not afraid of you two-legged things.*

If their packs hadn't still been weighed down with food, Kelael probably would have shot something. As it was, they were all too tired—even Kelael—to raise a weapon without immediate need. Finally, all grimy with sweat and bits of vegetation, the sun a lingering memory, they set down for the night in a small clearing, partially shielded by a rock outcropping. While they were building a fire, Bob saw Erto sitting cross-legged beneath a nearby rocky overhang. In the near-dark, the tiny purple flashes deep in the spirits eyes were like beacons.

Soon, Bernard had created a light-barrier so that none could see them from outside his invisible dome. They ate without much conversation. The two wizards prepared their pipes as Kelael stared sleepily at the crackling fire and Osivia hovered over *A Common History of Engoria*, which she'd propped open on a log. Bob had noticed Bernard looking at him throughout the day. Now, the old wizard was positively staring.

"Ok," said Bob. "What is it? You've been giving me the googly-eyes for hours. I mean, I know I'm pretty…"

Kelael snorted but didn't look up from the fire.

Bernard nodded as he lit his pipe. "There is something I need to tell you, Bob."

Osivia looked up from her book.

Bob, also lighting his pipe, sighed heavily out of his nostrils. "I was just thinking, we could all use some more bad news."

"There are many things," said the old wizard, "I discovered at Azenbul. There is bad news, yes. But also, good news."

"Bad news first," said Kelael.

BOB THE WIZARD

Bernard nodded at the suggestion but when he spoke, it was directly to Bob. "There are only three other Vigilants currently on Hub. Mostly, they have kept to the tower. When I arrived outside of Azenbul, courtesy of Faffle, I witnessed a disturbing event. Two crates, identical to the ones we'd taken to the Koreka that held firearms, being transported by a team of Engorians onto a wagon. They were moving the crates from the tower."

"But that means..." muttered Osivia.

"Someone at Azenbul," said Bernard, "is attempting to supply guns to King Flaire. As I'm sure I've mentioned, there are Gates at Azenbul. Only the Vigilants have access to them. I can only surmise that the British came through one of them at some point, just as they did at the Nexus, and that a cache of their weapons remains at Azenbul. It is worth noting that this is also when I saw Galvidon's drone. It seemed to be witnessing the transport. Overseeing it."

"One of the Vigilants is helping Galvidon?" said Bob.

"Possibly more than one," said Bernard.

"This word," said Kelael, "*Vigilants*. You keep saying it. What are you talking about?"

"He means the wizards," said Bob. "They... *we*, are all reincarnations of ancient astral bodies engineered by the Precedentials. We're called the Vigilantum. Individually, we're called Vigilants." Saying it aloud made him doubt it more than when he just held the idea in his head.

"And lo, he is capable of learning," muttered Bernard.

"I knew you weren't joking!" declared Osivia.

"Spirits, protect me from the lunacy of humans," said Kelael to the fire as Bernard continued.

"The three at Azenbul are Aterax, Kieren, and Priscilla. **A**, **K**, and **P**. My memories, which I remind you are necessarily incomplete, seem to offer me no clue as to which one of them would seemingly betray the Mandates in such a brash fashion. The gaps in my memories are mostly in the last several millennia, meaning any one of them could have had a change in character recently that I am currently unaware of."

"Sometime in the last few millennia is... recently?" said Osivia, her voice a higher pitch than usual.

"For my astral body," said Bernard, "yes, it is."

Bob scratched his beard. "What should we do about it? About this... traitor?"

Bernard shook his head. "For the time being, I have decided there is only one Vigilant on Hub, aside from myself, that I can trust."

"Who..." began Bob, before realizing the Bernard was talking about him. "Oh."

"Beyond that, I'm not sure. Any investigation must be done with utmost care. Aterax, Kieran, and Priscilla are all quite formidable. Alerting the traitor that we know what they are up to, could prove fatal. For now, we must concentrate on Galvidon. It seems our traitor's goals more or less align with his. By stopping him from opening the Nexus, we temporarily frustrate the efforts of the traitor."

For a long moment, the only sound was the snap and pop of the campfire.

"So, what is the good news?" asked Kelael.

"Ah, yes." Bernard reached into the breast-pocket of his cloak and pulled out a small object. He tossed it to Bob over the fire.

It landed in Bob's lap. He held it up. It was a small notebook, black leather, about the size of a wallet, bound at the spine.

"I believe," said Bernard, "there is a way to retrieve your memories at the Astral Core, in the Anterior. In those pages, I've written directions and maps for you to follow through the Astraverse, should you so choose."

Bob swiftly flipped through the pages, catching glimpses of diagrams and paragraphs written in Bernard's looping cursive. "Thanks, Bernard. But why don't you just come with me? I could definitely use your help."

"Alas, I cannot. Even if we stop Galvidon, the En'harae will still be enslaved. The traitor at Azenbul will remain. There is too much for me to deal with on Hub, I'm afraid. That is why I wrote down the instructions."

BOB THE WIZARD

"I'll go with you, Bob," said Osivia. "I still want to explore the Astraverse."

Bob grinned at her. "Wouldn't have it any other way."

<hr>

The following morning, they ate breakfast and struck camp. They donned their cloaks and coats. Kelael restrung his bow and Bob made sure the dragon pipe was packed and easy to pull from the jerkin. Bernard announced he had to rest his astral body at least a little bit. He was not yet fully recovered from his temporary coma, he explained, and using magic was more taxing on him than usual. So, he lowered the barriers that kept the party from being seen and heard. The party set out cautiously. They hadn't been walking five minutes when they were set upon by a swarm of snapping sherka.

M. V. PRINDLE

CHAPTER THIRTY-ONE:
THE SILENT STALKER

A gust of wind knocked back a few of the scaly creatures, but nonetheless the swarm was upon the party too fast for Kelael to get off any arrows. The Gasheera cursed and drew his sword, fighting even as he loosened his buckler from its strap on his back.

Walking backwards, Bob drew the pipe and a match and commenced producing a cloud of smoke. He and Erto immediately recreated the familiar trick of blinding the Gez Kar with earth. It worked, at least for a few seconds—enough time for Kelael to properly attach the buckler to his arm and dispatch a few of the enemy.

But it was not enough. The remaining sherka began sniffing the air and cocking their heads, soon leaping to the attack. Bernard and Bob barely fended them off with blasts of air and earth while Kelael sliced through scaled flesh, dancing through the sherka in a spinning maelstrom of steel, teeth, and blood. More sherka arrived. They were already racing full tilt through the forest, as if they were running from something....

In the gloom of the forest, a few yards beyond a wall of brambles, Bob saw a Sherka seemingly explode into viscera in midair. He caught a glimpse of a huge, grinning, bestial skull, floating high above the forest floor. Some undead, monstrous Gez Kar seemed to be tearing into its living counterparts. But it didn't move like a Gez Kar...

Bob unleashed a casual smoke ring as a shard of rock burst away from an outcropping behind him to impale a sherka through the chest, pinning its writhing body to the ground. He got three more with the same trick as, thanks to Bernard, a group of the creatures dropped to the ground, flailing and gasping like beached fish as they suffocated.

Off Bob's left, there it was again— a silent, towering form, its head apparently a huge white skull lined with teeth, lifting sherka by the handful and squeezing them easily to scaly mush or slamming its hands together to crush several sherka at once. Bob saw a hammer, its haft as tall as Bernard, swinging from the thing's waist. The monster's body was covered in scales. What manner of Gez Kar was this, that slew its own kind?

The remaining sherka bolted past the party into the forest, unleashing squeals and shrieks as they scampered over the underbrush. The huge skull-faced monster approached the party with long, silent, bipedal strides. Bob heard the sherka's cries fading into the distance. He poised, pipe in his teeth, a heartbeat away from unleashing a hail of deadly rocks at this new enemy. But then…

The monster reached up and removed its own head. Bob blinked. Suddenly, he felt incredibly stupid. The monster wasn't undead, wasn't a Gez Kar at all. And the skull was not its head. It was a helmet, apparently fashioned from the skull of an enormous Gez Kar—possibly a tortum. And the scales, Bob saw now, were overlapping skins—armor fashioned from slain Gez Kar. The so-called-monster's face was human enough, and it hit Bob just then…. It must be Skinner. He had earned his name.

Skinner the Gurdun stood fifteen feet tall. He was not bulky, but lean. Still, each of his arms was almost as wide as Bob's chest. His hair was festooned with bones and trinkets, his chin framed with dark-gray stubble. The Gez Kar skins that covered his body had been deftly connected in such a way as to give the wearer the appearance of having scaly skin. Closer inspection revealed darkened bones in clever places along the armor to catch incoming weapons or claws.

Skinner calmly held his skull-helmet under an arm and regarded the party. Suddenly he slapped his chest, leaving a bloody handprint.

"Behold, Skinner of the Gurdun!" he boomed.

A bird, apparently having arrived in the untimely interim between the attacking sherka and this moment, burst from its perch in a nearby tree and fluttered fearfully to a safer neighborhood.

"I, who have slain thousands of Gez Kar, who wear them as my clothing, who's very presence causes them to flee in terror. I, who have traveled long over the Endless Mountains, spoken to a dragon, and bested countless challengers in single combat. I, who am bonded to the earth spirit Burrin, who walks in the earth, allowing me to stride upon it without a sound, allowing me to follow any creature who makes but a mark upon the ground; bonded to the nature spirit Leelo, who walks in the trees, who can entangle my enemies, and who allows my passing to not disturb a single branch. I, Skinner, Eighth Fist of the Gurdun, bear myself to you, if you are able to withstand it!" He glared at them with wide, challenging eyes, puffing out his chest.

Bernard looked exhausted. He leaned on his staff like it was the only thing holding him up. Nevertheless, the old wizard cleared his throat and stepped forward. Bob eyed him warily and noticed Kelael doing the same.

"I behold you, Skinner, Eighth Fist of the Gurdun, yet I do not tremble," said Bernard. Bob flinched, but Bernard continued quickly. "You stand before Bernard Heathrow, of Montana. I, who have traveled to thirteen different realms in this lifetime alone, who have defeated hundreds of Gez Kar and men, who have fought alongside Gurdun, alongside En'harae. I, who have *battled* a dragon and lived to tell of it. I, who have bonded to sixteen air spirits before their disintegration. I, who am currently bonded to the air spirit Faffle, who walks in the winds and grants me fearsome control over them; bonded to the light spirit Asho, who walks in the light, and grants me powers over the visual perceptions of my enemies."

For a heartbeat, Bob thought Bernard was finished, and his own mind raced to remember what to say. But it seemed the old wizard was just getting started.

"And these" said Bernard, "are only the feats of one of my names, for my true nature so eclipses your own, should I reveal it to you, your mind would be crushed under its weight as an ant under a boulder. I lived countless lives of struggle and strife, of love and sacrifice, before even the Gurdun race drew a single breath. I have witnessed the rise and fall of civilizations, the destruction of worlds and the birth of new ones. I have seen the greatest atrocities living beings are capable of, and the most inspiring deeds of love. I have walked as a daughter, breathed as a father,

BOB THE WIZARD

dreamed as a mother, and died as a son. I look upon you, and all I feel is pity, mighty Gurdun, for I know, to my great displeasure, how each and every story ends. I, Bernard Heathrow, the Second Vigilant, and a thousand other names besides, bear myself to you." Bernard and Skinner stared into each other's eyes. Then, Bernard added softly, "if you can withstand it."

Bob held his breath. His heart was beating uncomfortably fast. His eyes involuntarily flicked between the five-foot wizard and the fifteen-foot Gurdun.

Skinner breathed a huge sigh and knelt onto one knee. He slowly placed his helmet onto the ground beside him. Bob saw a little creature—a little mud person, like Erto, but not Erto—scamper along the giant's shoulders. Faintly, with his astral ears, Bob could hear the little creature muttering gibberish to itself. Skinner regarded Bernard for another long moment before speaking.

"I am humbled," he said finally. "Such an impressive human you are, Bernard Heathrow of Montana. And polite as well. This pleases me. Tell me, Tiny Ancient Being, are your companions as impressive as you?" He turned his large gray eyes on Bob and Kelael, regarding them seriously, like a man appraising a new car.

Behind Skinner's back, Bernard waved a hand in a nudging gesture. His message was clear. *One of you start talking.*

Kelael stepped forward and met the Gurdun's eyes with his own. He spoke softly but firmly. "Behold, you stand before Kelael Ellaren. I, who have slain nearly a thousand Gez Kar, hundreds of men, and three En'harae. I, who have been across the continent of Sheral, from Borgamash to Tanatha to Engoria to the Endless Mountains. I, whose brother is the only remaining leader to my people; I, who travels with wizards, and who trusts the spirits in all things. I have bonded to no spirits, but that will not prevent me from slaying my enemies, for all I need is my hands." He glared dangerously at the Gurdun, showing not a glimmer of fear. "Even for one such as you."

Skinner pursed his lips, impressed.

"I, Kelael Ellaren, En'hari Gasheera, bear myself to you, if you can withstand it." Without taking his eyes off Skinner, Kelael offered a slight bow and stepped back.

Skinner grinned—a frightening sight. "I meet you as an equal, little Gasheera," said the giant, nodding his head in approval. He shifted his attention to Bob, who couldn't help but shrink back a step. "And who might you be, Shaggy One?" asked Skinner.

"Uh—" Bob was incredibly nervous. The giant's stare seemed to bear down on him. "Hi, I'm Bob…"

Skinner's expression began to darken.

Bob cleared his throat, "I mean… behold," he said lamely.

The giant arched an eyebrow.

"You stand before Bob the Wizard of Texas!" said Bob all in a rush. "I, who have, uh…" He scratched his beard.

Skinner crossed his six-foot arms.

"Traveled!" said Bob. "I've traveled. To many realms. I didn't learn a lot of the names. I, who…" Bob racked his brain. "Who is pretty good with firearms. Who was enslaved by the Engorians and escaped that slavery. I, who saved Torael Ellaren, who even now takes leadership of the En'harae." He was starting to get the hang of it, and he pushed forward. "I, who have befriended a faerie, who have battled alongside Harold Whitespring, soon to be King of Nine Peaks. I, who have chased my family's killer across the Astraverse, who have killed a few dozen Gez Kar, one En'hari…" his eyes flicked to Kelael and then back to the giant, "and more men than I'd like to think about. I, who am bonded to the earth spirit Erto, who, uh… is really old, and walks… in the earth."

Skinner's eyes had grown wide in shock. Bob's heart started hammering again. What did he say wrong? Why was this so hard?

"And," Bob continued, "who gives me control… over… rocks and such…"

The Gurdun's expression was growing ever darker by the second.

Bob gulped.

"Erto?" rumbled the giant. "Erto? You speak of the eldest of Hub's spirits! The most ancient and powerful! The spirit of this very world! You… lie." Skinner's voice held a dangerous edge.

Bob glanced at Bernard for help, but Bernard was tiredly watching the exchange. He offered no guidance. Frantically Bob scanned the forest, hoping to glimpse Erto. No sign of him, of course.

"Lie?" asked Bob in a strained voice. "To you? No, I wouldn't…." He withdrew the pipe from the jerkin. "Uh, may I smoke?"

The giant's scowl remained fixed. The fingers of his right hand twitched over the hammer at his waist.

Swiftly, Bob stuffed fresh tobacco in the pipe and lit it, keeping his eyes on the Gurdun. He sensed Kelael backing up ever so slightly, hand poised over the bow on his back.

"Erto and I," said Bob, "*are* bonded. You must forgive my manners, mighty Gurdun. It's just that your imposing presence has me distracted. Allow me to demonstrate by bond."

Streamers of smoke exited his nostrils and the earth around the giant began to swirl, as if caught in an eddy of wind. Skinner blinked and retreated a step.

Bob concentrated. He just hoped this worked. The dirt and bits of rock in the surrounding area began to take a shape in the air before Skinner. Brown and gray flecks danced and spiraled, clumping together, meeting to form lumps, then large chunks, like a sculpture of sand on the beach that went about building itself. Two large, lumpy brown feet and legs appeared, then a torso, then arms, and finally an oversized, rounded head. It was a sculpture of Erto, as large as Skinner was. The sculpture's empty eyes bore into the giant.

Skinner's expression had changed to curiosity. He inspected the sculpture and jumped when it turned to regard him. The Gurdun backed up again. The giant facsimile of Erto slowly extended a lumpy hand. Reluctantly, Skinner took the hand, and they shook. All the while, Skinner's eyes shone with disbelief. Then, the Erto sculpture dissolved into a cloud of dust.

M. V. PRINDLE

For a moment, Skinner stood in silent contemplation. Then he faced Bob. "I apologize for doubting you, Bob the Wizard of Texas. You are slightly rude, but you walk with polite companions. I accept that you have bonded to Erto, though I cannot understand why Erto would choose thusly…" He rubbed his chin. "In any case, now that introductions are complete—"

"Ahem."

The giant stopped and cocked his head at the sound. It was Osivia, from Bob's shoulder.

"Hello!" she called cheerfully.

Skinner lowered himself to one knee and peered down at the faerie. His face was uncomfortably close to Bob. His breath was dreadful. Each gray eye was as big around as Bob's entire face.

"I see," rumbled the Gurdun. "You must be the faerie Rude Bob has spoken of. I have heard tell of your kind but have never met one! Imagine the faces of my brethren when I boast of this encounter! Please, Infinitesimal One, who are you?"

"Osivia Glenbrook, pleased to meet you. I am rare among faeries for my curiosity. I was the first of my family, indeed my village, to attend school. I am the first faerie in written record to have spent so long away from the glens. Of course, our written records are atrocious, but that is neither here nor there. Let's see… Oh! Like all faeries, my body produces a substance called lumith, which has healing properties, and other properties I understand less fully. I travel with wizards, as you can see, and am considered a friend to the En'harae. The Niners didn't seem to mind me either. I'm afraid I've never killed anyone, but please don't hold that against me. Um… I, Osivia Glenbrook, faerie scientist, bear myself to you. If… if you can withstand it!" She giggled.

Skinner threw his head back and laughed long and hard. Bernard looked on with weary amusement. Kelael still looked about a split second away from springing into action. Bob nervously puffed on the pipe.

"Such a brave and tiny creature!" declared Skinner. "I meet you as an equal, Osivia Glenbrook."

"Thank you," said Osivia politely.

"Now," said the giant, "pray tell me, what are such impressive characters—and Rude Bob," he cast a pompous look in Bob's direction, "doing in my killing grounds?"

"We seek passage to the Nexus," said Bernard.

Skinner nodded. "Ah, then your journey is almost complete. Yet I wonder, impressive as you are, if you know what danger awaits you in that place."

"I know," said Bernard, "all too well. Axiis."

"That is so, Bernard of Montana. Axiis the Dragon is very polite. I like her very much. Unfortunately, that would not stop her from killing me should I journey into the Nexus. Nor would it stop me from killing her if given the opportunity, for who would not be impressed by such a tale? Tell me, have you the capability to face her?"

Bernard shook his head. "I do not know. Yet, we have little choice in the matter. We travel to the Nexus, not for the end of facing Axiis, but to stop the efforts of one called Galvidon."

"Intriguing. Who is this Galvidon?"

"A murderer," said Bob.

The Gurdun ignored him.

"He is," said Bernard, "a Galon Var. Have you heard of such a people?"

Skinner shook his massive head.

"They are a race from beyond this realm. Gray skin, they have, and black eyes."

The giant's face lit with recognition. Then, it darkened to a frown. "Ah, this Gray Man you speak of, I have met him… skulking near the entrances of the Nexus. He was very rude. I did not like him at all. I tried to kill him, but alas, he is slippery." Suddenly, he turned to Bob. "Tell me, Rude Bob, there was something you said about fire arms. I have not heard of these. Explain to me these arms of fire."

"It means guns," said Kelael from beside Bob. "Weapons from another realm. They make immense noise and can kill from great distance. I travel to the Nexus with these companions in order to procure these weapons for the En'harae."

"Intriguing," mused Skinner. "I would see such weapons." He bent over and picked up the skull helmet. "It seems there will be many opportunities for future boasting should I accompany you, Little Ones. The closest fissure is only a few hours walk. Allow me to escort you. Potentially, depending on how events transpire, perhaps we shall join in killing worthy opponents together."

"You are a most welcome addition to our party," said Bernard. "Please, mighty Gurdun, lead the way."

"It is an honor," said Skinner, and strode northward, melting silently into the forest. Bernard and Osivia started after him. Bob and Kelael took a moment to exchange a worried glance, before they too followed, stepping over broken foliage and sherka corpses to follow the Gurdun.

As they walked, Bob saw Skinner's spirits more closely. The little mud-person was thinner and smaller than Erto, and had but a single, hollow eye. Burrin—as Skinner had named him—scuttled and zipped alongside the party, muttering his gibberish in a gravelly voice. The other spirit, Leelo, was decidedly female in aspect, and much more difficult to detect. She appeared as an undersized little girl covered in swirling bark. She occasionally hopped from limb to limb like a ballet dancer. When she was still, she blended perfectly into the forest, invisible. She produced no sound that Bob could detect.

Eventually Bob and Kelael caught up to Skinner. Watching the giant move was hypnotic. Tree branches bent around him perfectly as he traversed the forest. His footfalls produced not a whisper, nor left a single track. Now, again wearing the monstrous skull atop his head, Skinner was an apparition—a cold, silent herald of Death itself.

Death does not follow you. You follow Death.

Erto's words. Now, so close to the Nexus, striding in the empty footsteps of the giant, it was hard to refute them.

Erto? You speak of the eldest of Hub's spirits! The most ancient and powerful!

BOB THE WIZARD

The spirit of this very world!

Could that be true? The Gurdun seemed to despise lying, so it must be what Skinner believed.

I, Erto, am old—so old I can remember the first souls arriving on Hub.

More of Erto's words from the dream of the Cave. Erto, the spirit of Hub? If that was true, Bob shared Skinner's confusion as to why the spirit had chosen him, Bob, of all people. But then again, Erto had seemed to recognize him.

You are new. Do you remember?

It dawned on Bob just then that **R** must have bonded to Erto as one of the Vigilant's previous incarnations. That's why Erto, of all the spirits, had shown himself to Bob in the first place. Why Erto had recognized him and asked him if he *remembered*. Erto and R could have a long and complicated history, for all Bob knew.

Yet another realization struck Bob. He'd never bragged about being a Vigilant to Skinner, the way Bernard had. Perhaps that's one reason why Skinner didn't trust him—the giant somehow sensed that Bob had not fully shared himself. It was just as well. Though Bob believed everything Bernard had told him about the Vigilants, he still didn't feel like that was who he was. Bob and **R** were separate people. Bob felt like he was just borrowing **R**'s astral body, and not even on purpose. If he could, he'd probably give it back. Well, not yet. Not until Galvidon was dead.

A single sherka appeared among the brambles, squealed in terror at the sight of Skinner, and was impaled by Kelael's sword before it could even turn around. The giant offered an approving grunt as the En'hari shook the blood from his blade. The party commenced its journey through the bramble-choked forest.

<hr />

Finally, daylight filtered through the leaves ahead of them. They reached a jagged tree-line and stepped out into the warmth of the sun. Ahead stood a mountain—effectively a sheer wall of solid rock. But directly before them was a massive fissure in the mountain, rock meeting earth at ninety-degree angles. The fissure was so perfectly rectangular that it had to be artificial. It was a stone hallway, long and wide, leading through the mountain. What technology could have managed such an impressive feat?

At the mouth of the fissure stood Erto, silently regarding them, as was his way.

Bob rolled his eyes. "*Now* you show up."

Skinner gasped. The giant fell to his knees, the impact producing no sound. "It is you," he said. "Why have you chosen this rude and hairy human? Am I not more impressive? Why, mighty Erto?"

Kelael was looking back and forth between the giant and the fissure with a scowl.

"We are bonded," replied Erto in his deep rumble. "It has always been so."

Skinner narrowed his eyes and glared at Bob, who just shrugged.

"I believe there is more to you than you let on, Rude Bob."

"Trust me, Skinner. Soon as I figure it all out, I'll let you know."

Skinner regained his feet. Bob noticed with zero surprise that Erto had vanished again.

"Very well," said the giant. He straightened his shoulders and addressed Bernard, who was sitting on a nearby rock, breathing heavily. "The Nexus lies just beyond the fissure. Come, mighty companions and Rude Bob, let us see what opportunities for impressive deeds present themselves this day."

CHAPTER THIRTY-TWO:
ASH AND ALLIANCE

"Alright, Bernard. Out with it. What's going on with you?" Bob was right behind the old wizard, just inside the mouth of the fissure. Bernard was sweating profusely. He walked as though the sanded wooden staff was barely keeping him up. At Bob's question, he ceased walking and leaned against the fissure's sheer wall. Just ahead, Skinner stood silently, watching them from underneath the grinning skull.

"I'm afraid," managed Bernard, "I may have understated the extent of the damage to my astral body. There is a connection between the astral and physical bodies, you see." He huffed and slid down the wall into a sitting position.

Bob knelt. "It's okay, Bernard. No need to go into lecture mode. You look fucking terrible. Maybe we should stay here and rest for a while."

Osivia fluttered over from the tree-line, where she'd been studying a cluster of large yellow flowers. "My goodness!" she said at the sight of Bernard, and swooped to hover over him, where she began to rub her hands together.

"Lumith, huh?" said Bob.

"That's what the Engorians call it. Faeries just call it, 'giving Light.'" The glob of white light dispersed over Bernard.

The old wizard closed his eyes and leaned his head against the wall. "Very nice. Just give me… a moment."

"You must be very desperate," said Skinner, "to come here in such a state. Normally I would call such a thing foolishness. But knowing who you are, Bernard of Montana, I see it for what it is—determination. Tenacity! Tell me, what is your true goal?"

"The wizard wishes to prevent an invasion," said Kelael. In the shadows of the fissure, his golden eyes gleamed like a cat's. "Galvidon is attempting to open the Nexus and bring forth an army."

The giant lifted himself to his full height. "An invasion, you say? I can only imagine what rude legions may pour forth, that one such as Bernard of Montana would fear it so! Truly, a terrifying notion!" His hand caressed the helmet over his face. "Defeating such a force would be a worthy tale, yet, knowing I might fail, I weep for my brethren should this invasion occur. The Gurdun grow ever rarer, our lands encroached upon more with each passing century. To allow yet another group of interlopers purchase in the Endless Mountains… no, I will not stand for such a thing. I wish only you had spoken of such matters sooner! Now, I am truly invested in this adventure!"

"Glad to hear it," said Bernard. Bob helped him to his feet. "I'm feeling much better, thanks to Osivia. Please, let us walk."

Skinner nodded once in unsurprised approval, then turned to lead them deeper into the fissure. Bob was growing more uncertain by the second. Warily keeping an eye on Bernard, he reluctantly stepped deeper into the shadowy corridor.

The fissure was wide and perfectly straight. Daylight shone from above, behind and ahead, yet provided little illumination, such was the magnitude of the fissure. It was only early afternoon, but it seemed they walked in twilight. Each wall was a full thirty feet away from the other, and coupled with the gloom, this produced the impression of walking through an endless, shapeless void.

Bob had tuned the astral voices as far down as they would go. Still, they sang around him, humming their constant, resonant melodies. The deeper into the fissure Bob walked, the more he felt a kind of pressure building in the air around him—an astral pressure. He felt it not with his physical body, but felt it nonetheless. It was like a heavy, leaden blanket slowly descending upon his soul.

"She knows we are here," murmured Bernard.

Skinner grunted in assent. Osivia blinked with dark purple light.

They walked for what seemed like an hour. One foot in front of the other. The sounds of Bob and Bernard's footfalls—and the *clunk* and *clack* of the staff as it struck the ground—echoed along the stone corridor. The astral pressure built and built. Bob developed a headache. Osivia's glow grew muted. Finally, the daylight ahead began to widen. At the mouth of the fissure, Bob could see vague swatches of green and gray.

Suddenly, Bob felt something move above him. It was an odd feeling. The astral pressure seemed to shift, as if it had a shape. He looked up and saw nothing but shadows and the straight line of daylight at the top of the fissure.

TRESSPASSERS, blared a voice in his head. He didn't hear it, so much as feel it. It was much like hearing the astral voices, but more violent, more… intelligent.

TURN BACK NOW OR DIE, commanded the voice. It sounded female, but not effeminate. This was the voice of an enraged mother, a slighted daughter, a vengeful sister. A matriarch.

Bob reached up to cradle his head, but it made no difference. The voice cut into him like an axe.

THE EYES OF AXIIS ARE UPON YOU. THREE OF YOU ARE KNOWN TO ME. THIS WILL NOT PROTECT YOU. TURN BACK NOW OR DIE.

The crystal atop Bernard's staff flared alight. Bob felt the astral pressure lessen. Dazed, he reached in the jerkin for the dragon pipe.

"Axiis," said Bernard calmly, "hear me out, please."

SECOND OF THE VIGILANTUM, roared the voice of Axiis, *I LEFT BEHIND MY PATIENCE LONG AGO. SPEAK QUICKLY.*

"We come seeking to defend the Nexus, not defile it. There is one called Galvidon—"

HE HAS COME. HE FACED ME AND RETREATED LIKE A COWARD. I DO NOT FEAR HIM. I FEAR NOTHING. THIS IS YOUR FINAL WARNING, VIGILANT. TURN BACK NOW OR DIE.

"Is she not magnificent?" muttered Skinner.

"Perhaps we ought to turn around," said Bernard, taking a step backward.

"The guns!" hissed Kelael. "I must have them!"

TRESSPASSERS, the voice bellowed.

"Run!" yelled Bernard.

A gout of flame burst from the shadows above them, barreling down at the party like an exploding train. Even as they ran, Bernard's mastery of wind saved them, the air gusting in a sheet above their heads, sweeping the flames aside. An animalistic roar erupted inside the fissure, and Bob was sure he'd heard it with his physical ears. He chanced a glance upward and saw a massive, bestial shape writhing in the shadows. Another gout of flame erupted at them. This time, Bob felt the heat of it bake his head as Bernard and Faffle were barely able to deflect it.

Bob's heart leapt into his throat as the huge shape lithely dropped onto the fissure floor just ahead of him like a descending snake. Its massive, batlike wings couldn't stretch to full span, but Bob saw the lizard-like, brutal face of Axiis come alight as her breath began to gather flame. A gust of wind slapped at her and she shook her head, flames momentarily abating, giving Bob the time he needed to light his pipe. He and Erto began to tear off pieces of the fissure wall and fling them at the dragon like railroad spikes out of a cannon. The sharp lances of stone pelted her armored skin, causing her to shriek in rage and leap deftly upward back into the shadows above. Bob concentrated and pulled on the stone in the walls, reforming it into a thin roof, separating the party from the dragon, at least temporarily.

"Well done," said Bernard, pushing past Bob. "Don't stop running!"

FOOLS. NOT EVEN YOU MAY ENTER. IT IS MANDATED.

BOB THE WIZARD

They ran. The astral pressure began to gradually loosen until it disappeared. Finally, they reached the entrance to the fissure, and raced out onto the grass, all panting but for Skinner.

The giant ambled out last, unhurried. "Such a polite creature. I can hear the truth in her every word."

"Skinner, behind you!" yelled Bernard.

Bob felt the astral pressure swell as the head of the dragon appeared out of the shadows like a stalking tiger, flame already burgeoning from her fanged maw. Bob was swept backward by a sudden gust of wind and lost his balance, teetered on his heels, dropped the pipe, and crashed onto his back. A blaring rush filled his ears, like the sound of a burning gas main. He pushed himself up in time to see Bernard alone at the mouth of the fissure, facing Axiis. Bob was reminded of the old wizard's battle with the tortum. Axiis's fiery breath blasted outward in a coruscating cascade of implacable heat and met an equally fierce torrent of wind. Bernard appeared to be pushing with his staff against an invisible barrier, pressing against the force of Axiis's breath with all his might. Bob fumbled for the pipe on the ground, unable to find it. He saw Erto beside the mountain wall, passively watching the contest. Skinner and Kelael had apparently also been knocked over by Bernard's gust, and only now were regaining their feet. Bob scanned the ground frantically. Bernard's wind was abating, growing weaker, while the flames were unremitting, relentless. They pounded against the barrier of air like hammers upon a crumbling shield. The pipe—there! Bob reached out—

There was a sound like a shattering crystal orb as Bernard's barrier buckled. The old wizard was engulfed in orange and white fire. A moment later, Axiis ceased her barrage. Where Bernard had stood, there was nothing but scorched earth and dancing ash. The dragon regarded Bob, Kelael, and Skinner with a sweep of her inhuman eyes, then melted back into the shadows of the fissure. Bob heard her voice with his astral ears as she receded through the mountain.

SUCH A FATE AWAITS YOU ALL.

Bob stared, unbelieving, at the blackened earth where just a moment before, Bernard had been alive and breathing.

M. V. PRINDLE

"No," whispered Bob. He stared, slack-jawed, at the fissure's mouth, at the site of the battle just past.

"What just happened?" asked Osivia shakily, from somewhere.

"I believe Bernard has saved our lives," said Kelael, having regained his composure.

"Aye," rumbled Skinner. "An honorable man, to the last! I expected nothing less. But what shall we do now? It seems Axiis has already rebuffed Galvidon. Should we not trust her to keep doing so?"

"My people continue to suffer," said Kelael darkly. "The weapons beyond the fissure are the only hope they have of defeating the Engorians and driving them from En'hirin. Bernard was a great man, and I mourn his loss. But I will not cease until I have exhausted every avenue in the pursuit of my goal. Even if I die in the attempt, as Bernard has."

Hands shaking, Bob relit the dragon pipe and took a deep draw. He had to think. *Think.*

"Oh, Bernard..." gasped Osivia. Bob saw her hovering over the smoldering patch of earth where the wizard had stood, hands to her mouth in disbelief and sorrow.

Then came another voice—a rich, male baritone. "It seems," said the voice, "we share a common enemy."

A dark form melted out of the tree-line into the daylight. Just under six feet tall and clothed in chitinous, interlocking black armor that gleamed in the sun, the figure took another step, his black eyes locked on Bob, his slate-gray skin smooth in the afternoon light, the small horns above his brow pointed like incisors. Twin black knives were cross-sheathed in the armor at his chest, and an assortment of weapons and pouches hung from his waist.

An explosion of rage erupted in Bob, rolling over his insides like a crashing wave. Involuntarily, he bellowed. Rocks and bits of the mountain flaked away from their purchases and shot at Galvidon in a deadly rain. The dirt swirled at Bob's feet.

BOB THE WIZARD

Galvidon swiftly raised an arm, and a gleaming black shield formed from shifting plates on his armor in the blink of an eye. Just as quickly, a black helmet sheathed his head and face, section by section. The volley of stone struck the black armor and caused Galvidon to stagger backward, rattled but unharmed. A nearby tree branch reached down and began to tangle over him. Roots in the earth twisted upward like snakes to wrap his legs.

"Wait," commanded Kelael.

The roots and branches ceased their motion. A stray stone pelted against Galvidon's chest plate. The Gray Man began ripping away at the flora that had assaulted him.

Kelael's order had been enough for Skinner, but Bob saw nothing but red. Earthen hands erupted from the ground at Galvidon's feet and attempted to grasp him, but suddenly he was hovering above the ground, his feet and small nodules on his armor producing a shimmering blue fire that seemed to propel him upward.

"Die!" screamed Bob, throwing yet more lances of stone. Galvidon weaved in the air, dodging some of the projectiles, while others landed glancing blows on his armor, leaving scuffs but no damage.

"Sora Kelai!" barked Kelael. He was directly in front of Bob now, right in his face. "You will cease your assault immediately!"

Bob growled something incomprehensible and launched himself bodily at Galvidon, who easily hovered back out of reach. Bob felt arms wrap around him and fling him to the ground. Then there was a sword point at his eye. Kelael stood over him, menacing, a gleam in his eyes that reached through the cloud of fury inside Bob and demanded calm.

"I suggest you take a deep breath."

Bob unconsciously followed the suggestion. Deep breaths in, deep breaths out. Finally, he managed to croak a single word. "Why?"

"It is clear to me that, had Galvidon wanted to kill us, he would not have begun by engaging us in conversation. I would hear him out. Tell me, Sora Kelai, may I put my sword away?"

Heartbeat slowing to a fast gallop, Bob eyed the sword point dangling inches from his face. Slowly, he nodded. The sword disappeared back into its sheath. Kelael held out a hand to help Bob up. Reluctantly, he accepted the assistance.

Galvidon had once again touched down to earth. The black helmet shield had disappeared. Skinner stood glowering over him, massive hammer in one hand, eyebrows twitching. "Rude Bob carries much hatred for this Galvidon. I would know why."

"He killed my family," breathed Bob.

Skinner considered. "Were they worthy opponents?"

"Worthy—my son was *nine*!"

The Gurdun's expression darkened. "I find myself sympathetic to Rude Bob," he declared. "I would crush this gray insect into a squishy puddle."

"You would fail," said Galvidon haughtily.

Skinner's throat produced a deep growl.

Osivia came to settle on Bob's shoulder. "You've waited this long," she whispered in his ear. "Just wait a little bit more."

Bob angrily rubbed a tear from his cheek.

"Alright, Galon Var," said Kelael. "Consider my protection extremely tenuous. Say what you have come to say before I unleash my companions upon you."

Only a cold smirk graced Galvidon's features. "Very well, En'hari, as you say. It appears, by the grace of God, our interests temporarily align. We all wish to enter the Nexus. Yet, none of us alone can hope to defeat the guardian. I propose an alliance."

Bob unleashed a cloud of spittle in Galvidon's direction. The Gray Man did not move his attention from Kelael.

"I will *never* ally with you!" declared Bob. "Fuck you."

Kelael turned to Bob, one eyebrow raised. "Tell me, Sora Kelai, do you wish the continued oppression of the En'harae?"

Bob said nothing.

"And do you not wish to reach the Astral Core to retrieve your memories?"

"Kind of a good point," muttered Osivia.

"You don't even know what's in there!" yelled Bob. "There could be no guns at all, for all you know!"

"Ah, is that your interest?" asked Galvidon politely. "The firearms? I assure you, my readings indicate a substantial number of them within the borders of the Nexus."

"And how," growled Bob at Kelael, "do you plan to move all of those weapons to En'hirin?"

"Fortunately," snapped the En'hari, "I am traveling with an extremely powerful wizard! We will think of something! We had better, or Torael's leadership will mean nothing. He will rule over chains and ash, only to be rooted out and killed as the others were before him. The Tessaeshi are all but extinct, the Gasheera mostly enslaved. The humans bring metal armor and weapons to bear against stone and wood and ivory. Do you not see, Bob? We have no way to defend ourselves, and we are almost beaten!"

Bob's mind was racing, trying to find an excuse to attack Galvidon again, trying to come up with alternatives to an alliance. What if he were to kill Galvidon now, and just walk away? What then? Assuming he managed to get past Kelael, he'd have condemned the En'harae. Even if he could live with that, what would he do next? Bernard had spoken of Gates at Azenbul. Maybe Bob could go there, find a Gate, try to follow Bernard's maps, starting at the Wizard's Tower instead of the Nexus. But Azenbul held its own dangers—the traitor, for one. And there were a host of problems waiting for him if he defied Kelael now. He'd be throwing away his allegiance to the En'harae, and by extension, probably the Niners as well. If forced to choose between Bob and Kelael, Harold would most likely choose the En'hari. Bob would be undoing every connection he'd made since arriving on Hub. He could see no way out. He turned to stare at the shadowy fissure, knowing that, should they proceed, death probably awaited them all.

"And what happens after?" asked Bob, turning back to Kelael. "After we defeat Axiis, what then?"

In response, Kelael turned a questioning look on Galvidon.

"After," said the Gray Man calmly, "we endeavor to complete our goals separately."

"I see," mused Skinner. "After we kill Axiis, we kill you." He snorted like a bull at Galvidon.

"You are certainly welcome in the attempt," drawled Galvidon, not even deigning to look at the Gurdun.

"A reasonable offer," said Kelael.

"Fine," said Bob. "To hell with all of us." He turned a hateful look on the creature he had trailed for years. "So, what's the plan?"

Bob hurried along the flat ground of the dark fissure behind Skinner and Kelael. Osivia fluttered cautiously at their rear. Somewhere high above, he felt the astral pressure of Axiis's presence shifting. Galvidon was up there somewhere, flying on those shimmering jets of blue fire, harassing the dragon, luring her toward the center of the Nexus, where open ground would even the odds against her. They had all agreed, fighting the dragon in the fissure would be collective suicide. In the cramped shadows, Axiis had all the advantages. Bob had a fantasy that involved drawing the dragon into the fissure and then collapsing it to crush her under the weight of the mountain. Unfortunately, he was still getting his bearings regarding magic, and he knew that such an attempt would probably fail. There was a distinct difference between manipulating small chunks of stone and commanding an entire mountain.

The more time he spent in the fissure, the more it seemed familiar, like strong memories of the place slithered just beneath the skein of his thoughts, threatening—but never quite managing—to break the surface. He had been here before, many times. He could feel it.

Axiis roared in the sky, the distant sound diffusing as it echoed down the fissure.

BOB THE WIZARD

"This Galvidon," remarked Skinner, "has a strong knack for irritating others."

"That's one way to put it," muttered Bob.

They shuffled along the stone corridor at a fast walk. The light of the exit widened slowly. The sounds of Axiis chasing Galvidon through the air floated down to them: blasts of fire, roars of rage, and the reports of the Gray Man's high-tech sidearm. Finally, the mouth of the fissure gave way to the Nexus.

Bob was unsure what he had expected, but the sights that greeted him were such an odd blend of the mundane and the surreal that he could do nothing for a moment but gawk at his surroundings.

The Nexus was a huge, open valley, hemmed on all sides by mountains. It was shaped like a hexagon. The fissure the party had entered by was one of four. They'd entered from the west, and directly across from them to the east—past the full mile-length of the valley— was a fissure through the mountains that led directly west. The other two fissures were located at the southwest and southeast corners of the hexagon, to the party's right as they entered via the western fissure. The entire northern stretch of the valley wall was solid rock—no fissures. Carved into the mountain walls on each side of the hexagon were enormous stone archways with shallow steps leading up to them. Beyond the mouths of each archway was solid rock. Bob knew Astral Gates when he saw them. At the exact center of the hexagonal valley was a dais and cylindrical stone platform. Beyond it, in the valley's northeastern quadrant, were two huge, concrete buildings. Bob could just barely make out a faded carving of a British flag along the side of one of them.

Apart from these oddities, the Nexus seemed a calm and natural place. Bright green grass grew in tufts across the flat, rocky ground. Here and there an occasional tree, ancient and gnarled, thrust itself toward the open sky. Ringing the top of the mountains along the hexagonal perimeter were wide, unnaturally flat stone ledges. Divots in the mountainside below acted as ladders up to them. Bob realized that, if one were to climb upon one of these ledges, one could look down upon enemies that encroached along the fissures.

"Magnificent," said Skinner. "Truly a baffling achievement of architecture."

"Where do those other fissures lead?" asked Bob, glancing at the sky as they walked toward the center of the valley.

Skinner pointed with his sizeable hammer toward the southwestern fissure. "That way leads to the east of Nine Peaks." He rotated, turning the hammer toward the southeastern fissure. "To the Northern Forest, a long stretch of forested valley." The hammer then pointed at the remaining fissure. "The western fissure is very long. It stretches for almost a hundred miles and opens up into a wide valley road that veers southward and connects to northern Engoria, only a few dozen miles north of a human city called Swearington." The hammer lowered to the ground.

"It leads straight to Swearington?" asked Bob, irritated. If that was true, why had Bernard not led them down that path?

"Mmm," said Skinner, "perhaps, 'straight to Swearington' is a bit generous, Rude Bob. It is fraught with twists and turns and is closely watched by Axiis. Additionally, there is a tribe of my small cousins who live near a stretch of it. The Engorians have not dared such a journey in living memory."

"I like the look of that ledge above the southeastern fissure," said Kelael. "Look, I can gain purchase on the ledge, giving me cover to shoot from. It is close to the wall, so Bob will have material to work with. There are two trees nearby, for your Leelo. What say you, Gurdun?"

Above the valley, the black silhouette of Galvidon jetted through the air in a tight spiral, Axiis close behind, riding the wind on her expansive wings, snapping and roaring and blasting fire.

"I say we should move quickly," replied Skinner.

Bob, Kelael, and Skinner ran toward the southeastern fissure. Bob had lost track of Osivia, but he trusted her to keep herself safe. He hoped she would stay hidden. Bob figured he, Kelael and Skinner had all earned a death from the dragon. They were killers, all three. But Osivia was not. If any of them deserved to get out of this alive, it was her.

They reached the area of the fissure and Kelael climbed a line of

BOB THE WIZARD

divots that led up the mountainside, where he reached the rocky ledge and dug in. Skinner positioned himself on Kelael's left flank near the base of a huge maple. Bob took the right flank. This way, they formed a triangular kill-zone. When Axiis approached the southeastern fissure, she'd be assailed on three sides—Skinner's branches, roots, and hammer on her right, Bob's stones and earth on her left, and Kelael's arrows from above in the center.

Galvidon had no doubt been monitoring their progress, for as soon as they were settled the Gray Man took a sharp turn in the sky above the valley and rocketed toward them, the massive, flowing form of the winged dragon snapping at his heels.

Bob could feel the astral pressure building. He puffed on his pipe. Skinner cracked his neck from side to side. Kelael was silent behind a shallow boulder atop the ridge.

Galvidon barreled out of the air like a comet, striking the earth just ahead of Skinner and Bob with an impact that threw dust into the air. Immediately he swiveled to face his pursuer, black helmet and shield forming even as he turned, and crouched behind his gleaming black shield as a torrent of fire exploded from Axiis's mouth, engulfing him. An arrow *thunk*ed across the dragon's brow, bouncing away. The astral pressure weighed heavily over the area like a shroud.

The torrent ceased, and Bob half-expected—and fully hoped—to see Galvidon disintegrated as Bernard had been. But the Gray Man remained, apparently unhurt in his interlocking armor.

In the open valley, Axiis now only feet away, Bob finally got a good look at her. The dragon was roughly sixty feet long and covered in grayish green ridged scales. She was essentially a winged serpent, the middle of her sinuous body as big around as a septic tank. Her pointed head—about the size of Bob's entire body—ended in a ridged beak, and her maw was lined with spiney fangs. She had no arms or legs, but the tip of her tail fanned into a brace of razor-thin spikes. Her mouth did not move as she spoke. Her words were entirely astral.

I TIRE OF THESE GAMES, declared the dragon. *NOW YOU SHALL DIE.*

M. V. PRINDLE

For the space of a single heartbeat, Bob, Galvidon, Kelael and Skinner faced the dragon Axiis, guardian of the Nexus. Then, as one, they attacked.

CHAPTER THIRTY-THREE:
KEYSTONE

Axiis opened her mouth to breathe fire and was rewarded with a mouthful of dirt that flew up from the ground in a cloud. She coughed—a sound like a choking lion—and tossed her head as a volley of red streaks rained upon her from Galvidon's pistol. A tree-root the size of Skinner's arm snaked from the ground to grapple the dragon's twisting body. Another arrow bounced harmlessly off the beast's scales near her eyes.

Axiis snapped at Galvidon as a section of her body whipped away from Skinner's hammer-blow. The tree-root was ripped violently asunder even as other, smaller roots worked to entangle the dragon. Flame once again gathered at her maw.

Bob and Erto shot a clump of mud and shale at her mouth again. This time, Axiis snapped her mouth shut only for the earthy projectile to clamp over her beak and jaw like a muzzle. She attempted a jet of flame anyway, baking the mud into hard, brittle clay. Then the spiked tail was swishing at Bob, cutting a swathe of razor-sharp death through the air. Skinner's hammer connected to a chunk of dragon-flesh, slamming it aside and cracking scales. Shards of gray-green armored skin flew into the air.

Bob threw a spike of rock that missed by inches as he was forced backward by the whipping tail. One of Kelael's arrows finally struck home, entering the dragons eye socket with a wet crunch, causing Axiis to writhe violently and roar in pain and rage. The clay muzzle still held, but Axiis attempted to breathe fire anyway, and a small gout erupted from the corner of the muzzle, spraying the left side of Skinner's face with white-hot flame. The giant barked in pain, throwing his smoldering helmet and dropping his hammer to clutch at his face and stumble backward. Axiis breathed once more, directly at Galvidon, who was slashing his knives at the dragon's writhing body. The muzzle glowed red and orange, flaking away at the sides, and the fire jetted askew, blasting a nearby maple branch as it reached for the beast under the command of Leelo. The branch ignited in an instant, the tree erupting in flames.

Bob raised a barrier of earth that barely blocked a strike from the tail. He found himself fighting right next to Galvidon. Out of instinct born from years of brooding hatred, Bob unleashed a volley of stone spikes at the Gray Man while his back was turned. The shards pelted his armor, knocking him to the ground, where he immediately was forced to roll away from Skinner's hammer as the giant swung it down upon him.

"You fools!" yelled Galvidon.

The muzzle broke and a line of fire exploded toward Bob, who dove aside just in time, feeling the inimical heat rush by him. The maple was fully aflame now. Bob saw an arrow pierce Axiis in the gums. There was an enormous cracking noise as a section of the maple began to teeter. The spiked tail came out of nowhere and Bob felt a sudden tear of bright pain along his right arm. The sleeve of the trench coat flopped, sheared apart. He cried out, and attempted to re-muzzle the dragon, who slithered her head away from the earthen projectile.

A chunk of burning maple branches fell, toppling backward to strike the ledge where Kelael lay. As he himself tumbled, Bob saw Kelael roll off the ledge and barely catch himself, dangling precariously over the drop from a single hand. Galvidon still struggled with Axiis, batting away the tail with his shield, absorbing blasts of fire with his armor, assaulting the dragon with sidearm and knife. Cradling his wounded arm—a seven-inch gash that was now oozing blood—Bob threw more shards at Galvidon before applying another mud-muzzle to the monster, this time successfully.

Axiis was finally slowing. Blind in one eye, muzzled, missing chunks of armored scales and bleeding from several places, the dragon's movements had become lethargic, plodding. Roots sprung from the ground to entangle both the beast and the Gray Man. Galvidon hovered on blue jets, ripping up the roots as he ascended. Axiis was less successful in her escape. The roots gained purchase along her dully thrashing body, drawing her ever closer to a position of utter vulnerability.

Kelael deftly swung himself from the burning ledge onto the nearby divots and began to descend. Skinner, the left side of his face a bright-red mess of flesh, stepped back to watch the maple fully collapse into a pyre. Galvidon hovered backward, keeping his eyes on Bob, Kelael and Skinner. The dragon struggled and released a dull roar that was muffled by the muzzle. A moment passed, Bob and his companions facing Galvidon, the restrained dragon between them.

A silvery metal orb the size of a basketball floated out of the southeastern fissure, ten feet above the ground. Bob became aware of a rhythmic thunder in the earth. If it weren't for the sounds of battling the dragon, he would've noticed it sooner. The flying orb produced an almost imperceptible *woosh* as it arrived and began to hover over Axiis. The roots tightened across the dragon's tangled body like boa constrictors. Galvidon landed in front of the dragon to face the party. Bob saw with barely retrained fury that the Gray Man was smiling.

"Perhaps," said Galvidon, "I neglected to mention that I have invited guests."

The rhythmic thunder continued, growing louder. *Boom…boom…boom.* There was a duller sound beneath it—the constant rumbling scrabble of thousands of claws striking stone.

Skinner's left eye was swollen shut. He turned a cyclopean glare on Bob. "In this instance, he is being quite polite."

Like waves upon a beach, hundreds of Gez Kar began to pour forth from the southeastern fissure. A flowing swarm of sherka was punctuated by dozens of the armored, man-sized lizards. Bob found Kelael at his side.

"Time to go," said Kelael with an inappropriate calm.

Bob, clutching his wounded arm, nodded, and the two of them began to skirt northeast. Galvidon stood stoically as the horde of Gez Kar trampled up to him. He remained unmoving as the waves of sherka darted between and around his legs. They began to leap onto the dragon. Skinner was on the opposite side of the swarm from Bob and Kelael, and Bob saw the giant bellow as he flung himself into the Gez Kar, hammer swinging and tossing up a dozen sherka with a single strike. The roots holding the dragon loosened, and Axiis flailed with bestial desperation as she was assaulted on all sides by Gez Kar. The *boom… boom…boom* continued unabated as still more Gez Kar erupted from the fissure's mouth.

Bob and Kelael made their way north and then west, skirting around the fray in an attempt to reach Skinner. As they passed around the northern section of the thrashing brawl and moved further west, the source of the thunderous noise made itself known.

A towering, reptilian monster stepped out of the shadowy fissure—a beast thirty feet tall with massive, piston-like legs and smaller but still formidable arms that ended in heavy talons. Its head was long and round and seemed to be mostly a huge, fanged mouth. Its eyes were slitted, and upon its head was an elaborate crown of fused bones. Its body was encased in a plated shell that dovetailed to spikes at the edges. It was an enormous tortum. The monster roared in a deep, resonant bellow that echoed across the Nexus.

"It's a God-damn Turtle-Tyrannosaurus!" declared Bob.

"It is Forr Ghaway," said Kelael. "King of the Gez Kar. Now would be a good time to run."

They ran. The tree-roots began to loosen around Axiis as her breath disintegrated a swathe of Gez Kar, but the lizard creatures kept on coming, relentlessly biting and clawing and piling on the dragon. Galvidon stood watching for long moments before finally ascending into the air. As Bob ran west, he saw the Gray Man fly over him toward the pedestal at the center of the Nexus.

"Shit." Bob changed direction.

"Sora Kelai!" called Kelael behind him.

Bob was running out of breath. His right arm was numb. As he ran, he forced his muscles to cooperate, roughly pulling out tobacco and spilling nearly an ounce as he worked to repack the dragon pipe. He had to pause for a moment and experienced a sharply terrifying second of stillness as his first match guttered out and he was forced to light a second. He heard Kelael's footfalls just behind him and concentrated. Kelael shouted in alarm as the earth beneath their feet rose like the crest of a wave and propelled the two of them after Galvidon like a supercharged earthen escalator. They surfed the wave of earth as it rushed them at the Gray Man and the pedestal.

Just ahead, Galvidon was reaching into a pouch at his waist. He pulled out a small baton of glimmering gray stone and reached out with it toward the pedestal. Bob launched off the rolling earth and tackled him from behind. It was like colliding with a concrete pillar. Bob felt something in his shoulder crack as it connected with black armor. Galvidon barely stumbled, but it was enough. He dropped the Hub Keystone.

Kelael grabbed the Keystone as he rolled by the pedestal on a shoulder. Galvidon snarled and lashed out an arm that connected with Bob's face and flung him backward with a broken nose. Adrenaline masked the pain, and he maintained a grip on the pipe. The Gray Man pulled his pistol and aimed where Kelael had been a moment before only for a leather-clad leg to strike at his hand from the side, knocking the weapon from his grip and onto the ground, where, thanks to Bob and Erto, the earth opened up and swallowed it.

Galvidon swiveled, reached with his left hand, grabbed Kelael by his patchwork leather jerkin, and flung him away from the pedestal. Bob climbed to his feet with difficulty. Galvidon snatched up the Hub Keystone and reached out with it toward a dimple at the center of the pedestal, but Bob concentrated, and the Keystone exploded in Galvidon's hand, pelting the Gray Man's face with shards. Galvidon exclaimed wordlessly in shock and pain. Kelael was pushing on Bob, thrusting him away from the pedestal.

"We must retreat!"

Kelael's voice seemed far away. Bob struggled to reach Galvidon, who stood, momentarily stunned, clutching his face. Suddenly Kelael dominated his vision.

"Bob! Look!"

Bob turned his head to wear the En'hari was pointing. The battle was a swirling mass of scaled flesh and glinting teeth and claws. Axiis was almost dead. Her breath produced no flame. She bled from a dozen places. With booming steps, Forr Ghaway approached her methodically, slitted eyes coldly watching the smaller Gez Kar struggle and pile on the dragon. As Bob watched, he saw Skinner tear a man-sized monster from his back. All the while, more Gez Kar skittered and tromped out of the southeastern fissure.

"There are too many! We must retreat!"

Reluctantly, Bob nodded. He allowed Kelael to drag him forward a few paces, then he and Erto recreated the rolling wave of earth, propelling them at high speed toward the western side of the battle.

"Skinner!" called Bob. "Skinner, we're leaving!" He skewered a stray sherka with a lance of stone.

The Gurdun either couldn't hear him or had no interest in retreating. He did not acknowledge the hail, instead electing to cut a large Gez Kar in half with a horizontal bludgeon of his hammer. Out of the corner of his eye, Bob saw Galvidon rise into the air by the pedestal, turning to pursue him.

As Bob and Kelael rode upon the earth, there came a blinding flash of light. It took Bob a moment to realize it was Axiis. White light was leaking from her wounds as she lay motionless, eaten alive, piece by piece, by the ravenous sherka. For a moment, Bob was sure her malicious eye was upon him, and him alone. Then her body erupted in a gust of light that shined for unabated seconds. The light seemed to vaporize everything it touched. Gez Kar skeletons became visible for a split second before their bodies disintegrated to ash. A wave of astral pressure washed over the area. The voice of Axiis came then, bellowing a death cry that was accompanied by words that chilled Bob to the bottom of his soul.

EIGHTEENTH OF THE VIGILANTUM. YOU DOOM THE WORLD YOU HELPED TO CREATE.

The following explosion knocked Bob tumbling to the ground. Dazed, he fumbled in the grass for the pipe, found it, and stumbled to his feet. His arm and face were throbbing. His whole body hurt. "Did you... did you hear that?" he asked thickly. Despite the deadly explosion, there were still plenty of Gez Kar, battling Skinner, mewling at the feet of Forr Ghaway, consolidating for another attack.

"Yes, Sora Kelai. I heard. We must keep moving."

Fortunately, they were now only a few strides from shelter—the southwestern fissure. Bob took a few halting steps into the shadows before turning around to close the entrance to the fissure. The rock pulled and stretched itself into a ten-inch-thick barrier of solid, mountainous stone. The fissure was thrown into near-darkness. Bob leaned against the sheer wall, breathing hard, and slid down onto his ass.

"Bob, Galvidon can fly."

Bob shook his head, panting. "He heard your speech. He knows we'll come back in, try to get the guns. Besides, he needs me alive now. To put the Keystone back together."

"You can put it back together? It exploded!"

"I think so. Its... I can hear the voices of its pieces, even now. It's hard to explain."

"Yes, Sora Kelai, I understand." He sighed. "I still have a small amount of food. Come, let us try to find a safe place to hide and recover."

Bob felt lightheaded. He flopped the ragged right sleeve of the trench coat aside and inspected his arm. It was a deep cut, still lightly bleeding. He realized blood was falling into his mouth from his nose. "I'm a fucking mess," he muttered, wiping his upper lip with his uninjured forearm.

Kelael helped him to stand. The En'hari seemed to be able to see fine, so Bob followed his dark blue form in the shadows, supporting himself with his left hand against the stone wall. The thunderous footsteps of Forr Ghaway occasionally rumbled through the ground to reach them. There was a moment when Bob grew afraid he was going blind, but then he realized the sun was setting. The daylight that provided the fissure's bare illumination was receding. Kelael walked on, unbothered. The fissure grew cool, and then cold. Even as his wounds throbbed like frayed nerves, Bob could barely keep himself awake.

Osivia arrived, silently swirling out of the darkness. She and Kelael had a conversation that Bob was beyond the ability to follow. He found himself sitting on the ground, leaning against the fissure wall, as Osivia's light bathed over his arm and face.

The world came into sharper focus. Osivia was sitting on his shoulder, yawning heavily. He looked at his arm. The wound was still swollen and yellowish, but the bleeding had stopped, and it appeared to be in the beginning stages of scabbing over.

"Thanks, Tinkerbell," said Bob tiredly.

"You're—" she yawned again, "welcome."

The faerie's glow had dimmed considerably. She crawled into the breast pocket of his coat, where, he assumed, she fell asleep. A few more minutes of walking led them to the mouth of the fissure and the night sky. It seemed they were back in the enormous, forested valley of hills, only further south and east from where they'd first entered the Nexus.

"A valley of lizard monsters or a forest full of wild animals," said Bob.

"I pick the wild animals," said Kelael, and set off into the tree-line.

"Like we've got a choice," muttered Bob. He followed Kelael into the forest.

After a few minutes of walking, Kelael suddenly halted, holding up a hand for Bob to do the same. Bob stood in weary silence, hoping with all his will that he would not have to fight again. Osivia, apparently not asleep, poked her head out of his pocket.

Kelael called out. It took a moment for Bob to realize he'd spoken Hari. The Gatekey was translating.

"*Brothers and sisters!*" called Kelael. "*The spirits walk with you.*"

Bob was confused. Who was he talking to?

The answer resolved itself into a figure approaching through the trees. It was the shape of a man, taller and heavier than Kelael but not by much. The figure's skin appeared blue in the moonlight. No—it wasn't the moonlight!

Gorrelai stepped out of the trees, followed by several other En'harae, all bristling with weapons. Bob was suddenly unsure if he'd fallen asleep,

BOB THE WIZARD

if maybe this was a dream.

A grin lit Gorrelai's face in the dark forest. "*And you, Kelael Ellaren.*" The two Gasheera grasped each other by the forearm. Gorrelai's eyes flicked from Kelael and found Bob. "Sora Kelai!"

Osivia darted into the air as Bob was swept into a brotherly hug. His arm flared with pain, but he couldn't help smiling. This was no dream.

"Sora Kelai," repeated Gorrelai, releasing him. "*I have prayed to the spirits we would find you!*" He chuckled. "*Torael says hello.*"

CHAPTER THIRTY-FOUR:
WEAPONS

"You look like shit," observed Gorrelai.

Bob blinked. Gorrelai had used an English curse word.

"Come, Sora Kelai, Kelael. We can set up camp and discuss the situation."

"How?" asked Bob as he followed Gorrelai and the other En'harae deeper into the forest. "How did you get here so fast?"

Gorrelai led them into a small clearing where more En'harae were waiting. Several of them held torches. "Senaesen Eeno," answered Gorrelai.

An elderly En'hari stepped forward. He wore a headdress of brown eagle feathers and a thick, hooded, black cloak. As was typical of the En'harae, his weathered, blue face was completely hairless. He approached leaning on a long staff wrapped with leather cord, atop which was bound the skull of a small bird of prey.

"Senaesen of Tribe Eeno," said Gorrelai, *"is one of the last of the Tessaeshi. A 'wind shaman,' you would say. It seems the Koreka's evacuation to the rendezvous was well timed. A contingent of Gasheera, led by this man, was there awaiting us. He says he heard our approach on the wind."* Gorrelai flashed a proud look at Bob. *"After some...consideration, Torael bid Senaesen bring us here. Fifty Gasheera—the last remaining true warriors of the En'harae—carried by the air spirits to the Nexus in pursuit of Kelael Ellaren and two Teserae. Imagine, Sora Kelai! Imagine the tales that will be told of this journey—this night, even!"*

"Got to live through it first," muttered Bob. Then, to Senaesen, he said, "Nice to meet you. I'd shake your hand, but I'm just a little bit covered in blood."

Senaesen Eeno glanced at Gorrelai. "*This hairy human can understand my words?*"

Gorrelai grinned. "*Very well, Uncle.*"

The old Tessaeshi turned back to Bob and affected an exaggerated way of speaking. "*I wish to speak to Bernard!*" he said loudly. "*Where is the famous Tesera?*"

"He's…" began Bob, glancing behind him. Then he remembered. Had that really happened? "He's…"

"*He is dead,*" said Kelael somberly in Hari. "*Destroyed by the dragon Axiis. May the spirits guide him home. He has been avenged, but sadly, not by us. Forr Ghaway and a large contingent of Gez Kar now occupy the Nexus. There are many sherka and karka. Forr Ghaway was the only tortum we saw, but more could have arrived since we left.*"

Senaesen shook his head, seemingly unperturbed by news of the Gez Kar. "*Dead? Most unfortunate. I had looked forward to discussing the finer points of air currents and weather pressure.*"

A new pain burgeoned in Bob. His mind demanded that he remember. The gust of wind that knocked him over. The standoff with the dragon. The barrier breaking. And then…

"*Sora Kelai,*" said Gorrelai, putting an arm around Bob, leading him deeper into the clearing. Bob winced as Gorrelai's hand touched the shoulder that had collided with Galvidon's armor. "*We are ready to fight, but I see that you have had a trying day. I would not attack the Gez Kar without your leave. Please, eat. Rest. Once you are enough recovered, we will follow you into battle.*"

Bob shot Gorrelai a surprised look. "Me? Don't you mean you'll follow Kelael into battle?"

Gorrelai grunted. "*Of course. I simply meant… well, Torael has commanded that, should his brother fall, command of the Gasheera would fall to Bernard for the duration of our stay at the Nexus. And if Bernard should fall…*" he shrugged.

"Me," finished Bob.

"As you say, Sora Kelai."

Bob glanced around at the En'harae as they set up camp with practiced efficiency. They wore fur and leather. Their swords and axes were fashioned of stone and ivory, their arrowheads tipped with the same. No metal was visible anywhere. They stole furtive glances at him, curious, no doubt wondering who he was, what made him so special that Torael would command them to follow him. Bob wondered the same.

He found himself staring at a campfire. There was a rotating wooden spit over the flames. The smell of roasting meat reached his nostrils, and he collapsed into a sitting position.

"I am sorry to hear about Bernard," said Gorrelai, standing behind him. "He was a great man. May the spirits guide him home."

Bob stared into the fire. In the licking flames, he could almost see the face of Axiis, maw widening, furious and regal. From somewhere in his mind came the sound of Bernard's barrier shattering.

Smoldering earth and dancing ash. Osivia's shaking voice.

What just happened?

Bob was too exhausted to cry. Nonetheless, sorrow suffused his bones.

———◉———

He sat by the fire beside Kelael. Osivia sleepily plucked a strand of roasted boar flesh from Bob's plate. The Gasheera and the Tessaeshi kept back at a distance in their tents. A kind of silent understanding seemed to permeate the camp. Bob and Kelael were apart from the others—on their own journeys, the En'harae would say. Even Gorrelai did not approach them. Instead, he stood guard somewhere beyond the rim of firelight.

"Did you hear?" Bob asked Kelael in a low voice. "Torael put you in charge."

Kelael's eyes reflected the dancing flames like twin mirrors. "Unfortunately, I see no logical alternative."

"Unfortunately? You're a born leader, Kel. Why do you run from it?"

Bob expected a witty retort, probably at his expense. Instead, Bob saw doubt cloud the En'hari's features. "I am unworthy," said Kelael softly. "The spirits do not deign to speak with me. Or even appear before me. The spirits do not make mistakes. If I was to be a worthy leader, they would have shown me so."

Bob snorted, causing Kelael to look up sharply in anger.

"Don't get me wrong, blue-boy. I only laugh because you're so wrong."

Kelael glared. "Explain."

"You ever consider that maybe you're just unlucky? Maybe the spirits would like nothing better than to talk to you, but for whatever reason, they just can't?"

Kelael looked back at the fire.

Bob bit off a chunk of boar, chewed, swallowed. "You know what your brother told me at the Koreka? He thought he might die in Swearington. Yeah, I know, don't look at me like that. Anyway, he made a big deal about it. He wanted me to make sure you took over for him. Said you were the only one that wouldn't accept it—you being Quaylen Dah, I mean. Your brother believes in you, Kel. The En'harae believe in you. And what's more, you're a damn good leader. You know what to do, when to do it, and you take charge. If the spirits didn't want you to lead, do you think so many of your people would want it?"

"What would you know of what the En'harae people want? You're just a human!"

"I'm trying to pay you a compliment, asshole."

Kelael looked irritated and embarrassed, yet a smile twitched at the corners of his mouth. Bob glanced at Osivia. She'd fallen asleep on a nearby log.

"So, anyway. You're calling the shots. And… I'm cool with that."

"Good, Bob. That is good." Kelael's eyes narrowed. "Because I have an idea."

M. V. PRINDLE

The dream, like so many others, began in the Cave. The rough walls of rock glistened with streaks of iron ore. A soft, ethereal light emanated from nowhere. From the shadowed mouth of the Cave, along the corridor in which Bob had saved Torael's life, a figure appeared.

It was Anna, barely visible in a pool of inky shadow. He knew it was her by her smell, the shape of her hair, the way she walked. She stood just outside a cast of light, watching him. He called her name, and she beckoned with a wave of the hand before retreating into the corridor. He called after her again, following.

The tunnels twisted a labyrinthine path deeper and deeper into the earth. The streaks of iron ore began to taper away and finally disappeared, replaced with long, throbbing blood vessels. The rock on all sides began to soften into moist, black earth. Occasionally, soupy blood dripped from the ceiling, splashing the muddy ground, pattering on Bob's body as he caught glimpses of Anna turning down the next branch of the maze. The light grew brighter, an ultraviolet blue, though no light source revealed itself.

He came to a dead end—a wide room with a high ceiling and rows of abandoned tables. Bob had the vague impression that it was the feast hall in Ninth Castle, its edges blurred with purple mist. He saw Anna lower herself into a hole in the center of the floor. He approached.

He stared down at an open manhole, a gaping wound in the ground beneath him. It oozed black blood and expanded and contracted in turns like a breathing throat. In the vague distance, Bob could hear the rumbles, grinds, and strident *beeps* of garbage trucks. The sounds of automobiles and footsteps floated down to him as though he stood beneath a modern city on Earth. He watched the manhole swell and shrink, swell and shrink. Anna had gone down there. He followed.

There was a ladder, slick with viscous fluid. He climbed down an esophagus, one slippery rung at a time. The air became thick and moist, cloying. He reached the bottom of the ladder and fell into darkness.

He found himself standing in the Cave again. This time, Anna faced him. She was covered in red and black goo, but her expression was friendly. Corridors stretched to her right and left. Along each corridor was a row of people, standing with their backs to the jagged rock, staring blankly ahead into the underground gloom. To his right, Bob saw Bernard standing expressionless next to Fan. Beyond Fan was Hirrell, and beyond Hirrell was Ellaria the keep slave. Then, Titchell and Guanam. There were others—so many others. Hundreds. Thousands. The line of people stretched off into the gloom as far as Bob could see.

To his left was another row of silently standing people. He saw the guard that had killed Fan at Oath Keep, the knight he'd shot in the head at Ransom Ridge, the bandits he'd killed upon arriving on Hub. Beyond them, there were more. So many more. Just like the other row, it seemed to stretch on forever.

"Bernard?" Bob heard his own voice, scratchy and raw.

Bernard did not respond. He stared blankly ahead, unmoving.

"They can't hear you," said Anna kindly. "They are just shadows."

He faced her. "Shadows?"

"Imprints," she said. "Memories."

Bob looked down the left row. In the middle distance, he could see Gez Kar standing among the others, as silent and stoic as the rest.

"There are so many," said Bob. "So many."

Anna extended an arm toward the row to Bob's right, the one that began with Bernard. "Those who have died for you." Then she indicated the row to his left. "Those you have killed."

He looked again at the rows of people. Each row stretched on and on into the dimly lit distance. "Impossible," said Bob. "There are too many!"

"Tell me," said Anna, "if you cannot remember something, does that mean that thing never occurred?"

He stared at her. "You're saying… all this… was **R**? The eighteenth Vigilant?"

Suddenly all the faces in the rows had turned toward him. Their faces remained blank, their eyes seeing through him, or nothing at all. Yet, they faced him. Bob retreated a step.

"Why?" he managed. "Why are you showing me this?"

"Oh, my love," Anna said sadly. "I am also a shadow. You control this dream, not I."

"You killed us," came a whisper from his left.

"We died for you," came a rasp from his right.

"Why, Bob?" asked Fan, staring blankly at him. "I warned you. You would not listen."

"If you were faster," said Bernard, "if you'd caught on quicker, I'd still be alive."

"No," whispered Bob. His heart hammered in his chest. The bluish light flickered in time with each beat.

"You didn't even know why we were there!" came a bandit's angry voice from his left.

"You killed me, and you don't even remember!" called another one of his victims.

"No!" cried Bob. He wheeled desperately, plunging into the darkness behind him.

He ran in pitch black. Soon there was silence but for his own heavy breath, the pounding of his heart. Sweat trickled down his forehead. His legs burned with effort. He ran. And ran.

Ahead in the black satin broke the image of Anna and Daniel, bloody and torn on the couch from his living room. Blood leaked from horizontal wounds at their necks, their chests. As had his own victims, their blank eyes stared at nothing. He tried to stop running but couldn't. The image of his freshly-murdered family drew ever closer. Then, as if from a hidden loudspeaker, came the voice of Farmer Willis.

Everybody needs a family. Right, Bob?

Then, he was falling. The grisly image of his wife and son rose above him, shrinking to a speck before disappearing entirely. The air resisted his fall, buffeting his hair and beard. He careened in empty blackness, falling.

Falling.

The Gatekey began to glow. Brighter. Brighter.

A flare of white light illuminated the empty void around him. He shut his eyes at the sudden glare. He fell hard on soft grass. Bounced.

Now then, he heard his disembodied voice say, *where the fuck am I?*

Smoke filled his lungs. It was pleasant at first, but soon became overwhelming, choking him. He gagged. He hacked and coughed. He was suffocating. He would die.

He gasped lungfuls of clean air and his eyes shot open. He was in the Cave again. Galvidon was tied to a chair, bound and gagged. He struggled, but to no avail. There was a gun in Bob's hand, a gleaming, black, nine-millimeter, semiautomatic pistol. Its weight was just right. The safety was disengaged. Before him, Galvidon struggled at his bonds. At the back of the Cave stood Erto, silently watching.

"Go ahead," said Anna from behind him. "*Do it*," she hissed, suddenly vicious. "*Kill him!*"

Bob lifted the weapon and pointed it at Galvidon. For some reason, Kelael was there now, standing in the way. Scowling, Bob moved a few feet around the Cave's perimeter. He raised the gun again. Yet again, Kelael was directly in the way of his shot.

"Get out of the way!" snarled Bob.

"It will not work," said Kelael, shaking his head sadly. "This way will not work."

"Move!"

Kelael did not move. Bob walked along the Cave's perimeter again. Now, he stood behind Galvidon, the back of the Gray Man's head making a perfect target. He pointed the pistol.

Kelael was in his way. Bob hissed in frustration.

"He is in the way!" declared Anna righteously. "Kill him too!"

Bob ignored her. He looked from the pistol to Kelael, over Kelael's shoulder to the bound Galvidon. There was only one way to solve the puzzle. Kelael reached out his hand, palm up, to receive the weapon.

Bob's eyes snapped open and met daylight. He lay on hard ground next to a dead fire in a small clearing, pines and elms towering on all sides. Birdsong and the buzz of insects mixed with voices—both physical and astral. He sat up coughing. His back and shoulder hurt. His forearm dully throbbed. His throat was sore. Bob hacked a ball of phlegm into the grass as he climbed to his feet.

For a moment, fragments of the strange nightmare still swimming in his head, he forgot where he was. Maybe outside the burned down Koreka, he thought. Maybe before that. Maybe he was in the Essen'aelo on the way to Ransom Ridge. No, this wasn't the Essen'aelo. The trees were wrong. More importantly, that was all over, the past. These En'harae around him were Gasheera, armed and armored, and he was outside the Nexus. Today was the day.

"You look awful, Bob." Osivia hovered nearby.

"That's funny, I feel like a million bucks," growled Bob, rubbing his shoulder.

"I'd offer to help, but I'm still recharging after yesterday. If I heal you now, I might not have enough Light to heal you later."

Bob nodded. "I get it. Thanks anyway. Is there breakfast?"

"Some leftovers." She hesitated. "Bob?"

"Yeah."

"Good luck."

It was well after sunrise. The tents were all packed. Kelael was standing in a knot of Gasheera, conversing in low tones. Gorrelai joined Bob as he sat in a bar of sunlight eating cold boar meat and then loading the pipe.

"Are we just waiting for me?" asked Bob.

"*Interesting,*" said Gorrelai, cocking his head.

"What's that?"

"*I hear your Engorian words, but I also hear them in Hari. If I was not so used to listening hard to what you say in your language, I would not have noticed. It is a strange sensation, to hear two contradictory things at once.*"

Bob, who could hear the astral voices singing over everything, yet also hear all the physical sounds around him, nodded. "Trust me, my friend, I understand what you mean. It's the Gatekey, I think. A kind of translation feature."

"*Very useful, this magic.*" Gorrelai reached for a bowl of leek-like vegetables that someone had left by the remains of the fire. "*Anyway, Sora Kelai, to answer your question, yes, the Gasheera wait for you. But do not feel that you are a hindrance. Our patience is practical. You are one of our most powerful weapons. To engage the enemy without you at peak strength would be foolish.*"

Gorrelai's phrasing brought Bob strange comfort. A weapon. Bob would rather think of himself as a weapon than a person, at least for the moment. It would be easier to wade into battle that way. He struck a match along Fan's jerkin and lit the pipe. "Well then," he said, glancing over at Kelael and the others, "five more minutes won't hurt."

As he smoked, he opened the trench coat and pulled the Gatekey out from underneath the jerkin by the chain. He lifted the key from his neck and held it in his palm, the chain dangling between his fingers. It was Mannix's chain. Bob had been using a shoestring. The little green meter indicated the Gatekey was fully charged. Enough for two jumps.

Gorrelai peered at the Gatekey with flat, half-lidded eyes. Bob realized they were both thinking about Fan. He was spared having to cross that particular conversational minefield by the arrival of Kelael. Bob cashed out the pipe and looked up as the Gasheera's shadow fell over him.

"It is time," said Kelael.

"Isn't it always?" muttered Bob.

Bob left his pack with the rest of the camping equipment, just inside the entrance to the western fissure. The fissure's interior seemed darker than usual. After a moment, Bob realized that was because he'd sealed the mouth of the fissure on the Nexus-side. Daylight had only two avenues to enter by, rather than three. Osivia fluttered soundlessly above the procession of warriors, notebook out, scribbling. Perhaps she was writing down everyone's name, recording the event like a journalist. Bob absently wondered if anyone who cared would ever read what she wrote.

Bob bumped into someone in the murk and muttered an apology. He nervously patted at the pipe in his pocket every thirty seconds, reminding himself it was still there, loaded and ready. He drank water from a skin provided by one of the Gasheera. He walked.

The further down the fissure he traveled, the more nervous he became. He felt great thumps and rumbles resounding through the earth beneath him. The Nexus was unquiet. The Gez Kar were stirring. Soon the shrieks of sherka and barking growls of the man-sized Gez Kar—karka, Kelael had called them—filtered over rock to reach his ears.

Kelael signaled for the procession to stop.

"*Sora Kelai the Tesera,*" called the old En'hari named Senaesen Eeno, "*you are required.*"

Bob saw a cherubic wind spirit flash briefly over the Tessaeshi as he pushed his way through the stoic Gasheera toward where Kelael waited at the rock wall that had once been the mouth of the fissure. Kelael met his eyes as he approached. They exchanged no words as Bob withdrew and lit the dragon pipe.

"*We are the claws of the spirits,*" intoned Kelael in Hari.

"*The spirits are our claws!*" called back the Gasheera in unison.

"*The spirits demand our blood,*" said Kelael.

"*Our blood is the spirit's blood!*" called the Gasheera.

"*We are the thrusting spears of the spirits.*"

"*The spirits are our thrusting spears!*"

BOB THE WIZARD

"We will die today."

"We will never die!"

"Our enemies are mighty."

"The spirits no know fear!"

"We are the arrow on the wind, the knife at the heart."

"Through us the spirits live! By our hands, our enemies are forgotten!"

"May the spirits guide our journeys."

The Gasheera responded to this last with a unanimous bellow.

Hands shaking, smoke trailing from his nostrils, Bob opened the fissure.

He was jostled and pushed out onto the grass as fifty Gasheera, led by Gorrelai and Senaesen Eeno, thrust into the Nexus grounds. They were still bellowing, clashing their weapons to their shields, roaring curses and entreaties to the spirits—a stampede of blue flesh, brown fur and leather, dull white ivory and bone. Bob followed Kelael eastward, skirting behind the crowd.

Off to the north was quite a sight. Skinner the Gurdun, scabbed and bruised and cut all over, stood battling the Gez Kar. They came at him in waves batted aside by hammer blows, dashes turned away by huge swatting arms. Had he been fighting all night? It seemed so.

Forr Ghaway stood back from the battle, apparently disinterested. The giant, crowned creature stood calmly between the two British buildings in the valley's northern half. He now intently watched the Gasheera as they charged toward the churning swarm of lizard creatures. And such a swarm it was. Looking upon it drained the blood from Bob's face. Hundreds of darting sherka, dozens of man-sized karka, and of course, the towering Forr Ghaway—a foe that appeared able to take on fifty Gasheera all by himself. Within the teeming horde, Bob saw a karka with twin fluttering torches strapped to its back—a fire shaman. This was suicide, the last stand of the En'harae. Everything Bob had been through, everything he'd learned, was all for nothing. They were all going to die.

"Sora Kelai," called Kelael. "Bob," he said, after getting no response.

Bob turned his head.

"Look, there."

In the distance, atop the ridge lining the mountains above and behind the eastern fissure, stood Galvidon, arms crossed, watching the arrival of the Gasheera with his black eyes.

"I see him," said Bob, and he and Kelael broke into a run, keeping along the eastern side of the valley. He held his hand over the pipe's bowl, allowing it to go out.

They slowed to a jog as they reached the eastern fissure. They were dangerously close to the mass of Gez Kar now, and a group of sherka cocked their heads and began to hop in their direction, snapping at the air. Shortly the scuttling creatures were joined by three karka, who rolled their shoulders and hissed and barked at each other in a thick, bestial language.

Kelael nocked an arrow in his bow as Bob popped a match to light against the jerkin.

"Keep moving," said Kelael. "We cannot allow them to prevent our advance."

They inched northward, the eastern fissure's mouth at their backs. Kelael shot a karka in the chest and Bob raised a wall of heavy earth that teetered and crashed upon a crowd of advancing sherka. One more arrow was loosed before the Gez Kar were upon them. To the west, Bob saw Skinner pick up a karka in one hand and hurl it toward Forr Ghaway. The limp, leathery carcass flew over sixty feet but still landed woefully short of the Lizard King, splattering and skidding on the rough ground. Forr Ghaway snorted disdainfully and did not advance.

Bob ducked and dodged. He blinded Gez Kar with earth, sucked some small sherka into the ground like it was quicksand, impaled countless enemies with shards of the mountain. Beside him, Kelael killed every scaled creature that came within the reach of his sword. The two of them pushed ever northward as they fought, closer to the divots that lead to the ridge upon which Galvidon stood.

BOB THE WIZARD

In the southwest, the Gasheera met the tide of teeth and claws. Though vastly outnumbered, they were fierce, competent, and cunning. They formed rings of fighters, their backs to each other, weapons outward. The rings slowly rotated, wading into the press of scaled bodies. Whenever a ring lost a member—for the Gasheera were not invulnerable—the others would immediately close the gap by moving closer together. Senaesen Eeno blasted the enemy with waves of flowing air. Even with their advantages, though, Bob could see the Gasheera would be overrun in a matter of minutes.

He stepped behind Kelael, who guarded him as he and Erto enacted a creative bit of magic. Bob thought of the animated statue of Erto he'd created to impress Skinner, and he willed the nearby earth to recreate the trick. But only one statue would not do.

Previously while using magic, Bob had felt as if he had an unlimited supply of energy to draw upon. The previous night, he'd been fatigued from both physical and astral exertion, but he never felt as if he'd reached a point where he could no longer engage in Astral Friction. However, after the fourth fifteen-foot Erto statue, he suddenly felt as if he'd reached into a well with a bucket and scraped the bottom. He knew then that if he made any more statues, he'd have nothing left with which to fight Galvidon. Four would have to do.

The statues formed near the mountainous valley walls, swirling into existence in a whirlwind of rocks and dirt. Their hollow eyes seemed to scowl as they began stomping toward the Gez Kar. Even as the statues plunged into the fray, Bob saw a handful of Gasheera fall.

"Galvidon is still a threat," said Kelael. The nearby Gez Kar were all dead.

"They're dying," said Bob, looking on in horror.

"Those buildings," Kelael pointed to the two British structures. "Are the guns in there?"

Bob nodded. "Guarded by Forr Ghaway."

"The Gez Kar do not simply help others for no reason. Galvidon has promised them something. Remove him, and Forr Ghaway can no longer get what he wants. He may simply leave."

"Allowing us access to the guns," said Bob quietly. "Even if all the Gasheera are dead."

"There is no greater purpose for a Gasheera than to die for the En'harae."

Bob glanced up to the ridge where Galvidon stood. He wasn't visible anymore, but Bob hadn't seen him fly away. He was up there, waiting. "I guess we keep on with the plan, then."

Kelael nodded. In the center of the valley, Skinner was down on one knee, sherka covering him like roaches. Senaesen Eeno battled the fire shaman. Only three wheels—each composed of a handful of Gasheera—remained. Bob caught a glimpse of green dreadlocks. Gorrelai still lived. But for how long?

"Come," said Kelael. "You have done all you can."

Another Gasheera fell. Bob tore his eyes away to follow Kelael to the mountainside, but a sudden sound caused him to snap his head back around.

It was a long, low trumpet blast, fanning its strident cry across the entire valley. It was followed by another. Then, another. The Gez Kar swiveled their leathery necks toward the western fissure. The sherka covering Skinner scattered away like frightened deer.

Then, out of the shadows of the western fissure, in a trample of oversized boots, came dozens of extremely tall humans. At the fore, clad in gold-filigreed breastplate, gauntlets and greaves, was Brumhilde, her long reddish hair in a tight ponytail, her spear Lady in one hand, a curved, ram's horn trumpet in the other.

The Niners had arrived.

BOB THE WIZARD

CHAPTER THIRTY-FIVE:
FACING THE DEMON

Now with thirty Niners and four giant dirt-statues with oversized heads to back them, the Gasheera's odds of survival—or even victory—increased dramatically. As the newcomers met the tide of scaley green, Skinner retreated to a section of mountain wall by the western fissure, sat down, and closed his eyes. He was too far away for Bob to tell if he was still breathing.

At the arrival of the Niners, Forr Ghaway took a single, thunderous step toward the battle. The giant shelled creature craned its neck to look back at the ridge where Galvidon waited, glanced back to the battle, then returned to his original position between the two buildings.

Bob saw Senaesen Eeno catch the fire shaman with a blast of air, sending the karka and his torches tumbling toward an approaching line of Niners. When the creature regained its feet, the metal edge of a bladed spear sliced through the air above its head, through the flames of the torches. Bob thought it was a miss—but then, seeming to plume out of the air between the torches, a writhing human-shaped fiery mass appeared, then exploded in a shockwave of coruscating, orange flame that blazed in concentric rings above the heads of the combatants. Bob realized he'd just witnessed the death of a fire spirit. The twin flames went out like snuffed candles and the shaman was quickly dispatched by a Niner's blade. Senaesen Eeno turned his attention to a nearby Erto statue, blasting sherka off its earthen back like a leaf-blower turned upon gnats. The Gasheera fell back and reformed into harassing lines, striking Gez Kar between the towering forms of the Niners. Brumhilde spun in a glinting, gold and silver whirlwind, Lady delivering swift death to all in her path. Bob saw one of his statues lift two karka off the ground—one in each clumpy hand—and smash their heads together.

Bob shook himself, turned to face Kelael. The En'hari was just as mesmerized by the carnage as he'd just been. "Kel," he said. His voice was husky and raw, as if he'd been shouting.

Kelael snapped his attention to Bob. "Yes. Yes, of course."

They began moving toward the ladder of divots that lead up the northeastern wall of the hexagonal valley. As they walked, Bob carefully packed the dragon pipe with a fresh bowl. He saw Forr Ghaway, now only about fifty yards away, eying them with a single, slitted pupil. The Lizard King watched, unmoving.

"Why is he just standing there? Its creeping me out."

"Do you remember what Bernard said about the Gurdun? That they value strength, but do not measure it in physical power? Well, the Gez Kar are *only* concerned with physical power. This is why Forr Ghaway is their king. None can defeat him. I think he waits, not just because Galvidon has assigned him the task of guarding the weapons, but also because he wishes to see who will come out on top in this conflict. If we defeat Galvidon, he will see Galvidon as weak, and therefore unable to follow through on his promises, even if he still lives."

"So, Forr Ghaway really will just leave if we win, then?"

Kelael shrugged as they reached the mountain wall. "Perhaps. I am just guessing, Sora Kelai. There is always a chance that we will defeat Galvidon only for Forr Ghaway to eat us."

Bob glanced back at the shelled Lizard King, who still watched them with his cold, inhuman stare. "Right."

Kelael reached for the lowest divot.

"Wait," said Bob. He drew a match across the front of his jerkin and lit the pipe with a series of puffs. He took a step toward Kelael so that they stood side by side next to the wall. Streamers of smoke exited his nostrils. The earth at their feet shivered, and they began to ascend. Kelael gripped Bob's arm for balance. Bob and Erto had made an earthen elevator—a round platform of earth and rock that attached to the mountain wall even as it slid upward along its face.

Bob looked directly upward. A little head watched their ascent from the lip of the ridge. For a moment, Bob thought it was Galvidon, but it was just Erto, his round, hollow, unblinking eyes upon them as they rose higher and higher above the ground.

This particular section of ridge seemed to be exceptionally high up. Bob judged it to be equivalent in height to the roof of a five-story building. Perhaps that was why Galvidon had chosen it to be the site of the confrontation—a fall from this height would be deadly to Bob or Kelael, whereas if Galvidon fell, he could simply fly to safety.

"Kel?"

"Yes, Bob?"

"May the spirits guide our journeys."

"As you say, my friend."

Erto disappeared again. Kelael made sure his buckler was tightly strapped to his forearm, then drew his sword. The lip of the ridge grew closer. Closer. Now that the moment had arrived, Bob felt a deadly calm fall over him. Unlike his previous confrontations with Galvidon, in which he'd been twisted up with rage, he now felt only an icy determination. Anna's vicious shadow was silent. He thought maybe she was gone.

They reached the ridge. It was about fifteen feet deep, ending in sheer mountain along its northern edge. It stretched in a lazy curve for the entire length of the Nexus's northeastern wall, even continuing several hundred feet eastward to overlook a section of the eastern fissure. The stone ground was almost perfectly flat, though dust, pebbles, and the occasional large rocks were scattered along its surface. Galvidon stood, back to the wall, helmet retracted, a gleaming black knife in each hand. The left side of his face was marred with red welts where shards of the Hub Keystone had struck. As soon as Bob and Kelael stepped off the earthen elevator, it crumbled to dust behind them.

"Bob the Wizard," drawled Galvidon. "I see you've returned to rebuild my Keystone."

Bob puffed casually on the pipe as Kelael inched around to his flank.

"I see you're still a little bitch."

Galvidon's black eyes gleamed with subtle anger. Bob Smiled.

"Tell me, Vigilant, do you miss your family? I still do not remember them, but I'm sure they were ever so sweet."

The rock of the ridge's floor stretched, clamping down upon the Gray Man's feet. Immediately, there was a hissing rush of sound as Galvidon activated his flying boots. The rock manacles resisted, cracking. Kelael struck at Galvidon with a swift overhand slash. The black helmet appeared, and Galvidon twisted his shoulders. The sword glanced off a section of interlocking armor by an elbow. The rock manacles began to glow red hot.

Galvidon struck out at Kelael with a black knife in reverse grip but fell short as the En'hari simply backed up a step. Bob and Erto threw stone lances at the Gray Man, but they clattered against his armor, and the clamping rock at his feet finally split. Galvidon spiraled into the air, hovering just above the ground. A hand of stone the size of a parasol reached out from the mountain wall to grasp him, but he spun away.

The ridge became a maelstrom of frenetic combat. Galvidon rocketed around into attacks, dodges, parries. Kelael landed strike after strike on the black armor. Each time the gleaming plate held, chipping tiny flakes off the En'hari's sword. Bob struggled to entangle Galvidon with stone hands, to pelt him with projectiles. The armor showed wear, but it was slight. It took a beating from every angle, yet Galvidon fought on, seemingly at full strength. Bob began to feel his cold calm begin to strip away, replaced, heartbeat by heartbeat, by a familiar, smoldering rage. He screamed and a torrent of dust and pebbles rushed over Galvidon. The Gray Man teetered. Kelael's sword came down, perfectly aimed at the joint where helmet met neck armor. It struck true, clean and strong enough to have decapitated any unarmored creature. The blade shattered.

Kelael dropped backward into a roll, and Galvidon pounced, daggers plunging down at the En'hari like fangs. Kelael came out of the roll into a sidestep, and the knives struck stone. A leather boot crushed down upon Galvidon's right hand. Bob was preparing an assault on Galvidon's back when a static shock erupted through his body. It felt like he'd stuck a fork in an electrical socket. His hands seized, dropping the pipe. He managed to turn onto his back as he collapsed.

Just behind where he'd been standing was a floating silver orb the size of a basketball. Bob could see his distorted reflection on its surface. It lowered toward him, and the air gathered with intensity as, Bob knew, it prepared another attack. Bob willed his muscles to move, but they refused to unclench. The orb floated closer, a warbling charge gathering along it surface.

And then Osivia was there. She swooped out of the air to hover just above the orb, rubbing her hands together. A drop of white light fell onto the top of the orb, landing with a small patter. There was a huge popping sound and flash of electric discharge, then the orb fell to the ground at Bob's feet with a thud, smoking.

"Oops!" lamented Osivia, one hand to her mouth. Then she was gone.

Bob rolled onto his hands and knees, breathing hard. The scuffles and grunts of Galvidon and Kelael pressed on his ears. He pushed himself up. The pipe... where was the pipe?

Bob looked up in time to see Kelael's foot kick a black dagger along the ridge floor and right off the edge, where it disappeared beyond the lethal drop. Galvidon's right hand seemed to be crippled. He fought with his left, slashing in tight circles with the remaining dagger. Kelael, unarmed but for a tattered buckler, kept at a distance, ducking away from each attack, waiting for an opening. Bob made it to his feet, spotted the pipe... only to see Galvidon's armored foot kick it off the side of the ridge, just as Kelael had done to the dagger.

Bob tested his connection with Erto. It felt tenuous, strained. He glanced out into the valley. The battle raged on. He saw one of the earthen statues spontaneously begin to crumble.

Beside him, Galvidon overextended into a long stab. Kelael stepped aside, placed his right hand at Galvidon's wrist, then stepped right up next to him like they were dance partners, left hand gripping the Gray Man's left shoulder. Then Kelael twisted, using Galvidon's own momentum against him. Galvidon's arm buckled, elbow bending, knife-wielding fist turned inexorably to point at his own body. Guided by Kelael's hand, Galvidon stabbed himself in the ribs. The black dagger slid right through the black armor. Kelael stepped away. It had all happened in the space of a heartbeat.

Draining the bottom of his well of power, Bob gathered stone around his fists, creating a pair of jagged gloves. He stepped toward Galvidon, slamming a punch into the black helmet. Galvidon staggered but pulled the knife free of his side, slashing at Kelael, who once again maintained distance, biding his time. Blood seeped from the wound in the Gray Man's left side. Bob closed in swinging.

But Galvidon easily blocked his blows. A heavy gray fist cracked Bob in the cheek. He stumbled back, dazed. Undeterred, Bob attacked again. Kelael stepped behind Galvidon.

This time, Bob found his arm knocked away. A spike of pain shot through his right side as the remaining dagger slammed into the space between his shoulder blade and collar bone. He cried out, falling backward. The stone knuckles dissolved around his hands.

Kelael used Galvidon's attack as an opportunity. He threw his body into a tackle, attempting to push the Gray Man toward the edge of the ridge. But Galvidon had anticipated this. He spun as the En'hari collided with him, deflecting the weight. Kelael slammed into the rocky ground. Bob's feet scrabbled on dust and pebbles as he attempted to get his back to the wall. He gripped the dagger in his shoulder with his left hand, gathering the willpower to pull it out.

"Leave it in," said Osivia from somewhere above him. "The blade is plugging the wound. If you take it out, it will bleed a lot more."

Moaning, Bob's hand dropped from the dagger's hilt.

Galvidon and Kelael had squared off. Kelael had shed the ruined buckler. The two warriors circled each other. Kelael refused to make the first move. Galvidon lashed out with his uninjured hand. Missed. Lashed out again. Missed again. He kicked. Suddenly Kelael was right up next to him again, pressing his knee into the side of Galvidon's own bent knee, grabbing Galvidon's shoulders and heaving. The Gray Man lost his balance, tumbled. Kelael attempted to stomp on the uninjured left hand. Missed. Galvidon grabbed his ankle, tossed him onto his back.

Kelael rolled back to his shoulders and sprung onto his feet, but

BOB THE WIZARD

Galvidon did not relent. A gray fist connected with Kelael's stomach. Kelael doubled over, forward, sidestepped another strike. Caught a slam from an armored elbow in the side of head. Reeled. A thick, black-armored leg shot out like a piston. Connected with a leather-clad chest. Kelael flew backward. Outward. Over the edge of the drop. Bob caught a horrible look of surprise on the En'hari's face just before gravity gained its implacable grip. Kelael plummeted out of sight.

Slowly, Galvidon turned to face Bob. The black helmet retracted as he methodically marched to where Bob sat against the mountain wall. Waves of pain rolled across him from the knife in his right shoulder. Galvidon's gray face glistened with sweat. The livid pock marks on his face gleamed wetly. His expression was flat, emotionless.

"A worthy test that God has placed before me," said the Gray Man. His heavy, sheathed feet crunched upon gravel as he approached.

That old rage still smoldered in Bob. He tried to say something. Only ragged breaths escaped his lips. Galvidon stood over him.

"Now, Bob the Wizard, you will rebuild the Hub Keystone."

Bob managed to spit in Galvidon's general direction.

"Very well." Galvidon reached to his belt and withdrew a small object. It was a little black cylinder. Bob recognized it as the device he'd been tortured with in Oath Keep's dungeon. Galvidon held it up lightly in his hand—only for it to be plucked away by Osivia. She zipped toward the valley, the little device dangling from her double-handed grip. Galvidon snarled. The blue jets erupted as he began to hover, eyeing Osivia's path through the air. Then, he seemed to think better of it, and landed once more. "No matter," he said calmly. "I do not need a machine to cause you pain."

Bob came home from work in his truck. Went to check the mail.

Galvidon knelt. Gripped the hilt of the dagger in Bob's shoulder. Twisted.

The front door to the house was standing open.

Bob cried out in pain, lashing out with his arms. They connected with dense armor. More pain.

He pushed the door open the rest of the way. The mail fell from his hands onto the floor.

"Why do you resist me? Do you not see, Vigilant? My will is the Order's will. And the Order's will, is God's will." He relented his grip on the knife. "I shall have plenty of time to make you obey."

Something was wrong. Someone was here. Someone—oh God, what is that creature?

"For now, I believe I will take your Astral Key." He reached to Bob's chest, patted around. Felt his neck for a chain. Rifled through his pockets, pulling out matches, a pouch of tobacco. There was nothing else.

There they were. Anna and Daniel. On the couch. He was only nine.

"Where is it?" hissed Galvidon. "Where—" His black eyes widened with realization. Too late.

A wiry, blue forearm wrapped around Galvidon's forehead. A blue fist plunged a gleaming, black dagger into Galvidon's throat, then drew it across his neck in one swift motion. A sheet of hot blood sprayed over Bob's neck and chest, but he did not blink, did not flinch. He was unable, in that moment, to feel triumph, or relief. He was filled only with his fury, throbbing, seemingly bottomless.

Galvidon staggered backward, gripping his bleeding throat. Kelael stepped away, allowing him room. Adrenaline drenching his nerves, Bob surged to his feet straight at Galvidon. He looked in the Gray Man's eyes and saw fear. "Where is God now?" demanded Bob.

Galvidon tried to speak. More blood shot from the deep red line at his neck. He was struggling to stand. Bob, ignoring his own pain, grabbed Galvidon by the shoulders and shook him. "Where is He?!" he screamed.

Galvidon fell, pitching forward into Bob. Bob collapsed onto his back. "Where are you?" he asked God. The sun was at a perfect apex, a perfect circle in a perfectly blue sky. "Where were you?"

He repeated the question in a wrenching, guttural bellow that spread over the valley, echoing in the ears of every living creature in the Nexus.

Where were you?

BOB THE WIZARD

Then Kelael was standing over him, his silhouette blotting the sun, silently holding out a helping hand. The Gatekey dangled from a chain around his neck. The little green meter was depleted.

"Ready?" Osivia's voice pierced through Bob's fitful sleep. "Now!"

There was a slicing sensation in his right shoulder. The pain brought him fully awake, gasping. Kelael was pressing a clean rag to his wound.

"Do not move!" barked the En'hari.

Bob forced himself to be still. Osivia fluttered over him. There was a white glow. A warm sensation.

"Hold it for about five minutes," she said. "After that, he should be okay to walk on his own."

Bob blinked up at Kelael as the Gasheera pressed the rag to the place where Galvidon's dagger had just been lodged. "What… how long was I out?"

"Only a few minutes, Sora Kelai."

"Galvidon, he's…"

Kelael nodded. "Quite dead, thank the spirits."

Bob closed his eyes. "Thank you," he whispered, completely without irony. When he opened his eyes again Kelael was smirking down at him.

"Tell me, Bob, have you converted to the En'hari religion?" Golden eyes glittered with amusement.

"At this point, Kel, I don't know what to believe."

"Ah, so you are the same then."

Bob started to chuckle, but it hurt. "Well… I got a few more friends than I used to."

"Really?" Kelael made a show of looking around. "Where?"

Bob and Kelael stood at the point where the northeastern and northwestern ridges met. Below, between the two British buildings, Forr Ghaway stood with his domelike back to them. The remainder of the Gez Kar swarm now cowered at his feet. Beyond, to the southwest, the combined forces of the Gasheera and the Niners were consolidating. Against a mountain wall by the mouth of the western fissure lay Skinner, apparently asleep, scratching his nose. The Erto statues had all disintegrated.

"Ready?" asked Kelael.

"As I'll ever be." They bent down. Bob grabbed the arms of Galvidon's corpse, while Kelael grabbed the legs. "Oh, fuck me, he's heavy." They swung once and heaved. Bob cupped a hand to his mouth and shouted, "Hey! Forr Ghaway!"

The Lizard King turned toward him as Galvidon's body plummeted through the air. Bob watched it fall. It tumbled under the weight of the armor. The corpse landed head-first on a huge boulder. Blood and brains exploded outward, splattering the rocks with a starburst of gore.

Kelael winced and grunted sympathetically.

"Fuckin' A," said Bob, grinning.

Forr Ghaway stared at the crumpled, smashed corpse of Galvidon. He snorted and turned away, lifting his head. He produced a rhythmic, growling roar. Was he laughing? The giant, shelled creature then swung its round head eastward. For a moment, he seemed to stare at the eastern fissure.

The Lizard King began to trundle away. *Boom. Boom. Boom.*

The limping remnants of the Gez Kar followed. In the southwest, the Gasheera and the Niners backed into a defensive position, eyes on the procession of lizard creatures. The valley watched, thunderous footstep by thunderous footstep, as Forr Ghaway led the Gez Kar all the way to the southeastern fissure, where finally the Lizard King, and his unruly children, disappeared into the shadows.

Bob reached the lowest divot on the mountain wall and finally hopped to the ground. Kelael was right behind him, Galvidon's twin daggers in his belt.

Bob eyed the knives. "So, what exactly happened, Kel?"

Kelael shrugged. "As I was falling, I remembered the Gatekey. I had little time, so I used it to appear on the ground, right over there." He pointed to a grassy section of the valley just under the drop from the ridge. "When I arrived, I was pleasantly surprised to find the dagger I had just kicked off the edge. The rest should be obvious." He cleared his throat. "Anyway, Axiis is dead. Galvidon is dead. Forr Ghaway is gone. Now we can finally get into those buildings."

"I could really use some water," said Bob, hands on his knees. He felt light-headed.

"Bob!" It was Osivia. She came swirling out of the air.

Bob recognized the look on her face. "Okay," he said, exasperated. "What now?"

"They're coming! No... they're here!" she sounded frightened. "They're here, Bob!"

"Who?" demanded Kelael, suddenly alert. "Who is here, faerie?"

Osivia flashed with bright red light. "The Engorians! From the eastern fissure! Oh, Bob, its Mannix!"

CHAPTER THIRTY-SIX:
GATES

"Mannix?!" Surprise and anger were evident in Kelael's features. He glared at Bob. "Mannix is... still alive?"

"About that—"

"Why is he still alive, Bob?" There was a dangerous edge to Kelael's voice.

Exhausted, Bob sighed. "It didn't seem right to kill him, at the time."

"Didn't seem—" Kelael grabbed a handful of Bob's collar and shouted in his face. "He enslaved Torael, Bob!"

Bob provided no resistance to being accosted. He offered Kelael a flat stare. "Little more complex than that. He didn't personally put the chains on your brother."

Growling, Kelael released his grip. "No, he just gladly held them. It seems you made a mistake, Sora Kelai. It seems that mistake may cost us dearly."

"Look." Bob held up his hands in a placating gesture. "I know you're mad." He glanced at the nearby concrete buildings. "But I think I know something that will cheer you up." He tried a tentative smile.

Kelael followed his gaze and sighed. "As you say."

"Osivia, are Brumhilde and Gorrelai still alive?"

"Last time I checked."

"Good. Can you do me a couple favors?"

"Seems likely," replied the faerie, still sounding worried.

"Go tell them what's going on. Get somebody to bring me some water. And then see if you can find my pipe."

"Got it." She began to hover away.

"Oh, and Osivia?"

She stopped. "Yes?"

"For God's sake, wake up Skinner."

Bob and Kelael approached the concrete buildings. The one further west was smaller, about the size of a house in the suburbs. Along its weathered front was the faded, colorless semblance of a carved British Flag. There was a rectangular slab of concrete, barely visible in the encroaching grass, that stretched from this western building southward along the ground. Bob could almost see the rows of camouflaged tents that would have been there about a hundred years previous.

The eastern building was much larger. It was a long, rectangular, windowless structure with a curved roof of corrugated metal. A large pair of steel loading-doors on its western face was the only entrance. To Bob's eye, it was clearly a warehouse—if there were crates of firearms here, they had to be in this building.

As they arrived at the steel doors, Bob held out a hand to Kelael. "The Gatekey, if you please, sir," he said with mock-formality.

Kelael, still scowling, slowly removed the Gatekey from his neck and then slapped it into Bob's outstretched hand.

Bob approached the thick loading-doors and tried the handle. It creaked and swung ninety degrees, but the doors wouldn't budge. There were two keyholes in the square metal frame that held the handle. Bob wiped powdery rust on his pantleg.

"Will you teleport inside?" asked Kelael.

Bob shook his head. "Too dangerous. I can't see in." He held up the Gatekey to inspect the green meter. Though Kelael's jumps had drained it, it had already begun to refill. It wasn't much, but it should be enough for what Bob had in mind. "However, there is one more trick I know this puppy can do."

He stepped to the locks, set the Gatekey against the metal handle-frame, and pushed the appropriate button. There were two heavy clicks in quick succession from inside the metal of the doors. Bob reached out to the handle, twisted, pushed. The doors swung inward with a deep shriek. Rust rained down in a flaky powder. The air inside was dry and cool.

Bob hesitated in the doorway as his eyes attempted to adjust to the gloom. Kelael pushed past him impatiently. Bob saw him withdraw a black knife from his belt. The room came into dim focus. It was a warehouse, alright—a single, wide room that stretched the entire fifty-foot length of the building. Along its sides were row upon row of wooden shelves, supported by rusted steel scaffolding. Upon the shelves were stacked rectangular wooden crates, each identical to those from which the Small Magazine Lee-Enfield Mk. III's had been taken. At a glance, Bob estimated the warehouse contained roughly two hundred and fifty firearms. Not an impressive arsenal by modern-Earth standards. But for Hub, it was a veritable treasure trove.

Kelael jammed the knife into the seam in a crate's lid and pried it open. He tossed aside handfuls of hay, reached inside, and pulled out a rifle. He held it in both hands for a moment, drinking it in with his eyes.

"Quickly now, Sora Kelai. Show me how it works."

Bob and Kelael made their way toward the center of the hexagonal valley, rifles on their shoulders. Whinnies of horses and the clop of their hooves floated out of the eastern fissure to Bob's ears. He realized vaguely that the fissures must act as a sound amplifier, carrying the sounds of those approaching into the valley well ahead of their arrival. Gorrelai and Brumhilde awaited just east of the central dais, accompanied by Osivia, Senaesen Eeno, and a sleepy-eyed Skinner. Only a few yards behind them were the remaining Gasheera and Niners. It seemed the Niners had been relatively unscathed, as twenty-four remained alive and standing. The Gasheera had not fared as well. Only thirteen of them, including Gorrelai, remained. Everyone, barring the faerie, was covered in gore, injuries, dirt, and sweat. Skinner looked especially bad—like he'd been tossed in a woodchipper and somehow come out the other side whole.

Gorrelai whooped at the sight of Bob and Kelael carrying guns. Brumhilde leaned upon Lady, bearing a look of deep concern.

"Ah," rumbled Skinner, eying them with the unburned side of his face. "Tell me, Rude Bob, Little Gasheera, did you squash the gray insect?"

Bob cleared his throat. "Kelael slit his throat. Then we tossed his corpse off the ridge, and his skull exploded when it struck the rocks." He offered the Gurdun a wan smile.

Skinner's half-destroyed face split into a wide grin. It was truly ghastly. Bob had to stop himself from taking a step back.

"Wonderful! Congratulations on your victory, Rude Bob! And also, it is nice to see you in such a polite mood!"

Bob found himself grinning. "Tell me, Skinner, were you fighting the Gez Kar all night?"

Skinner chuckled. "Nearly, my rude friend, nearly. I took a small break for a few hours. They would not follow me into the western fissure, it seems. I wished to face Forr Ghaway, for what a feat defeating such a one would be! Alas, he judged himself too magnificent a foe, even for me. Perhaps, one day…" He looked off wistfully toward the fissure down which the Gez Kar had fled.

"Look on the bright side," said Bob. "At least you got to fight the dragon."

"Excuse me, aye?" said Brumhilde. "I hate to interrupt this lovely cultural exchange, but we've got more company."

The sounds of the Engorian's mounts had been joined by the stomping of booted feet, the clank of armor, the murmur of conversation.

One of the Gasheera—a young, fit En'hari—came jogging up from the southwestern fissure. Fourteen, Bob amended. Fourteen Gasheera had survived. The young En'hari stopped right next to Bob, dropped to one knee, bowed his head, and held up a waterskin. "Your water, Tesera," he said in a thick accent.

"Thanks" said Bob, taking the water. "But don't kneel to me. It's weird."

"*Gaeren, in formation,*" murmured Gorrelai in Hari. The young Gasheera hurried to obey.

"Here they come," said Brumhilde.

The Engorians began to file out of the eastern fissure. First came dozens of lightly armored archers. They dashed to form a series of lines as a group of men on horses cantered into the valley behind them. Most of the mounted men were blond. Bob drank deeply from the waterskin as he studied the newcomers.

Kelael set the butt of the rifle to his shoulder and took aim.

"Woah there, cowboy," said Bob. "Those archers aren't drawing their bows."

"You would wait for them to begin shooting?" Kelael asked tersely.

"We only have ten bullets each. There's like a hundred of them. You can't shoot them all. Besides, look at them. They don't look eager to fight."

The archers had completed organizing into three rows. Mounted men in black and white armor paced behind them. Bob noticed that the black and white of Swearington was everywhere on the Engorian's adornments. The green capes—those bearing the color of Tortellan—were nowhere to be seen. The fist of Swearington fluttered from their banners. No other iconography was present.

Behind the riders came almost a dozen wagons, which pulled up behind the archers, next to the mountain wall. One of the mounted men shouted a command, and as one, the archers stood at attention, bows propped at their sides. Kelael growled.

"*Prepare to charge,*" called Gorrelai over his shoulder. Among the Gasheera and Niners, weapons were drawn, armor was tightened.

BOB THE WIZARD

Sighing, Bob set the rifle-butt to his shoulder. He hoped he didn't have to fire it. It would probably only take one shot to reopen the wound where Galvidon had stabbed him.

A single, blond rider broke away from the gathered Engorians and trotted casually toward Bob and his retinue. The man held his head high, his back straight. He slowed as he approached and halted a few yards away.

He seemed to stare past them as he announced loudly, "The honorable and majestic Fulton Mannix, King of Engoria, requests an audience with a representative of the elves." His eyes flicked to Bob. "Furthermore, upon seeing Bob the Wizard, the honorable and majestic Fulton Mannix, King of Engoria, requests that said wizard accompany such a representative. He gladly awaits you for an audience. All who approach will leave their weapons or be destroyed. Hail the Sun! Hail Engoria! Hail King Mannix!"

Having made his announcement, the rider wheeled to trot back to the line of archers. Bob scanned the blonde riders, trying to pick out Mannix, but they were too far away.

"King?" Bob wondered aloud.

"King?" demanded Kelael.

Gorrelai looked thoughtful. *"Do you not remember? Swearington's forces, they destroyed the Koreka, but then headed south..."*

"To Tortellan," finished Bob.

"Mannix has taken the crown from Flaire?" asked Kelael, incredulous.

"Isn't this good news?" asked Brumhilde. "After all, hard to get a worse king than Martimus, aye?"

"Maybe," said Bob.

"One human king is as good as another," grated Kelael.

"Oh, really?" threw back Bob. "What about Harold?"

"He does not count," said Kelael defensively.

"Why? Because he's only part human? So, you only hate him part-ways?"

"This is not the time!" declared Brumhilde, stepping between them. "Thick headed bastards, the both of you."

Skinner watched the entire exchange in silence.

Bob sighed. "Alright. Kel, Brum, Senaesen Eeno, and Osivia, you're with me. Everyone else watch carefully. If the shit hits the fan, book it."

Gorrelai and Brumhilde were staring at him in confusion.

Bob cleared his throat. "If they attack us, run away."

"*Leave you to die?*" demanded Gorrelai.

"Better than dying yourselves."

"*Only just, Sora Kelai.*"

Bob handed his rifle to Gaeren the Gasheera, who accepted it with wide eyes.

"This end kills," said Bob, indicating the barrel. "Don't point it at anybody."

Gaeren nodded in stunned silence.

Not looking back, Bob strode toward the gathered Engorians. After a few strides, he heard the others fall in behind him.

As they approached the line of archers, a man behind the line dismounted and pushed his way to the fore. He was resplendent in filigreed black and white armor. His blond beard was perfectly cropped, and his familiar smirk was just as unbearable as it had always been. Fulton Mannix stepped forward, a simple crown of dark brown wood upon his head.

"Nice crown," said Bob.

"Nice giant," replied Mannix, eying the crowd around the central dais.

"How's your face?"

"Much better, thank you. How's your inflated sense of righteous

BOB THE WIZARD

superiority?"

"Diminished."

"What do you want, Mannix?" interjected Kelael. "Why are you here?"

"And how," added Bob, "did you manage to become king of Engoria?"

Mannix sighed, bringing a finger to his chin in exaggerated contemplation. "Questions, questions. You make bold demands of a king with two hundred men at his back."

"*Shall I kill him?*" asked Senaesen Eeno quietly in Hari.

Kelael tossed a reply over his shoulder. "*Not yet, Uncle.*"

Mannix moved suspicious eyes between the two En'harae, then continued to address Bob. "However, I find myself lacking recently in amusing conversation. I shall answer your questions. Then, I shall make a proposal. Since I believe you to be wise, Bob the Wizard, I think you will accept. Now, where to begin… Oh, I know, I'll begin with the destruction of your hidden base."

Bob could feel the hatred radiating from Kelael.

"Our mutual friend, Galvidon, discovered the location of said base using a fascinating flying-machine. I've never before seen its like. Anyway, this flying, silver orb arrived at Oath Keep and revealed to me, in the voice of its owner, the location of the invisible base within Shepherd's Forest. As you undoubtedly know, I sent my remaining forces to that location just before your own timely arrival at the keep. My men then joined with sections of Lighton's forces to the north of Tortellan, to continue a plan set in motion long before your arrival to our great kingdom, Bob the Wizard—the removal and replacement of Martimus Flaire.

"Most of Tortellan's forces were, and still are, inside the Borders of En'hirin. The city's defenses were paltry. Why wouldn't they be? The elves have been mostly defeated, their country occupied. Martimus certainly didn't see us coming." He paused to flash a magnanimous grin. "Or rather, he didn't see Archlector Stephen Carosel coming. Since then, Stephen gladly holds the title of Chief Counselor to the King, as he occupies Tortellan in my name. A much more fitting crown than this awaits me there.

"Anyway, two events of significant import occurred thereafter. The first was the Gez Kar entering Engoria. For weeks, they've been sending small armies across the border to test our defenses. Yesterday, I received word that Swearington just barely repelled an attack. The nerve! I never thought I'd have to order the Darkhairs to rebuild the moat, but here we are. I warned Flaire against making deals with the lizards, but he was characteristically deaf to reason.

"The second event was the arrival of our mutual friend's orb in Tortellan. No doubt it was meant to speak with Flaire. However, it instead found Chief Counselor Carosel. Stephen, deliciously devious man that he is, pretended as though Martimus were off hunting to the south, in Turtle Forest. It seems Galvidon wished the former king to send forces to the Nexus in order to help him secure advanced weapons for the armies of Engoria. According to Stephen, Galvidon had become aware that several guns on the way to Flaire were intercepted mid-transport by the elf rebels. Furthermore, he knew the rebellion had acquired information as to his plans. He did, after all, send the orb to follow a spy of some kind, and that is how he discovered the location of your hidden base. For these reasons, our mutual friend was convinced that the En'harae would send an army to the Nexus in order to disrupt his plans and take the guns for themselves. It appears he was correct about that. Anyway, Carosel informed the orb—and thus our mutual friend—that relief forces would be forthcoming. The Chief Counselor then immediately dispatched a messenger to Swearington to inform me of this turn of events.

"Well, having held a gun in my hand, I could hardly contain my excitement. The Gez Kar could not hope to defeat us if we possessed such weapons. I gathered some of the men coming in from the eastern cities and set off myself. Easy enough, I thought, to arrive at the Nexus, allow Galvidon to defeat the guardian, then kill the pesky, gray bastard and take the guns. Imagine my surprise to find, when I arrived, not only a gathering of elves and half-giants, but my old friend Bob the Wizard, here in the Nexus. Tell me, am I to conclude that Axiis has been defeated?"

Bob nodded.

"And Galvidon?"

"Dead as shit," replied Bob.

BOB THE WIZARD

Mannix's grinned. "Excellent! I am almost to my proposal. Bear with me for a moment longer, if you please. It has occurred to me on more than one occasion that the status quo established by Flaire's betrayal of the En'harae has become untenable. Engoria grew to such heights because we were successful merchants. Honestly, enslaving potential customers is simply bad for business. For this reason, I have released all the slaves in the Swearington Mines."

Kelael released an audible gasp.

Mannix's eyes shone with excitement. "Oh yes, elf. Your brothers and sisters are free. At least, several hundred of them. There are many thousands of slaves in the other cities. However, I am prepared to use my newfound power to have them released."

"And what would you ask in return for such... *generosity*?" Kelael's final word was dripping with sarcasm.

"I'm glad we understand each other, Mr. Elf. First, I ask that we sign a treaty, here and now, that I have prepared. The terms are simple. Engoria releases all En'hari slaves, and our armies within En'hirin will be repurposed for the defense of both our countries. The war between us ends. Yet, the war with the Gez Kar continues. Our peoples, elf—yours and mine—henceforth will be allies, as we swore to each other so long ago. We will renew the alliance that was shattered by Flaire's betrayal. And...we will take the guns."

Kelael burst out laughing, a rueful sound. "You are dreaming, human!"

"*Is he saying what I think he is saying?*" asked Senaesen Eeno.

Bob answered, knowing the Gatekey would translate for him. "He freed a bunch of the slaves. He offers to free the rest and end the occupation in exchange for an alliance against the Gez Kar, and possession of the guns."

The shaman's eyes were wide as he swung a look on Kelael. "*What are you waiting for, you thick-headed warrior! Accept! Accept!*"

"No," said Kelael flatly. "We keep the guns." He and Mannix stared at each other for a long moment.

"Okay," said Bob, "we split them. Fifty-fifty. Both sides get guns, the

En'harae get their freedom, and the Engorians get their allies against the Gez Kar."

Mannix and Kelael continued to stare at each other.

Mannix's smirk was unwavering. He cleared his throat. "Agreed."

Kelael looked about ready to burst.

"*Accept*," repeated Senaesen Eeno softly. "*Think of the lives you will save with but a single word.*"

Brumhilde watched with her arms crossed. Osivia hovered nervously.

Kelael held out a hand to Mannix. "Agreed."

The new King of Engoria grinned and shook. "Excellent!" He turned his head and bellowed a command. The Lighthair that had delivered Mannix's call to parley pushed his way forward, a thick parchment dangling from one hand. "Now," said Mannix, "we sign a historic treaty. Then, my new friends, we shall all enjoy a much-needed rest. I've brought wine!" He turned to Brumhilde, craning his neck upward. "Tell me, my lady, are all women in your village so beautiful?"

Brumhilde's lip curled into a grimace of disgust.

Bob volunteered to go with the group assigned to retrieve the camping supplies from the southwestern fissure. Brumhilde, Gorrelai, and Kelael had all stayed behind to oversee the removal of the guns from the warehouse. Mannix had agreed to allow the En'harae several of his wagons in order to transport their own half of the weapons. Skinner loped slowly beside Bob, pausing after every step in order to not overtake him.

"Skinner, are you okay? You're very... wounded."

"I am honored by your worry, Rude Bob, but it is for naught. We Gurdun have mighty constitutions. I will heal, in time."

"Glad to hear it."

"I shall return to the wilds now," declared the Gurdun tiredly. "For one thing, I left all my knives at a camp to the northwest. For another, proximity to so many rude individuals tries my patience. Though I admit, you have somewhat changed my view of rude behavior."

"Oh?"

"Yes. There is an honorable man in you somewhere, that much is clear to me. Perhaps the teachings of my people are slightly too harsh on those who do not think as we do."

"Maybe. Or maybe its everyone else who's wrong. You value honesty. Very few humans know how to do that."

"Perhaps, Rude Bob, perhaps. Though I know now, humans can learn to be honest. Bernard of Montana, for example. And to a lesser extent, yourself. Perhaps most humans do not even realize how dishonest they are being. It is difficult to place judgement upon those who know not what they do. You have given me much to contemplate, and for that, I thank you."

"It was an honor to meet you, Skinner of the Gurdun."

"And you, Bob the Wizard of Texas. And you."

The giant easily quickened his pace and advanced in utter silence, melding into the shadows of the fissure. Then, like an unspoken word, he was gone.

⸻

Two camps were erected in the valley—the En'harae and the Niners on the western side, the Engorians on the eastern. Everyone set about dragging the corpses of the Gez Kar into the southeastern fissure. At some point, Osivia approached with Bob's dragon pipe, dropping it into his hands with a relieved huff. Bob smoked his first bowl of tobacco since Galvidon's death. Everything, he realized, was new. Some kind of internal pressure that had been propelling him for the last few years was gone. In a sense, he was more free than he'd ever been.

He had these thoughts as he sealed the mouth of the southeastern fissure, entombing the bodies of the Gez Kar. He was free of Galvidon, yes, but not free. He was still bound by the future, obligated to push on. He still had to retrieve **R**'s memories. Still had to find a way to take down the Order of Tag Nah. Hub would never be safe until the Order was defeated.

Bob and Erto made graves for the fallen En'harae and Niners. Bob could not stand a funeral. Not right now. As Kelael led the funeral rites, the sky reddening with sunset, Bob approached Galvidon's battered corpse at the northern peak of the hexagon. For long moments he stood, staring down at the dead form of the thing that had killed Anna and Daniel.

He sat down next to the body. He curled his arms around his legs, an unconsciously childlike posture. He stared at Galvidon's shattered skull, his mangled right hand, his blood-splattered armor. Bob wept tears of joy. Then, he just wept.

At some point, Erto arrived on his little brown legs. The sun had gone down, but the valley was alight with dozens of campfires.

Bob hastily wiped his eyes, cleared his throat, and stood. "I guess I owe you my gratitude."

The earth spirit cocked his oversized head. "Unnecessary. We are bonded."

Man and spirit regarded each other.

Erto spoke again. "You will leave soon."

Bob nodded. "Tomorrow, I think."

"I cannot follow. Perhaps, when you reach the central realm, I will find you once more."

"Why would you want to? Don't you have anything better to do?"

Hollow eyes bore into his own. "We are bonded," repeated the spirit. Then he dissolved into a clump of dirt.

Bob commenced the grisly task of scouring Galvidon's corpse for useful items. He found a pouch of black beads, a small device that looked a bit like a cell phone, and a Gatekey. Osivia arrived and dropped the cylindrical torture device at his feet. He lit some tobacco, tentatively felt for Erto, found the connection still there, and called upon the earth to swallow the cylinder, the phone-like device, and the black beads. He buried them all deep, so deep they'd never be found by a sentient being. He figured the phone thing was a control interface for the orb. He didn't know what the black beads were —all the more reason to get rid of them. Then, he subsumed Galvidon's body in the earth. Not out of any kind of respect. He buried the Gray Man's corpse as deep as it would go because he didn't want anyone finding the black armor. Ever.

"Hey, Tinkerbell?"

"Yes?"

"How'd you take out the orb like that? Saved my ass…"

She smiled. "It's hard to explain. I could feel it give off a kind of energy. It felt… like the opposite of Lumith. I had a feeling it wouldn't respond well to contact with the Light. Thankfully, my hypothesis yielded positive results."

"Thankfully," repeated Bob, tucking Galvidon's Gatekey in his breast pocket. "Lets go get some grub."

She made a face. "They're serving grubs?"

Bob chuckled. "God, I hope not."

Bob enjoyed the evening. The Engorians and the En'harae mingled, cautiously at first, then enthusiastically. The Niners seemed to have no problem engaging their shorter cousins in conversation. Mannix's barrels of wine undoubtedly helped. The young Gaeren approached Bob at one point and offered him a mug of wine.

"Get that away from him before I cut off your hand!" barked Kelael from nearby.

The young Gasheera scampered away like a frightened rabbit. Bob turned an amused stare on Kelael, who winked at him in the firelight.

Bob spent most of the night reading through the little notebook Bernard had given him. It took only a few pages to find what he was looking for: details about the Hub Keystone and the Nexus. He read the information over and over, making sure he understood it. He fell asleep beside one of the fires to the sound of Brumhilde regaling Kelael and a group of Niners with embarrassing stories about Harold. The sound of their laughter echoed as he drifted into unconsciousness.

He dreamed he was under an open blue sky. The sun shone pleasantly above him. He sat on a plaid picknick blanket. Anna lay next to him, eating grapes. In the grassy field next to them, Torael helped Danny get a kite of leather and bone off the ground. Off in the middle-distance, a group of Engorians tossed around a frisbee with a group of En'harae. Bob saw the young Gaeren make an impressive, jumping catch. As Danny and Torael ran, laughing, and the kite rose into the sky, Bob noticed Kelael standing quietly off to the side, watching his brother and Daniel as they played.

"I told you he was a good man," said Anna.

"And I told *you*. I know." He grinned.

"Oh, I forgot, you know everything."

"That's why I married you. You see me for who I really am."

She threw a grape at him. There was a pleasant moment of silence.

"Can you move on now, Bob? Forget about me, find another woman?"

"Oh, please. I could never forget you."

"You can't hold on to this love forever."

"Just watch me."

She sat up onto her elbows, green eyes sparkling. "Be realistic, Bob. Or should I say, **R**. It's silly to be so hung up on me. How long will you cling to such a small fraction of your existence? I mean, how long until you forget all about me anyway? One lifetime? A dozen lifetimes? A hundred?"

"Anna, I couldn't stop loving you in a million lifetimes."

BOB THE WIZARD

She offered a soft smile. "Well then, you'll just have to let the love fade into the background."

He sighed, not taking his eyes off her. "I guess I will."

"But right now, let's just have a picknick."

The sound of Danny's laughter floated on the breeze.

The next day, Bob stood at the valley's central dais, smoke streaming lazily from the pipe in his teeth. He concentrated, holding out an upward palm. Shard by shard, mote by mote, the Hub Keystone formed in his hand.

According to the notebook, there was no immediate danger in activating the Gates at the Nexus for a brief time. Once powered by the plugged-in Keystone, the Gates would be available to be opened by an Astral Key. However, it would take an outside realm several hours to detect the subtle shift in energies from their side of the Gate. So, Bob could turn on the Nexus, open a Gate, and step through. Someone still within the valley could then remove the Keystone, shutting down the Gates once again, ensuring nothing would come through.

He'd explained all this to Kelael. In fact, he'd given him Galvidon's Gatekey, and bid him take the Hub Keystone—to be guarded by the En'harae —once he'd stepped through the Gate.

"A potentially very evil wizard might come searching for it," Bob warned him.

"A potentially very dead wizard, you mean," replied Kelael, "if he tries to take anything from me."

Bob chuckled and slapped him on the back, noting Galvidon's black knives still in the En'hari's belt.

Presently, Bob tentatively inserted the Hub Keystone into the slot in the center of the dais. An odd warble momentarily disrupted the songs of the astral voices. Bob could detect a faint hum from within the dais. That was it.

M. V. PRINDLE

Bernard's notebook had a diagram of the Nexus, labelling each Gate. Bob stared at the one that led to Earth. He silently said goodbye to the realm in which he was born. At that moment, he felt he'd never return.

There was a crowd to either side of the Gate that Bob would leave by. To one side was Mannix and a smattering of Engorians, both Darkhair and Lighthair. To the other, the En'harae and the Niners. Brumhilde, Gorrelai, and Kelael stood at the fore.

Bob wore the trench coat over Fan's jerkin, which snugly held his matches, pipe, and tobacco. The sunglasses were perched on his face. The brown backpack was slung on his back, a tied British rifle dangling from its left side. His boots were tied, his belt cinched. The breeze tugged at his graying beard. The Gatekey swung from the chain around his neck.

"This is so exciting!" breathed Osivia from his shoulder.

"Just got to triple check this is the right Gate," muttered Bob. As he opened the notebook, his finger slipped slightly, and the little book shuffled to the final page. There, in Bernard's loopy scrawl, was the following:

See you in another life.

-B

Bob sighed. He remembered something Bernard had said to Skinner in the woods. *I know, to my great displeasure, how each and every story ends.* Had he truly known he would soon die? Or, had he simply written this note as a way of saying goodbye? Questions that may never be answered. At any rate, Bob found the appropriate page and confirmed that he and Osivia were about to walk through the correct Gate.

He commenced walking forward. The Gatekey began to glow slightly. The crowds to either side of him grew thicker. He heard some of the Engorians whispering to each other.

"What's that on his eyes?" said one. "Can he even see?"

"You idiot, don't you know nothing? Them's called Wizard Glasses!"

"I ain't heard of no Wizard Glasses."

BOB THE WIZARD

Mannix watched him approach with naked eagerness. "Could you imagine, Bob," he said quietly, "when we first met, that such a thing as this moment could ever occur?"

"Hell no," said Bob. He glared at Mannix. "You better free those slaves like you promised, or so help me, I will find a way back here just to kick your ass again."

Mannix simply smiled. "Of course, Bob the Wizard. Of course."

Brumhilde shook his hand. The Gatekey's glow had brightened.

"Tell Harold I said thanks. Tell him… I owe him a big favor."

She arched an eyebrow, grinning. "Oh, he knows you owe him though, don't he? You owe me as well, you wee, hairy bastard. Just make sure you stay alive so we can collect, aye?"

"*Sora Kelai!*" Gorrelai tackled him with a hug. "*I will miss facing enemies alongside you! Will you return?*"

"I guess I will, Gorrelai. There's some unfinished business for me at Azenbul. But first, I have a lot to figure out about myself."

"*May the spirits guide your journey, Sora Kelai.*"

"And yours."

Bob caught Kelael staring at him. They locked eyes. Bob remembered seeing him for the first time, on a hill covered in khaki-grass. They'd stared each other down, the corpse of Willis Bailey ripening in the wagon. They shared a similar moment now, but all the preconceived notions about one another they'd had on that day had been erased. Kelael offered a nod. Bob returned it.

Then finally, the time had come. Bob approached the large arch set against the side of the mountain. He took a deep breath and removed the Gatekey from his neck. The area within the arch swirled with subtle light. The Gatekey blazed like a little sun.

"Make sure you're touching me," he said to Osivia. He felt her little hands gripping his neck hairs. "And whatever you do, don't let go."

"Oh, you're making me nervous!"

M. V. PRINDLE

Bob held up the shining Gatekey and stepped closer to the archway. Closer. He was a single step away from entering. The mountain wall swirled with astral eddies, right in front of his face.

Bob reached out with the glowing Gatekey, as if for a lock, and turned his hand. Then, everything shifted.

The End,

For Now.

BOB THE WIZARD

M. V. PRINDLE

The Language of Hari

Chess'no Baka .... *(CHESS-NO-BAKKA)*
                    Mammoths

Devoh Sheral .... *(DEV-OH-SHER-ALL)*
                 The Great Home (the world)

En'harae .... *(EN-HARR-EYE)*
                   The elvish people

En'hari .... *(EN-HARR-EE)*
                       An elf

En'hirin .... *(EN-HEER-INN)*
                   The elvish nation

Essen'aelo .... *(ESS-INN-AY-LOH)*
                A great, ancestral forest

Forijja .... *(FOR-EE-JAH)*
                     A dancer

Gasheera .... *(GASH-EE-RAH)*
             A member of the warrior caste

Gez Kar .... *(GEZ-KARR)*
            A race of intelligent reptilians

Kafeh .... *(KAH-FEH)*
               Vocation/Caste/Job/Calling

Kes .... *(KESS)*
                      Real/True

BOB the WIZARD

Ketra .... *(KET-RAH)*
A member of the leader class

Koreka .... *(KOH-REE-KAH)*
A hidden base of operations

Por'chei .... *(PORR-CHE)*
Exactly/Precisely

Quaylen .... *(QUAY-LIN)*
The ruling council of the elves

Quaylen Dah .... *(QUAY-LIN-DAH)*
The figurehead of the Quaylen

Sheral .... *(SHER-ALL)*
Home

Sifah .... *(SEE-FAH)*
Wait/Halt

Sora Kelai .... *(SORR-AH-KEL-EYE)*
Face hair

Tessaeshi .... *(TESS-EYE-EE-SHEE)*
The elvish shamans

Tessat(.... *TESS-AT)*
The Spirits

Tesera .... *(TESS-EH-RAH)*
A wizard

M. V. PRINDLE

PHRASES

En'do senna ....My name is/I am called

En kes tesera ne don vohant ....I knew you were a real wizard

En vohan fa ....I knew it

Et tessat sheera sheral .... May the spirits guide them home

Et tessat sheerat morae .... May the spirits guide our journeys

BOB THE WIZARD

M. V. PRINDLE

Author Bio

Matthew Prindle was born in 1984, and quickly became enamored with Science Fiction and Fantasy. He grew up on a steady diet of *Star Trek*, *The Lord of the Rings*, and *X-Men*. He messed around a little too much in his youth, until finally, in his early thirties, he graduated from Southwestern University in Georgetown, Texas with a bachelor's degree in Education. *Bob the Wizard* is the first novel he has written that doesn't belong in a trunk. He is currently writing an Epic Fantasy called The Outer Darkness and the second installment of *Bob*. He lives in Austin, Texas with his wife, two children, and a mother who makes a pretty good editor. He still messes around a little too much, and his love for fiction has only grown.

Printed in Great Britain
by Amazon